SAVING THE WORLD
AND BEING HAPPY
(The Computer Ager)

R. Eric Swanepoel

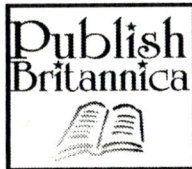

Publish Britannica

PublishBritannica

London   Baltimore

First printing

ISBN: 1-4137-1756-X
PUBLISHED BY PUBLISHBRITANNICA
www.publishbritannica.com
London   Baltimore

Dedication

This book is dedicated to the memory of three uncles,
all remarkable men:

James "Jim" Alfred Phillips
Wilhelmus Jacobus "William James" Swanepoel
Frank Taylor Thomas

Acknowledgements

Huge thanks are due to my parents, whose life-long support and encouragement I hope will at last be seen to have been at least not entirely wasted. Mark, thank you so much for your advice and your belief in me. Jane, Karsten, Heike, Siemen and Traute, many thanks *und Vielen Dank!* to all of you for the warmth of your hospitality, and to the first two for giving me such great nephews! Erica, Robin, Dorothy and Margaret—it's been wonderful to know that you were always there.

Christoph and Jo, fab friends and top-notch professional photographers, thank you for taking my mugshot and for everything else—I owe you more than one favour!

Bettina, thanks so much for the IT assistance, and thanks to both you and Oliver for your valued friendship. Good luck in Denmark!

Carolyn, big thanks for being the first brave soul to read this book (and, for years, the only one). Your comments were invaluable. I shall always be grateful. Keep fiddling!

À mes amis français : alors, sans vous…! Bises et remerciements. Il faut boire un coup prochainement!

Eddie, you're a great poet and a great friend, and you beat me to it, twice over—you b*stard!

Warm acknowledgements to those who have helped my literary career: to the Lemon Tree Writers (and especially to Todd McEwen, novelist and former Aberdeen writer-in-residence), to *Deliberately Thirsty*, *New Writing from the North*, *Cutting Teeth*, and *Pushing Out the Boat*, and to the abctales website (www.abctales.com).

Thanks to *The Observer* for permission to quote an extract in Chapter Thirty-Four, which remains their copyright, and an especially big thanks to Lenono Music for their decision to waive fees for permission to quote from John Lennon's "Imagine" in Chapter Seven ("Imagine" lyrics ©1971, renewed 1999 by Lenono Music, all rights reserved)—would that a certain other company had been as kind!

Thank you for the music, all you musicians out there! Thank you for the art, all you artists!

Finally, to my teachers and to all my other friends, pardon me for not naming you, but I could not put you in order and you know who you are and how much you mean to me—elephant skins of gratitude for everything! (Read the book to understand this.) Many of you assured me that I would be published eventually—you knew more than I did!

SAVING THE WORLD
AND BEING HAPPY
(The Computer Ager)

For Loren and John

Many thanks for your support
and friendship!

Love and best wishes

Eric

PART ONE
The River

CHAPTER ONE
The Source and Some Tributaries (Time, Rosemary, and BASIC)

If the truth be told, there was no single moment that led to it all, but it is human nature always to seek a unique starting point and a direct line of causation. For example, to find "the" (i.e. one and only) source of the Nile was the obsession of supposedly intelligent men. (Women were wiser.) Was the reasoning of such brave explorers impaired by heat and/ or swamp fever such that they couldn't sit down and think about their stupidity? A few moments of sober meditation, if this were possible under their sweltering solar topees, would have told them that rivers are the sums of their tributaries, that one source is as good as another, and that even raindrops might be counted as sources, to say nothing of the urine streams of natives micturating bilharzia into the water, through which the paler-skinned discoverers were later to wade heedless.

The truth is that the notion of "the" source of a river is artificial. It is necessary for men (not women) to compete. To compete they need a goal, preferably arbitrary. Men are said to be superior to animals because of their capacity for abstract thought. That is debatable, but it is true that few concepts could be as abstract as that of "the" source. Like cricket, football and war-gaming, there is plenty of room for so-called heroism (and a lot more for rivalry, jealousy, and assorted forms of malice) in the race to discover the source of a river. And it's all nicely useless.

Why do something worthwhile, such as making a minimal effort to understand the culture of those who live beside "the" source, when it is so much more satisfying and simpler to plant a flag, take the appropriate compass bearings, and sing the national anthem of one's mother/father land, rejoicing in the knowledge that one has beaten some other poor jaundiced anaemic dysenteric schistosomiatic febrile die-hard imperialist to the spot? Competitive culture comprehension could not hold a candle to such a magnificently perverse delight.

The spread of European civilization—or "syphilization"—was a secondary justification. Ultimately one succeeded in getting the local, relatively melanotically undeprived peoples ("the darkies") to drape themselves in clothing dependent on intensive laundering and industrial chemicals for its mandatory whiteness, so that they would then be fit to accompany one in one's subordinate obsession: the ligneous implement-assisted rapid relocation of pigskin-covered balls of string, also known as the English rain-making ritual, "cricket."

Nathaniel E. Papulous could not be accused of these absurdities. He didn't play cricket, hated football, and hadn't been farther afield than London or Manchester when the whole thing started. He only came up with "the" source of his revolutionary and planet-saving ideas when he got tired of the disappointment on female journalists' faces in response to his standard, "I don't really know…" mumble. His journalist-pleasing concoction wasn't entirely untrue, as the grandfather clock and the oil paintings had had some influence. Probably.

The story was that as a four-year-old he'd been taken by his aunt to see the former home of a great man, then converted into a museum. He'd been awed by the size of the rooms, the height of the ceilings, the gilt-framed oil paintings of the uniformly fair women and uniformed fairly ugly men, the musty smell of the grim-looking volumes on the bookshelves (fairly informed men!), and, more than anything, the grandfather clock in the hall—formidable! When one is used to the rapid and trivial tick-tick-tick mouse heartbeat of little clocks and, especially, from a more recent perspective, when semi-habituated to the hideous silent plastic slickness of electronic timepieces broken irritatingly by their evil little beeps insidiously pressurising one's already hectic existence, the measured, deep, stately "tock, tock, tock…" of a grandfather clock is impressive, more so when the noble quality of its ancient mechanism's vital signs and casement are set off by a mahogany parquet floor and an ornate vaulted ceiling.

Of course, Nathaniel didn't quite use these words in his interviews (and electronic watches weren't around when he was four), but he did convey something of the impact the enormous clock had made on his four-year-old self. If he had had full recall he would have mentioned the pendulum. No little boy viewing a grandfather clock for the first time could fail to be mesmerized by that measured swing. Be that as it may, the gist of his hack-fodder story was that this childhood museum visit made him aware of the passage of time, and thereby of change.

Come the height of Nathaniel's fame, the museum visit story had become more elaborate still. He had extended his analysis of the effect of the tocking on his infant consciousness, and would say that the grandfather clock's genteel beats had spoken to him of the importance of the correct use of time. That is, that while they hinted at mortality, their leisureliness intimated that what time remained to mortals was perhaps not best employed by precipitate action but rather by weighty and deliberate deeds, considered at length and seriously undertaken. Concordantly, the steady persistence both of the ancient clock's mechanism and of its housing had suggested to him that a measured approach to life might extend it, that a hasty bull-at-a-gate lifestyle might abbreviate it. His treatment of the effect of the oil paintings on his young self also found itself embroidered. The portraits of successive generations, he stated, had made a considerable impact—the features being visibly passed on (or not, when aristocratic inbreeding necessitated a little judicious covert outbreeding) from parents to hapless or happy offspring—leading him to pose himself at the time a juvenile version of the nature-or-nurture question. His own physiognomical inheritance had been, to put it charitably, mediocre: a weak chin, poor skin, premature alopecia—the essential attributes of the computer expert. No surprise, then, that computers would be his life, or at least a major part of it.

Apart from the question of genes, he'd been particularly fascinated, so he said, by multiple portraits of the same sitter, showing the effects of age. That he had been conscious of all he claimed to have been conscious of at the rude and raucous age of four is surely not true. Rather than call him outright a liar, though, we might imagine that his accompanying aunt (who died a few months later) had said something along the lines of, "Look, Nathaniel, there's the same man at twenty, thirty-five, fifty-one and eighty years old! Can you see? Look, see his hair is greyer here, and you can see how this wrinkle grew! He probably did a lot of frowning! But I'm sure he looked even worse than that. The painters tried to make them look as young and as handsome as possible or they wouldn't get paid!"

The full truth of the source of Nathaniel's ideas will never be known, for while the superficial physical appearance and location of things may, within limits, be described, the chimerical electrochemical workings of the human brain can only be approximated, especially those of a child many years since matured. However, if one insists on finding a single source for the Nathaniel Papulous saga then the tale outlined above should be good enough for most purposes. (It is certainly more accurate than "the source of the Nile"—*de Nyl zijn Oog*—as "discovered" by the *voortrekkers*, not vastly north of Pretoria in South Africa, half a continent south of "the genuine" source. At least the wretched *voortrekkers*, like Nathaniel, never inflicted cricket on anyone.) A more complete account of the ontogeny of Nathaniel's ideas forms much of the rest of this book.

Nathaniel was born in the sixties, but the most important years of his childhood were the seventies. Never has a decade unfairly suffered so much opprobrium as the poor seventies. Granted, the clothes were not "practical" or "restrained," but who needs practical and restrained? Neither were the sideburns particularly aesthetic, but muttonchop whiskers had been around before, and would come back again, and the ties came in damn handy if something had to be mopped up.

The seventies had none of that ghastly sixties half-hearted pseudo-rebellion of rich kids which was blamed for every evil in society for the next few decades and thereby killed sympathy for genuine reform, being used to justify repression and promote reactionary attitudes by numerous right-wing bigots, and, worse, launched the career of that most appalling "singer," the adenoidally hinge-voiced Bob Dylan. OK, granted, his lyrics had some merit, and someone had to be "the voice" of that generation. The glorious seventies were also untainted by the crass materialism of the eighties. Indeed, this and "yuppie" power had yet to rear their conjoined, hideous, short-back-and-sided Thatcherite heads.

The seventies yielded the shamelessly hedonistic but touchingly innocent Bay City Rollers in flamboyant tartan. Bowie was at his camp best. Abba were the slickest popsters ever. The sufferings of poor old Elvis mercifully came to an end. Motown was motoring, and Nixon got his fixin'. The residues of the best aspects of flower power were still there at the start and AIDS was nowhere. A veil should perhaps be drawn tactfully over the Mods and the Rockers in the UK (mostly gone by then anyway), and the Partridge Family in the USA, but, overall, the picture is clear: the seventies were fab! Even if the Beatles had ceded to Wings.

The seventies weren't quite like that for Nathaniel. At least not at first, though he benefited in some ways. Being the only child of professional parents (that is, his parents had professions; they were only too conscious of the fact that they received no money for raising Nathaniel!) he didn't want for material comfort, and, provided what he requested had some perceived educational benefit, it was his.

He asked for a computer. In those days computers didn't come with games consoles and a vast assortment of glitzy noisy wham-bang games. If you wanted to play a game you typed in the programme yourself, or you might possibly have been able to procure a taped version of paddle tennis—yawn! In short, if you had a computer you learned to programme it. Sitting in front of the poor quality screen of the black-and-white portable TV in his upstairs bedroom, this is precisely what Nathaniel did.

There was only one other kid in Nathaniel's class at school who had access to a computer. They were, therefore, special—an elite club of two. Jason and Nathaniel shared the subscription to a computer magazine, and one of Nathaniel's annually renewed Christmas presents (provided he passed all his exams, which he always did) was a subscription to *Scientific American* (which had "Computer Recreations" and "Metamagical Themas" columns, the latter being an anagram of "mathematical games"). Together the two boys would translate the programmes given in these magazines into the appropriate versions of BASIC for their humble though expensive machines. For the really long programmes this would take a couple of evenings of painful hunt-and-peck, and then there'd be the even more painful and frustrating process of debugging. There was nothing to beat the adrenalin-endorphin rush, however, when a new programme ran for the first time! Nothing, that is, until Rosemary appeared.

Rosemary and her family arrived in Thrackston with a bang one wintry afternoon. They moved in next door to the Papulouses, empty since the Martins had gone, taking their obnoxious yapping pug with them. The Taylors had a cat, but no dog. There was a boy, several years older than Nathaniel (a super-macho sports freak of a guy, it later emerged), a little girl about five years old (who plays no part in the story at all, but is listed here for completeness), and Rosemary, fourteen like Nathaniel.

Nathaniel had been waiting for the Mandelbrot pattern to appear on his screen (which took ages when generated by a BASIC programme running on a seventies computer) when, from the vantage point of his bedroom window, he had seen them disembark from the once white Peugeot estate. It was as if he had been shot. For fundamental and ancient things like human emotions, the old metaphors are often the best, and the Cupid's arrow one still has some mileage left in it, unlike the Taylors' estate car which was backfiring and belching smoke and, indeed, didn't see the following spring, at least not as a possession of the Taylors.

Perhaps the backfiring had something to do with Cupid's arrow. It is said that heightened emotion, whatever the cause, increases a person's vulnerability to pulchritude, and, certainly, the fantastic racket of the old banger had Nathaniel's heart racing even before he had seen his soon-to-be beloved. The back of her complaining chariot was stuffed with bedding and suitcases, and was low on its axle. The front was riding high and proud, as well it might for the princess who emerged from it, a seventies princess in the full glory of the appropriate regalia: bell-bottom jeans, massive orange platform-soled shoes, a satin-sheened orange boob-tube under a fake fur-trimmed wasp-wasted suede jacket. Her fair hair, as he later described it, paraphrasing the words from what became the most important song in the universe ("Passion Proliferates Where My

Rosemary Perambulates") was "somewhat flamboyant and unrestrained."
Perfection.

Nathaniel watched intensely for the next few hours, as the estate car
and a removals van were unloaded, and as that wonderful incarnation of
all the important virtues (those of importance, that is, to a young man in
early testosterone flush) appeared and disappeared: visible as she
collected small items from the vehicles, gone as she entered the house,
and intermittently visible again through the uncurtained windows of the
rooms facing him. And then the significance of the patterns of movement
in the house, which he had been observing without any attempt at
analysis, became clear. The room directly opposite his was to be hers! It
was the second bolt from the beneficent blue! The hanging of curtains all
too soon eclipsed his view, but not before he'd seen her putting posters
on her walls: David Cassidy, Abba, Mungo Jerry and Gilbert O'Sullivan.

She seemed to notice him for the first time as she was about to pull
the curtain closed, and peered for a few seconds at the shadowy face lit
from the side by the glow of a television screen. First eye contact—pity
it was so dark! Nathaniel turned reluctantly back into his pop poster-free
room and was surprised to see an elaborate and elegant pattern on his
screen. He had forgotten all about it! Yes, the Mandelbrot pattern was
beautiful, but not as beautiful as....

As is often the way in "real" life, and as novelists are often fearful of
admitting lest they destroy their tales by pushing the sceptical reader's
credulity too far, there was a "genuine" coincidence that day. "Passion
Proliferates Where My Rosemary Perambulates" had actually been
playing on the radio (in Jack Rind's *Hits of the Decade* show) as the Taylors
unpacked their possessions, though at the time Nathaniel hadn't known
that to be her name. Until the Rosemary era, Nathaniel had listened
rather indifferently to music, Jason's enthusiasm having not entirely
rubbed off on him.

That changed the following day, when the new girl in his class was
introduced. He immediately identified himself as her neighbour, though
blushing furiously. She was polite, but not obviously over-delighted.

Still, they had spoken. That evening Nathaniel re-ran the brief conversation in his head, repeatedly whispering her name to himself, disappointed that she'd been picked up from school by her mother and apparently hadn't come home until it was dark, but deliciously anticipating the morrow. In the future, he thought, there would be so many opportunities! His radio was on and as he lay on his bed only half listening to the re-broadcast of the *Hits of the Decade* show, he was blasted back into awareness of the present by the heart-seeking missile that "Passion Proliferates Where My Rosemary Perambulates" inevitably now constituted. He had become a real teenager—he must buy a record player! His computer had its first night's rest since its purchase.

The computer was idle for a long time. It found itself languishing in a cupboard, cruelly displaced by the upstart record player. If it had not been relegated to the sheltering darkness it would have witnessed a shocking change in its environment, as newspaper cuttings about the US and Soviet space programmes were displaced by huge images of David Cassidy, Abba, Mungo Jerry, Gilbert O'Sullivan, and—to show his independence and shameless machismo—Gary Glitter (then not revealed as a paedophile). Nathaniel's bank account converted itself into vinyl.

His parents were not entirely gruntled, but were wise enough to voice only mild displeasure, thus enabling their adolescent progeny to experience the essential developmental phase of rebellion without its extreme manifestation in the form of repeated all-out screaming matches. Under such circumstances Nathaniel had, therefore, sufficient reason to closet himself with his friends and mutter darkly about lack of parental understanding, but could not legitimately slam his door more than five times a day. And he did have more "friends," now that he was up on pop music and had one of the best collections in the class. To some extent it achieved its primary aim, in that the gorgeous Rosemary became a "friend," and would drop by from time to time, accompanied or alone.

They would talk about the inevitable subjects—parents, pop music and school—but Nathaniel never quite mustered his courage sufficiently to tell her directly that she was more than a friend to him. He would play

"Passion Proliferates Where My Rosemary Perambulates" whenever she visited, but then others had taken this up too, despite the song being a few years old—it was a standing joke which, like the record, was wearing rather thin.

He would wave to her from his bedroom, when she was ensconced in hers. He would hear what record she was playing, and try to synchronise his record player. They walked to school together. Nathaniel started to believe that his feelings were reciprocated, that they had an understanding that obviated verbal description, and yet he did want to tell her, and he wanted to hold her hand, to kiss her. He wanted to know for certain that the feelings were shared and that they would be together forever. Seeing her so often, talking to her without taking it any further was making life hell. He decided, then, that he had to act, some time, somehow, although part of him knew that he might lose everything.

Rosemary was a balanced, healthy, outgoing girl. She had many friends (of which Nathaniel was painfully aware). She was also leagues ahead of her would-be suitor in terms of psycho-sexual development, indeed in her understanding of human beings, and of Nathaniel himself, even. She was a girl, after all. She was not unaware of what the classroom stares, the perpetual solicitude, of her neighbour signified. She liked Nathaniel, but was beginning to find him irritating, and, physically, sexually, he was a non-entity to her. She had debated the ins-and-outs of the whole thing *ad nauseam* with her coterie of female friends—she even had them visit her bedroom with the express purpose of showing them Nathaniel's constant vigilant presence—how to drop him gently? Though she had sworn them to secrecy, these things have a way of coming out, and it wasn't long before Nathaniel became an object of pity amongst the more kind-hearted girls in the class, and an object of fun amongst the rest—most of them in fact. Rosemary's emotions were increasingly perturbed: pity, pride in her power over someone else's existence, frustration, anger at being subjected to all of this, and even hatred. They churned inside her but no butter of salvation formed. She couldn't bring herself to tell him directly to get lost, she couldn't be cruel to be kind. The next few months were difficult.

Rosemary's curtains were closed more often than not, even in daylight. Rosemary was always involved in intense discussions with others at school, and would sit as far from Nathaniel as possible. Rosemary was out a lot. Nathaniel was losing his appetite. From being in the top five in most of his subjects at school, he fell to average, and was even doing poorly in history and French. He would try to concentrate on the texts of his school books, up there in his Rosemary-pop shrine, but seconds of concentration were the limit, then the love-obsessed lyrics of some pop song would redirect him to reflect again on his misery, his gaze would revert to the house next door. At times he would doze, and hallucinate that Rosemary was there, coming home, or opening her curtains, but it was seldom true.

The day came when she swapped her bedroom with that of her brother, and Manchester United and Status Quo posters replaced Rosemary's. If big brother Neil caught Nathaniel looking out of his window towards the Taylors' house, hoping to see Rosemary entering or leaving, he would glower and shake his fist, and once, humiliatingly, called him aside in the school playground, and stood over the puny Nathaniel: "Leave my sister alone! She's sick to death of you. She wants nothing to do with you!"

But that couldn't be true! The problem was that he hadn't declared the true depth of his feelings! If she really knew him, knew how deeply he cared, she would change her mind. They had all poisoned her against him. It was her brother, and her brother's friends, and her friends. The pain increased daily. And then she was picked up one evening by a rugby first team mate of her brother's, and carried away on the back of a motorbike. Nathaniel was too young for even a learner's licence. To be a shining knight in Rosemary's eyes he must have a charger, or do valiant deeds? *Something heroic.*

One Saturday morning the Taylors had all gone somewhere, and Nathaniel was able to stare at his beloved's territory unthreatened: the hated curtains of her hated brother's room radiated all that was malign, but not powerfully enough to swamp Rosemary's magic influence on the dwelling as a whole; the lucky sparrows, nesting under the eaves of a house that contained the glory that was Rosemary; the washing line, sanctified through its contact with her glad-rags; the fishpond, which reminded him of a failed conversational gambit about goldfish; the garden shed, where, in his wildest late-night imaginings, he and Rosemary might…; the decaying poplar tree, where…their cat was stuck!

The pathetic miaows transmuted themselves almost instantly in Nathaniel's lovesick mind into the breathless voice of Rosemary: "Oh, Nathaniel, how can I ever thank you enough? Nathaniel, I have been so wrong about you. Please forgive me! Nathaniel, I love you!" He almost lost himself in reverie. Who'd have thought that that hated cat, which had for years (probably) undeservingly and unappreciatively experienced the caresses of Rosemary's sensual, slim, beautifully manicured fingers, the warm pressure of her breasts as she hugged it…that that very same despised bird-murdering felid would now be the agent of his experiencing similar sensory stimulation? He would simply rescue it, and become a hero!

Theory and practice are rarely identical, there's many a slip 'twixt cup and lip, and other apposite old saws….The truth is that that ancient poplar could have done with an apposite old saw a few years before Nathaniel's attempted epic chivalric feat. He was halfway up the thing when a branch gave way beneath his feet. He slipped a bit, and grazed a knee, but his hand grip was secure and he did not fall. The significance of the break would only register later. At the time the powerful libido-driven limbic system of his brain had enslaved the higher faculties of reason. Rescuing the cat to gain the fair maiden was all what mattered. Ever onward, ever upward.

A yard higher: what if no one believed he had rescued the cat? Rosemary would probably—no, definitely—imagine that the whole story had been contrived to impress her, nothing but a cowardly braggart's empty and desperate boast! *Ah ha!* He would wait in the tree until his loved one returned, and then effectuate the swashbuckling rescue in front of her pale brow and tremulous lip, her fair hands writhing in an agony of suspense, her warm heart expanding with repentance and admiration like the Mandelbrot pattern gradually emblazoning itself in all its wonderful intricacy on the screen of his black-and-white portable television set.

Three hours is a long time to cling to the trunk of a tree, particularly if it is raining, which it was towards lunchtime. Still, "Faint heart ne'er won fair maid!" Nathaniel repeated to himself. Disregarding the trivial irritation of the wetness, there were two immediate problems with this tree-clinging business. Firstly, he was terrified of heights, and, secondly, he was suffering terrible cramps. The first problem he tried to overcome by telling himself that height was nothing but vertical distance, and that it was silly to be afraid of distance, distance being the necessary means by which objects avoid being superimposed (not that he'd have minded being superimposed on Rosemary!). Without distance nothing would exist, because everything would be one, back to before the big bang. In general, it would be more logical to fear extreme proximity! Verticality, too, was not that bad, because it was only forty-five degrees away from being a slope of forty-five degrees, and who woke up at night having experienced the nasty sensation of sliding down a slope of forty-five degrees? No one. Forty-five degrees was nothing, not far off horizontal in fact, and you couldn't be anything but laid-back about horizontality! So there was nothing at all to fear about vertical distance, QED!

Nathaniel was almost light-headed about the whole thing now. Hey, once he got down he could sell this idea of how to combat fear of heights! Heights? Oh, my god, look how high! God, the leg pain! Was it better to concentrate on the arm cramp or the leg cramp? Perhaps if he just imagined he was hugging the grateful Rosemary on solid ground rather than a rotting old tree eight yards skyward of *terra firma*. It would probably be a good thing if he moved, he thought. He should keep the circulation going. The cat was still a couple of yards away, anyway. A bit more climbing....

Zebedee watched the appalling anorak monster approaching him. He had tolerated its relatively static presence a few yards away, and had almost got to the point of finding its intermittent sighs and hums ("Passion proliferates where my Rosemary perambulates...") soothing rather than disturbing, but the intense and apparently malevolent stare that was fixed to the front of this ghastly apparition as it approached to

22

within a yard was just too much. Zebedee decided to get down from the tree. A cheeky bound on the monster's shoulders, a light scrabble down the trunk, and Zebedee was through the cat flap and curled up next to the radiator.

The Taylors' new (second-hand) blue Citroën pulled up. By twisting his head Nathaniel could see the whole family disembark. "Nathaniel, what the blazes are you playing at? That tree's far too dangerous to climb, and it's on our property! Get down at once!" called Mr. Taylor.

Humiliation. Nathaniel, cramped and terrified and wretched as he was, descended to the point where the branch had broken, following the shouted instructions of a gleeful Neil and a wrathful Mr. Taylor. Then he could go no farther. It was Neil who fetched the ladder and carried him down to safety, to ignominy, to humiliation in its extreme abject depths. Naturally he told them what he'd been trying to do. He didn't know whether they believed him or not, and hardly cared now anyway. Everything was hopeless.

No, it was never entirely hopeless. Nathaniel bought and borrowed self-help manuals, and pop psychology texts, and, unfortunately, Richard Bach's books about the power of love, and from all his reading he only took in what he wanted to have confirmed: that true love (which, of course, was his variety) would ultimately win through. How and when? Rosemary was now so remote, he couldn't even speak to her. He wrote letters, and posted them through her letterbox, and stuffed them in her bag at school, when she left it unguarded. After the first three she wrote a reply: "Nathaniel, please leave me alone. I don't know how you can love me. You don't really know me. I can never love you. You are only hurting yourself by going on like this."

His next letter professed that he would die for her, if necessary. Shortly thereafter her parents called to have a serious discussion with his. The depths of hell, that was, to have his parents poking around in his soul! They took him to a psychiatrist, but he remained uncommunicative, staring at the table. From where he sat, he could read the graffiti inscribed by previous beneficiaries of the good man's services: "F***ing p*** tried to f*** me!" and "Suicide would be better than this!" Returning from the shrink in the back of his parents' Austin Maestro, he suffered their reprimands: "You might, at the very least, have greeted the man, Nathaniel!" It was then that he resolved to send the world to Coventry. When they arrived home he also put himself on indefinite hunger strike in his bedroom, for good measure.

At dinner time (7.30 p.m. on the dot) his parents sat over their healthy portions of balanced high-fibre low-fat food. Mr. Papulous swallowed the second of his daily allocation of two glasses of red wine, an expression of distaste distorting his thin lips. Both the older Papulouses hated wine, but had thought it prudent for their son to witness moderate and responsible drinking at home, and never deviated from the two-glasses-a-day rule. According to Nathaniel's recollections of his parents, the conversation might have run something like this:

"Mathilda, I think we may possibly have strayed a little too far towards Rousseau in our approach to the rearing of the boy."

"You mean, I presume, Everard, that we have not been involved enough, that we have failed to interact sufficiently? A bit too *laissez-faire*."

"Precisely. Heaven knows we studied everything we could find on child-rearing, but perhaps our moderate approach was...miscalculated?"

"But we didn't just try a moderate approach, did we? I mean...the years we spent trying different methods—the Spock approach in '67 and '68, for example? No one could have done more!"

"Mmmn, yes. There is one more thing we could try, Mathilda...."

"Spit it out, man!"

"Well, I've read...there's this idea that one should hug one's child, and inform it that one...that one loves it!" Mr. Papulous mouthed the word "love" with as little relish as he had the wine.

"Well," said Mrs. Papulous with a sigh, "we've definitely tried everything else! I suppose it couldn't do any harm to try that too, although it does...ahh...it does seem a little far-fetched! If that doesn't work we really will have to have the child committed though! We could always try again with another one, you know. It's not too late yet!"

Mr. Papulous muttered under his breath, looking at his severe and unadorned spouse, "So much touching involved—whichever way!"

—

Meanwhile, in his room above their heads, their son, barely conscious of what he was doing, was extracting his long-forsaken computer from its place of internment. He plugged it in to the mains, connected it to the television and the tape recorder, and switched it on. Mechanically, he rewound the tape and loaded the old Mandelbrot programme again, typed "RUN" and pressed "ENTER." He was staring at it as it developed, remembering again the day Rosemary had arrived, when the world had been full of promise and joy (this was one of his favourite memories), when his parents knocked and entered directly.

Nathaniel didn't move a muscle (apart from those of his diaphragm and his heart, of course, which were not under his conscious control at that moment, so it is debatable whether he, or rather his will, moved them anyway, but this is not the place to launch into a metaphysical discussion...).

The senior Papulouses stood awkwardly just inside the doorway. "Nathaniel, your mother—that is we—have something to tell you...."

Mr. Papulous was nudged sharply by his wife, who muttered, "No, no, Everard!" and gestured towards Nathaniel. Mr. Papulous looked uncertainly at her. She gestured more vigorously. He advanced, haltingly, towards Nathaniel (still resolutely refusing to look at them) and stood for a moment behind his son's chair. Further eyes-to-the-skies-accompanied gesticulations from his spouse caused Mr. Papulous to raise his arms, and shakily deposit his hands on Nathaniel's shoulders.

In the seventies they would have likened Nathaniel's expression to that of a startled rabbit. The language has since been enriched by the activities of a certain artist of zoo-sectional tendencies, and today Nathaniel's expression would be described as being akin to that of a farmyard animal which has just been informed that it is about to meet Damien Hirst. In short, Nathaniel was terrified, his father scarcely less so. Mr. Papulous' trembling transmitted itself to Nathaniel, who perceived that the Mandelbrot pattern was now jiggling.

Mr. Papulous tried to speak. "Na, Na, Nath, Nathan...."

Mrs. Papulous had had enough, and, very rapidly, she blurted, "Oh, for goodness' sake, Everard! Nathaniel, we've come to tell you that we

25

love you!" Then, more quietly but with the same celerity, she said to her husband, "Right, that's it. We've done it. Let's go!"

Mr. Papulous whipped his hands off his son's shoulders and left in a hurry. For the first time in his life he heard himself say, "God, I need a drink!" No objection emerged from the ashen face of his wife, and that day the two of them increased their alcohol intake by a whopping fifty percent—a whole glass extra! They lay awake that night, worried that they were well along the road to becoming hopeless alcoholics.

As it turned out, their visit had afforded some comfort to Nathaniel. His parents meant nothing to him, and their absurd performance did not, as it was meant to, immediately fill him with even the tepid inkling of a feeling that he might be wanted. It did, however, relieve his gloom slightly to know that no matter how crazy he was at times, there were people crazier than himself. He would eat, after all, if not speak. The Mandelbrot pattern was steady again. How he wished it could be Rosemary's face, rather than the representation of a mathematical formula.

CHAPTER TWO
A Confluence (BASIC Meets Rosemary)

When a tributary joins a river (or, to be unbiased, when two streams merge) the mixed water retains characteristics of each contributing body, yet gains in power and possibility. Salmon, entering a river mouth together, may part company at upstream junctions, depending on which tributaries furnished their individual nurseries. They taste home equally in the conjoined flow of the lower reaches, but some will taste it in one branch at each potential parting of the ways, and some in another. The taste of home is all-encompassing when they reach the little gravel-bedded becks of their infancy, and of their later rapidly succeeding concupiscence, senescence and death.

For mankind, a river generally becomes more useful, certainly more navigable, as it nears its debouchment in the briny. We have tasted the distinct flavours of the three major headwaters of the Nathaniel E. Papulous saga: an awareness of time, an interest in computing, and the love of Rosemary. This chapter details the first confluence. The next relates the usefulness of the augmented water body.

Nathaniel's wish to have Rosemary stare back at him from the screen would have been increased, had that been possible, by his parents' chosen therapy for his condition: the Papulous family moved, lock, stock and re-corked wine bottle. Why waste a glass-and-a-half of perfectly drinkable red wine?

Rosemary was now, on average, 67.23 miles away, Nathaniel estimated. By this stage even he realised that he had nothing to gain by seeing her in the flesh, at least not in the short term, and he made no effort to travel back to Thrackston by the two bus rides and the one train journey that would have been required (although he could have afforded the £3.93 he calculated was necessary).

His apparent improvement in the new environment of Utter Glopwort was spectacular. Little did his parents know, that far from this being due to the abandonment of his obsession, Nathaniel's "recovery" was due merely to a channelling of his ever-present pain into activity; in short, a plan.

The idea dated from Thrackston days, when Nathaniel had been wishing Rosemary's features onto his screen. It was not a stroke of genius. A sub-eureka experience would be a fair description, as it was simply the thought: "Well then, why not put them there?" Newly unpacked in Utter Glopwort, and before even the pop posters had been erected, he spent an hour trying to draw a fair likeness of Miss Taylor's face on grid paper, in order to transfer the X,Y coordinates of the comely features to his computer. Nathaniel discovered that he wasn't an artist. No matter how clear the image of this reluctant Juliet was in this too-willing Romeo's brain, it did not compensate for a lack of drafting skills. The clean new sheet of graph paper rapidly became a grey eczematous cellulosification of failure: so many rubbings out, so many millimetres of pencil lead—all wasted.

Adopting the classic pose of the despair-wracked (elbows on the table, eyes closed, head in hands), Nathaniel sobbed. All the treasured images of Rosemary cascaded through what remained of his mind: Rosemary arriving in Thrackston, Rosemary putting up posters in her bedroom, Rosemary laughing next to him as they listened to music together, Rosemary walking with him to school, Rosemary playing netball....BINGO! That was it! Rosemary was the star of the junior netball team so there'd almost certainly be a photograph of her in the school magazine, due out next week!

Nathaniel was on the phone to Jason in seconds, "Hi, Jason! It's Nathaniel. Yes, we've arrived in Utter Glopwort. Look, I'm really sorry about the way I've been behaving, but I'm getting over it." Nathaniel was not good at lying, but Jason let it pass.

"Jason, um, I don't really want to go back to Thrackston, but it would be good to see you some time, you know. I promise I won't talk about Rosemary. You know you could come over for the weekend. I'm sure my parents won't mind." (They associated Jason primarily with Nathaniel's computing activities, and so approved of him.) "Umm….It'd be good to hear how you're all doing! Umm….The school magazine comes out next week, right? Why don't you come over next weekend and bring a copy with you? OK, speak to your parents…."

As the next weekend was almost certain to bring him a picture of Rosemary, whatever his new school had been like Nathaniel would have tolerated it. It turned out to be small and quiet, and, although his mind was largely elsewhere, Nathaniel managed to pass himself off as an innocuous lad of mediocre ability, with a good knowledge of pop music.

On Friday he was jittery, and the mathematics teacher, Mr. Barker, a huge man with a mane of black hair and a crushingly dominant personality, reprimanded him for tapping his heel on the floor, his right knee bouncing up and down. (Nathaniel had long been aware of the time-killing joys of the tendon-stretch reflex, though, at the time, did not understand the physiological principles behind it. Particularly pleasant was to find a piece of music to which the rapid and rhythmic contraction and relaxation of the gastrocnemius muscle could be synchronised. He never did spot the connection between this harmless habit of his and the more staid but equally regular swings of the pendulum of the grandfather clock of his youth—a pity, as the source story could have been more satisfactorily embroidered.)

Nathaniel knew for a fact that Jason would be bringing the magazine. Jason had confirmed this when he'd phoned to say that his mother would drop him at Nathaniel's place at seven that evening. Nathaniel drew a clock in the margin of his math exercise book and marked off the minutes. How he hated trigonometry!

Until the Utter Glopwort days, Jason was not a major player in Nathaniel's story. Though frequently in Nathaniel's company and sharing his less passionate interests, he had not been crucial to any of the developmental stages. Nathaniel's displacement changed all that.

Jason was a scrawny lad, slightly taller than Nathaniel, with a dirty poodle's crop of tangled hair above his high forehead and bottle glasses. If Nathaniel had not been a classmate of his he probably would have found himself isolated and bullied, but Nathaniel had, in the early days, taken most of the flak.

More recently, Jason's known connection with Nathaniel had boosted his cachet as Nathaniel's ridiculous obsession and its various manifestations had become big news, and everyone had wanted to hear the details. On one occasion Rosemary had even asked Jason to intercede on her behalf, to persuade Nathaniel to leave her alone. Jason rather liked the standing all this had given him, but, at the same time, felt loyal to Nathaniel, his computer buddy of old, and fellow filler of the obligatory role of classroom nerd.

When Nathaniel had left Thrackston, Jason had allowed himself to talk a bit more freely about Nathaniel's—and his parents'—eccentricities, and so he was feeling rather guilty as he sat next to his mother in their old Ford as they approached Utter Glopwort. He must try to make up for his semi-betrayal by being as considerate and supportive as possible.

Nathaniel's smile of welcome was genuine, even if it was for what Jason represented rather than for Jason himself. Nathaniel took him up to his bedroom immediately, "…So you can get rid of your things!" A camp bed had been laid out for Jason, and the latter deposited his holdall on the end of it, fossicking in a pocket for Nathaniel's promised magazine. He handed it over, and received a falsely casual, "Oh, thanks."

Nathaniel forced himself to point out the view from the window first, then to look at the cover of the tightly gripped magazine with apparent interest, and scan page one, and then to make a remark or two about the introduction and the photograph of the headmaster, and "read" an article on page two…and page three, and four, and….

"Jason, there's a page missing here!" Nathaniel looked at Jason, and knew the truth at once.

"Well, Nathaniel, there was a picture of Rosemary there. I thought it might not be good for you." A needless explanation.

That was a difficult moment. On the one hand, the whole purpose of living for the last week had been as a necessary preliminary to possessing a photograph of the lovely Rosemary at the end of it. On the other hand, his only reliable link with this future Cleopatra to his Anthony was Jason, and Jason believed that Nathaniel was getting over Rosemary, and that any reminder of her would be bad for him. Nathaniel could not afford to alienate Jason, and yet how was he to use him for Rosemarious purposes without letting him know that she was still the centre of his existence? Nathaniel just managed to maintain his self-control and presence of mind, and said, "Oh, yes. You probably did the right thing. That was thoughtful of you." In his mind he was screaming, *Shit, shit, shit!*

The solution didn't take long to come: bribery, combined with just enough of the truth to make his plea convincing without totally offending Jason's conscience. "Sit down, Jason," he said. "I'm going to be honest with you. I still love Rosemary. I want her more than anything, but I sort of do realise now that I can't have her. But if I can't see her I feel I haven't the strength to go on. This last week of cold turkey has been terrible, terrible...." Nathaniel felt that the desperate circumstances had improved his ability to dissimulate, and was almost starting to enjoy his semi-deception, "...so I have been wondering how I can wean myself off her....I think a gradual approach might work. So, OK, I didn't tell you why I wanted the magazine. Yes, I knew there'd be a picture of Rosemary there, and that's why I wanted it. But it's only to stop me...." Nathaniel faked a tragic sob at this point, "...It's only to stop me...ummm....It's only to stop me doing something foolish. I must take things gradually. Now I know it'll cost you to get another magazine, but I'll pay for it. Better than that, you can help yourself to a record—a couple of records from this box!"

Nathaniel pulled over a cardboard box, split under the pressure of the singles stuffed into it. "I've hardly played these. Go ahead and choose a couple!" For the last few months it had been his practice to buy two copies of all the new singles as soon as they came out, in the hope that if Rosemary ever asked if he had a record he could reply in the affirmative and give it to her, and then (joy of joys!) he could play his copy, knowing she was playing hers.

The records in the split box were those she had effected to despise (in fact all those he'd bought in the last fourteen weeks, which, strangely, included some new songs by groups she'd previously liked!), and which were consequently of no interest to himself. Indeed, until this moment they had been worse than useless as they all exuded the miasmatic gas of Rosemary's disdain. Now they represented a vast treasure trove of future Rosemarious activities enacted by Jason on his behalf. Little did Jason know!

The magazine arrived in the post on Tuesday, as promised, and was waiting for Nathaniel when he got home, fresh from a bawl-out from Barker for his ignorance of tangents. His apparent complete *sang froid* in the face of monumental ire considerably enhanced his status amongst his classmates, but this too left him unmoved. What did anything matter when he was going to see Rosemary again? Curled up around the magazine on his bed, he gloried over her heavenly image for nearly an hour, occasionally allowing himself the supplementary pleasures of kissing her lips and reading her name on the caption, "Rosemary Taylor." Beautiful it was. Almost as beautiful as "Rosemary Papulous"!

Sighing, he got off his bed, and propped the photograph up on his table, where he could see it as he set up his computer and searched for a ruler and pencil. The tracing paper had been purchased days previously, but he needed to increase the resolution of the grid he'd drawn on it as he'd imagined a larger picture.

Hours of labour later Nathaniel was staring at a crude likeness of his love on the flickering screen. It was slightly too wide and squat. The addition of two lines to the programme, and he could squash and stretch the image as he wished. Rosemary was his! At his mercy! He saved her on tape, and tried to sleep, the magazine in bed with him. More than once that night he found himself switching on his bedside light and drooling anew over the photograph, and at 3.24 a.m. he just had to switch his computer on again and look at the digitalized version. His performance at school the next day was even worse than usual. He was exhausted, true, but it was more than that. He was unsatisfied with the oblique view of his beloved's features offered by the magazine photograph. He wanted her face full on, so that kissing her would be more realistic, and he wanted better resolution.

"Jason. Hi, it's Nathaniel. How're things? Good. Listen, Jason, thanks a lot for the magazine. Yup, it's great. Did you like the records? Boney M isn't bad, huh? Listen, Jason, I was wondering if you could do me another favour. Could you take a couple of photographs for me? The sideways view in the magazine is lovely, but it isn't quite…ummm…quite strong enough for me. Do you think you could try and take a photograph for me, a straight-on view? You can use my camera, and, of course, I'll pay for the film and development, and you can have another couple of records if you want. Please, Jason! Look, I'm not bothering her, am I? I'm not really bothering anyone except you, and if you don't help me….Great! Thanks a lot! I'll post the camera and film to you right away!"

The photographs, when they arrived at last, were unsatisfactory. Not one was a clear frontal view. Everything but. In the last three she looked really angry, and in the very last one her hands were reaching towards the camera, half-obscuring her enraged features. There was a curt note from Jason in the envelope: "You owe me £1.67 for development, postage and packing. Rosemary has your camera and the second film and I'm not going to get it back. Be happy that you have the first film anyway—it was lucky that I'd finished it and loaded the second before she got the camera! Forget the records. That's the last time I help you."

When Nathaniel phoned, Jason's mother, in an embarrassed voice, described him as "out," after a muffled conversation with someone. Nathaniel knew what the truth was. Hell, at least he had the photographs, and at least it was Rosemary who had his camera! She was touching what he had held! He might even be able to think of a way of using the camera to get to see her in the flesh, but in the meantime the new photographs: how she had looked only last week! Better than nothing!

Nathaniel selected the three best pictures and translated the familiar curves into digits. Now he could, at the touch of a few buttons, flick between four images of the hallowed features. Two showed her facing to the left, two to the right. He could magnify them or reduce them, squash them or extend them. If only there were a full-on view! As he stared at the screen, his hill of satisfaction gradually eroding into a talus of frustration, a real, full-blown, as genuine as Abba's intra-group marital problems, eureka experience exploded upon him. Of course, what an idiot he'd been! To determine the position of an object in two dimensions one needed two fixes, to determine the position of an object in three dimensions one needed three. There must be a way of using the information in the four slightly different views he possessed to construct a three-dimensional description of Rosemary's lovely-beyond-imagining face! But how?

Mr. Barker was astounded. The transformation was amazing. Not only had Nathaniel metamorphosed overnight into his most attentive pupil, but he had also come up to him after the lesson to ask for more information! It must have been that row he'd given the boy. Yes, he'd always believed in putting the fear of God (or, at least, of himself) into them, and here was the proof of it working! Or was it just that the poor lad had needed time to settle in to the new school? Whatever—his teaching methods were clearly succeeding.

Within two weeks Nathaniel was the star pupil in the mathematics class, and Mr. Barker was singing his praises in the staff room. It is perhaps worth taking some time to consider all the psychology that was at work here. If there is one concept in human psychology beyond all others of which the understanding enhances one's ability to get on with people, then it is that of self-esteem. Boost someone's ego and one makes a friend. Damage an ego and one destroys that person, or one makes an enemy. Those with self-esteem are outgoing, sociable, and willing to try new things. Those who lack it are reactionary, negative stay-at-homes. Had Nathaniel arrived at Utter Glopwort Comprehensive as a fully fledged mathematical prodigy, it is likely that Mr. Barker would have felt insecure, and, therefore, consciously or subconsciously, would have set about making Nathaniel's life harder, in effect have taken him down a peg or two. As it was, Mr. Barker believed that Nathaniel's dramatic progress was largely due to himself. Identifying thus with Nathaniel's apparently logarithmically growing capacities, Mr. Barker took Nathaniel under his wing in a big way.

Mr. Barker had been the most outspoken frequenter of the staff room almost since his arrival from college seven years previously. Utter Glopwort Comprehensive was a small school and there were not that many teachers, which prevented the usual cliques forming. Within the staff room everyone was on first-name terms. Even the usual school staff room division of stuffy old stick-in-the-muds and timorous-but-enthusiastic new bloods allied to the odd older rebel did not exist. Mr. Barker (John) was well known to all, and liked (or at worst tolerated) as an outspoken, honest and competent man. Though given to occasional outbursts, these were usually justified. His position, then, was one of influence. This was particularly the case with the more junior female members of staff (none more so than Miss Grimshaw, a recently graduated English teacher), who were all conscious of his eligible bachelor status. While Mr. Barker's classes generally did well (for he was gentle, encouraging and laudatory towards his female pupils and he only ever aggressively perorated for the benefit of deserving inattentive males) and he derived some satisfaction from this success, he was starting to feel that he needed more of a challenge.

Mr. Barker could not have met Nathaniel at a more appropriate time. Nathaniel could not have met Mr. Barker at a more appropriate time. A mutual ego boost of gigantic dimensions was about to occur.

CHAPTER THREE
Combined Forces, Smoother Waters, and the Entry of Time

Never has someone's opinion on a subject changed as quickly as Nathaniel's did on mathematics. Trigonometry, geometry and algebra were no longer associated with miserable hours on hard school seats enduring high-volume abuse and dodging chalk dusters, no longer with fear-inspiring dog-eared textbooks seemingly designed to lock the abstruse knowledge on their yellowing pages rather than disseminate it. Now these subjects meant the delectable three-dimensional curves of Rosemary's nose, her lips, her eyes (and why not her whole body?) at Nathaniel's command—literally at his fingertips.

Mathematics is unfairly stereotyped as cold and hard. More fairly, so are its teachers. In fact the latter fact gives rise to the former: many children's early classroom encounters with mathematics put them off for life. Negative emotions block cognition. How unfortunate, when, with a bit of imagination and small class sizes, it should be possible for the enlightened, well-paid, and unconstrained teacher to discover what special interests each pupil has, and to link mathematics with these interests. Nathaniel was lucky enough to discover a link himself and, under the powerful drive of libido and the competent tutelage of Mr. Barker, he soon had Rosemary's face in any position he wanted it—or, at least, the representation of it could be oriented at his whim.

Nathaniel was obtaining great satisfaction from his mastery of his computer and mathematics. As the manipulable digital representation of

Rosemary improved, the Rosemary-in-the-flesh-shaped hole in his life was becoming less tangible, the vacuum less avid.

Mr. Barker couldn't restrain his curiosity about his star pupil's intense interest in his subject. Nathaniel had told him only that he was interested in rotating three-dimensional shapes on his computer. Mr. Barker asked if Nathaniel might bring his computer to school. Nathaniel complied but only allowed him to see banal pyramids and a hastily entered crude representation of a car, rotating with painful slowness on the small fuzzy screen.

Within a month Mr. Barker had become a computer nut himself, a computer club had been set up, two spanking new top-of-the-range ZX Tandybrain microcomputers had been ordered, and Nathaniel and Mr. B (as Nathaniel began to call him) set about infecting other pupils and staff members with their disease. Their success amongst the males was sufficient for Nathaniel to acquire a substantial body of friendly—even admiring—acquaintances, including some senior boys. Thus he was protected from bullying as surely as if he'd carried a howitzer on his person. Nathaniel walked the playground with confidence for the first time in his life.

It wasn't just in mathematics and the new subject of computing that Nathaniel was shining. He was doubly fortunate in his English classes. Not only was Miss Grimshaw favourably disposed towards him because of her admiration of and close association with Mr. Barker, but also the play they happened to be studying in Nathaniel's first term was *Romeo and Juliet*.

Nathaniel naturally enough identified with Romeo, and his insightful comments on the emotions of the characters were streets ahead of anything any of the other boys could produce. Of course the girls were up there with him in this respect, but they could not substantiate the arguments in their essays by referring to all the psychology books (cod though they might have been) that Nathaniel knew backwards.

With Miss Grimshaw and Mr. Barker both convinced of his brilliance, it was not long before other staff members fell under the spell. Give a dog a bad name, they say, but the reverse is at least as true. Although

Nathaniel was bright, he was not, in fact, a genius. Nevertheless the respect that teachers showed him—their obvious high expectations—acted as a powerful drug. Nathaniel, almost to his astonishment, found all his schoolwork easy and a delight. Within a few months he was top in all his subjects, and even trying to play sport. His parents were pleased with his academic progress, but worried that he might injure himself on the sports field. It was not, however, a physical injury that should have been concerning them. Underneath all the success and the new-found self-confidence, Nathaniel still craved Rosemary. Her three-dimensional manipulable image on the screen of his new computer would do for the time being, but it was not a long-term solution.

Close relationships with other human beings, however, were not totally lacking. Mr. B drifted into the role of friendly uncle. Sensing Nathaniel's need for such a figure in his life, but aware of the necessity of appearing professional, Mr. B used the computer club as an excuse for organising social events at which they could converse on a more relaxed basis. With lots of other boys around, there would be no danger of accusations of favouritism, and yet Mr. B could befriend Nathaniel in a more profound way than was possible in the classroom.

Miss Grimshaw would attend these events, and it became apparent that they constituted a couple. In fact they became parent substitutes for Nathaniel, his own suffering from the peculiarities previously described. The once-a-term computer club pizza parties at Mr. B's house (described as *Bites and Bytes* on the posters) became the highlight of Nathaniel's school years. It was at one of these that he was introduced to the Beatles.

Mr. B despised most of the music of the seventies, but for his other virtues, and for his tact in hiding this fact, one can try to forgive him. Mr. B was very much of the Beatles-Stones-Hendrix-Doors era, and he was not ashamed to play this music at his pizza parties. Although all present had heard it before, this was the most intense exposure any of the pupils had had.

Familiarity is supposed to breed contempt, and absence to make the heart grow fonder. It is time these trite epigrams (and most others) were discarded, because life is seldom so black and white. They are particularly inappropriate to describe the response to pop music, which is multifactorial to a high degree. The time of narrowest musical tastes is the teenage period. This may to some extent be physiological (a directly age-related modification of the aesthetic faculties?), but a large part of it can surely be explained as the adolescent need to distance oneself from one's elders and to reinforce one's identity by rejecting the touchstones of previous generations, however temporarily. Another fact is that very few tunes evoke much reaction on first hearing, if this is not dislike. A few listenings later, though, and the listener is humming along, or rhythmically displacing some portion of his or her anatomy in time to the predominant beat. Hundreds of replays down the line, and the music is boring. Give it a rest for a while, and it becomes nostalgic. Add to this the knowledge derived from the experiments of Pavlov on his dogs (which were offered food when a bell was rung, and subsequently would salivate merely upon hearing a bell) and Skinner on his rats (which were conditioned, amongst other things, to push levers for food), and a still more complete picture emerges. Animals and therefore human beings, these scientists argued, can learn to associate specific stimuli with punishments or rewards, and they can be conditioned to respond to these stimuli in various ways. With this background one may consider Nathaniel's response to Mr. B's music.

Nathaniel's parents never listened to music at all, and openly expressed their disdain of people wasting time on such "a frivolous thing." For Nathaniel, then, all music was free of contaminating parental associations. He experienced the same rebellious buzz from listening to Doris Day and to Gary Glitter. Mozart was no more to be scorned than ZZ Top or *vice versa.*

While Nathaniel had no negative associations with music then (apart from those tunes Rosemary had rejected, but even those, depending on his mood, had a certain not totally unappealing bitter-sweetness about them, particularly as some had, in an admittedly roundabout way, procured him Rosemary's photographs), he certainly had positive ones. There were those songs associated with the more pleasant Rosemary moments, naturally. There were those associated with other friends (to be pedantic, with friendly acquaintances, because the word "friend" connotes a level of intimacy, of exchange of personal information, of which Nathaniel had not yet proved himself capable, except with Rosemary and Jason, both of whom he'd alienated). And there was the Beatles' music (the *Sergeant Pepper's* album) which was playing right then, as he munched a superb deep-pan pineapple, avocado and prawn pizza, and chatted to Mr. B and Miss Grimshaw about the joys of machine code programming. Miss Grimshaw looked restless; she examined her nails, sighed repeatedly and eventually tugged at Mr. B's sleeve and whispered something into the latter's ear. "That's very interesting, Nathaniel," said Mr. B, "but I'm afraid we'll have to break off there for the moment. Alison and I have an announcement to make."

Mr. B turned down the music and joined Miss Grimshaw again in front of the drinks table. He called for quiet. Holding her hand in the hushed room, he spoke, "Now, you've known for some time that Miss Grimshaw and I have…well…taken an interest in each other. You all mean a lot to us so we've decided to tell you something important. You're the first to know that we're going to get married!"

The applause and cheering were as loud as they might have hoped for. Miss Grimshaw tore her shining eyes away from Mr. B's. "Now, people. We've decided to do something very naughty this evening, and you must promise us that you won't tell your parents! Do you promise?"

This was tremendously exciting, and they chorused, "Yes!", wondering if they were going to make love in front of them.

"Underneath the drinks table there's something a bit stronger than orange juice and coke—there's some cider! Have some if you want, but no more than two glasses each, mind! Mr. Barker will pour it for you."

Half the youngsters had never had more than a mouthful from their parents' wine glasses and this was more exciting for them than if the engaged couple had worked their way through the entire *Kama Sutra* right there and then. Through Nathaniel's cider-hazed eyes he could see Mr. B kissing Miss Grimshaw. The loudspeakers were blaring out McCartney's lyrics querying the continuation of his partner's adoration into old age. Well, Mr. B and Miss Grimshaw obviously believed that their mutual affection would last that long.

Nathaniel's thoughts and emotions were tangled but, with the benefit of the psychological perspective that has been established, they may be understood. The strongest emotion was happiness. Nathaniel was well fed and experiencing his first alcohol-associated endorphin rush in the company of people he liked and who, on the whole, liked him. The music, which he had heard a few times before on his radio, was now associated with a feeling of well-being and invested with a depth of meaning it had heretofore lacked. Mr. B and Miss Grimshaw were, it appeared, going to experience a lifetime of happiness together. They had certainly committed themselves to each other for the rest of their lives...into old age, even if they became wrinkled and bald. Somewhere in the background of Nathaniel's mind the memory of those oil paintings of his childhood museum visit was flickering. An awareness of time thus entered the Nathaniel E. Papulous stream, which was strongly to influence the rest of his career. For better or worse, thenceforth he was wedded to an intense awareness of the fourth dimension, initially, at least, with happy associations.

The same life-changing evening had produced another Pavlovian-Skinnerian phenomenon. Nathaniel had not only discovered the Beatles, he had discovered alcohol, linked in his psyche to pleasant events.

Woven into the happiness was a fainter but not insignificant strand of melancholy. Miss Grimshaw and Mr. B would be together and happy for the foreseeable future—why not Rosemary and himself? He was sure he would love her until and beyond the vast age of four to the power of three that the Beatles sang about. But, of course, that was the one thing he had not explicitly told her! That he would love her come what may.

CHAPTER FOUR

Unexpected Turbulence

Back in his bedroom the next evening, the Beatles blasting from the record player and the psychoactive fraction of half a bottle of illegally obtained cider in his bloodstream, Nathaniel was hunched over his computer. He wanted his camera back, he wanted Rosemary, and he'd worked out how to kill these two birds with one stone.

Two days later Rosemary came home from school to find a letter waiting for her on her bed. (It was her mother's practice to leave Rosemary's mail thus.) She put Zebedee down, whom she'd been fondling, and picked up the letter. The name and address were printed, the postmark was illegible, and there was no return address on the back of the large brown envelope. She ran her comb along the seal.

The following Monday, Nathaniel received a notice informing him that an item too large for delivery was waiting for him at the post office. Exhilarated as he hadn't been since the first time Rosemary had visited his bedroom in Thrackston to listen to his music, he sprinted all the way there immediately. Five minutes later, still feeling a bit winded, he stood outside the post office clutching a parcel. To open it then or to take it home? He decided to postpone the pleasure, and forced himself to walk home very slowly. Strange—had the parcel rattled when he'd turned it?

There was a note:

> *Undear Nathaniel,*
> *No thanks for the Beatles record, and your pictures of myself in fifty years, assuring me of your "long-term fidelity" despite my "likely*

appearance at the age of sixty-four"! I have pleasure in showing you what
your record and your camera would have been likely to look like in fifty
years. Get out of my life, completely and forever! I hate you and I always
will!

NOT yours, with no affection whatsoever,
Rosemary (Mike's girlfriend!)

The box contained the smashed fragments of his camera and the
Sergeant Pepper's album. In the stunned aftermath feeling, before the full
horror really hit him, he found himself wondering whether the real import
of the message might have been in the flower-patterned scented
notepaper. But even he was incapable of this level of self-delusion.

His extreme lassitude did not go undetected at school, and Mr. B and
Miss Grimshaw called him aside at the end of the next day. Nathaniel sat
at a desk in Mr. B's classroom, staring ahead at nothing. Mr. B had a hand
on his right shoulder, Miss Grimshaw stood at his left. "Tell us what's
wrong, Nathaniel."

Nathaniel sighed and breathed deeply for a while. If the world had
ended, what harm would it do for them to know? Over the next forty
minutes the saga emerged. Miss Grimshaw's face contorted as Nathaniel
related his naïve attempt to woo Rosemary by sending her images of
herself as a wrinkled hag, but she just about managed to prevent herself
laughing, spluttering ambiguously into a handkerchief at one point. Mr.
B's face was better controlled, but Nathaniel wouldn't have noticed
anyway, so engrossed was he in re-living the tragedies of his short
existence.

When Nathaniel had been silent for a couple of minutes, Miss
Grimshaw felt that she should say something, "Nathaniel. I'm afraid,
painful as it is, you'll have to accept that she's not interested in you. I
know it's not much consolation at present, but I can assure you that your
pain will fade as you get older. Besides, there are lots more fish in the
sea."

"Hah! None like Rosemary. I won't ever feel as strongly again, and if
not then life isn't worth living…."

Miss Grimshaw sighed, and then she brightened and bit her lower lip, her eyes sideways and travelling. "Look, Nathaniel, there is another way of looking at this whole thing. I'm a woman, and I know how women think, or feel. The last thing a woman finds attractive is a man who's totally emotionally dependent on her. Women are attracted to strong, independent, successful men. If you are serious about Rosemary, and you're prepared to wait for her...."

"Yes, yes, I am. If I knew I was going to get her in the end...."

"Well, you won't necessarily get her in the end, but there is only one way that you might stand a chance...."

Nathaniel was looking alive and alert now for the first time since he had opened the beautifully neat package. "Yes, OK, but what is it?"

"Well, the only way you'll stand a chance—and I know it sounds strange—but it's if you care less about her, and throw yourself whole-heartedly into other activities.... If you become very successful, famous, well-liked, you might eventually win her. But in order to do this, you must put her out of your mind for now. By the way, have you noticed how Angela has been looking at you?"

Nathaniel was livid. "Look. I'm not interested in other girls. I can try and put Rosemary out of my mind, and try the other things, but I can't just switch my interest to someone else!"

"No, no, of course not." Miss Grimshaw was delighted with the anger. She had succeeded in resuscitating him. Her eyes met Mr. B's admiring gaze.

Mr. B cleared his throat. "Nathaniel, there's a business matter I need to discuss with you." He signalled for Miss Grimshaw to leave them. "You know the computer club has received a lot of visitors recently?"

Nathaniel could remember the nodding men in suits.

"Well, the Ministry's very impressed with what we've been doing. They want me to help them set up a proper computing syllabus, and to help other schools develop their own computer clubs. This means I won't be around next term, so you'll have to take on the running of the club yourself. Do you think you could manage it?"

Nathaniel affirmed that he could. The hymn at Friday's assembly had new meaning for him: "Ransomed, healed, restored, forgiven...."

CHAPTER FIVE
Beatled but Not Beaten

Heartened by Miss Grimshaw's words, Nathaniel collected all his possessions having some link with Rosemary: the photographs, the computer tapes and disks containing her digitalized image, the records rejected by her, those of his books that he'd forced her to borrow (and had been returned largely unread), and the pop posters bought in emulation of her. He transferred them to a large cardboard box, which he sealed with masking tape, and then he slipped this into a plastic bag. He fetched a ladder from the garage, and, with difficulty, transferred the box to the attic, inching up the ladder with one arm around the heavy box. The only Rosemary-connected item which escaped this wholesale clear-out was his replacement copy of *Sergeant Pepper's*. In a spirit of exorcism he listened to the whole album three times non-stop, taking particular pleasure in "Getting Better" despite the fact that the perceived amelioration of circumstances had, according to the lyrics, only occurred since the girl had become the singer's.

The rest of Nathaniel's school career was relatively untroubled. His stewardship of the computer club was exemplary, he was consistently first or second in all his subjects, and he was deputy head boy—the top job going to an outgoing sports type with a large female following. Nathaniel did not resent this—David had been a friend of his since he'd asked Nathaniel for help with maths and Nathaniel was not in competition for the female attention. Besides, he didn't particularly like public speaking, on which David thrived.

For his A-levels Nathaniel took mathematics, English, biology and the new option, computing science. This was an easy year for him, as he knew the maths and computing science backwards, so, in effect, had only two subjects requiring any effort. As Mrs. Barker was taking English, his course there, although slightly uphill, was smooth and scenic. The only really hard graft was biology. Nathaniel was not lazy, as such, but preferred subjects where comprehension was more important than memory. This did not apply to school biology, unfortunately, but he bought a few books on memory improvement, and worked out mnemonics for the entire syllabus (Kingly Philanderers Can Oppress Foolishly Genuflecting Serfs, for example, one of the more pretentious and less image-based, for Kingdom, Phylum, Class, Order, Family, Genus, Species). The biology project loomed on the horizon as the major challenge of the year. They had been warned repeatedly that they needed to choose a topic by the end of March. The day came and Nathaniel hadn't thought of anything.

The previous evening had seen him, as usual, quaffing cider and listening to the Beatles—*Sergeant Pepper's* again, as it happened. The reference to balding in the song that had made such an impression on him at the *Bites and Bytes* party was starting to worry him, as he thought he could detect signs of his own hairline receding! His sleep had been troubled, and he'd woken just after three in the morning with the horrible vision of Rosemary's rotating sixty-four-year-old head leering at him. The nightmare was troubling in more than one way. Not only was it a reminder of Rosemary, whom he was trying to put to the back of his mind, but he realised also, if he were honest, that he did not find the wrinkled version attractive. How could he reconcile this with his conviction that his love for her was undying?

Cognitive dissonance, the simultaneous belief in contradictory concepts, is a double-edged sword. On the one hand it may be associated with the most outrageous hypocrisy or "schizophrenia" in the popularly accepted meaning of the word, and *in vino veritas*-type (alcohol-induced) character changes (or revelations of character), sometimes violent. On the other hand, the struggle to reconcile two or more apparently mutually exclusive ideas is what provides the fuel for some of the most creative minds. When it is conscious it may serve to enhance one's understanding of others, rendering one less judgmental, or, in other words, promote humility. Nathaniel's conscious cognitive dissonance was to make him one of the most creative thinkers the world has ever known. Whether it contributed to his happiness along the route to his ultimate success remains an open question.

Sitting exhausted and depressed anew (and slightly hungover) at the front of the biology classroom, Nathaniel's name reached his ears. He was surprised to hear himself answer: "Ageing. I'll do ageing, Miss Doherty."

Miss Doherty chuckled. "Yes, that's something we'll all do, Nathaniel, if we're lucky. Alas." Nathaniel's face was blank.

Whatever his naïve ideas of ageing had been at the start of the project (loss of skin elasticity, general wasting, and an increased susceptibility to cancer, possibly), within a week Nathaniel was to be both horrified and fascinated by the immensity of the subject he'd chosen, or rather which had been thrust on him by fate or by his subconscious. His collection of *Scientific American*s were, until then, his only experience of general scientific writing, but an unimaginably vast world opened up before his persistent questioning of the local librarian, and, subsequently, of the librarians at Bexford Heath University. Used to understanding at least ninety percent of what he read in his own rapidly growing computer library, and unused to much disagreement in this literature, apart from in the more philosophical corners of artificial intelligence, Nathaniel felt his sympathetic nervous system go into turbo-boost (fight-flight, knot in the stomach, dry-mouth, pounding heart) when the thousands of virtually incomprehensible, inter-related and disputatious articles all more or less with a bearing on his hugely ambitious project came to light. He sat in the university biology library, surrounded by insouciant students, all, he imagined, competently and blithely working their way through their reading lists. He felt very small. His ears reddened as he imagined himself exposed in the way he'd been a few years before, clinging to the trunk of a dead poplar tree. At least this time he could climb down himself.

As it turned out, Miss Doherty was only too happy for him to change his project title to "Aspects of Fibroblast Activity in the Ageing of Human Skin"—much more manageable although still ambitious. The finished work was no more than satisfactory. Nathaniel ran out of time at the end, wasting three days trying to produce a fancy computer graphics cover picture, and had to rush the concluding section. A lot of the technical parts went over Miss Doherty's head, as they would have Nathaniel's not long previously, but her criticisms of the structure of his work were valid. Nathaniel received 68%, the lowest mark for any of his work for a long time, but a safe pass.

And so at the end of his school career, Nathaniel was, on the surface, both academically and socially successful. In fact, after a time when his academic ego, at least, had known no bounds, he was feeling rather chastened. He was conscious that he couldn't know everything, and that his view of the universe had its flaws, possibly intractable. He still wanted Rosemary, but could not, in full conscience, claim that he loved her unconditionally and forever. At least he could keep her out of his thoughts to the extent that she no longer affected his day-to-day functioning.

Nathaniel E. Papulous obtained four A-levels, all of them As, and had the pick of the universities.

CHAPTER SIX
Student Daze

Universities pride themselves on their academic reputations and their traditions. Their brochures also mention location, access to public transport, the pleasant nature of their constantly sunny campuses (at least that's what the photographs imply) and the salubrity of their modern student accommodation.

While these things are important to some, for many potential students other factors, over which the universities have little control or ability to dissimulate, take precedence. These include the destinations of school chums or girlfriends/boyfriends and the proximity of families.

In the late 1980s and the nineties, when government money was drained by such plutocracy-directed initiatives as tax cuts for the rich and the privatisation of state monopolies, many students were constrained by the paltriness of their grants to stay at home. Nathaniel was fortunate to be going to university before Mrs. Thatcher, the World Bank, the IMF, the MAI, and the subordinate treaties of Amsterdam and Maastricht had done any major damage to proletariat education, but the proximity of his parents was also important in his choice of university. Like most sensible students, but possibly with more reason, he wanted to get as far from them as possible. The most distant establishment offering a degree in computer science was Inverdon University in the northeast of Scotland.

Like many south of the border, Nathaniel knew little about Scotland before arriving there. He was familiar with the Bay City Rollers, of course, and had heard of the rival Glaswegian football teams Rangers and Celtic. Billy Connolly, Sean Connery, whisky, kilts and tartan had their origins in Caledonia so he'd heard, but he had no idea that the single most important thing about Scotland was that it was NOT England. He was allocated a place in a predominantly English-occupied hall of residence, and never did manage to work out whether the English students had been thus concentrated to reduce their inevitable feelings of alienation as expatriates, to protect them from victimisation, or to minimize the amount of contact with the hated English that the Scots had to endure. For the first time in his life Nathaniel found himself having to apologise for his place of birth. If he went out for a drink in a pub he was expected to knock back pint after pint of McEwlose's Export, Rusty Nails and Whisky Macs, and, at closing time, stand up and sing, "Oh, flower of Scotland…" (or, more accurately, "Oh floo-err o' Sco'land!") which celebrated not only the defeat of "proud Edward's army" by the Scots hundreds of years ago but also, in the way it was sung on the streets, the recently acquired and grotesque glottal stop. He'd always assumed that he was British, and that everyone else in Great Britain felt British as well. Now he realised his mistake.

Conditions in the halls were cramped, which did nothing to alleviate the siege mentality suffered by many of the foreigners. Rumour had it that the accommodation blocks shared their design with East German prisons, but instead of the four rooms per kitchen unit in which German anti-communists presumably luxuriated (the lucky, lucky bastards!), there were six, with the same total floor space. At least this avoided any ambiguity when a girl asked one to visit her room—there was only room for one thing, and it wasn't swinging cats! As it happened, Nathaniel was not asked to visit a girl's room for some time and, unsurprisingly in view of his history, he did not want any dealings with cats.

Sharing a tiny kitchen and bathroom with five bachelors would be difficult for most people; for Nathaniel, with his near-obsessional nature, it was a nightmare. His *idées fixes* unfortunately extended to matters of hygiene and tidiness. With regard to these aspects of life Nathaniel found himself unusual; the adolescent and post-adolescent male of the species *Homo sapiens* is not generally known for fastidiousness. One could describe Nathaniel's initial attempts to keep the bathroom and kitchen clean, one could specify the proportion of his student grant spent on disinfectant, one could quantify the pubic hair he removed from the shower, the mass of fungal material he harvested from crockery and assorted cooking utensils (when he managed to find them), one could enumerate the rotting pieces of flesh he tracked down under the refrigerator, one could provide a transcript of the rows Nathaniel had with his fellow inmates pertaining to these matters....All this would be easy because Nathaniel recorded all these things himself, in his diary and in his letters to Mr. and Mrs. B. Their replies, while sympathetic, could be summarized by the words: "Too bad. Grit your teeth. When in Rome...."

Nathaniel held out a while. After giving up on his attempts at enforcing operating theatre standards of hygiene, he tried to live as much as possible in his own room, but he found there was a limit to the culinary applications of a toaster, a radiator and a kettle. It was too expensive to eat out more than a couple of nights a week. At least one couldn't do that if one wanted to drink as well....Nathaniel did begin to notice that beyond three pints his ability to tolerate sub-optimal sanitation started to improve. In fact it was after a six-pint spree one night that he found himself chatting to Gavin (his immediate neighbour) in the kitchen over a fridge-raiding session.

"You know, Gavin...." said Nathaniel.

"Yah?" replied Gavin.

"You know, Gav, I've just...hic...realised...I've just rea...I've just realised shomething 'portant."

"Yah?" said Gavin again, as interrogatively as before.

"You know what dirt is?"

"Yah, course," said Gavin, affirmatively this time.

"All it is...hic...all it is, ish jusht clean stuff, but ver' small!"

"Thatsh right!"

"So a crumb...like...a crumb, say...."

"Yah...." said Gavin ambiguously, perhaps encouragingly.

"Crumb's jusht small piece bread!"

"Yah....I'm gonna be sick...."

Fortunately Gavin made it to the WC, thus not immediately forcing Nathaniel to reappraise his new-found philosophy.

Drink helped reduce tensions in the flat in other ways. There was a sense of solidarity between hangover sufferers of a more concentrated form than that to be had from being The-Hated-English together in Scotland. Drinking excesses and hangover cures provided an endless and safe conversational territory. True, the endlessness was more subjective than objective, the same ground being re-trodden time after time, but the sober analysis of these issues was not important.

Thus, with the help of ethanol, the neuronal plasmalemma permeability-altering excretory product of the oxygen-starved yeast organism, Nathaniel found himself gradually drifting into a normal student lifestyle. A propensity for indulging in half-baked philosophical discussions with his flatmates and a tolerance of filthy living conditions were two of the necessary components of this. In parallel with the erosion of Nathaniel's sense of isolation within the mini-community of his flat, the English students were gradually being absorbed into the mainstream student community. Not only was this acclimation to Caledonia due to their habituation to anti-English songs (a concomitant of much pub-drinking in the land the Gaels call Alba, and therefore associated with pleasant experiences *à la* Pavlov's drooling dogs), but also to that wonder drug, testosterone.

It has been said that, under the influence of oestrogen, women become unpredictable for a few days every month, but that men are permanently under the more dangerous thrall of testosterone. Yes, most crimes are committed by men, but one must balance the scales by considering the influence of testosterone on the behaviour of English students on Scottish campuses. The attractions of Scottish women for the testosterone-driven existed long before the words "bonnie" and "lassie" found themselves juxtaposed. (Indeed, etymology suggests that the very word "bonnie" testifies to the powerlessness of the French to resist feminine Caledonian charms.) The problem for an Englishman is how to approach these beguiling creatures dubbed "bonnie lassies." What are the appropriate rituals?

Scotland is a harsh land of mountains, moors and forests, periodically swept by Arctic winds. What's more, it is permanently wet. To survive in this inhospitable place the wildlife must be tough, and no female creature would dream of pairing with anything other than the hardiest of males, so ensuring the fitness of her offspring. To assist the selection process nature has developed elaborate courtship behaviours. Once a year the deer have their rut. Once a year the capercaillies have their lek. Most people will be familiar with the notion of two thick-necked, muscle-bound and shaggy-coated stags, antlers locked, pirouetting and snorting misty-breathed as they fight for the control of a harem of seemingly indifferent does. Who, having heard a stag bugling his challenge or his victory, can forget the spectacle? The lek of the capercaillies is scarcely less awe-inspiring though it is a more civilised procedure. These huge black grouse, denizens of the dark pine forests, assemble in clearings where the males enact an ancient dance display, tails fanned, and throats pulsing as they produce a sound of the same timbre as that produced by a pebble hitting the water at the bottom of a very deep and narrow well. It is the mysterious, tingle-producing pulse of pre-history. At the end of this transfixing, tremulous, Terpsichorean veiled velitation it is to the spectating hen-birds to decide which male's performance collects the coveted carnal congratulations.

The people of Scotland, subject no less to the vicissitudes of these northern climes than the fauna, have a similarly rigorous mate-selection procedure. It is called the ceilidh (pronounced "kay-lee"), and it differs in only two details from the rituals described above. Firstly, as the connubial antics of the human species are not seasonally restricted, the ceilidh takes place throughout the year (although it is ideally suited to winter). Secondly, the mate-seeking Scottish female (the above-mentioned lassie) is not content to judge purely from the sidelines, she must participate, palpate male muscles directly, and compare the grip strengths of her potential inseminators. Together with the pub, the ceilidh is the most important institution in Caledonia.

Entering the student bar one Thursday evening, Nathaniel and Gavin were fortunate to spot a poster before their blood-alcohol levels would have rendered reading impossible. It was advertising a freshers' "see-lide" (as they pronounced it), and whatever a "see-lide" was, they decided they would go. Colin, the most gung-ho of their flatmates, said that he would accompany them, when he heard later of their plans.

Saturday evening found them entering what had been the familiar central refectory, now transformed by the dimming of lights, by the dress of the students, and by something no less tangible to those present but more difficult to describe, the ceilidh-expectation atmosphere. The bar was one familiar beacon in this unnerving, exciting environment, and Gavin, Nathaniel and Colin propped themselves there to spy out the land. The lassies were particularly ravishing that evening, in longish skirts and with their pale northern skins delicately tinted with carefully applied make-up. Their eyes sparkled. The laddies were no less colourful, in kilts, Prince Charlie jackets, and dagger-bearing socks, which weaponry they later discovered were called *skean-dhus*. Jokes about men wearing skirts were clearly unwise! Fortunately there were many men more conventionally attired, from an English point of view, so the be-trousered Nathaniel & Co. did not feel themselves overly conspicuous. A band was tuning up on a raised platform: two fiddlers, an accordion player, and a bass player with the characteristic disenchanted fag-in-the-corner-of-the-mouth mien of his calling, and there seemed to be a couple of other band-associated types hanging around. A Scotsman was ordering a round next to them, and obviously heard their accents, "Have you loons ever been to a ceilidh before?"

Why was he calling them "loons," and what on earth was a "kaylee"? Nathaniel & Co. looked blank until they realised that he must be referring to a "see-lide." "No," said Gavin, before adding (unnecessarily from a semantic point-of-view, but wisely from the point of view of not wanting to sound too curt), "this is the first time."

"Och, well. I think you'll enjoy it. There's really nothing to it. They'll call out the steps and you just follow along. Besides you'll find that your partner will probably know what to do anyway. By the way, the name's Euan."

Nathaniel & Co. introduced themselves, delighted that they had stumbled upon a tame Scot with an intelligible accent. Euan took them over to his table and introduced them to Shelagh, a petite blue-eyed blonde with a bob and a huge smile, and to Mary, a tall dark-haired and dark-eyed creature possessed of a regal grace and an arch turn of phrase.

Sarah was a short-haired brunette with a tom-boyish pizazz about her—
she didn't wait to be introduced! Conversation was easily started, the
standard questions ("Where are you from?" and "What are you
studying?") providing enough leads for an evening's interchanges. Only
Nathaniel's answers failed to raise much interest. He felt compelled to
fill the embarrassing silences that followed "Computing science" and
"Utter Glopwort" with something. Wisely, rather than providing further
unwanted details of his own biography, he followed up others' answers.

It is a curious fact that whereas it is generally accepted that self-
confidence is a good thing, it is often the slightly insecure who make the
better conversationalists, and, in consequence, often make the better
first impressions. Gavin and Colin were better looking than Nathaniel,
but Nathaniel's apparent interest in the lassies' histories and thoughts
contrasted with the other lads' relative air of vacant complacency and
tended to cancel their physiognomical advantages. Barriers down, and
the playing field level, all three young Englishmen found themselves
regularly hauled onto the dance floor.

Ceilidh dancing is better watched than read about, and better
performed than watched. One can buy, it is true, how-to-do-it books on
Scottish country dancing, which is to ceilidh dancing what English
thoroughbreds are to Shetland ponies. However this analogy is not
perfect as there exists abundant literature on all matters equestrian.
There are Thelwell-illustrated manuals galore on the stubborn and
malicious little Shelties, informing one in detail of the likely bruises and
bumps of mini-equestrianship, and giving one thereby some idea of how
to avoid them. Even if one could interpret the semi-abstract black
footprints spelling out Scottish country dance steps in the appropriate
manuals this would be a poor preparation for a ceilidh, as useful as
perusing a Dick Francis novel would be, say, as preparation for a heather-
bashing pony trek on the Isle of Skye. Watching a ceilidh is diverting, but
for a novice the dances appear off-puttingly complex and violent, the
grins of the participants bizarrely at odds with the torture they appear to
be putting themselves through. No, the only way to experience a ceilidh
is to get up and dance.

—

Nathaniel found himself being whirled down the middle of two lines of glowing faces: on the one side laddies, on the other, lassies. The latter creatures would individually grab him, spin him round, and pass him back to his partner (Sarah) and she would whirl him again and pass him to the next pair of hands reaching avariciously from the waiting row. This dance seemed to go on forever, with some variation. At the end of a whirling session or three he would find himself in the laddies' line, clapping away to the drug-like music. Then it was the whirling again: the first time—down the way—it was his partner being whirled by the men and he just had to whirl her on the rebounds, the next time, up the way, it was himself being whirled all the time, the next time, down the way again it was the two of them….Gradually everything fell into place, and Nathaniel was at home with his first ceilidh dance, the Strip-the-Willow. It was too late to go back now, Nathaniel E. Papulous was infected with Caledoniaphilia.

The disease of Caledoniaphilia may progress in a number of ways, but the ceilidh is the most common method of infection, whisky seriously retards recovery, and exile aggravates the symptoms to a painful extent. (More of that later….) It is possible to subdivide the infection stage. The starting point is passivity, a willingness to be pulled onto the dance floor, and be flung about. Then comes a desire to fling others about (which Nathaniel was developing at the end of the Strip-the-Willow). The real enjoyment starts with this more active phase, when the lassie will giggle and catch the laddie's eye if his grip is manly and the torque he imparts sufficient. Things are hotting up when one is driven to utter the traditional ceilidh cry, often rendered on paper as "Hooch!" but, sounding, in reality, nothing like the oxymoronic "alcoholic soft drink" which shares that orthography. The roaring of the stags and the plocking of the capercaillies has little on this feral and atavistic vocable. Almost contemporary with the hooching is the show-off stage. This can manifest in more than one way. The real snobs will refuse to dance anything less challenging than a Schottische, the more everyday show-offs will relish that part of the Eightsome Reel when they can gyrate, gesticulate and raise the hems of their kilts in the middle of an admiring (they imagine) ring of seven other dancers, four being of the opposite gender.

Nathaniel went through all of these phases barring the Schottische, which eluded him altogether. Colin drank too much and didn't make it through his first Strip-the-Willow, despite the fact that it was an ordinary one and did not involve the marathon spins of the Orcadian version. Gavin developed a particular affection for the Dashing White Sergeant, perhaps because this involved dancing with most of the people in the room and thus gave him the opportunity of close—if transient—contact with a lass he'd spotted in the corner earlier. Having smiled very obviously at her, *en passant*, he plucked up the courage to go and chat to her. He waited until she was near the bar so that the encounter would look accidental, took his courage in his hands, and ventured forth. "So, is this your first ceilidh?"

This was a terrible line from a novice Englander to an experienced lassie, but she smiled. "No. Is it yours? They're great, aren't they?"

Gavin hadn't prepared any other lines, so fell back on slight variants of the standard ones. "So…you're local are you?"

"Well, not really. I'm from Edinburgh."

"I've only been there once, on my way here by train—beautiful!"

"Yes, it's worth a proper visit!"

The lass was looking restless, so Gavin had to ask another question, but wanted to put a spark into it. "Let me guess what you're studying, it's a hobby of mine. Ummm… I'd say English and philosophy!"

She laughed prettily. "No, it's psychology actually. Listen it's been nice chatting to you, but my boyfriend's waiting for his drink….Ah, here he is. Luke, this is, ah…?"

Gavin introduced himself, disappointed to meet what he learned was the boyfriend of Cynthia, but happy not to have committed any major impropriety. When Luke asked him if he'd care to join himself and Cynthia in what sounded like the "Hooligan's Jig," he naïvely agreed to this apparently friendly gesture. He was instructed to find another woman to join them, and the ever-willing Sarah stood in. Poor Gavin was to learn a lesson that night that almost cured him of Caledoniaphilia.

One can see parallels between various ceilidh dances and the agonistic antics of highland beasts, but there is no correspondence as close as that of the "Hooligan's Jig" (in fact, "Hulichan's") to the locked-antler spinning sessions of red deer stags. In approaching the doe-eyed Cynthia, Gavin had unwittingly crossed the challenge threshold of her possessive partner, and the latter had accepted the perceived challenge in the way natural to an acolyte of St. Andrew.

Nathaniel, fortunately sitting out this dance, watched his flatmate's humiliating destruction. A cat complacently falling asleep in a spin-dryer could not have had a ruder awakening than did the hapless centrifugally vanquished Gavin. He staggered towards the toilets and reappeared fifteen minutes later, whey-faced and trembling. Sympathetic words from the friendly faces at Euan's table helped restore some confidence, but Gavin did not dance again that evening. Shelagh, Mary and Sarah weren't at all bad looking themselves, he thought nauseously—what the hell had he seen in Cynthia?

The closing event was the singing of "Auld lang syne." Everyone joined hands, and the circle thus formed moved inwards and outwards to the music, the whole gradually accelerating until wild abandon took over. Nathaniel & Co. were no longer the isolated inhabitants of an English enclave, and the University of Inverdon was starting to look like an enormously good choice. They slept well that night, comely lassies cavorting captivatingly in their drunken dreams.

CHAPTER SEVEN
High Pressure, a Low, and an Ambivalent Alliance

Little has been said about Nathaniel's academic progress at university. At first there wasn't much. He was, however, having a damn good time, and progressing apace in the more important school of life. All very well, but it doesn't pay the rent.

With only a handful of lectures under his belt, Nathaniel found the first-year exams approaching. At least, he thought to himself, he knew how to operate a photocopier.

In any class one finds a broad range of aptitude, commitment and self-confidence. These characteristics are more or less randomly distributed. For example one may find a very capable student who doesn't particularly care if he passes or fails, but is very confident that he will pass. Equally, there may be totally incompetent students who believe that they are likely to fail and therefore attend every lecture and conscientiously note down every word (or at least suffer from the delusion that they have faithfully transcribed every word). Nathaniel, as a consequence of his success at school, and of the previously mentioned distractions, found himself in the former category, that of the over-confident. At the end of the year he decided that it might be an idea to have some notes. Unfortunately, he borrowed them from a student in the last-described category, that of the diligent but intellectually challenged slogger.

Edward McDonald, apart from having been cursed with an embarrassing combination of English and Scottish epithets, had the misfortune to have been under-supplied with grey matter (for the more literal minded, his neural circuitry was not as efficiently connected as it might have been, intra-specific brain mass not in fact being highly correlated with intellectual performance in young adulthood, although senile performance does appear to be...). He was a good lad, nonetheless, and his thick-witted perseverance had seen him into university. *Peter's Principle* states that people rise to the level of their incompetence. Edward had risen to his. His notes, generously lent to whomsoever wished to borrow them, were virtually useless. (They were not entirely useless as the paper was yet serviceable for the construction of model aircraft.) Nathaniel, like numerous other classmates, borrowed and photocopied Edward's deficient but neat scripts. The members of this "Edward McDonald Photocopy Clan" failed their exams. All of them. All the clan members and all the exams.

Nathaniel was devastated. His hours of waiting in the photocopier queue and his two nights of caffeine-fuelled cramming had been in vain. For the first time in his life he had failed a major academic challenge. Not only had he failed to win the affections of Rosemary (years previously, but still rankling) but he had failed in the one area he had believed himself secure. *Failed, failed, failed!* He walked through Ushant Park, back to the student residences from the campus, glorious flowers singing in technicolour under the crystalline light of the far northern midsummer, but all he saw was black. *Shit, shit, shit!*

Logical positivism will out. Eventually. Nathaniel (he of the fear-of-heights remedy) manoeuvred the situation in his mind. If he had to re-sit his exams he did not have to return home for the time being. As most of the other students had disappeared he would have fewer distractions, and under those circumstances he should easily catch up. Mary and Shelagh lived in Inverdon, so if he did feel lonely he could see them. Things could be worse.

The hall authorities were determined to make them so. In a ploy possibly obtained from the East German prison regime (as a job lot along with the plans for the hostels?) they insisted that all students staying for the summer holiday had to move out of their term-time blocks and in to the Stalag Teuchter building. Their justification for this considerable disruption was that they were going to hire out the university facilities for a conference. *Trust them to stage a conference just to legitimise this act of wanton barbarity!* thought Nathaniel, as he carted bags of empty beer and cider bottles and cans out of his room to the refuse collection point, and took down his posters. Despite doing his best to clean the room he was fined for miscellaneous damage. It possibly had something to do with his attempts to cook fillets of cod by suspending them from shoelaces between the front and rear panels of his radiator. How was he to have known that fish loses its tensile strength when cooked? Besides it wasn't as if one couldn't habituate to the smell! It was scarcely more noticeable than the pile of sweaty socks and underwear found in most male students' rooms.

Once re-settled, Nathaniel started studying again in earnest. He managed to get hold of the phone number of one of the students who'd passed, and by dint of this capable and conscientious one's expensive notes (a bottle of Deep Shit Single Malt), and the textbooks in the library, he plugged the breach in the armour of his knowledge. He found he was sharing his new block with Kenyans, Indonesians and a chap from Hong Kong. Through these new acquaintances Nathaniel discovered African music and eastern cuisine. In turn, Nathaniel infected them all with belated Beatlemania (and if there had been a ceilidh on over the summer he'd probably have succeeded in infecting them with Caledoniaphilia as well). When Nathaniel eventually passed his re-sits they had an all-night party. The non-Africans found themselves learning an East African song, "Malaika, ndakupenda malaika…" about love unrequited owing to the suitor's poverty. Nathaniel taught them John Lennon's "Imagine all the people, living for today…." It ended in a maudlin fashion with them mumbling drunken inanities about brotherly love and the wretched contrariness of women. And there were three women in particular on Nathaniel's mind.

—

There are many types of love/obsession/attraction. What one experiences of these emotions is determined not only by individual circumstances but also by one's culture. Some cultures have no notion of falling in love, as Nathaniel learned from Samuel, one of his Kenyan flatmates, who although himself westernized in this respect was aware of his forebears' traditions. In other cultures the importance and centrality of this concept is beyond questioning. It would be fatuous to attribute the rise in the divorce rate in the western Anglophone world to Hollywood and Mills-and-Boon fairytale-fed propagandizing and parasitism on this notion of One True Love and its corollary (that once the couple has been established there is no more work to be done—one is bound to live happily ever after). There is indisputably, however, a degree of commercial self-interest in the hyping of the OTL myth. There is also a rising divorce rate. Nathaniel, like most westerners unconsciously inhaling the notion from birth, had expectations of finding his OTL, and verged on believing he had found her in the form of Rosemary—it only remained for her to realise this. With this notion underlying his psyche, it would have been very difficult for him to fall "deeply in love" with anyone else.

To revert to river metaphors, if one considers the "true love" of a life to be the lining of the canal which directs the waters of that life, then the height of the water above the unsilted bottom corresponds to the depth of love. Unfortunately most such waterways need regular dredging and frequent maintenance if they are not to become sclerotically silted or cracked. Nathaniel had had no positive feedback or contact with Rosemary for years. His canal was still there but it was heavily silted, which meant that his awareness of Rosemary was no longer pervasive; he could almost forget at times what constituted the lining of the waterway. Ideally Nathaniel would have gone through the process of constructing an entirely new canal, lined by someone else. He was content, however, to try to fit a false bottom under the shallow water and above the silt of his old one.

Nathaniel-the-student thought occasionally about Rosemary, and more often about Shelagh and Mary. Shelagh, all bubble and sparkle.

Mary, seemingly calm waters upon which one embarked with serenity only to find oneself sucked into a whirlpool; the depths were fascinating, the lure irresistible. Nathaniel found himself drawn to both of them, and allowed himself to see each at least once a week during his pre-re-exam cram. The problem was they were close friends in their own right, having been to school together. Which one should he "make a pass at" and how and when? He only knew how to fail.

Mary-the-magnetic. Some afternoons they would go for a hot chocolate together in a café at the beach, and she would sit next to the window, staring far out to sea, seemingly oblivious of her immediate surroundings—and of Nathaniel even—for minutes at a time. She was always elegantly dressed, in long skirts, cashmere sweaters and chic silk scarves draped with flair. Her neatly plucked—but not overdone—arched and dark little eyebrows, epitomising refined femininity, added a whimsical air to her languorous but intense gaze. Her conversation seemed to reach beyond the superficial in that same beguiling way—never explicit, but carrying so much weight, and going to the core of things. Things which one hadn't been consciously aware existed, but which one recognised as important and real as soon as she spoke. Nathaniel would ask her if she'd enjoyed the last ceilidh, for example, and she would turn slowly from the sea, exhale the smoke from her slim cigarette in a narrow and seemingly endless plume, and reply, "Nathaniel, do you never see the sadness in desperate joy-seeking?"

Slightly discomfited he would say something about it not being desperate joy-seeking at all, and what was wrong with fun anyway?

She would murmur, "Fun...." Yes, she was discomfiting, but that kind of disturbance was addictive.

One day, she turned to Nathaniel, as he was rabbiting on towards her perfect and mournful profile about the quirks of his flatmates. Her tantalising voice conveyed the same question as the words it carried. "Nathaniel, do you think you could really love me?" Her dark, hungry eyes briefly scoured his soul. He couldn't reply, so she spoke for him, one corner of her neat pale pink lips curled briefly, just short of scorn. "No. I thought not. I'm never going to find anyone, Nathaniel. I can't live in the surface world which you others inhabit. Don't get me wrong, I'm not saying I'm better than you. I'm worse, even. I don't know where I begin and where I end, so how could anyone else know that for me…of me? How could I be loved? I envy you. Nathaniel, you and Shelagh would be good for each other. Sometimes knowing less is knowing more, is wiser. There is no ultimate meaning, so enjoy, enjoy." And as she spoke, Nathaniel knew that she could also have been describing him. He was attracted to her because part of him was like her, and he had been hiding it from her, and he'd only managed to do this because he'd been hiding it from himself also. He told her about Rosemary. For the first time since he'd met her, Mary laughed.

Meetings with Shelagh were so different. She did most of the talking, and most of the laughing. Nathaniel could rest in her company. There was no work to be done: a bask in the sun, coasting with the engine switched off. But Shelagh was sometimes a "desperate joy-seeker," and one evening, when Nathaniel returned from the bar with her lager and lime and his oatmeal stout, she told him, "Nathaniel, I sometimes feel so…so inadequate when I'm around you and Mary. You laugh, but sometimes I wonder whether you're laughing at me. You two know so much!"

And then Nathaniel saw Shelagh clearly for the first time. "Shelagh, you are so wrong! We love you, both of us. And we need you!"

Nathaniel would not manage to fit a false bottom called Shelagh or Mary to his love canal. Whether they saw each other every day or only every few weeks, for the rest of their university careers the three of them formed a stable *ménage-à-trois*. Each of them needed the others, but was, at the same time, held prisoner by them. They were emotionally set; the only possibly progress was in the understanding of their problems, not in their resolution. They had one regular rendezvous. Once a month, on a Sunday, they would go for a walk on the beach together, elegant Mary, scarf billowing in the wind, on Nathaniel's right arm, and jaunty little Shelagh, in jeans and a brightly checked jersey, on his left arm. Shelagh would chatter away, Mary would be silent, and Nathaniel would be torn between the two of them, wishing that they could all really love.

There are two possible explanations for Nathaniel's situation. The implication of the narrative so far is that his inability to even temporarily fall for Mary or Shelagh was due to chance: it was chance that they both turned out to be unavailable, and hopelessly dependent on each other, so that the only possible role for Nathaniel was that of piggy-in-the-middle mutual confidante. The other explanation would be that subconsciously Nathaniel perceived that they were unavailable, possibly even from the time of the first meeting. Something in the way they interacted with each other, with him and with the world, told him that evening that their personalities were like the two halves of a mould into which his personality could slip, and be protected. No danger of painful change. No real growth. Just a comfortable and safe cocoon from which to long for it. Perhaps he was looking for an ideal beyond any real woman. Rosemary-of-his-mind.

CHAPTER EIGHT
John Lennon

Nathaniel went home a week after his last re-sit. His parents' home was as cheerless as ever. He visited the Barkers. Their world seemed small and petty. He was desperate to get back to Inverdon.

By December 1980, towards the end of the first term of his second year at university, things were settling into a comfortable routine. He had some good friends. He did not feel the need to go out drinking every night. He was a member of the Celtic Society. He'd decided it would be a good idea to attend the odd lecture. On Tuesday the ninth of December he had no lectures. He rose late, had a couple of slices of toast and some coffee in the kitchen. Then he took a shower, shaved himself and brushed his teeth. He was listening to the Beatles' *Abbey Road* album and going through his lecture notes when Shelagh burst in. She was distraught. Her red eyes took in the calmness of the scene. "Have you not heard? John's dead! Lennon—he's dead! Some madman's shot him!"

For a long time they sat on Nathaniel's bed, hugging each other, crying and letting the album play on in the background. Alas, it wasn't even an argent mallet—such as the one alluded to in the lyrics—that had ensured the demise of the Liverpudlian bard and peacenik. It was an unglamorous gun. (For the rest of their lives even a few bars of any of the songs on that album would cause them to cry.) Nathaniel poured them each a whisky. Then, leaving Shelagh to sip hers, he went outside and phoned the Barkers, forgetting that they'd both be at school. He came back and drank more whisky. He tried to tell Shelagh what the Beatles, and especially John Lennon, had meant to him, but he was almost incoherent. They cried until they were exhausted.

Around six o'clock, feeling drained, they bought themselves a meal at the student canteen: chips with misery. They phoned Mary, and the three of them sat in the student bar together. Mary was dry-eyed and she had obviously not been crying, but her customary gloom was a bit deeper than usual. At first Nathaniel was almost angry at her for apparently not sharing the depth of his and Shelagh's pain, but while he was trying to analyse the unfocussed rage inside him, without knowing how he'd come to it he suddenly found he understood something about her. She did not appear particularly distressed, particularly shocked, because she lived with a constant awareness of death, and of the futility of life. John Lennon's demise was no news to her, no surprise. It just confirmed her in her beliefs. As this revelation hit him, Nathaniel started crying anew, this time as much for Mary as for anything else. Mary's dark eyes met his, and he knew that she knew what he'd discovered about her. She managed a half smile.

No matter how much pain he was experiencing now, or had experienced in the past, it could not amount to a forged farthing compared to the horror of the constant awareness of the void, with which Mary lived. Luckily, unlike poor Mary, Nathaniel knew he could still, from time to time, throw himself into the pleasures of the here-and-now—superficial admittedly—but what was life apart from the summation of the here-and-nows? Nathaniel resolved to let himself go even more, to live even more in the world of ephemeral delights and therefore of equally transient pain. He did not realise the paradox of resolving, in effect, to make fewer resolutions. He attended as many ceilidhs as he could, he even kissed a few girls afterwards; he continued to enjoy a drink, the nights of carousing with his male flatmates, and his strange walks on the beach with Shelagh and Mary, the actual and symbolic poles of his existence. Despite the valuable philosophical insights that Nathaniel believed he'd had, there no further significant changes in what remained of his undergraduate career.

There is another way to look at Nathaniel's undergraduate years. Form a paperclip into an S-shape. Grasp the upper end of the S between the forefinger and thumb of your right hand and the lower end between the forefinger and thumb of your left hand. Now pull your right hand up and to the right, and your left hand down and to the left. You have created a sigmoid curve. The sigmoid curve is one of the most useful curves in the sciences. It describes the speed of chemical reactions, the growth of an animal from conception to maturity, the growth of a bacterial colony in a Petri-dish from inoculation to maximum density, and it also describes the learning curve in a new environment.

When Nathaniel arrived at the University of Inverdon he was overwhelmed by new stimuli, by the strangeness of it all. At first he closeted himself in his room and clung to old ways of life, but he couldn't help being influenced, gradually, by diffusion. (We are on the lower left end of the distorted paperclip and it has only a slight upward slope to the right.) With time he felt more secure and opened himself to new ways of thinking (for example as far as tidiness was concerned) and he took some brave steps, such as going to a ceilidh. This was a good experience and his self-confidence grew. In order to satisfy his social and other cravings he was prepared to take bolder and bolder actions. He met more and more people and learnt new things at a great rate. (We are in the middle of the paperclip, and it is steeply climbing.) With time he found that there was no great need to meet any more people—he had a good circle of friends, and, besides, he only had so much time and energy and his studies needed a certain amount of this. There was also less left to discover: he knew the Inverdon area well, particularly its pubs. (We are approaching the end of the undergraduate paperclip, and it is almost horizontal.) Lennon's death came about three-quarters of the way along the paperclip. The recollection of the assassination would help inaugurate the middle section of the most important paperclip of Nathaniel's life but this, the real impact of John Winston Lennon's death on the life of Nathaniel E. Papulous, was not to happen for another fifteen years.

Nathaniel graduated without difficulty, obtaining a 2.1. The door was open to a career in computing or to further study. A decision had to be made.

CHAPTER NINE
Unhappy Days

If one looks forward too much to the achievement of an ambition, if one sees its realisation as an end and not just as a mildly pleasant stopping-off point, then one is bound to feel anti-climactic when that goal is reached. Like many students in the relatively golden years of the early eighties, Nathaniel was guilty of focussing on his final exams to the extent that he had no idea what he was going to do after graduation. The first couple of days were pleasant enough: guilt-free drinking sprees with similarly successful friends. Then came the vacuum. He knew what he didn't want to do: move back down to England and away from the hard-won territory of his new adulthood. Obviously, then, he needed to find a job in the Inverdon area, but how and where? Fortunately Inverdon was at the heart of the North Sea oil industry, which, like every other business in the eighties, was obsessed with computers and computerising. They were gagging for computer "experts." Nathaniel was snapped up as soon as he dipped a toe in the job-seeking water. One day he had been wondering what he was going to do, the next he was working for Dutch-Anglo Petrochemicals Ltd.

DAP owned a brash skyscraper on the outskirts of Inverdon. From his office on the tenth floor Nathaniel could see far out to sea. This was a problem. Being a "computer expert" and knowing more about his job than anyone else, Nathaniel had no one breathing down his neck to check what he was up to. He was unique amongst DAP employees in this respect. As computing was changing so fast, even people who had graduated three years before him did not feel qualified to supervise—

they were terrified that they would reveal their own ignorance.

Nathaniel had been used to the pressure of exams. Now there were no pressures, but there was a lovely sea vista. He would stare out the window and think of Mary, marine-musing Mary. He would think of Mary and Shelagh and their walks along the beach. He would think of how the waves crashing against the beach had not changed in millennia, but how the hamlet-village-town-city of Inverdon had evolved, and even the beach, now held in place with perpendicular fences, like the little sticks that assured the integrity of roll-mops…even the beach must have changed beyond recognition and eaten its way west into the land. He would think of the fish that came out of that sea to make the roll-mops, and of the first time he had tasted Scottish fish—haddock from the takeaway on Queen Street—and of his ludicrous attempts to cook fish himself on the student residence radiator. Sometimes he would think about how they cleaned the windows of the DAP building. The men who did that would certainly not be scared of heights—were they naturally bereft of that phobia, or had they discovered some psychological trick for overcoming it in the same way as he had in his youth? Was it Dutch-Anglo courage? (Ha!) Did they have to pay more for their life insurance? In short, Nathaniel would think about anything and everything except his work.

What he was supposed to be doing was working on a new database which would enable DAP to improve its efficiency. Ultimately the company wanted to be able to analyse the present and projected costs of labour, the probability of political and labour instability, current and projected costs of extraction equipment, the probability of future oil finds, the present and future activities of its competitors, the present and future statuses of various markets, etc., etc., on a global basis, in order, of course, to maximise profits. This super-analysis was a long way from being completed and Nathaniel was not, of course, expected to achieve this huge task himself. His job was to improve the international labour cost comparison module of the database.

A huge collection of economic facts and figures sat in front of him in numerous files. He did not need to concern himself with their absolute values, nor with what they represented in terms of the exploitation of poverty, but he did need to think about how the abstract figures related to each other, in order to make the interrogation of the future database as easy as possible. A few ideas had been suggested to him. For example it would be useful to question the database about the relationships within a country (and internationally) between the equality of income distribution, the level of unemployment, the development of a social security system, the degree of organisation of trade unions, and the minimum wage which could be paid and still guarantee sufficient employees of any given level of training.

For Nathaniel it was as boring as the routine tasks of dentists and oil drillers, and the significance of it all eluded him. Three weeks into the job he'd had enough of staring out the window, or, to be more precise, he'd had enough of feeling guilty about staring out of the window. He'd decided he needed a break from brain work. He tore his eyes from the seascape, put the few scraps of paper on which he'd written anything vaguely useful into a cardboard file, picked it up and walked to his superior's secretary's office, which constituted the antechamber to the boss's room, and knocked on the door. A flushed young woman opened the door and brushed past him. He could hear her sobbing as her heels clicked into the distance. Mr. Morgan was notoriously undiplomatic, but at least he had the decency to tell people face-to-face that they had been fired, unlike the big boss, Sir George "The Dragon" (knighted for donations to a political party), who rarely deigned to show himself to anyone more than two ranks down unless he particularly felt the need to humiliate.

Mr. Morgan's secretary was pale-faced and tight-lipped. Her voice seemed a little shaky as she asked Nathaniel to sit. She buzzed through to the monstrous Morgan, who indicated that Nathaniel should go straight through.

"Yes?" Morgan didn't even look up from his notes.

Nathaniel had been about to offer his resignation on the mythical grounds of emotional disturbance owing to the death of a relative, but something in the cowed attitudes of the lachrymose one and of the secretary goaded him to stand up to the ogre, and to simply state the truth: "Mr. Morgan. I resign. I find the work too boring. Here are my ideas. Goodbye." Managing to put an insolent lilt to the last word, he dropped the file on Morgan's desk, catching a glimpse of his astonished face as he turned and walked out. The lassitude that had claimed him since the post-exam festivities was left in pieces on the gaping Morgan's floor.

He caught the bus back to Junction Street, and strode buoyantly from there to his little rented flat on Granite Place. This was a stupid name in Inverdon, he reflected, as the whole city could have been called "Granite Place." In overcast weather it was grey and miserable. Now it was sunny and the mica chips were glistening from every surface. The air was cool and clear and the seagulls were calling. Nathaniel was in positive-thinking mode: "It's good to be alive! I have no job, but I love this place and I'm young and free and healthy and here! Things will work out." If it had been raining he probably would have executed a Gene Kelly impersonation.

Once home and listening to the Beatles—could it have been the album whose cover semaphored for emergency assistance?—the reality of his situation began to sink in. He needed to pay his rent. To eat and drink. As he had resigned he was not eligible for the dole. But he wanted to take a break from mental labour. Three days later he found himself working as a check-out operator at Steptoe's, the little supermarket on Junction Street. For the first time in his life Nathaniel found himself meeting a cross-section of humanity.

There will be no heart-warming morality tale about how Nathaniel E. Papulous came to appreciate that, while not everyone was particularly bright, the less intellectually gifted often possess the more-than-compensatory virtues of compassion and humour, enabling them to cope with their otherwise drab and *dreich* existences and bring a bit of light and joy into the world. Bollocks. Granted some of the check-out girls were fun—occasionally—but for Nathaniel there was little light and joy from the constant conversation about dieting, boyfriends and Australian soap operas in an almost unintelligible northeastern Scottish dialect. As for the more senior staff and the shelf-stackers...Mr. Tough (pronounced "Tooch," the final sound being the same as the guttural "ch" in "loch"), the manager, was a spindly stooped little man with thick glasses, who would come up and say, "Now, how are we doing today then, Nathaniel? Mmmn, mmmn…." The "Mmmn, mmmn…" constituted a tic, having no connection at all to the digestion of information, nor was it a cue for the addressee to continue talking, as it was produced before the addressee had opened his/her mouth. If it had any explanation at all it was that it signalled a mild displeasure, as it often preceded a complaint, usually of the most pedantic nature, such as, "Mmmn, mmmn…you know, Nathaniel, if you looked at your watch occasionally you would find it easier to avoid saying 'Good morning' when it is actually the afternoon. I make it three minutes past twelve, Nathaniel, and yet you have just greeted that lady with 'Good morning.' People notice these things, Nathaniel. Mmmn, mmmn…." Sniffing, he would stalk off to spy on another staff member, petty officialdom at its worst, self-important incompetence and treachery to the working class personified.

He never watched anyone without making a derogatory comment of some nature, as a result of which all the junior staff were panicked by his presence into making mistakes. The hardened senior staff, sensing his bleary gaze, would stop work and stare him out, and he would sniff loudly and turn away, hands behind his back, to find a weaker victim. He was loathed, but at least when he was at the other end of the supermarket he was an easy man to impersonate, to great hilarity. Nathaniel's real enemy was a shelf-stacker called Calum.

Calum grew up on the wrong side of the railway tracks, metaphorically at least. On principle he hated those he suspected of growing up on the other side. Nathaniel, being English and having gone to university, was several railway tracks away from being acceptable. It had been years since Nathaniel had consciously thought of himself as English. His adoption of the more important aspects of Scottish culture, his circle of local friends who saw him now as "Nathaniel" rather than as "English," and his avoidance of "real" Inverdonian pubs (as opposed to studenty ones) had contributed to this forgetfulness. Calum was to remind him of the land of his birth.

The first evidence of Calum's malign intentions were the hostile stares. Whenever Nathaniel found his till idle, he would, naturally enough, allow his eyes to wander. If he were lucky they would come to rest on some aesthetically agreeable member of the opposite sex. If he were unlucky he'd find himself staring into the uni-eyebrowed brutal countenance of Calum. It wasn't that Calum lacked supra-ocular hair, in fact being of hirsute Celtic stock (most of his great-grandparents had been Glaswegian) what otherwise would have been separate eyebrows were fused in the middle, and the conjoined bristles served to accentuate his beetlebrow to Neanderthalian effect. His dull and shallow brown eyes found themselves rather close together, sheltering under the middle of the frontal thatch, like two rats in a rainstorm. Shallow though they were, they were capable of radiating an extraordinary amount of hatred. They say that opposites attract, but the weak-chinned, slight and balding Nathaniel attracted only enmity from the slope-foreheaded, stocky and shaggy Calum. Calum never insulted Nathaniel on the supermarket floor, contenting himself with the basilisk glare, but should their paths cross in the changing room or outside the shop (and Calum made sure they did), it was a different matter. An index finger would jab Nathaniel repeatedly in the stomach to the tune of, "What's a f——ing English jessie like you daein' here? Are ye nae happy wi' stealing a place in oor university, and stealin' oor oil minnie, ya poof? Ye're takin' a guid Scottish job fae simbiddie fa deserves it! Ya f——ing English scum! Ah tell you, if ye're nae f——ing oot o' here by the end of the month I'll hae you! Ye widna like 'at. Ah'll gie ye three weeks. Three weeks, mind!" To emphasize his dearth of universal brotherly love, this would be followed by forceful expectoration in Nathaniel's direction.

Inverdonian anti-Sassanach graffiti, to which Nathaniel had formerly turned a blind eye, now seemed pervasive: "English out! Free Scotland!" Within a few days of feeling that it was good to be alive, and that he loved Inverdon, Nathaniel was feeling very isolated and foreign. There was, after all, only a small amount of comfort to be had from muttering "…in every packet of cornflakes" whenever he saw "Free Scotland"! It also didn't help that Shelagh was away on holiday, and Mary had left to start a job at the Victor Ear and Herb Alpert Museum in London. Maybe he'd made a huge mistake. The supermarket was at least as insufferable as the DAP job, even if Calum were put to one side…and what was Calum going to do to him? Was it worth contacting the police? It was his word against Calum's, and why make trouble if he was wanting to leave the job anyway? But how was he going to pay his rent? Everything he'd done had turned out badly. He was a failure. He must think.

What did he want out of life? He wasn't sure exactly how he felt about Rosemary anymore. He had no idea where she was or what she was doing, and, after all, it had been eight years since they'd last had any contact! It was surely ridiculous to hanker after a fourteen-year-old!? But, even if he had no idea what he would feel about the twenty-two-year-old Rosemary, it would be wonderful if he made it big one day, and if she bitterly regretted the way she had treated him. And even if it weren't to be Rosemary, the only way he could be sure to have something juicy would be if he were tremendously successful. He recognised he was no great shakes in the looks department, so he had to become rich and famous, or rich and powerful, or, better still, rich, famous and powerful. How? Although he was low at the moment, he still believed that he had the makings of greatness. "Where there's a will there's a way!" the all-knowing "they" said, but how to find this "way"?

There was no point in him trying to make it in a field where his heart was not. He'd tried that. So what was his heart in? When had he most enjoyed his work? He had enjoyed the three-dimensional modelling of Rosemary. He had been so excited when he'd had the idea of showing her as an old woman. If he were honest and he separated his self-disgust and embarrassment at his earlier naïveté about the way to gain a woman's affection, and his negative associations with the idea because of Rosemary's response, then that had genuinely given him a buzz. So what then? Biological modelling? The computing associated with CAT and ultrasonic scanning? Yes, but it would be frustrating to approach it solely from a computing point of view. He didn't want to be condescended to by the likes of those egotistical drunken bastards called doctors—he'd seen what they were like as medical students, God! What about that idea of ageing? He hadn't really enjoyed the biology project at school but if he wanted to carve out a niche for himself how about one at the frontier of biology and computing, doing, in effect, exactly what he'd tried to do with Rosemary's image, but in a much more scientific way? If he applied himself he could surely learn the anatomy and physiology to the extent of being able to hold his own with the white-coated fraternity…and it would be such a sexy subject! He could see the women's magazines begging him to show them what models and pop stars would look like in ten, twenty, forty years….Then he'd become a consultant to the vain rich on how to stay young and beautiful. And he could imagine some nubile young starlets would pay in kind! Yes!

So, now that he knew where he wanted to go, how exactly was he going to get there? He needed some concrete plans. He took the pad of notepaper from his telephone and wrote:

1. LEAVE SUPERMARKET AT END OF MONTH
2. STUDY BIOLOGY—DEGREE? FINANCE?

He underlined FINANCE and put the pen down in disgust. Having just obtained one degree he wouldn't be eligible for another grant. Why did everything have to come down to bloody money? He was going to have to prostitute himself, metaphorically at least. What would be the least painful way of doing it? In his mind he walked along Junction Street, looking at all the businesses and asking himself which of them he could tolerate working in. Ah ha! A bookshop! He took up the pen again, scored out what he'd written after 2., and wrote:

DO DEGREE IN BIOLOGY THROUGH OPEN COLLEGE, FINANCING IT BY WORKING IN BOOKSHOP

He chewed the end of the pen for a moment, spitting out a fragment of plastic, and added:

SUPPLEMENTED BY COMPUTER CONSULTATION WORK AS AVAILABLE.
3. DO PH.D. IN AGEING (COMPUTING + BIOLOGY AT LAST!)
4. BECOME RICH AND FAMOUS
5. FIND ROSEMARY AND RUB HER FACE IN IT/ MARRY HER!

"The best laid schemes o' mice an' men gang aft a-gley," said Burns. Fortunately Nathaniel's scribblings did not constitute a well-laid scheme, and he succeeded. Burns had a lot to do with it too.

CHAPTER TEN
Books and Biology

You don't just walk into a bookshop and say, "Give me a job!" and they give you one straight off. Oh no. Nathaniel modified his c.v. on his computer to try to make it look like that of an ideal bookshop employee. He knew about filing systems and computers, he read books and he'd held a semi-managerial position in the computer club at school. What more could they want? He couldn't think of anything else, so he printed several copies and visited all the bookstores in Inverdon to advertise his abilities and availability in person.

Blackstones was a large, dingy and slightly chaotic shop with an appealingly eccentric feel to it. The assistants always knew whether a book was in stock and where to find it, even if it turned out to be at the bottom of a miscellaneous and forgotten-looking pile in the corner. What's more if it was a work of fiction you were after they'd probably have read it and you would have to stop them enthusing if you wanted the denouement to be a surprise. The staff turnover was almost non-existent—someone had been replaced five years previously, it was rumoured.

Frillons was a modern, glitzy and bright competitor. They had a bang-up-to-date computerized filing system which the predominantly young, part-time and inexperienced staff were still learning to use. The working atmosphere was great if one was into giggling one moment and cursing the computer the next. It was not a place for perfectionists, or, for that matter, clients. The staff turnover was zero, because it had only just opened.

Waterfriar's was a small dull place which no one had been into for years. Judging by the window it specialised in second-hand Reader's Digest Condensed Books at new-book prices. It was rumoured to be a front for laundering drug money but was, in fact, the pipe-dream project of Mildred and Archibald Waterfriar. Captain Waterfriar had retired from the army fifteen years previously and as he and his wife had always wanted a bookshop they'd jolly well gone ahead and bought one. There they lived happily ever after, pottering away in the back shop, occasionally emerging to swap Charlotte Brontë with Rider Haggard in the window display. The staff turnover was one in fifteen years (the cat had died of kidney failure and had been replaced by a budgie, whose excretions were less noxious to Reader's Digest Condensed Books).

Whyte's was the university bookshop, with branches on both the Queen's Chapel and the Medical campuses. The branches were small, efficient and soulless places with only two members of staff at each. Their combined average turnover was one staff member every 4.2 years, or approximately 0.2381 members of staff per year. Generally, however, the turnover took the form of whole people leaving every now and again, rather than a gradual changeover of staff in the form of body parts, although they once had a double amputee working from a wheelchair, and at another time nearly employed someone who had a transplanted kidney.

Alas, none of the shops needed Nathaniel at the time but all of them politely took his c.v. and said they'd contact him if they had a vacancy. Feeling footsore but worthy, Nathaniel went for a drink at The Prisoner of War, the most famous and historic pub in Inverdon, traditionally threatened with destruction and saved by petition every five years or so—what better means of advertising? Nathaniel peeled open a beermat and on the fresh surfaces thus created he wrote down the names of the bookshops in his order of preference, and then in the order of probability of finding employment in them. His lists looked like this:

PREFERENCE: [beerstain]
WHYTE'S, BLACKSTONES, FRILLONS, WATERF.
LIKELIHOOD: F, WH, B, WA

For obvious reasons he'd have preferred the Medical Campus branch of Whyte's but the chances of getting a job anywhere other than Frillons were tiny. He circled FRILLONS and tried to think positively about it. There were some OK-looking girls on the staff. He'd easily get the hang of the computer—he might even create an "indispensable" role for himself there as the expert. Mmmn, it might not be too bad. Nathaniel looked up from the beermat and took a swig of 85/-. The barman was polishing a glass. Behind him on the wall there was a notice:

BAR STAFF REQUIRED. APPLY HERE.

Nathaniel applied there. He worked for two months at the POW, as the pub was affectionately known (or unaffectionately, by those who'd been short-changed, refused service or forcibly expelled). He got on well with the staff, and also with most of the clients. Whenever there was any difficulty (such as when the mono-browed Calum showed up drunk one night) the staff supported each other, and Nathaniel found that it was possible to enjoy being a team member, something he never would have believed previously. (There will not be, however, any expository saccharine tales of amity in adversity.) In the meantime the Open College sent him their prospectus and Nathaniel registered to study for a bachelor's degree in medical sciences. Then Frillons got in touch and Nathaniel's sketchily planned show was on the road again.

For many, working in a bookshop has a romantic appeal to it—it's almost the grown-up and intellectual version of being a fireman. However, as with most things possessed of romantic appeal, the reality is not glamorous, and like all jobs which involve working with the public it can be tedious and unpleasant. Nathaniel distracted himself from the worst aspects with his habitual mental games, such as attempting to guess which section of the bookshop each new entrant would make for, whether they would purchase a book, and what it would be. When he encountered particularly obnoxious customers he would imagine replacing their chosen volumes with ones more appropriate to the defects in their conduct. *How to Win Friends and Influence People* featured high on his list of wishful prescriptions. When the thrill of these covert imaginings started to wear off, he began to po-facedly suggest such therapeutic titles directly to the most offensive clients. Usually they looked at him blankly and would say something like, "No, that's not the sort of thing I'm looking for at all!"

Once the victim of one his exasperation-driven "suggestions" spotted the intended insult and had him pinned against the wall. The manager had to separate the shocked Nathaniel from the fuming dirty-raincoated insultee. When Nathaniel's taunt had been explained, the manager insisted that the "gentleman" take his chosen book for free *(Mass Murderers Through the Ages, with Full Colour Photographs)*, the money to be docked from Nathaniel's pay. (Nathaniel had recommended the non-existent *Sexual Inadequacy and the Genesis of Psychopaths*.)

After this experience Nathaniel restricted his wit to harmless-looking individuals in clean and permeable garments, and refined his techniques to the extent that his now largely genuine suggestions were sometimes even taken up by the clients. He had a few successes selling books on time management to those apparently hastily looking for last-minute presents, and discovered that an excellent way to chat up attractive women was to suggest that they might want to buy a book called *How Not to Let Your Astonishing Beauty Spoil Your Friendships*. Somehow, however, he found he couldn't take it beyond the point at which they smiled at him.

After a few months it was noticeable that Nathaniel sold more books than other members of staff. The pleasure that this gave him helped to balance his lack of social success with his colleagues, and a creeping deeper unease, arising from the books themselves.

Superficially the image of an intellectual in a library or bookshop conjures similar feelings to that of a cow in clover. Both connote joy. A farmer, however, would be worried if his hay-fed cows broke into a spring field of rich sweet clover. He would know that the resulting glutinous mash of clover in their rumens would trap the fermentation gas, preventing them from eructating (burping) and causing them to bloat, possibly fatally. The dangers faced by an open-minded intellectual in a bookshop are different, but no less serious: the idea-hungry reader has to decide which books to read. One mouthful of clover in a field is much like another, the only differences being that consecutive mouthfuls are spread about the field, requiring locomotion to attain them, and that a few potential mouthfuls are better eschewed than chewed, being fouled by the ordure of earlier grazers: sniff, munch, step, sniff, munch, step....The decision-making process of a book-bound reader is more complex. Books are not consumed by being read, nor fouled by their readers (not usually, anyway). Except in totalitarian regimes, they survive for decades. Thousands of new titles are printed every day. Not all of these books are equal, in fact they are almost infinitely varied in the quality and nature of their content. The average reader will know that even were he to spend every moment of every day of his life reading, he would never manage to read more than a fraction of the books available. Thus the mere existence of so many books thrusts his mortality in his face. And, if he is aware of the difficulty of choosing which books to read, will he not also become aware of the difficulty of making any decision in life? From there it is a small step to asking about the meaning of life. This line of reasoning will lead some troubled bibliophiles to the sections marked "religion" and "philosophy," and possibly to those marked "the occult" and "mysticism." Others will despair of finding a solution to the dilemma and will attempt to drown their unhelpful intellects in drink and drugs, or to seek sensory overload in other ways. At least then the resulting problems point the way to specifically helpful titles, such as *Cocktails Galore, Living with Alcoholism, Fifty Years of Playboy* and *Seventy-Seven Surefire Suicides.*

Nathaniel's strategy was to read the ten bestsellers of every month (of course, he only read them "ironically," to "keep in touch with the proletariat") and also those books of which the author's back cover biography/photograph appealed to him. Naturally, he read everything on the Beatles in his first month at Frillons. Occasionally a customer recommended something to him, and he would add this to his reading list. His conscience still prodded him, however, about other books he ought to be reading, such as "the classics," but then Homer and Kipling had waited so long anyway, a few more years wouldn't bother them (Kipling was surely "prepared" for every eventuality anyway, even not being read). And after all, Nathaniel thought, his studies had to take priority, and he had to find time for his ongoing experiments on the effects of the excrement of air-deprived yeast on cognitive function in his favourite pub, the good old POW.

Of the old uni crowd, Shelagh was still around to aid in this research, though increasingly less bubbly as her unemployed status gnawed at her self-esteem, and enhanced her *misère de vivre*. So much for a history degree. Sometimes she would turn down his invitations to the pub, claiming that she had to see a friend, or that she was feeling unwell. Nathaniel guessed it was really because she couldn't afford to buy a round, and that she felt bad about letting him "sponsor" her all the time. He tried to explain to her that it gave him pleasure to buy her the odd drink, and that he would have let her buy his drinks had their positions been reversed, but there was only so much persuading he could do.

Hitting the books and the bottle (pint glass) were, for Nathaniel, not strange activities, and not necessarily mutually exclusive. Previously, however, he'd been one among many struggling supping scholars. Now he had no one to share the agonies of his after-hours knowledge acquisition, although drinking partners were abundant even if one set aside Shelagh. As the day of his first Open College exam approached, Nathaniel realised that his time allocation had reflected the present availability of companions in his two main spheres of activity, and that while his fondness for social bibulousness comfortingly indicated that he probably was of the human species (unlike his parents) it also predisposed him to academic failure. It was time to remind himself why he'd set out to do what he was doing, to give himself a boot up the backside.

If he pared away all his petty day-to-day concerns, he knew that he was still, at heart, driven by the advice of Miss Grimshaw/Mrs. B. Although in his mind "Rosemary" had to some extent ceased to be the individual Rosemary Taylor, and had come to represent the ideal woman, whatever her name might be, he was still determined to capture her. It had become an article of faith that he would only be able to have her once he had attained worldly success. It was perhaps for this reason that his attempts to woo other women, such as Frillons staff and customers, had failed: all his attempts had been half-hearted. He neither expected amorous success, nor, in truth, wanted it at this point in his life. If the ideal woman existed then it was unlikely that he would stumble across her by accident, his profile as a junior shop assistant not standing above the average man in the street, his weak signal being swamped by noise, to borrow a metaphor from electronics. In order to be sure of attracting the rare Rosemary moth to his lantern, from however far afield she might have strayed, he'd have to increase his glow from that of a feeble flickering birthday cake candle to that of a carbon-arc lamp in a lighthouse. He must become famous. If a woman were attracted to him in his present dim pre-glorious manifestation then she must either have uncanny perspicacity (which even the egotistical side of himself found difficult to believe), or, to respond to the lukewarm come-ons of an ill-dressed and unprepossessing junior bookshop attendant, she must be a crawling, tatter-winged and desperate Lepidopteran indeed, and he couldn't be attracted to one such as that. He was only interested in the ideal woman, and his course was chosen: obtain his biology degree, then do a Ph.D. in ageing. The fame would follow. Forget the cheap thrills from his "ironic" reading of salacious Jackie Barrelmaker bonkbusters. Forget the pedestrian attractions of the women around him. Forget even the transient mellowness issuing from a good malt in the POW: Nathaniel had to study. His months of coasting were over.

Nathaniel had almost forgotten the horrors of memorising screeds of seemingly incompressible biological facts. (After all, schooldays had been a long time ago, and his computer studies had had a more logical underpinning.) However, his old study methods were de-mothballed as the occasion called for them. This time round, he found he had to be parsimonious in his use of mnemonics because the invention of more and more colourful and elaborate aides-memoire could become a diverting thief of time. It might be more efficient, he came to realise, to learn the muscles of the leg directly, than to spend an hour developing a phantasmagoric Dali-esque memory jogger, fun though the latter might be. His playful and creative side had to be crushed for the time being. His Open College books and the passage of time constituted the Spartan fabric of his un-materialistic evenings. Every hour on the hour he'd allow himself a mug of strong coffee, a visit to the loo and a brief daydream about what would be waiting for him at the end of this purgatory.

The remaining Open College/Frillons years passed soberly and successfully. When the more extravagant side of his shopfloor behaviour had been tamed by a combination of chastening experience, managerial intervention and study-induced fatigue, Nathaniel emerged as the obvious candidate for the position of Assistant Manager. Duly promoted, his enhanced income enabled him to set a little money aside to supplement his future presumed starvation-level Ph.D. grant. The likelihood of his being accepted as a Ph.D. candidate was good, if his OC marks were anything to go by. When he at last obtained his biology degree and was free to go further it came as a bit of a shock. Until that point he had taken the finding of a Ph.D. studentship for granted.

CHAPTER ELEVEN
Towards Researching Time's Losses

Trawling through the advertisements in *Nature* and *New Scientist* became an increasingly desperate activity. Nathaniel had handed in his notice at Frillons, but no suitable Ph.D. positions appeared in the journals. It dawned on him that he was unlikely to find a single institution possessing expertise in both computing and the biology of ageing. He would have to design his Ph.D. himself, and then look for supervisors in each of these fields, perhaps approaching a cosmetics company for sponsorship?

Three months of speculative phone calls, and numerous railway journeys and interviews later, Nathaniel found himself the proud compiler of a patchwork Ph.D. project. This brought together the three-dimensional image computing skills of the world-renowned Cambridge Computing Centre (his supervisor there was to be Dr. Hugh C. Well), expertise in the field of ageing provided by the Faculty of Medicine at the University of Inverdon (Prof. Vance Hall-Crumble MBE, geriatrician to the Royal Family when in residence at Balmoral, would be Nathaniel's mentor there) and the plastic surgery *savoir-faire* of the London Institute of Maxillo-Facial Surgery (under Prof. Iolanthe R. Gnoze). Nathaniel's project was to be sponsored by the cosmetics company Hardley-Dreamlon International. By the rules of Ph.D. sponsorship HDI would not only cover the direct costs of Nathaniel's Ph.D. and his maintenance requirements, but would also make a generous contribution to each of the three institutions involved. In fact, once Nathaniel had persuaded HDI of the commercial potential of his ideas, and they had agreed to sponsor him (they were as much motivated by what they stood to lose should one of their competitors snap him up, as by what they would gain directly from his research), he found that research bodies were falling over each other to court him as a student. He narrowed it down to the three abovementioned on the basis of their scientific standing (number of articles published in high-impact journals such as *Nature*), the relevance of their work to his proposed Ph.D. project, and his personal feelings towards his future supervisors.

Dr. Well was a short and youthful dynamo of a man, with curly black hair and a New York accent. He was given to extravagant gesticulation, oozed enthusiasm and never seemed tired. Tact and subtlety were not his strong points, but his sense of humour and inability to hold a grudge (or to recognise when others were doing so) ensured that he was well-liked by at least some of those who had more than superficial contact with him and that the Cambridge Computing Centre (known as "Three Cs" by its staff, and as "Faeces" by its bitter and less successful competitors) had a relatively convivial atmosphere. The tea room (always a measure of an organisation's state of health, Nathaniel had found) was well attended and its walls not unused to echoing laughter. Nathaniel was not to know that those directly supervised by Dr. Well had a rather different opinion of him.

Prof. Hall-Crumble was a tall dour man who had made an art of conveying a great deal in a few words (when he chose to utter them). His habitual taciturnity stemmed possibly from long experience as a physician, in which job a concerned face and the miserly dispensation of a few "Ahs" and "Mmmns" rapidly earn one the reputation of being caring and wise. In that the impression of being listened to is therapeutically beneficial, and in that this enhanced his clinical success and his reputation, Prof. Hall-Crumble was undoubtedly wise. His lack of loquacity did not serve him so well amongst colleagues, however, for while his economically expressed opinions were respected, he always gave them the feeling that he was sitting in judgement on them, superior and aloof. No one knew what made him tick. At his interview Nathaniel couldn't escape from the feeling that he'd met the professor somewhere before. Though slightly unsettled by this notion, Nathaniel had not found the eminent man's silences intimidating as he had prepared his sales pitch well, and his notes obviated embarrassing hiatuses. When

Nathaniel had come to the end of his spiel he said as much, and the professor had no option but to speak: "Fine. That'll do. You've convinced me." No beating around the bush. Nathaniel liked that.

Prof. Gnoze was intermediate in her volubility, and volatile in her moods. Like a few women in hostile, traditionally male territories, she veered between the deployment of feminine wiles (coquetry, tears and contrived displays of vulnerability) and an over-compensatory, macho, autocratic style of management. Her team (if the loose assemblage of doctors, nurses and medical students around her could be dignified as such) was in a constant state of nervousness and insecurity, which she was a genius at fostering and exploiting. If individuals A and B were inveighing against her, for example, having both been offended by some Gnozian outburst, she would summon A to her office (the male if they were of different genders) and explain in confiding tones, touching his arm frequently and tilting her head imploringly, that it was the other party who had earned her wrath and that she had had to lambast the two of them to avoid accusations of favouritism, but that he, A, had her "full confidence and trust," and could she rely on his? The innocent Nathaniel, a new man in her realm and the expediter of a lucrative contract, received the full Iolanthe charm assault, and as she was passably young and attractive he emerged from her office with dilated pupils and an addled brain. He failed to notice the smug-faced trio of interns hanging around an open doorway just along the passage. "Another poor fool!" one of them murmured.

Once Nathaniel had arranged the supervision and financing of his Ph.D. he had to plan the execution of it in detail, on the basis of the facilities and expertise of each the parties involved. He was given a month to draft his proposals, after which all his supervisors would meet in Inverdon to hear him present them. Nathaniel's euphoria dwindled as he struggled with the logistic jigsaw of his project, envisaged in three stages. The first stage was simply the description and quantification of the macroscopic (large-scale) and microscopic age-related changes in human skin (of women's faces, in particular, as this was where the commercial potential lay). During this phase he would be asking such questions as whether women all tended to wrinkle in the same way, or whether there was a large random or individual component to line formation (the notorious "Prune or Pattern" question), and, if a general pattern existed, whether it could be described mathematically. The second stage was to look for associations between age-related changes and genetic and environmental factors (such as diet, climate, exposure to the sun, and the use of cosmetics). The third stage, and perhaps the vaguest, was to come up with some ideas as to how his findings could be put to commercial advantage by a cosmetics company—Hardley-Dreamlon International, of course!

How was he to obtain any meaningful results in the standard three years of a British Ph.D.? One approach he could rule out immediately: there'd be little point in following the changes in the skin of individual women over a mere three years as they'd surely be barely detectable! If he couldn't follow individuals over a useful period of time he could at least compare the members of a family across generations. As mothers shared only half their genes with their daughters, and as environmental factors experienced by one generation weren't necessarily the same as those experienced by the next, this wasn't ideal, but if he interviewed enough women this wouldn't matter so much. It should also be possible to reconstruct the appearance of people as they had been years previously, as long as they could provide him with a few clear photographs. In this, his Rosemary experience would serve him well.

How to start? He'd need to devise a questionnaire for his "subjects" (this was the word Nathaniel used to describe the women whose epidermises were to earn him the three new letters after his name), and to advertise for these volunteers. It would make sense, he thought, to obtain half his interviewees in the south of England, and the other half in Scotland. That way he'd be sure to have contrasting environmental factors within his sample. (What he didn't realise at the time was that Scottish women were not only exposed to a colder climate, but also tended to eat more fat and less fruit and vegetables, and to smoke more than southerners. This meant that it would be difficult for Nathaniel to disentangle the influences of these factors with certainty.) The interviewees would need to be bribed somehow. Perhaps HDI could be persuaded to give them some cosmetics? Exactly what sort of subject was he looking to attract?

The ideal interviewee would bring along her mother, thirty years older than her, and her daughter, thirty years younger. (A bonus would be the availability of sisters in any of the generations.) This trio would supply numerous old photographs of themselves, which would include multiple views taken on the same day. They would know the focal length of the lenses and the format of film used for each of these photographs. They would be able to describe their diets and use of cosmetics over their lifetimes, and to quantify exposure to the elements, particularly any episodes of sunburn. They'd authorise their doctors to provide Nathaniel with their full medical records. They'd be willing to have skin samples taken so that the cells could be cultured and characterised in Inverdon, and would willingly travel to London (if they weren't Londoners), at a time that suited Nathaniel, so that they could be scanned in Prof. Gnoze's unit. These data would then enable Nathaniel, ensconced in his natural habitat of old (behind a computer console), to answer the questions he had set himself.

Nathaniel allowed himself a dream of the fame that this would garner—the television interviews, the cheques from *Vague* and *Cosmopolitan* for lead stories on "Sun, sagging and sex appeal," the desperate phone calls from twenty-five-year-old models, horribly aware that their wrinkle-free time was running out: "Please, Dr. Papulous, can you help me? I'll do anything for you, anything!"

Whole hours and then days were lost to such daydreams. Unsurprisingly, the timetable for the huge project failed to compile itself while Nathaniel was performing, in his mind's eye, thorough professional examinations of every square centimetre of the virtually flawless surfaces of young ("ageing") models' skins. The day before the big meeting with his supervisors Nathaniel tore himself from his reveries sufficiently long enough to jot down this arbitrary timetable:

Nov. to April—Inverdon—interviews, skin samples and set up skin cell culture
May to Oct.—London—interviews, skin samples and scans

Nov. to April—Inverdon—work on skin cultures
May to Oct.—analysis at Cambridge
Nov. to April—obtain more data as revealed necessary by
analysis
Last few months—write up Ph.D. (Cambridge and Inverdon)

To this he added a few ideas concerning the work he might perform on the skin samples, spicing it with references to Prof. Hall-Crumble's recent papers. With that he considered himself ready for the meeting, to be hosted by the professor himself.

Nathaniel was the first to arrive at the office. His knocking embodied, he hoped, just the right compromise between respectful forbearance and no-nonsense firmness. "Come in!" The professor looked up from his papers, his spectacles (balanced on the tip of his nose in suitable clichéd professorial fashion, thought Nathaniel) and his unkempt grey eyebrows framing a penetrating appraisal by his glacier eyes. "Ah, Nathaniel! Come in, and take a seat at the table there. You're a bit early and I've some papers to go through yet." With that he returned to his paperwork, and Nathaniel was at liberty to peruse the large room. It reeked of academe. The walls were lined by a heterogeneous collection of old bookshelves stuffed with thousands of books, journals and files, to which a couple of old microscopes and a few specimen bottles containing pickled portions of humanity added some variety. His desk, and the low table in front of it at which Nathaniel had sat himself, were also piled with papers. A faded old photograph of a woman in her forties was prominent on top of a stack of microscope slide boxes in the middle of the desk, from which vantage point the woman appeared to survey the room quizzically, probably because she'd been photographed looking towards the sun. (Nathaniel was to discover later that this woman had been the professor's wife, and that she'd died in a car crash some twenty-five years previously.) There was no computer to be seen, although a modern-looking telephone had established a territory next to the slide boxes. Nathaniel opened his document case and extracted the copies of his proposal. He refreshed his forthcoming speech in his mind. He was nervous.

91

The next knock was more hesitant than Nathaniel's. The professor's invitation to enter revealed Prof. Gnoze at her ingratiating best. She smiled a lateral greeting at Nathaniel as she came in, and the professor stood to shake her hand. They'd never met, but his words to her were only marginally more solicitous than Nathaniel's peremptory directions had been earlier, and she was obviously disconcerted to be relegated to the table with Nathaniel while the great man occupied himself with weightier affairs. She was unsure whether she should talk aloud to Nathaniel, and contented herself with a whispered salutation before following Nathaniel's example and leafing through her notes. Her lips rubbed against each other—she'd apparently just applied her lipstick.

Five minutes after the appointed time of the meeting, a sharp rap made them all jump. The door opened immediately and an ambulatory affability offensive burst in. It was Dr. Well. He made his way immediately to Prof. Gnoze, dropping a "Hiya!" to Nathaniel *en route*. "You must be the famous Prof. Gnoze, whom everybody knows!" he said, smiling at his joke. She was delighted with this warmth after the professor's coldness, and radiated gratitude as she stood to shake his hand. The professor was left standing for a while, looking a bit foolish, but Dr. Well bounded over to him, shaking his hand vigorously and squeezing the professor's right elbow with his left hand (in what later would have been described as Bill Clinton-fashion) as he did so, "Pleased to meet you, Prof!" The professor was thrown completely. Full marks to Dr. Well, thought Nathaniel.

Greetings over, the professor asked his visitors whether they would care for tea or coffee, and summoned the requisite beverages using his phone. They arranged themselves around the table, the professor removing several of the piles of papers to make room. "Well, we're all here because of the initiative of this young man, and I'm sure that none of us can wait to hear his plans in more detail. Over to you, Nathaniel."

Nathaniel distributed the copies of his proposals, and started to speak. His concentration was not helped by Dr. Well's apparently frenetic scribbling, all over Nathaniel's recently pristine handout, nor by the not-that-covert glances Prof. Gnoze was throwing at these hieroglyphics. Only the professor seemed to be entirely focussed on what

Nathaniel was saying, his skewering eyes making Nathaniel doubt the worth of his own words. By the time he came to the end of his speech, and had suffered the further interruption of the distribution of the beverages, he was stuttering. The professor said nothing. Prof. Gnoze pursed her lips. They all knew that they were waiting for Dr. Well to speak, but he kept scribbling, scoring out and underlining. He looked up, apparently startled to find everyone looking at him. "Well," he began, "we have a very ambitious young fellow here. I think you'll be lucky to get all of this done, Nathaniel. Tell me, have you any experience of research?"

Nathaniel was angry at this question as his supervisors had received a copy of his c.v., in which all his previous experiences had been detailed. "At the end of my Open University degree I did a short research project comparing various suntan lotions."

"And what did you learn about research from this project?"

"Ummm…that you need a large sample size to get meaningful results?"

"Didn't you find that you needed a lot more time for analysis than you'd imagined, and that once you'd done your analysis you wished you had collected slightly different data?"

"Yes. I suppose so."

"Well then, I suggest you do a short pilot project first. Just interview a few women and then try to analyse your findings. Spend, say, a month interviewing—I'm sure the professor here can find you plenty of subjects around the medical school—and then come down to Cambridge and we'll take it from there. OK?" The question was directed at the other two supervisors as much as at Nathaniel, and Dr. Well had established himself so forcefully that they found themselves wrong-footed and unable to offer any objection, far less able to ask why so much furious scribbling had seemingly contributed to so little speech. Thus ended the first of what Nathaniel later called "The Supervisor Skirmishes": an unequivocal victory for Dr. Well.

CHAPTER TWELVE
Ph.D.: Pettiness, hardship and Disillusion?

A river some distance from its sources (forget the "unique source" nonsense) but not yet in the lazy meanderings of its senility, may nonetheless give an impression of tranquillity, particularly when viewed from a distance. From close up, its forceful purposiveness becomes apparent. Approach to within a few yards, and eddy currents and miniature whirlpools become visible. If one has the courage or foolhardiness to plunge into the waters, one will find that the so-called "bed" is not a place of rest, but of chaotic motion, abrasion and change. So it was with Nathaniel's Ph.D. His parents were delighted to hear of their son's academic progress, and imagined that having arranged his doctoral studies the rest would be a matter of course. Viewed from their perspective, Nathaniel's river was smooth—content in its cradling channel. The frictional and turbulent aspects of the river's passage through Ph.D. country, hidden to them, were to become only too manifest to Nathaniel.

Inverdon

Slightly thrown by the reception his talk had received, but no more disturbed than the professor and Prof. Gnoze had been by the usurpation of the reins of authority by the brash American, Nathaniel unchained his bicycle from the railings opposite the medical faculty. He was soon locking it again outside the art gallery and entering the calm atmosphere of the fountained entrance hall. They say that chimpanzees, on feeling

94

unwell, will consume the leaves of medicinal plants. They cannot be fully aware of the pharmacological justification for their actions—presumably it simply makes them feel better and that's why they do it. Analogously, Nathaniel found himself visiting the art gallery at times of stress (generally the diurnal ones, the POW being an efficient furnisher of his nocturnal medicine). As he mounted the stairs to view his favourite paintings, he tried to order his jumbled emotions.

The meeting had not been what he'd expected. He had imagined that each of his scientific proposals would have been carefully dissected by what he still thought of as the keen scientific minds of his supervisors, the discussion lasting several hours, not just a few seconds. He had hoped for a few words of praise for what he thought was a reasonably good project, from which, after all, they all stood to gain. He had expected that his supervisors would have managed a bit of an informal chat, seeing as they had never met each other, but as far as he knew Dr. Well and Prof. Gnoze had left at the same time as himself. Dr. Well's effusiveness appeared to go hand-in-hand with a streak of dominance unmoderated by ruth, against which even Prof. Hall-Crumble's control-by-remoteness stratagem was ineffective. The only one who had shown any real warmth was Prof. Gnoze, and she had seemed just a bit too keen to please, down to the last-minute touching-up of her make-up. What had he let himself in for?

Nathaniel tried to let these matters sink to his subconscious, and let the familiar canvasses soothe him. He adored the Pre-Raphaelites. In front of him was the lovely *Bright Eyes*, a bit sentimental perhaps, but a beautiful picture by Millais, a man who had dallied with the Pre-Raphaelite Brotherhood. It was virtually photographic in its detail (if one excepted the rather odd murky grey background), and showed a young girl possibly twelve years old. She was smartly dressed and wore a red cape, which might be a reference to Little Red Riding Hood? Wide-eyed, she stared out at the viewer, intelligence, goodness, confidence and innocence on her exquisite features: "Here I am. This is me. Who are you?" To judge by the date on the painting she'd have been dead at least fifty years, even if she'd lived to be an old woman, Nathaniel thought.

Had her youthful idealism lasted, or had it been swamped by the exigencies of an acquisitive and egotistical world? Had she died horribly in childbirth? Nathaniel moved on. There was a swathe of paintings of nymphs and swains in unlikely mythical settings, all with strangely prominent sculpted lips—was it true that Rossetti had believed that the lips were the seat of the sensual, the eyes the seat of the spiritual? There was another Millais painting, this one of a little girl in a white flannel nightgown: *The Convalescent.* She looked familiar. Yes, it must be Bright Eyes—why hadn't he noticed that on previous visits? She looked a bit younger and frailer here—had she really been ill or had the artist created her illness with his paintbox? Convalescence wasn't a word used much these days, perhaps reserved for those recovering from major operations? The painting had been made in the days before antibiotics, when childhood diseases could be killers, even for the well-to-do.

Nathaniel had the feeling that there was a message lying somewhere in all this but he couldn't put his finger on it. Yes, there was the ageing process visible in the two paintings of the *Bright Eyes* girl, which recalled his childhood experience of paintings, and, yes, there was a message about perseverance, but there was something else there too. Perhaps *Bright Eyes* was a representation of his ideal woman in her childhood? It would be a few years before he would understand. Excited, elevated and frustrated rather than calmed, Nathaniel left the art gallery. He'd be damned if Dr. Well and the rest of them would get him down!

They did get him down, repeatedly, but fortunately only in small ways and for short periods. Nathaniel composed his trial questionnaire, and deposited it in the professor's in-tray for his approval, together with a list of queries about how he should find his subjects, how he should take skin samples, how they should be processed after collection and so on. Knowing how busy the professor was, he booked an appointment through his secretary to see him a week after the submission of his queries. This would, he thought, give the great man plenty of time to consider his suggestions and formulate his responses.

At five minutes to two on Friday afternoon Nathaniel dutifully arrived at the professor's secretary's office. The secretary advised him that his meeting would have to be slightly delayed, as a visiting research fellow was having a few words with the professor.

At half-past two the secretary's phone/intercom buzzed. Nathaniel imagined that it would be the professor requesting his entry, but, no, some tea was required. Nathaniel politely asked the secretary whether he should come back later. She promised to chivvy him when she took the tea through. When she returned she said that the professor sent his apologies, and he would see Nathaniel in ten minutes—would Nathaniel like some tea?

Two cups of tea later, and nearly an hour after the original time of the appointment, Nathaniel was summoned into the arena of the first "Supervisor Skirmish." This time the professor was happy to remain the unbearded lion in his den. He briefly apologised to Nathaniel for keeping him waiting, and had just asked him what the purpose of the meeting was when the telephone rang. It was his secretary informing him of an important call. The professor took it. It was apparently from a friend and colleague with whom the professor had not communicated for some time, to judge by the chitchat about relatives and holidays which proceeded the chitchat about numbers of research students, research grants, numbers of papers published and the like. For the forty-three minutes of the phone call Nathaniel let his mind wander. He speculated whether his body language portrayed boredom, and whether he could, just for the sake of it, fake not being bored and at the same time make it plain that he was not consciously eavesdropping on the conversation. He leafed through the journals lying on the low table, and asked himself whether it would make a good party trick to recite the nucleotide sequence of the most recently discovered oncogenes. He suspected not. He wondered what the professor's long-dead wife had seen in the man, whether she would have liked him these days, and what she would have looked like had she not died in that car accident. When at last the phone call ended, Nathaniel was almost shocked and a surge of adrenalin had him ready to give the professor a rapid oral summary of his written submissions. But, no, the professor had to go to the toilet first.

It was nearly four o'clock before Nathaniel got the professor's attention. He hadn't seen Nathaniel's papers at all, or so he claimed, but managed to unearth them from one of his piles. In order to save time Nathaniel attempted to talk him through them, but the professor would have none of it and irritatedly signalled that he should be quiet while he read them. This seemed to take an inordinately long time. Through the window Nathaniel could see the happy student masses leaving early for their weekends of hedonism. The angled sunlight spoke of the lateness of the day. Here Nathaniel was, two degrees already under his belt, and he was still a nothing and a nobody, waiting for a few morsels of attention from the table of the likes of Professor V. Hall-Crumble M.B.E. The great man gave his deeply considered and profound response: "The questionnaire's fine. See my chief technician, Annabelle, about the rest of it. You've got your personal licence sorted, haven't you?"

No, Nathaniel hadn't, and he didn't have a clue what such a thing was. The professor, now apparently angry, explained to Nathaniel, as if to a child, that most experimental work involving human or animal subjects needed to be licensed by the Home Office. Each research project had a project licence, and in order to carry out certain procedures defined by the project licence individuals needed to have personal licences. Nathaniel's work would be covered by the professor's project licence, but he would need to apply for a personal licence if he wanted to take skin samples himself. The professor was sure that this would be a formality, but Nathaniel needed to get a move on. Nathaniel left the professor's office in a foul mood. He needed to get a move on—the cheek of it! He, who had submitted his questions a week ago, and who had waited two hours to be seen! Why couldn't he have been told all that earlier? Yet mixed in with his righteous indignation were feelings of guilt and incompetence. How had the professor managed to foist these on him?

Annabelle had left for the weekend by the time Nathaniel emerged steaming from the professor's office. At least there was little he could do until Monday, other than write to HDI to inform them of progress so far, and to request they donate some make-up to entice interviewees. He'd do that on Saturday afternoon. By God, he needed to hit the pub that evening!

Walking into the warm smoky atmosphere of the POW Nathaniel immediately felt better. He chatted to Graham, an old friend behind the bar, and engulfed the first Guinness of the evening, as welcome as the first Inverdonian daffodil in spring. He had phoned Shelagh and she'd said that she would show up later. He hadn't seen her for several weeks. She could be his first interviewee!

Shelagh was in good form. She'd been offered a temporary job in a stationery shop, reason enough for a celebration. Nathaniel was surprised at quite how well she was looking. He said as much to her.

She laughed. "No, I'm just back to normal now, to what I used to be like. I've been feeling pretty low for a long time, you know, with not having a job and all!"

They toasted each other's success. Having worked in a shop, Nathaniel wasn't sure that it merited huge rejoicing, but kept this thought to himself. But then, come to think of it, he'd never experienced the rumoured horrors of long-term unemployment, and the way things were going, a Ph.D. might turn out to be less pleasant than working in a shop! Guinnesses were sunk, to be joined by a good few and a few good malt whiskies. "Oh floo-errr o' Sco'land…!"

Saturday morning was a write-off for Nathaniel. So was the afternoon. And half of the evening. He was still weak at 8 p.m but no longer nauseous or in pain, and managed a trip to the nearest fish and chip shop. By 10 p.m. he was strong enough to write the letter to HDI. His conscience clear for the weekend, he went back to bed.

Most head technicians have never heard of Dale Carnegie. Annabelle was no exception, to judge by her initial non-approach to winning Nathaniel's friendship. No, the professor had not had a word with her about Nathaniel's project. No, she couldn't see herself finding time to maintain Nathaniel's proposed cell cultures, not with all the professor's work to be done. No, she thought the professor was wrong about Nathaniel easily obtaining a personal licence. As he wasn't a nurse or a medical doctor (unlike the professor's previous postgraduate students) he'd need to be specially trained, and the Home Office was slow at processing applications. It would probably be more practical if he could get the help of one of the doctors or nurses for this aspect of his work.

However, Annabelle did reluctantly consent to showing Nathaniel around "her" laboratory on the quietest day of the week (Thursday) and to giving him a rundown on the maintenance of cell cultures. Nathaniel, realising that she would be a very firm filbert to fissure, but a vital one if he were to do any useful work in Inverdon, thanked her profusely. He resolved to make the most of his opportunity to expose any kernel of kindness that might be lurking inside her harridan's husk. He would be at his charming best.

Nathaniel turned up five minutes early for his conducted tour, thinking he had nothing to lose by giving Annabelle the benefit of the temporal doubt. She was sitting in the technicians' stuffy little tea room waiting for him. She stubbed out her cigarette and pushed her *Daily Repress* aside. "Right, Nathaniel," she said, "let's get going!" She looked weary but there was, perhaps, a trace of friendliness in her voice. She led the way towards the laboratory, directing Nathaniel to enter via the men's changing room where a cap, mask, gown and overshoes would be waiting for him.

Within a few seconds of emerging into the laboratory, Nathaniel understood Annabelle. She took a tremendous pride in the smooth and efficient running of her little fiefdom. Nothing ever got in the way of that. Outside the world might be chaotic, unpredictable, but in Annabelle's domain everything ran like quartz chronometry. The junior technicians acknowledged her entry with a raising of their eyebrows, and continued their pipetting.

Nathaniel realised that no subterfuge or pretence was necessary to get on the right side of Annabelle. In fact it would have been counterproductive. All he needed to do was to express his genuine admiration for what was obviously a smoothly run ship, and, in the long run, show that he was competent himself. Nathaniel couldn't help but wonder how much of the famous V. Hall-Crumble's work would have been possible had Annabelle not been around. Another thought struck him: looking at the speed at which the technicians worked it didn't seem realistic for him to acquire their skills in the small amount of time his Ph.D. allowed. And if they didn't have time to maintain his cultures for him...? What if he merely preserved his samples for postdoctoral study, and cut the tissue culture aspect out of his Ph.D.? Would the professor hit the roof at this idea? What would HDI make of this? At the end of the tour Nathaniel thanked Annabelle, genuinely grateful for the most useful experience of his Ph.D. so far. He asked her opinion on the practicality of storing his samples for later analysis as opposed to culturing and studying them right away. Her reply confirmed that the postponement idea held merit.

It wasn't as bad as Nathaniel had feared. The professor seemed relieved, if anything, that Nathaniel would not require much supervision from him in the next few years, but would be doing the work eventually. HDI was happy to postpone the allocation of some of the professor's money. Nathaniel was delighted at the reduction of his burden. So all he had to do in Inverdon for the time being was to interview his subjects, and find a nurse or doctor to take the skin samples for him. He knew that it would be a waste of time asking Hall-Crumble for further help of any magnitude. Annabelle might be able to find someone for him if he asked her nicely.

As it turned out, Annabelle remembered that a niece of hers, who was a nurse in the cardiology unit, was looking for a bit of extra cash. She could help Nathaniel on three weekday evenings, and HDI was happy to pay her for her time. She filled out her personal licence application form, and Nathaniel doorstepped the professor until he countersigned it. He even went to the trouble of phoning the Home Office inspector to request that the matter be expedited. Possibly his conscience was troubling him about the way he'd thus far failed to facilitate Nathaniel's Ph.D.

Shelagh, Annabelle, and her niece, Sue, were Nathaniel's first interviewees. Fortunately Sue was not squeamish about taking a needleful of skin from her own face. Nathaniel photographed them with his specially purchased camera, rigorously double-checking his angles, illumination, exposure and focus. They each received an HDI "Wrinklebuster kit" and went forth to gather more subjects from amongst their friends and colleagues. Many nurses and a few doctors volunteered. Sue had what seemed at the time the bright idea of recruiting some of the patients in the geriatric ward, "…after all, it'll do them good to be the centre of attention!" It did do them good, but it was impossible to stop them talking. No one had asked them about their lives for years, and it all came out. Four of the five aged interviewees were able to supply old photographs of themselves, but only one had a daughter willing to take part. Return on the time invested in the old women, in terms of data, was poor, but the nurses on the geriatric ward reported a marked improvement in the condition of all those who had been interviewed, emotionally, mentally and physically.

Nathaniel's month of trial data gathering was soon over. Sorting and packing his things took longer than he'd imagined. He kept the taxi waiting, and just made the train. It was only when it had pulled out of Inverdon, and the rugged coastal scenery was flashing past his window that the fact that he was leaving what had been his home for nine years really sank in. No more Inverdon Art Gallery, no more Shelagh, no more POW, no more ceilidhs, at least not for several months. Back to what was for him the bleak and straitening Land of the Engs. At least the chances were that he would be closer to Rosemary, who was presumably still somewhere in the land of her birth, and in London he'd be able to see Mary.

Cambridge

Cambridge, that Mecca of suicidal bicyclists (most of them veterinary students at Girton College) and Japanese tourist-video camera units, seemed to Nathaniel to be a place crushed between the weight of its history and the pressures of the modern world. Dr. Well had sent one of his doctoral students to meet Nathaniel at the station. At the rate Geoff's decrepit Avenger Estate crawled along the clogged roads, they would have been better off walking to the digs, suitcase and all. Geoff's insouciance suggested that the roads were no worse than usual. Nathaniel was already homesick for Inverdon, but tried to keep up a bright conversation with the tall and haggard Geoff; after all, they were to be both flatmates and colleagues: "So what's it like working at Three Cs?"

Geoff snorted. "It's OK, if you can take Hugh. He's rather good at what he does, there's no doubt about that, but he's a bit one-tracked. If you don't agree with him he doesn't bawl you out, as such, but he has this way of…of getting to you. It's subtle, you know, the odd sly joke here and there, but it gets you down. He has his little fan club—sycophantic little….Most people think he's great for the first year or two, and then they see what he's really like. By the time you're into your third year you might well hate him, but you have little choice but to go along with him. Certainly, if you follow his advice you'll get your Ph.D., but it may not feel like it's your Ph.D. if you know what I mean. He's a control freak. It's difficult…." Geoff's voice trailed off.

Nathaniel's worst fears about Dr. Well seemed justified. He felt he should change the subject. "So what's the social life like?"

"Oh, not bad, I suppose. Last year's batch of postgrads are good for a laugh. The pubs are OK. Not that you've much time for that sort of thing in your final year. God, Nathaniel, if I knew what it was going to be like I would never have started. Hell, I'm sorry, I'm not very good company at the moment. Look, I could do with a drink. The chaps are going out tonight…."

Nathaniel's room turned out to be the smallest and darkest one in a five-bedroom semi-detached traditionally rented by CCC postgraduates. Geoff explained that as students left, Nathaniel would move up the hierarchy and get a better room. If he wanted to, he was free to look for lodgings elsewhere but it'd probably cost him a lot more. Nathaniel dumped his baggage, scenting and surveying the familiar disorder of communal bachelor living. A wave of nostalgia for those early days in Inverdon almost brought him to his knees, but he didn't really want to go through a similar experience again here and now….Geoff interrupted his ruminations. "Look I've got to get back to Three Cs. You can have a lift with me now, or stay and unpack." Nathaniel accepted the lift.

Dr. Well (Nathaniel felt awkward calling him Hugh) welcomed him in his ebullient way, and gave him a whirlwind tour of CCC, introducing him to more faces than Nathaniel could remember the names for, mnemonical skills or not. He was struck by the lack of women. There were only two female postgraduate students and one lecturer/researcher. Nathaniel's tour ended at what was to be his desk, supplied complete with graffiti, a view of a flaking wall, and a computer terminal. The most prominent graffito was "Guaranteed 100% Effective Debugging Device: Place bug on this spot ==> [X] Press firmly." If only it were that simple! More than once Nathaniel was to curse the author of that little piece of malice.

That evening in the pub Nathaniel failed to feel at home. It was strange but his ear had become attuned to the harsh Scottish consonants and gutturals overlain on that soft lilt, so appropriate to the Caledonian landscape. To hear his own voice merging now with the muted Southern English phonic background in the flat East Anglian fens, far from being a relief to the returning exile, was disturbing. Paradoxically it accentuated his fundamental sense of otherness. But apart from that there was a lack of something, an additional flatness, in the atmosphere, in the conversation. Part of it might have been attributable to the all-male nature of the gathering. Large single-sex congregations were, in his experience, seldom the forums for enlightened or inspiring philosophical debate, and this one was no exception, but it wasn't just that....

Of course Nathaniel had no long-term acquaintances there, so that while the banter and gossip were of interest to him in that they informed him about his new environment, the personalities, the cliques and the hierarchy, it was an abstract interest, "disinterest," in fact, in its original and most useful sense. This too, though, was only part of the hollowness he was feeling. Could it have been that Nathaniel was fresh from an occupied and self-aware land, itching under the yoke, whereas England was an apathetic and defeatist post-imperial nation in decline, a land where all horizons were perceived to be narrow, and therefore where foreigners with a modicum of chutzpah could cut a swathe through the grumbling but essentially anally retentive and complacent natives (provided, of course that these conquerors-aspirant were white-skinned, or if not white-skinned then sportsmen)? Nathaniel, looking at the listless and marginalized Geoff hunched over his half pint of bitter, found that his loathing and disgust were putting up a good fight against his sympathy. Perhaps Geoff deserved his miserable lot. He'd be damned if Dr. Well would turn him into a Geoff.

It is not possible to say whether Nathaniel would have had a better time in Cambridge had the foregoing thoughts never crossed his mind. Did these negative feelings inevitably entrain a vicious circle, maintaining him in an essentially isolated, friendless state? He did try, to some extent, to develop a social circle. There was a Caledonian Society at one of the colleges, and Nathaniel went to one of their ceilidhs, but the upperclass braying of the pseudo-Scots public school Hooray Henrys and Henriettas, and their (possibly imagined) disdain for his lack of Scottish pedigree and garb turned his stomach, and he left within half an hour. That was not what he was seeking. Strangely enough, the deepest sense of kinship he experienced during his entire Cambridge sojourn was with a Japanese tourist. It was this episode that saw the metaphorical river of his life significantly intertwining with a real river.

One of the near-obligatory tourist activities in historic little Cambridge is punting on the River Cam. Punting, like playing the triangle or cymbals in an orchestra, belongs to that category of activities wrongly pooh-poohed by those who have never attempted them. Punting is a deal more difficult than it looks, particularly if one is required to perform it for the first time before an audience of hundreds. Nathaniel's meaningful encounter with these flat-bottomed boats occurred towards the end of his first stay in Cambridge, when he treated himself to an Inverdon Art Gallery/POW-substitute-type walk along the banks of the Cam.

He had at last successfully debugged his computer programme—dubbed "conveRT"—for converting photographs into three-dimensional representations. (The last two letters of its name were in uppercase as they stood for Rosemary Taylor, although Nathaniel variously told people it was because the programme was "Really Terrific," that the first time he'd typed it he'd hit the "caps lock" key by mistake and couldn't be bothered changing it, that the programme "Reliably found Three-dimensional co-ordinates" or that by the time he'd eventually perfected it he was "Really Tired.") Be that as it may, after months hunched over his computer he felt he deserved a pleasant stroll. It was Sunday, after all, and a sunny Sunday to boot (and not, therefore, one on which to boot up his computer). A tipsy mixture of students and tourists overflowed from the pubs and sprinkled the banks of the Cam. The river itself was almost as chock-a-block with punts as its Canadian equivalent might be with logs in the felling season.

Amongst this waterborne mêlée was a hapless Japanese salaryman, his young wife, and their one-year-old daughter. Perhaps he had just been promoted and allowed the tremendous concession of a holiday? Manfully grappling with the cumbersome pole, the intrepid Yokohaman was only just capable of balancing, far less directing his craft in any useful direction. Professional puntoliers ferrying indolent obese American tourists gave him a wide berth. Less capable amateurs did not.

Although of course he didn't know the man's personal details, Nathaniel did know a little about Japanese culture, this being one of the many topics that had arisen on his beach walks with Shelagh and Mary so many years ago. Apparently, the Japanese were desperately conscious of "face," and the importance of maintaining it. According to Mary, they would smile at events that would appal Westerners, not because they delighted in horror, but because it was impolite to reveal oneself to be upset.

The salaryman was smiling widely as the inebriate masses on the banks jeered and clapped his floundering and the collisions this incompetence engendered. All the time the current was carrying him inexorably backwards. His wife was clasping their sole and precious offspring. Psychologically she had closed herself off to humiliation, a mother-child unit against the barbarian world. The salaryman grinned ingratiatingly at an oncoming craft and poled himself vigorously backwards, trying to get out of the way. His head smacked against the low bridge, an event which had been anticipated for some time by the brutal hordes, and he fell forwards, stunned, towards his numb wife. The audience roared with laughter. The salaryman struggled to his feet, wobbling alarmingly, somehow still managing to maintain that ghastly valiant and vacant grin. The spectators applauded. Nathaniel had to turn away. He wished he'd had sunglasses with him, and hoped he wouldn't bump into anyone he knew. How he detested the land of his birth.

London

Nathaniel was in a relatively good mood as the train carried him southwards. He took stock of the progress he had made with his work. He had reached the point where, at the touch of a button, he could summon the images of all those he had interviewed in Inverdon onto his computer screen. After struggling to come up with an objective way of eliminating the distorting effect of facial expressions he had decided to limit the photographs he used to those with neutral expressions, admitting the small inevitable element of subjectivity in this categorization. Further, he could play with these images at will. If he had a good set of photographs of a Ms. X at twenty, thirty and forty years of age, he could create (with his "conveRT" computer programme) three-dimensional representations of her face at these ages. He could then electronically blend these images at will ("morph" them). This enabled him to check, say, whether a fifty-fifty blend of the representations at twenty and forty years of age accurately reflected the same person as she was known to have been at thirty. This was an excellent starting point from which to ask questions about ageing patterns. What he needed to do, however, was to find a mathematical way of summarizing wrinkle physiognomy, so that he could enter this into a database together with the biographical information. Once that had been achieved it would be possible, using multivariate analysis, to answer all sorts of questions about the ageing process and make accurate predictions about future appearance. Nathaniel realised that he was genuinely enthralled by his work. He could see it all coming together! The clickety-clack, clickety-clack of the train accompanied, in his daydream, images of progressively computer-aged faces: twenty years old, twenty-five, thirty…eighty….

As London approached, Nathaniel's thoughts turned to the immediate future. London couldn't be worse than Cambridge. Prof. Gnoze couldn't be worse than Dr. Well. He would be able to see Mary. What would his accommodation be like?

London was more congenial than Cambridge. The London Institute of Maxillo-Facial Surgery (LIMFS) was attached to Saul's, one of the largest teaching hospitals in the country and virtually a town in its own right. Structurally Saul's was not particularly easy on the eye, consisting of an agglomeration of heterogeneous and variously decaying concrete and brick institutes, wards and clinics. Ironically it made up for its lack of aesthetic appeal, as far as Nathaniel was concerned, by the similarly varied nature of its cultural and social side. It was a relief to be out of what he had experienced as the narrow, silver-spoon-fed, academic snob-hole of Cambridge, and to be part of the bigger world, even if the price that had to be paid was the tolerance of Prof. Gnoze's occasional histrionics.

Nathaniel had a *déjà vu* experience immediately on arrival at LIMFS. Ever courteous, he presented himself at Prof. Gnoze's office to announce his presence. There followed a replay of his experience at Dutch-Anglo Petroleum, when he had gone to Mr. Morgan's office to tender his resignation. Exactly as on that occasion, a flushed young woman emerged from the potentate's den and brushed past him to disappear down the passage, all the while sobbing. Nathaniel was thrown by this experience and had to spend a couple of minutes pulling himself together before he could bring himself to knock on the potential ogress' door.

The "Come in!" was cold and imperious, rather than angry, but the charm Nathaniel had encountered on the two previous occasions he had met her was instantly reinstated. Prof. Gnoze enquired about his journey and his time in Cambridge, and then, just as Dr. Well had done, gave him a conducted tour.

LIMFS was physically smaller than Three Cs, but as its work merged with that of Saul's, the edges, in terms of the personnel, were fuzzier, and Nathaniel sensed that Prof. Gnoze was not well acquainted with all those to whom she introduced him. Nathaniel was delighted when this tour ended with the discovery that his desk was in a far more pleasant location than he'd had in Cambridge. He shared a large bright room with five other postgraduates (all young medical doctors) and had a view over a little courtyard garden, no less. His office-mates included a Zimbabwean of Indian ancestry (dubbed "Gopi"), two Londoners, the one being a Sikh (Anita) and the other a Rastafarian (unimaginatively nicknamed "Bob") and a Glaswegian (Robert, not nicknamed "Bob," presumably to avoid confusion). The fifth and largely theoretical roommate only appeared once during all Nathaniel's time in London. This unfortunate chap was an occasional topic of discussion. His name was apparently Ibrahim and he hailed from Iraq. He acted pretty strangely, according to the others, and there were rumours about his family being tortured by Saddam Hussein's regime, and his possibly consequent mental instability. The one time Nathaniel saw him he came in looking exhausted and sat down at the mainframe terminal. He spent two hours intently staring at the screen and punching keys, and Nathaniel guessed he was reading and responding to E-mail. Then he gathered some papers and left. All this without once acknowledging Nathaniel's presence.

Nathaniel's almost instant rapport with his other roommates paid dividends in terms of his accommodation. Prof. Gnoze had arranged for him to lodge in the spare bedroom of an elderly acquaintance of hers. Unfortunately this old woman was talkative to the extent that even if her verbal output and the sparse vocalisations of Hall-Crumble had been averaged, the result would still have been defined as logorrhoea. But this inconvenience was trivial, and laughably so, compared to the other horrors of her house, which Nathaniel couldn't believe Prof. Gnoze had ever visited. Ms. Mildred Scraddler was a longstanding and fanatical member of the "Cats' Defence Union," or had been until one of the inevitable feuds pertaining to those organisations that attract the mentally unstable had split the local branch into three. Ms. Scraddler constituted one of these new fragments.

The description of Ms. Scraddler's abode is perhaps best approached in the form of a recipe. Take the entire stock of several junk shops, full of ancient commemorative crockery, hideous vases, brass bric-à-brac and mock Grecian gimcracks. Add the contents of a bookshop and of a newsagent from the first half of the 20th century. Add seventeen cats, preferably faeco-urinally challenged and reproductively intact. Close all windows and doors, and turn up the heating. Mix well and leave to fester for at least forty years. If the air cannot be cut with a knife, sprinkle liberally with cat urine and milk, tread some miscellaneous faecal material into the carpet, and let a few forgotten kittens, blackbirds, sparrows and a one-legged pigeon decompose behind the wardrobe.

Not long after a wide-eyed and nose-covering Nathaniel had entered this den of decrepitude, a vision from hell roused itself from its apparent rigor mortis on the carpet, hissed and scuttled off into the nether regions. Patchily both bald and matted, skeletal and drooling blood and pus, Rosemary, Nathaniel learnt, was possibly the fittest cat in the place and the twenty-year-old apple of her mistress' eye. At her rickety flight, Ms. Scraddler almost succeeded in interrupting her merciless train of *non-sequiturs*: "Oh, dear. Poor Rosemary. Would you like a cup of tea, dear? Poor dear, she's terrified...." Rosemary! Nathaniel gagged, made his excuses and left.

The next day Prof. Gnoze was profusely apologetic, and Nathaniel's roommates were amused to hear of his experiences. Gopi suggested that he stay with him as one of his flatmates was away for a few weeks and wouldn't mind if his room was used. Nathaniel acted as if he were carefully weighing up a finely balanced set of pros and cons. It was only when his pensive expression cracked that the others saw the joke. Midst the laughter, Nathaniel accepted Gopi's offer with gratitude.

It came as a pleasant contrast to Hall-Crumble's off-handedness that Prof. Gnoze herself had arranged a long meeting with Nathaniel, to take place at the end of his first week. There was no hanging around waiting either, and she even had an agenda!

"Well, Nathaniel," she said, "how're you settling in? I'm sorry again about Ms. Scraddler—she seemed such a nice woman! You've managed to find somewhere else to stay, I believe?" (Pleasant Chitchat was One on her agenda, Nathaniel presumed, as he could see her put a tick next to what looked like a one on the sheet of paper in front of her.) Nathaniel replied in the amicable tone he believed was required, but was desperate to know what two would be.

"Now, Nathaniel, I don't know how you'll feel about this, but I have some suggestions to make regarding the direction of your project. Judging by what you told me earlier, you are making excellent progress with the computing, so that's up and running. As things stand at present, you are going to be concentrating on the external appearance of the face as it ages, and you will be adding to this some CAT scans, which are, fundamentally, static images of the facial tissues. This is what we'd planned, right?"

Nathaniel confirmed that it was.

Prof. Gnoze continued, "Additionally you are intending to study the microscopic characteristics of fibroblasts and epidermal cells once you've completed your Ph.D. It seems to me that there's an obvious gap in all this…." Prof. Gnoze paused dramatically.

Nathaniel, dutifully responsive, leaned forward and widened his eyes. To this he added what he imagined was a sage pursing of the lips.

Prof. Gnoze, subconsciously gratified, resumed, "We have all the facilities of a big teaching hospital on our doorstep here. It would be easy for you to carry out some work on the physical properties of facial tissues, and I think that this is very relevant to your work. You can hardly talk about the effects of ageing without having quantified elasticity, for example, can you?"

Nathaniel was engulfed by a wave of despair and nausea. It seemed that she was right, but in his own mind he had budgeted his time such that he didn't see that he could fit in more work without his Ph.D. running late. True, his was a self-organised Ph.D. so that the three-year deadline was more a self-imposed one than anything (provided he could persuade HDI to continue his funding), but the thought of all that extra work before he could call himself a doctor! Besides, he didn't quite agree with Prof. Gnoze's assessment of the computing situation. Yes, the "conveRT" programme was fine, but he hadn't started to analyse any of the few data he had collected so far. What about measuring elasticity? He knew very little about mechanics, but he could imagine that it wouldn't be quite as straightforward as Prof. Gnoze had suggested. Of course it suited her purposes to get as much out of him as possible while he was a self-funding generator of papers with her name on them! What could he do? He needed to stall for time….He became aware that Prof. Gnoze was still talking: "…so I think it would be an idea for you to see the facilities first. Apart from ourselves (because, obviously, during the course of our surgery we generate quite a few fresh samples of facial tissues) it would be worth seeing the pathology lab, and the A and E

Department. I don't know how good your anatomy is, but you might also want to join the medical students with their dissections. You'll also need to visit Followby. I'm sure you've heard of Professor Arthur Podd? You'll have seen his work on dinosaur locomotion—it was all over the popular media? Anyhow he's probably the best bio-engineer in the country and he can give you a quick rundown on elasticity testing. I've already contacted him and he's more than willing. Of course you'll want to put his name on your papers...."

Nathaniel was dismayed to see that Prof. Gnoze had still not reached the end of her wretched list. What more could she possibly wish to say? Strangely she seemed nervous, her immaculate lips twitching as she considered her agenda. As if pulling herself together and resolving something she circled an item on her paper and spoke, "So...ummm...." She cleared her throat. Now Nathaniel was nervous. "So...ummm, you had a good time in Cambridge then?"

Nathaniel had already told her about Cambridge—what the devil was she getting at? "Yes, it was OK. The work went well enough although it did take longer than I'd thought. Dr. Well was right about that...."

"You got on with him alright?"

"Yes, I'd say so, though...."

"Though what?" Prof. Gnoze seemed excited, her breathing slightly heavier than would normally have been required by sitting and talking.

"Well, he's not the easiest of people in some ways. I mean you saw what he was like at that meeting in Inverdon....?"

"Yes. Probably more than you did. Look, Nathaniel, I don't know whether I should tell you this or not...but I have a feeling that I can trust you, am I right?" She gave him the full benefit of her hazel eyes, and a soft warm hand placed itself on one of his, and squeezed it gently. Her generous lips, slightly parted, were coated in a glossy lipstick whose colour Nathaniel placed about midway between scarlet and chocolate. The slender pink tip of her tongue moistened them superfluously and languorously. Suddenly it withdrew between the perfect teeth. "Nathaniel, he was scribbling nonsense at that meeting. I could read some of it. It seemed to be string of random words!" Her lips closed.

Was that all? Nathaniel was disappointed. "Well, perhaps it was an elaborate system of mnemonics—his own method of shorthand?"

"Not much of a shorthand to judge by the quantity of it!"

"Perhaps it wasn't what I was saying that he was noting down, but his own thoughts?"

Prof. Gnoze snorted. "I don't think so. Let's leave it there for now. Don't discuss it with anyone else for now, will you? Come and see me in two weeks once you've put together some ideas."

Nathaniel rose and was almost at the door when she spoke again, "Oh, by the way, Nathaniel...." She waited until he'd turned around, "Please call me Iolanthe."

Nathaniel flushed and left, not sure what to make of anything anymore. It was clear that Prof. Gnoze, or rather Iolanthe, was pretty sharp in every respect, and he could see her point about his work. She was also pretty. Very pretty. What the hell had Well been writing? Had that just been power play? Had he been writing so frantically just to throw them all off balance? If so, why did he feel the need for it? How ridiculously petty! Nathaniel was losing any respect he'd had for the man. He couldn't quite bring himself to think of him as "Hugh," but the respectful "Dr." had gone. So, two out of three of his supervisors were a bit dodgy...but he thought he liked Iolanthe. Iolanthe, what a lovely name....

Nathaniel knew that he was perilously close to fancying her in an extreme way. This was both good and bad. To the extent that it meant that he might at last be breaking free of the reins of the mythical Rosemary, it was good, perhaps. But did this mean that he might be about to pedestalise Iolanthe in place of Rosemary? Was she perfect? She was getting on, after all: thirty-five, forty....Nathaniel made an effort to switch off his computer-influenced imagination. He wrenched himself back to an important question: what effect would a sexual relationship have on the working relationship? Should he hide his feelings until he graduated? Could he do this? What could be wrong with it if their feelings were mutual? She seemed to be giving him the right signals, after all....Strange, he felt more alive than he had for a long time.

CHAPTER THIRTEEN
The "Tartan Terrors" and the Torment of Thyme

Fortunately, within four days all the anguished analysis of the Iolanthe-Rosemary question was obsolete. Indirectly, this was due to Iolanthe herself, for she was the one who had suggested that Nathaniel acquaint himself with the finer points of facial anatomy. He had just emerged from the formaldehyde-laden atmosphere of the dissection hall where he had sat in on the second-year medical students' dissections. (By a stroke of luck, they happened to be peeling off the layers of the face at the time.) He had stayed back long after the others had departed in a pubwards direction, committing to memory the musculature, innervation and vasculature of the human visage (and incidentally thereby fulfilling the age-old role of the over-intense mature student, bane of lecturers and irritant of younger classmates). He was walking back towards the LIMFS building, mentally superimposing some of his computer-generated images on his fresh knowledge of the underlying muscles, trying to imagine how their patterns of contraction over the years would generate the wrinkles (partly as a way of taking his mind off Iolanthe), when his adrenergic system sent his heart racing and gave him the sensation of several flying foxes, rather than butterflies, doing aerobatics in his stomach.

The subconscious is a fascinating topic. What happens to generate an emotional response to stimuli in that period between their perception by the senses and their analysis by the higher faculties? Nathaniel was virtually solar-plexused before he could attempt to work out what had happened to him, but the combination of stimuli present at the burns unit side entrance could hardly have been better designed to cure him of incipient Iolanth-o-mania. Underneath the "Burns Unit—Staff Only!" sign was a trio of the loveliest young women Nathaniel had ever seen (with the possible exception of Rosemary, although she was arguably still a girl when he'd known her). Their white nurses' uniforms were held tight to their perfect figures by tartan belts, and they were wearing little tartan berets, decorated with heather sprigs and jauntily angled on their neatly taken-up hair: a redhead, a brunette and a black-haired lass, and all of them too gorgeously curvaceous to be fashion models! Two of them were smoking, the way they held their cigarettes emphasizing their femininity: elbows of their cigarette-bearing arms in to their waists, the pale smooth curves of the erect forearms ending in the backward flexure of their slender wrists. Add to this the fact that the door of the burns unit was open, and synchronous with his perception of the siren-nymph-goddesses had been his detection of the unmistakable strains of ceilidh music issuing from within. As he came up behind the brunette, almost in a state of shock, he registered that the immaculate maidens were conversing in warm and soft Scottish tones, and he caught some words: "Och, Ah'd be careful wi' him, he's a richt wee monster, so he is!"

Nathaniel knew he had to talk to them, but he was so shaken that he couldn't think what to say. Trembling, he heard himself mumble, "What's a wee corner of Scotland doing down here, then?"

The redhead laughed, and then smiled at Nathaniel, mischievous and delicious dimples appearing. She took a quick sip at her cigarette, blew the smoke sideways and spoke, "So you noticed then? I'll give you a clue. Today is a very important day for the Scots...."

Nathaniel was delighted by her archness. He tried to think—25 January—it wasn't Hogmanay, or St. Andrew's Day, so it must be..."A Burns Supper!" As he uttered it he remembered that this was the burns unit. He pointed at the sign, laughing.

"Aye. It started as a wee joke three years ago, when we realised that by chance most of us were Scots! We thought well, we are the burns unit after all, so why not? This year we've got almost no patients and a ward's empty, so we thought we might as well go the whole bang-shoot, so to speak, with the address to the haggis, the toast to the lassies, and the like....By the way how did you ken...?"

"I lived in Inverdon for many years. I've only recently come back to England. I'm English by birth but I almost feel more Scottish than anything. I've really been missing the ceilidhs and things...."

"Well, why don't you come in and join us? You're very welcome and ye'll find ye're nae the only Sassanach! The speeches are finished, and so's the haggis, but there's some chappit neeps and tatties left, more than a few drams of whisky I'm sure...and it'll as like go on all evening....There'll be plenty of dancing too! Come on!" They took a last drag on their cigarettes, stuffed them into an already full wall-mounted ash-tray unit next to the entrance, and led Nathaniel in to their little Caledonian Bohemia, their feet already skipping in anticipation of the next dance.

Nathaniel was in raptures. This was what ceilidhs were about, not that horrible exclusiveness of Cambridge, but a "Hail fellow, well met!/A man's a man for a' that!"-ness! Melanie (the redhead, a Glaswegian) had him on the dance floor immediately, then Kirsty (the brunette, also Glaswegian) and Lorraine (the black-haired one, from Edinburgh) had him up for dances. He got chatting to one of the two fiddlers (Gregor from Stornoway), and the accordionist (Sandy from Stonehaven). The latter had obtained his medical degree in Inverdon and remembered being lectured by Prof. Hall-Crumble. The bass player was a Londoner, but claimed to love Celtic music by virtue of his Irish parents. There was also a female piper, and an impassive-looking but adept bodhran player with whom Nathaniel never spoke.

Thus, within two weeks of his arrival in London, Nathaniel had nearly fallen for one woman, been pulled back from the brink of this by the attractions of three others, and had established two new circles of friends. Melanie, Kirsty and Lorraine (known within the burns unit as the "Tartan Terrors") turned out to be what might be called "social facilitators." They introduced Nathaniel to the jam sessions in a nearby Irish pub, the Galway Bay, which then gave him an opportunity to do the same for his roommates. It was particularly gratifying for Nathaniel to be able to introduce his office-mate Robert, a Scot long resident in London, to this scene. All was not blissful, however.

First, and most obvious, was the fact that he had a prodigious amount of work to do. Although intelligent and generally well-educated, he found that getting his head around the engineering aspects of his modified project (Prof. Hall-Crumble and Dr. Well had conceded that Iolanthe's arguments were valid) demanded a deal of time and effort. Second, he found that money was tight. Despite the fact that HDI were giving him £9,000 a year (three times what the average SERC or NERC Ph.D. student might receive) he found that his social life, and the exorbitance of London rent (he'd moved in permanently at Gopi's place as, conveniently, another of his co-renters had left), were driving him into debt. He tried not to let this worry him. The bank, on the strength of his record and the two degrees already under his belt, seemed happy to lend him more. Third, and most problematic, was his confusion over his sexual desires.

Once the initial froth of the post-Burns Supper euphoria had died away, Nathaniel's habitual torturing self-analysis rose to the surface. What did this powerful attraction to members of the opposite sex mean, he asked himself, if it were so labile, so fragile? A few days previously he had been on the verge of falling for Iolanthe, and now he couldn't stop thinking about Lorraine, Kirsty, and particularly Melanie! It was so superficial…but so damn powerful! Had Rosemary really been no better than these other women, and if that were the case how could he choose any one woman? But you only lived once, and if you didn't enjoy yourself what was life for? Nathaniel was possessed of remarkable (or remarkably eccentric?) analytic abilities, but his imagination was even more powerful. Little did he know at the time that the latter was to put paid to such analytic meditations, and submerge him in yet deeper anguish. Events shall be related in their chronological order (bearing in mind the implacable unidirectionalism of rivers above their tidal zones) and enlightenment on this point postponed.

Two months into his first spell in London, Nathaniel realised with surprise that he had forgotten to look up Mary—Mary who had been with him through some of the most influential years of his life! He had been so wrapped up in his work, and his seemingly self-generating new social life. Nathaniel obtained the number of the Victor Ear and Herb Alpert Museum from directory enquiries. Mary answered her extension in professional tones but sounded delighted when she recognised Nathaniel's voice. They arranged for Nathaniel to meet her in the museum's restaurant at lunchtime.

Nathaniel arrived a bit early, and decided to explore the impressive building. Up to this time he had never given the museum or its curious title a second's thought, merely thinking of it as the location of one of his friends, but now the unconsidered mystery would be explained. He learned that Dr. Hildegard Victor (his doctorate was honorary) had been a rich but hyper-stressed entrepreneur, dead five years previously. Other than medication, the only effective means of relaxing himself, he had found, was through listening to what may euphemistically be called "easy listening" music ("muzak" or "lift/elevator" music). Over the last ten years of his pecunious but unfortunate life he had gradually lost his hearing, and thus his chief pleasure. Consequently he had donated millions of pounds towards research into deafness, setting up an internationally famous institution. In his will he had left the rest of his considerable fortune for the establishment of this museum, whose aims were "to promote the recognition of the importance of easy listening music, and particularly the genius of Herb Alpert" and "to inform the public about the wonders of human hearing." Nathaniel gleaned all this from the big display case in the entrance hall, which, in addition to biographical details, featured a few photographs of the latterly auditorily challenged gentleman. Nathaniel glanced at his watch, and saw that he would have to proceed forthwith to his rendezvous.

Mary was sitting at a table waiting for him, but it was a moment before he recognised her. She was as stylishly dressed as ever (this time in a black cashmere sweater and short black skirt), but her long dark tresses had given way to a bob, under which pearl earrings could be glimpsed in her neat little ears. In front of her was a tall glass of sparkling mineral water. She was toying with the lemon and the ice with her swizzle stick.

It wasn't long before they were over the awkward greeting phase. Nathaniel was amazed by how much Mary had changed. Her previous air of languor and perpetual pensiveness seemed to have been swept away. She was positively vivacious, there was colour in her cheeks, and she oozed enthusiasm about her new job. In fact it was difficult for Nathaniel to get a word in, not that he particularly felt the need to.

"Yes, it could have been a bit daunting. The executors had this mandate for the museum but no ideas at all as to what to do about it. There were five of us on the shortlist. I must have impressed them. You know I didn't think I really stood a chance because I had no experience whatsoever, so I went in there with the attitude that I had nothing to lose, and I just let fly with some of the ideas I'd had. They obviously liked me, and I liked them. They asked me some questions about how I would implement some of my wackier schemes. We laughed, we joked. I really enjoyed the interview and they told me the same day that the job was mine! Incredible, really, because from being an unemployed graduate with no experience I was virtually in charge of a museum! Of course my suggestions have to be passed by the steering committee, but that's turned out to be a formality, so, in fact, I have a completely free hand. There's even an allowance for visiting other museums, and going to conferences. Next month I'm off to the Getty...."

Nathaniel had finished his meal before Mary was halfway through hers. Realising this, she laughed self-deprecatingly and let her vocal cords rest, increasing the work load of her jaw muscles. Nathaniel took the opportunity to bring her up to date with his life, and to give her news of Shelagh, but somehow didn't feel it was the right occasion to talk about the strange Ph.D.-related tensions he was starting to feel. After lunch, Mary was keen to show Nathaniel her latest exhibits.

"So you can see what I've done here. I've used water as a metaphor for music. You see the dirty water spurting in at the top left there? We have a team of YTSs, young people placed under the Youth Training Scheme—a cheap method of keeping them out of the unemployment statistics—taking it in turn to empty buckets of it into that funnel. We've got to find something for them to do! Anyhow, that muck is equivalent to the music you can hear through Headphones A."

Nathaniel obediently donned the headphones, and immediately grinned. "It's 'Hey Jude'!"

"Yes, the original version. As pointed out by the notice, this song is what I call textured, that is the emotional pitch of it is varied. There are changes in tempo and intensity, particularly with respect to the singing and towards the end, and so it takes you on an emotional journey. From our perspective, this is crude and unrefined product which is unsettling to the stressed person. Now, you can see the water passing through a filter there, and when it emerges it's a bit cleaner and the flow is more even. Here you need to put on Headphones B."

Nathaniel complied and was rewarded with a mellifluous Richard Elevatorman piano version of the same tune.

"Now that's a lot closer to what we're aiming for. Most of the variability is gone. It's probably the equivalent of a low dose of Valium, to use another metaphor. Right, then we come to the next and last filter. You can see that the water emerging from it is crystal clear and the flow rate is constant...."

Nathaniel couldn't wait to know how much further this bleaching process could be taken. What could possibly be more eviscerated than Richard Elevatorman? He put the headphones on and was immediately drenched in the aural equivalent of syrup. It was a Jamaican steelband. They'd converted the Lennon/McCartney classic into an insipid burble.

Mary was enthusiastic. "So this final version is the equivalent of a really powerful sedative—a barbiturate if you will—but with none of the side effects. If I were marketing the product, which I think we will be doing soon, my slogan would be 'Soporific sound effects without side effects!' You see, we have described and quantified the whole process. We can take any piece of music and scientifically process it into an aural comfort blanket. We've even coined a term for this. We call it 'blandification.' Ultimately our idea is to market collections of scientifically blandified music under the museum's own record label. Victor's legacy was generous but we could always do with a bit more income, and we don't want to charge entrance fees or cut back on our services like all the other museums in the country will have to soon. You know, Nathaniel, the sky's the limit, because with the loss of job security these days, and the growing numbers of stressed and poor people, this is exactly the sort of thing that will sell, and after all, it's better for them to spend what little money they have on this, rather than on gambling or drugs, at least they get some benefit and it's safe...."

Nathaniel felt queasy. He sensed that there was something immoral in this, but couldn't work out what it was. In any case, it was obvious that Mary had "found herself," and he didn't want to puncture her balloon even if he could find the arguments to do so. Why did he prefer the unfound Mary, though? Mary was keen to carry on and show him some of the displays relating to hearing and its loss, but Nathaniel made his excuses and left.

The essential ingredients of Nathaniel's Ph.D. years have now been chucked into the pot. It only remains to describe what happened to that simmering casserole. Nathaniel spent roughly half his Ph.D. years (they stretched to just over four) in London, a third in Cambridge, the rest of the time being divided between Followby and Inverdon. That is unless one counts a couple of weekend trips to see his parents, who seemed even more eccentric than ever. (Admittedly this might have been an illusion, resulting from Nathaniel's ongoing exposure to more "normal" people.)

Cambridge was as it had been previously, though Geoff-the-misery had finished his Ph.D. and left and consequently Nathaniel's room there was better. By the time of his second Cambridge visit, Nathaniel had a good grip on his project and felt able to let a lot of Well's spoutings pass over him. Essentially he used Well only as a resource to mine when he ran into a problem with the computing, but he tactfully let him think that he had a major influence on his work.

Nathaniel only visited Followby (in Yorkshire) once, and for two weeks. He found the little bio-engineering unit fascinating, and the people there utterly professional and enthused by their work (apart from one of the technicians who spent half his time E-mailing terrible jokes to imagined friends). Thoroughly cynical by now, however, he realised that this impression might be related to the brevity of his stay, and that if he stayed longer masks might slip. Nonetheless Prof. Podd was most helpful, and he mentally thanked Iolanthe for what might prove a useful future contact.

While in Followby, curiosity took Nathaniel to see the students' union and, of course, the student bars. He was impressed by the number of clubs available. To judge by the noticeboards there was a club for almost every conceivable activity, interest and sexual and religious orientation! He wondered what the ideal club for himself might be, to the same level of precision—"The Association for Cynical Anglo-Saxon Heterosexual-but-Tormented Atheistic Computer-Literate Caledoniaphiles Fond of the Odd Pint," perhaps? How many members would that attract?

After London, and Followby even, Inverdon seemed small and parochial, but walking along Junction Street (in rain or sun) he still felt completely at home. It was like nowhere else. Yes, Inverdon was a good place to be nostalgic about...when away from it. He felt almost guilty when he realised he was looking forward to returning to London. It is possible that some of this had to do with Shelagh. Nathaniel was shocked by the deterioration in her. Her temporary job in a stationery shop had lived up to its adjective, and the dole queues with their rude dehumanizing interrogations, the endless and seemingly useless filling out of job applications, the scrimping and making-do, and the meals consisting largely of the contents of discounted dented tins from Steptoe's had all apparently taken their toll. She seemed to have physically shrunk...and aged! Noticing this, Nathaniel decided to incorporate the socio-economic status of his subjects into his growing mountain of data.

Nathaniel found he was virtually powerless to retrieve her from her listlessness and apathy, no matter how many pints he insisted on buying for her. In fact his careless liberality with his money (not that he was well off—he already owed the bank £3,000) might even have exacerbated her depression. When he left Inverdon, having interviewed a sufficient number of women for his northern sample, he gave her a demonstration tape produced by Mary, a compilation of some of her horrible blandified music. He lied, and said that Mary had made it specially for her. The sad truth was that Mary hadn't seemed the least bit interested in hearing about Shelagh, far less in giving her anything.

His research, despite being more taxing than he'd imagined, was going well. In fact he was becoming possessed by it. It was getting to the point where almost everything he saw or heard would seem relevant to his work. The musical sessions (or *sesíuns*) in the Galway Bay no longer served as diversions for him, as so many of the songs dealt with the same subject as his work. For example, "A Bunch of Thyme," it seemed to him, could only be a parable about ageing. If one looked below the song's ridiculous pastoral surface a clear theme emerged: women only have a short period in which they are attractive to the opposite sex. Therefore they should choose their life partners well, the narrow window of opportunity only allowing one choice:
"Thyme it is a precious thing....
Once I had a bunch of thyme,
I thought it never would decay.
Then came a lusty sailor,
who chanced to pass my way,
and stole my thyme away."

Similarly, "Will ye go, lassie, go?" was a nostalgia-tinged ballad about the ripeness of a young maiden for love. The song constituted an invitation to her, presumably by a young man, to go gathering "wild mountain thyme." Its implication, that the "wild mountain thyme" would soon not be fit for gathering, and "the blooming heather" would soon no longer be blooming, was clear to Nathaniel. The song ended, rather cheekily, by suggesting that the man "...would surely find another...." Nathaniel, quaintly idealistic, could not stomach this use-'em-up-and-replace-'em idea.

Hearing these songs, Nathaniel would look across the table, through the pub haze, at the lovely young faces of Lorraine, Kirsty, and especially Melanie (O glorious vision!), and imagine that he saw them wrinkling and distorting, aged to eighty-year-olds in the space of a few seconds. He struggled to switch these imaginings off. He tried to force on himself the sentiment of the Beatles song of that computer club party so long ago, alluding to love in old age. In this song, it was the man who was sure his love would last; his concern was whether the woman would still love him! But this attempted antidote was impotent.

The tragedy was that during his first return trip to Inverdon, Nathaniel had decided that as soon as he got back to London he would, at long, long last, muster his courage and take things further with Melanie (his Rosemary/perfect woman hang-up be damned!) but now every time he wanted to drop a hint, or stroke her silky thigh under the table, the spectre of her as an eighty-year-old would superimpose itself on her elfin features, and he would turn away revolted. The girls would ask him what the matter was, and he found himself denying that there was anything wrong, or claiming stomach cramp or some other trivial ailment, but these excuses wore thin. The more Nathaniel tried to fight the phantom images, the worse they became, until he could no longer stand to be in the company of attractive young women, and spent most of his time hunched over a computer, pouring over his horde of genuinely age-ravaged visages and the huge matrix of data which accompanied them. For all he knew he might be in possession of the elixir of youth…if he could but wrest its arcane formula from the inscrutable figures.

It was not just his career, or his supervisors' reputations, or the price of HDI shares that were at stake here. It was much more important than that: it was his long-delayed sexual fulfilment. Unless he could discover how to retard the ageing process in women, and thus in his chosen woman, his supercharged imagination would prevent him from consummating his latent passion. Unless…unless he killed her afterwards, and thus stopped her ageing….Nathaniel was appalled to find this thought sneaking into his already turbid psyche. He did not believe that he would ever resort to something that drastic, but the horror that this idea could even occur drove him deeper yet into his obsessional workaholism: he MUST discover how to halt this terrible phenomenon of ageing.

It was fortunate that Nathaniel had long ceased to think of Iolanthe in a sexual way, in fact from the evening of the Burns Supper. In this way he was spared the horror of seeing someone he had lusted after turning into someone who repelled him but with whom he nonetheless had to interact on a regular basis. Iolanthe had probably sensed that her hold over Nathaniel had gone, to judge by a subtle coldness towards him. No longer blinded by the eyes of love/lust, Nathaniel could not help but become aware of her generally manipulative (not to say bitchy) behaviour, and of her reputation for this amongst the other LIMFS people. In fact he was shaken to see how close he had come to making a monstrous and possibly irretrievable gaffe. With time the relationship between himself and Iolanthe settled into what it should have been from the start, a businesslike one. Iolanthe could not help but respect Nathaniel's dedication to his work (from which she would, of course, benefit), and therefore, over the latter part of his Ph.D., she was scrupulously proper in her dealings with him, even returning the manuscripts of his draft chapters on time, unlike his other supervisors.

Prof. Hall-Crumble, on the other hand, took weeks to review each chapter, but only suggested minor changes. In fairness to him, Nathaniel's thesis barely touched on his own territory (cytology), and many of his little points were valid ones.

Well was infuriatingly slow at reading Nathaniel's work. He had such heavy lecturing responsibilities, and such an extensive paper-writing schedule, that Nathaniel formed the opinion that it was criminal for him to have been allowed to supervise so many research students. There was nothing Nathaniel could do about it. His frustration and anger with Well spilled out in a phone call to Iolanthe from Cambridge. She was sympathetic, and said that he wasn't to worry and she would sort things out for him. By the end of that week Nathaniel had all his chapters back from Well, thoroughly reviewed. Nathaniel wondered whether a little bit of blackmail had taken place there, a teasing mention of his "notes" at Nathaniel's maiden speech perhaps? He did look a bit sheepish when he called Nathaniel in to discuss his work. Nonetheless Well felt sufficiently self-confident to insist on a major re-write of two chapters. Nathaniel was angry and a bit depressed as he'd been kicking his heels for weeks waiting for Well to finish, and he was already a year past his notional deadline! Still, his findings, while not exactly revelatory of the elixir of youth, were exciting, and he tried to cheer himself with this thought.

CHAPTER FOURTEEN
Frustration and Fortune

God, that whisky was good! Soaring spirits needed to be accompanied by downing them, Nathaniel thought, and he had treated himself to two miniatures on the train back to Inverdon, with just a touch of water to bring out the flavour as he had been taught. At last his thesis had received the approval of all his supervisors. Iolanthe had wanted further changes after Well's suggestions had been incorporated, but eventually—astonishingly—everyone was more or less happy. Even his persistent psycho-sexual problems failed to hold down those soaring spirits of his as he watched the similarly occupied gulls and fulmars wheeling in the updrafts along the cliffs south of Inverdon.

Disembarking, Nathaniel caught a taxi directly to the university and set about printing his thesis. Two weeks later, after various printer problems, the correction of numerous typographical errors, and the re-binding of his thesis after the university binding service had misspelled his name on the cover, an elated Nathaniel held six softbound copies in his arms, relishing their weight and substance. Two were for submission, one for each for his supervisors, and one for himself. If (he preferred "if" to the arrogant "when") he passed his *viva voce* he would have it hardbound in red.

He submitted his thesis at the Inverdon University Postgraduate Office, making a joke to the middle-aged woman who received it about the importance of not losing the valuable fruit of his toils, the child of his labours. She forced a smile—it was no special event for her to receive theses.

Outside, Nathaniel thought that the fish-scented Inverdon air had never been so invigorating, the clouds never so lovely…so many shades of grey. It was just a matter of waiting for his *viva*, then. Of course he ought to be writing papers, but then he deserved some time off. The POW was almost empty at that time of the day, and Nathaniel didn't know the barman.

He had a pint of 85/- on his own and, feeling a bit deflated, and then strangely tense, decided to head for the art gallery. On the way he realised why he was going there, and he was frightened. He wanted to see whether his hallucinations were triggered by paintings as much as by people. He delayed the ordeal by paying a trip to the lavatory on the ground floor. He was trembling as he mounted the stairs to the mezzanine floor, and had to stop halfway and breathe deeply. He was in a cold sweat as he left the mezzanine floor and entered the side gallery where the enchanting Bright Eyes was lurking.

Keeping his eyes averted, he sat on the seat opposite the compelling canvas. He tried to wipe his mind clean of anticipation. He concentrated on his breathing: in, hold it…and out, in, hold it…and out. He was oblivious of the curious look of a tweeded matron. Slowly he raised his eyes. The lower reaches of the painting were safe, it was the face….

But there she was in all her youthful perfection! Nathaniel was weak with relief. He laughed at himself, and stood up, a song in his heart— *Things are "getting better…."* It was going to be OK. He turned lightly away and almost bounced back towards the stairs, spinning in the doorway for one last look at those sub-erotically exquisite features.

Horror! An evil-looking crone grinned back at him through blackened teeth, a distillation of all that was corrupt, decrepit and malign. Nathaniel stumbled down the stairs to the toilets, where he threw up, wretched and retching. He was sick in the soul. He had to do something about this obsession. He couldn't go on like this. Ashen, he somehow made it back to his flat, barely aware of the journey, just conscious that it was unpleasantly cold and dark—ugly clouds overhead—and that there was a stench of putrefying fish in the air.

For two days Nathaniel did not emerge. He told himself that he was intelligent, that somehow he'd got himself into this state, and that therefore he ought to be able to extricate himself. There was certainly no way he could expose his foul imaginings to anyone else! Perhaps the most obvious solution would be simply to reverse the way he looked at his images. Naturally enough he had always considered them in chronological order—old age following youth—but if he could invert that? After all, time was but one dimension of four-dimensional space-time, and it was easy enough to mentally manipulate the other ones (as his experience in a poplar tree so many years before had taught him), so. . . .

Nathaniel loaded half of his "conveRT" image set into his computer and concentrated on old faces. He couldn't mentally push those any further, no matter how hard he tried, so, though ugly, they held no horror for him. It helped that five of these women were now dead and cremated; even in reality they hadn't aged much beyond their computerized images before they'd become ash. And he could just about remember, looking at those haggard, ancient countenances, what their more youthful appearance had been. To jog his memory he allowed himself brief exposure to their younger images, not long enough for his daymares to interpose themselves, then it was back to the old faces, whose precedents he could imagine with more and more clarity.

Now to test whether he was really making progress! He loaded the other half of his image data set into his computer, and called up some fresh geriatric visages. Yes, he could imagine what they might have looked like. He retrieved the real images of these people as young women, to check the accuracy of his visions. Bingo! After thirty-six hours of tormented key-punching and screen-staring the red-eyed Nathaniel stumbled to his bed.

He rose at noon after fourteen hours of sleep, not aware of having dreamed. He remembered the art gallery, and then, with a lightening of his spirits, his partial rectification of the situation. He thought it wouldn't do any harm to physically cleanse himself: *mens sana in corpore sano*, and all that. He emerged from the shower feeling better; shaved, felt better still, and popped out to buy a carton of orange juice and a couple of those traditional Inverdon fast-breakers called "butteries." These salty bread-pastry hybrids were an acquired taste, but Nathaniel had acquired it. In addition to the purifying orange juice, Nathaniel allowed himself a good caffeine boost in the form of an infusion of a particularly delicious tea blended and packed in, of all places, Northern Ireland. He had been introduced to this variety of his favourite non-alcoholic beverage by an Ulsterman he'd met in the Galway Bay. As he gulped this magical liquid he reflected with pleasure that the tea was a metaphor for his current situation—something good from a tortured land. Could this thought vaticinate an upturn in his life?

Regaled in body and mind, he planned the next step in his rehabilitation. It would probably be a mistake to force the pace. From his avaricious consumption of pop psychology texts in the worst days of his Rosemary obsession, he recalled that the desensitization of phobics to the objects of their phobia needed to be taken very slowly and gently. In effect, he had become phobic with respect to attractive young women. Perhaps it would be wise to expose himself to old women first, and see whether his new inverted imagination worked as well with real old women as it did with their images? Yes, that made good sense. So where to go? He couldn't go around the hospital because he was too well known and the last thing he felt like doing was being sociable, or trying to answer tricky questions.

Nathaniel found himself stationed outside an old people's home. Thanks to the differential mortality of the genders these could surely be relied upon to be particularly well-stocked with the requisite one—women—he surmised. He was not wrong, and as the elderly women shuffled around the bleak garden, or Zimmered past on the pavement, Nathaniel let his eyes casually rise from his copy of the local rag, *The Morning Mercury*. He reckoned that a five-second gaze would not seem too suspicious, particularly if his expression matched that of a man absent-mindedly letting his eyes rest, while pondering a particularly weighty item of news. His lips twisted at this thought, because, according to Shelagh, the *MM* was produced by a handful of scab hacks, willing to work for next-to-nothing without the protection of a union (thereby doing tens of their erstwhile colleagues out of their jobs), and it was unlikely that such mediocre, immoral and overworked media men (and women) would be able to find a good story without it having been handed to them processed and shrink-wrapped by the Conservative Party, *The Scottish Sin* or *The Daily Torygraph* newspapers, or Channel 3 News! Nathaniel's wry expression persisted as he realised that by purchasing this jejune journal he was indirectly kicking people like Shelagh in the face. Could he never escape from anguish?

He pulled himself back to the present, and jumped to see a bony hand reaching out to touch him. "Ye a' richt, ma dear?" The old lady's expression was a composite of sympathy and pity, with a trace of apprehension sprinkled on top, like chocolate powder on cappuccino.

Nathaniel felt the superficial vasculature of his face involuntarily dilate. This was no good, he couldn't stay here! He hurried home, trying to think of a practical alternative to old people's residences, but persistently intruding into and diverting his thoughts (perhaps as a result of his blushing?) were the words of a Burns' poem: "O my love is like a red, red rose, that's newly sprung in June...." Oh, why, why, why, could he not see Melanie as she was, a lovely-beyond-the-singing-of-it red rose newly sprung in June? His wild eyes alighted briefly on a lollipop sign— a straggle of mixed infants was crossing the road under its aegis—"Stop/ Children." *If one really wanted to stop children,* Nathaniel's fugacious mind suggested, *one should use a condom, or, better still, abstain from sex. God, back to sex!* Nathaniel was twenty yards down the road when the answer to his immediate problem crystallised: *Of course, lollipop ladies!* He could walk the streets just before the schools opened in the mornings, and then again just after they closed in the evenings! He could work out the optimal route, to take in as many of them as possible! A safe and dependable supply of geriatric femininity. *Yes, yes, yes!*

The strategy worked. Better than he'd imagined. With regular exposure to the old lollipop women, not only did the degradation of old age become less abhorrent, but he became more and more adept at perceiving the young and often attractive faces that must have preceded the old ones. It was inevitable that he should pass some of these crumbly communitarian traffic regulators at times when they were unoccupied, and as his face had become familiar to them, that one or two should engage him in conversation. He was chatting to Martha one afternoon, the last Mars bar-munching schoolkid having traversed the tar (the adolescent Marlboro mob of course found Martha's services beneath their dignity), when it happened.…

Nathaniel was electrified to feel a tumescence in his trunks. *Oh, jumping Jehosephat!* This had gone way too far: senility had become sexy! Nathaniel made his excuses to Martha, and retreated homewards, hoping that by thrusting his hands into his pockets he could disguise his arousal. Disgusted with himself, and more disturbed than he'd been in his life, he tremblingly downed a quarter of a bottle of Notorious Whinge blended whisky, then a bit more. He woke with a cruel hangover. He deserved it, he told himself. Evacuating the meagre contents of his stomach, he tried to think of this act as a symbolic purging of his system of the new sickness. He couldn't go much lower. Sweating, he rifled through a pile of old newspapers looking for a photograph of a celebrating centenarian he'd remembered seeing. That would be a good test! And there she was.…*Mmmn, vaguely attractive, pity about the acne.…* One thing was certain, young women could not disturb him any more than old ones now!

As the weeks elapsed, Nathaniel's psycho-sexual response to women of various antiquities evened out…to zero. He found that no one (and, fortunately, nothing) stimulated him sexually anymore, at least not to any great extent. For the most part he saw women's faces as they were, this perception unpredictably interrupted by flashes of those same features at assorted ages. He was complacent. His state of lassitude was modified only slightly by a persistent dull ache. There was a void which he was coming to accept might never be satisfactorily filled. And his long-awaited *viva voce* was imminent, that must take precedence—he had put it to the back of his mind for so long.

In the week before the examination Nathaniel re-read his thesis. He had forgotten how good it was! *Yes, damn good!* He ought to be able to extract fame and fortune from this little lot. And fame and fortune would have to serve as ends in themselves now, seeing as he no longer had any interest in using them to bait the ideal woman. Well, he could indulge his other desires—food and drink, travel.…He would cope without sex. In any case, he could only dimly remember what lust had felt like. He supposed he must have psychologically castrated himself. He laughed, only semi-bitterly.

Nathaniel was standing outside Prof. Hall-Crumble's office waiting to be summoned for his grilling, mouth-dessicatingly nervous. He'd had a bad night's sleep as it had occurred to him the previous afternoon that he'd forgotten to check whether his data were normally distributed. If they weren't this might invalidate his parametric statistics, and therefore the whole of his thesis! He'd started to check them the previous evening but had soon realised that it was too late to re-analyse everything anyway. Fortunately the few things he'd checked had been normally distributed, but....

He heard Prof. Hall-Crumble's voice through the door, "Well, we'll call the young man in then, shall we?" (Why did they always call him a "young man" at times such as this?) And then he remembered. For the entire four years of his Ph.D. he'd had this nagging feeling that he'd met the professor somewhere before, and something in the almost apologetic cadence of his voice there had triggered the memory. The professor had been a customer at Frillons (and probably still was for that matter)...for erotic literature! Nathaniel could picture him now, coming in the first time and hanging around hesitantly, then approaching with a hang-dog look, and asking, "Ummm, you wouldn't ummm...you wouldn't have any books, with ummm...with *saucy* photographs in them, if you know what I mean?" The word "saucy" had been emphasized in such a way as to make the meaning unambiguous. Had the professor been living in fear of exposure ever since Nathaniel had started his Ph.D., or had he forgotten Nathaniel's earlier intersection with his life?

Nathaniel was elated and amused by this thought. While the professor was officially not an examiner, merely a tolerated observer of the *viva*, he was a highly respected and powerful man in his field. Only a very foolhardy (or aberrantly scrupulous) examiner would cross such a man. The professor obviously already had some stake in Nathaniel passing (Nathaniel was his supervisee after all) but if things got sticky Nathaniel only had to subtly remind the old man what he knew about him. Yippee! Nathaniel marched into the room full of confidence, and sailed through what Ph.D. students call "a dream *viva*." In fact he never even felt the need to slip the word "saucy" into his answers. There was not a single mention of how his data were distributed! At the end of it, his external examiner shook his hand and said, "It's been an honour to meet you, Dr. Papulous! I wish you good luck with the papers, which I look forward to reading soon."

For the first time since the early post-Burns Supper days, Nathaniel had a taste of happiness. He telephoned his parents, who were genuinely pleased. (They could respond enthusiastically over the telephone to academic success without embarrassment.) Well and Iolanthe were similarly congratulatory. Then Nathaniel headed for the POW. Under the circumstances Shelagh was happy to let Nathaniel buy her all her drinks, and she made an effort to be upbeat.

What had Nathaniel discovered? By far the most significant correlate of the facial manifestations of ageing (and presumably, therefore, a major factor in modifying the extent and rate of wrinkling) was socio-economic status. When this had first dropped out of his analysis Nathaniel had been incredulous, but he had checked it and there was no doubt! Next he had asked himself whether socio-economic status and rate of wrinkling correlated with longevity. Although not enough of his subjects (or their mothers) had died to enable this to be proven, the data tended to support this hypothesis. Nathaniel dutifully performed his literature search with respect to this question. He had mixed feelings when he discovered that he was not the only scientist who had reached the conclusion that the single most important determinant of lifespan appeared to be socio-economic status. (There were some data which suggested that it was relative and not absolute socio-economic status that mattered: Albania, with a very low per capita GDP but a relatively even distribution of income, had a similar average longevity to the UK!)

Unsurprisingly, the next most significant predictor of ageing was the wrinkling history of a subject's mother. Major predictors also, but not quite as useful, were the subject's smoking habits and her record of exposure to ultraviolet radiation. After this, diet was significant, but did not appear to have quite the same impact as the forementioned influences. High consumption of alcohol accompanied rapid ageing. Moderate consumption was correlated with retarded ageing. Marginally significant was the subject's use of cosmetics (apart from UV blockers, which definitely reduced the impact of sun exposure). There was slight evidence that regular use of moisturizers might ameliorate the development of wrinkles. This was significant at the level of $P = 0.054$, which, strictly speaking, would not have been enough to convince most scientists—convention dictates that P should be less than 0.050 for the results to be admissible.

The whole picture was complicated by the fact that many of these factors could not be disentangled unambiguously using Nathaniel's relatively small number of samples. For example, smokers tended to be more careless about their exposure to the sun, and the moderate consumption of wine was highly correlated with socio-economic status. The regional question (Scotland vs. Southern England) was similarly confounded, as Scottish women smoked more, drank more spirits and ate less healthily, but had lower exposure to UV radiation. When Nathaniel came up with this he had to admit that from his own direct experience that it seemed right enough. He could picture Melanie & Co.—Scottish albeit expatriate—crunching their crisps, puffing away on their beloved fags, and knocking back the whiskies in the fuggy confines of the Galway Bay.

However, whatever other areas of uncertainty existed, the massive influence of socio-economic status could not be entirely explained by suggesting that the poor and unemployed ate badly, and smoked and drank more. Put simply, a wealthy aristocrat, a member of one of the professions or a business magnate could drink half a bottle of whisky a day, sunbathe regularly, chain-smoke and live on deep-fried battered Mars bars, and still look more youthful than a relatively healthy-living but unemployed sun-avoider.

Nathaniel couldn't help thinking of Shelagh as he pondered these findings. A factor in her case, surely, might be her council flat, which was a horrible cold and damp hole. A few more years living like that...? Unfortunately he hadn't asked his subjects about their accommodation so couldn't test this idea. To ask people about their homes had seemed just too intrusive, or had he just been trying to justify this omission to himself, the real reason being that he hadn't wanted to burden himself with yet more mountains of data to analyse? Setting accommodation aside, his intuition was that long-term unemployment was by far the most important ageing accelerator, because it broke people's spirits. To judge by Shelagh, after a while they seemed to just give up on life.

Having quantified the apparent influences of most of these factors, Nathaniel had gone on to develop a programme capable of producing accurate representations of a woman at any requested age, given a few photographs of her and her mother (preferably as an old woman), and the relevant biographical details. Predictions could, of course, still be made without a full set of information, with some loss of accuracy.

Nathaniel, his supervisors and his examiners were not slow to see the potential. The problem was that one of the conditions of HDI's funding had been that the cosmetics company had the right to veto the publication of any of it. During his studies Nathaniel had sent regular summaries to HDI. The lack of response had suggested to him that they were satisfied, so he did not anticipate any interference. He was wrong.

Nathaniel had dispatched two hardbacked copies of his thesis to HDI, as requested. The next week he'd received a phone call from the CEO's secretary, congratulating him on his work, and informing him that HDI would be grateful if he would visit them "as soon as possible" at their UK headquarters in Surrey. They would cover the costs of his transport by plane, train or automobile; if he flew they'd be happy to collect him from Heathrow. Nathaniel had booked his flight immediately.

He was met by a red BMW sports car, with a tasteful little HDI logo on the doors. It was driven by what the un-psychologically castrated Nathaniel would have described as a tasty little blonde in a cream Chanel suit. She wore large dark sunglasses, which pleased Nathaniel as this reduced the chances of those irritating "age flashes" obscuring her face. She was not very talkative, and after introducing herself as "Michelle, the CEO's chauffeur," she responded monosyllabically to Nathaniel's questions about the route and what it was like to work for HDI. These few murmured words, the occasional sigh and the chinking of a gold bracelet against the gear lever were the only sounds that came from her on the entire hour-long smooth and air-conditioned trip.

Michelle declared Nathaniel's presence to the guard at the huge fortified gates. He waved them in. This was a real little kingdom, rather like Saul's Hospital, Nathaniel was thinking, but this had a smart corporate identity to it, buildings appeared to match, and there was a large manicured garden in front of the main office. This looked familiar! Yes, he thought, it must be a recreation of Monet's garden in Giverny, to judge by the waterlily pond, the bridge and the willows in the centre of it! And, yes, Nathaniel could remember seeing a couple of advertisements for HDI cosmetics set in such a place.

Michelle coasted up to the office building and told Nathaniel to report to the central desk. Nathaniel thanked her and alighted. She nodded coolly and drove off.

The receptionist seemed warmer: "Ah, Dr. Papulous! I'm glad you're with us. How was your journey? If you'd just take this ID badge, and sign here...."

Nathaniel was ushered into a bright waiting room with a wide window overlooking the currently sun-soaked Giverny-esque garden. The walls of this luxuriously upholstered modern room (low furniture in chrome, blue and green leather, and glass) were lined with huge colour photographs from HDI's advertising campaigns. Amongst these were five enlarged *Vague* covers. Nathaniel guessed that the exquisite models had been decorated with HDI products. A couple of them flickered into geriatricity in response to his gaze. Ho-hum, thought Nathaniel. Excrutiatingly serene music, that would have appealed to Mary, trickled in from somewhere. There was a subtle perfume in the air. In the corner of the room was a coffee machine, a drinks cabinet, and an assortment of sweet and savoury nibbles. The receptionist had told him to help himself. He felt a bit self-conscious, so avoided the alcoholic beverages, although he would have loved a shot of whisky, and poured himself a tomato juice. He timidly helped himself to a couple of olives, and sipped his juice, sitting at one of the tables to flick through HDI's corporate magazine for that year. Nathaniel was impressed by the slickness of it, and by the apparent absence of spelling mistakes. Even the apostrophes were in place! All the staff featured looked so clean and wholesome and groomed, including the white-coated brigade. Nathaniel was feeling increasingly ill-at-ease in his ill-fitting and far-from-new cords and non-matching shirt. Not to mention his scuffed shoes.

He was wondering what to do with his olive stones when the door opened and in strode Mr. Tyrone Silversmith himself, the CEO of the vast HDI empire, whom Nathaniel had met briefly at a London office when he'd been arranging his Ph.D. Nathaniel slipped the olive stones into his pocket. Though well-groomed, it seemed that Silversmith was exempt from the youth-and-beauty requirement. He was a squat man with large jowls. Contrasting with his pale blue-and-cream pinstriped shirt his complexion was almost supernaturally ruddy. His voice was deep, but strangely narrow and reedy, like a mildly peeved boar heard through a thick oaken door perhaps. He seemed jovial enough, and his small but prominent black eyebrows approached each other as he greeted his *protégé*: "Dr. Papulous—Nathaniel! Congratulations! But what's that you're drinking? A Bloody Mary? Been out celebrating every night have we? No—just a tomato juice!? That won't do! Champagne's what you want! There should be some in the fridge over there….Here we go! Moët and Chandon do you? It's a reasonable vintage."

Within three minutes of Silversmith's entry Nathaniel was light-headed and glowing. Nothing felt real. As if in a dream, he was swept along on a tour of the mini-kingdom that was HDI's English base. There were huge laboratories much better equipped than anything he'd seen in the academic world or the health service, a gigantic animal house (whose presence probably explained much of the impressive security hardware in evidence—everything from good old-fashioned closed-circuit television cameras to eardrum-destroying alarm loudspeakers, infra-red sensors and retinal scanners at access points—all this expense in honour of the animal rights movement!) and a fairly up-to-date mainframe computer, linked to monitors in every office and, by an elaborate coded Internet link, to the company's computers elsewhere in the world. As a finale, Silversmith took Nathaniel by lift to the top of the office building. There, a little paradise was laid out around a swimming pool, complete with a mini-beach and palm trees! Silversmith seemed more concerned with showing Nathaniel the view, and took him over to a railing to point out the full extent of the HDI territory. Looking at the triple razor-wire security fence, electrified and liberally sprinkled with remotely controlled cameras, spotlights and loudspeakers, Nathaniel couldn't help but think of a prisoner-of-war camp. This carried his mind away north to the POW in far-off Inverdon, and its comforting familiarity. Just what sort of world was he entering now?

"Now you've seen our little place let's talk business." Silversmith took Nathaniel down a floor to his office. He had his secretary (a Michelle lookalike) bring them coffee.

"Nathaniel. Your work is excellent, but we have to be careful how we manage it. Here's what we're going to do: firstly, we will market your wrinkle-predicting computer programme. I've had a word with Dr. Well, and we've agreed the commercial aspects of it. What we propose is that you write a manual on how you developed your programme, and how best to use it. Once you've done that there will be no need for you to spend any more time on updates and improvements. Dr. Well says he can find M.Sc. students to do that—it would be a waste of your obvious genius! By the way, we've already been negotiating with a few police forces who are keen to use it for improving their descriptions of criminals and missing persons. We ourselves will of course be using the programme at our commercial outlets. We will be running it in tandem with our make-up and hair preview programme, so that we can show our clients not only what they might look like immediately, through the use of our products, but also what they might look like years into the future." Silversmith smiled.

Nathaniel was feeling very strange indeed. He was pleased to be complimented, but the way Silversmith was talking it was as if he belonged to HDI, as if he had already sold his soul. The champagne buzz contributed to this sense of rudderlessness.

"Prof. Gnoze has suggested that it would be possible to incorporate the effects of selected plastic surgery into the programme. Now that would be beyond the ability of mere computer programmers, so we'll be looking to you to do that for us." This was an idea that Nathaniel had kicked around with Iolanthe, and its mention didn't surprise him.

"Then we come to your proposed cytological work. We would like you to discuss that with our team here. Unsurprisingly for a cosmetics company, we are already running some trials on the effects of potential cosmetic ingredients on cell biology." All this seemed to make sense to Nathaniel, but what a workload already!

"…and this brings me to another point. There is no reason why we can't continue monitoring the women that you used for your research, but perhaps we should carry out some long-term double-blind cosmetic trials at the same time. I'm not going to go into all the details now— they're beyond me, to be honest—but our chief scientist, Roland Greece, will have a word with you about that."

Nathaniel's head was swimming with all the ideas and projects, but he particularly wanted to ask what he would be paid, and what would happen if he chose not to stay with HDI, but Silversmith continued, "Now we come to the publication of your results. You realise, Nathaniel, that we are a business? Now, while your results are all fascinating, they're not all of commercial interest. Our idea is to mount a big advertising campaign based on your work, and we would like a clean scientific publication to refer to."

Nathaniel was open-mouthed, but Silversmith forestalled him. "Now, I know what you're thinking, but no, I'm not suggesting we suppress any of your findings, far from it. Perhaps it's best if I explain exactly what we envisage. We see the face of a lovely young woman on the left of a poster, this is labelled 'You today.' On the right there are two smaller images of her. The top one is labelled 'You in twenty years' and shows, well—not to put too fine a point on it—a hag. The bottom picture is similar to the big one on the left, just looking marginally older and perhaps a bit more elegantly made up, and it's labelled, 'You in twenty years, with HDI.' The small print details that with our sun-block cosmetics, our moisturizer, our dietary supplements and our aids to stopping smoking, scientific research has proven that this age retardation is possible. Now we would like you to publish those of your findings relevant to this scenario before you publish anything else, and publish them without the extraneous details. You follow?"

Nathaniel's lips were slightly twisted. He looked sideways for a moment, before replying, "You're asking me to publish my work in such a way that you can suppress the information that poverty is by far the most significant correlate of ageing, that everything else is trivial by comparison with poverty?"

"Nathaniel, that's not the way to look at it!" Silversmith sighed and bit his lower lip, rubbing his nose at the same time. "Look at it this way, we're relatively powerless to tackle the major evils in society. You know anyway that we're one of the most generous corporate donors to charity? But we can help women in our own small way. Now there's no point complicating the message. If we give people too much information they won't be able to digest it all, and we'll end up by helping no one, least of all ourselves. We're in a competitive business, and what we don't sell, another company does. There is nothing wrong with keeping the issues simple. I'm not suggesting that you suppress your findings—just publish them in their entirety at a later date, and give us a 'clean' reference for our ad campaign! Oh, there is one small point...."

"Yes?" Nathaniel was fascinated by the business approach. It was such a different world to the one he'd been inhabiting!

"I see that you found that the influence of moisturizers was...ummm...marginal?"

"Well...yes. That was one of the most difficult aspects to quantify, though. Some women were pretty vague about what they'd used over the years, and how often. So, to be homest, I'd say the question's fairly open yet."

"Good, good. So it's not impossible that we'll find, eventually, with a better set of information, that moisturizers in fact do have a significant impact?"

"Well, yes, I suppose so."

"OK. Good. Now, Nathaniel, is there anything to stop one from rounding figures, particularly when there's a lot of uncertainty anyway?"

Nathaniel suddenly realised what all this was about. "You mean that I should state that I found the impact of moisturizers to be significant at the 5% level!? That's what you're getting at, isn't it?"

"You are following my line of thinking. I won't deny it."

Nathaniel found himself floundering in turbid and uncharted moral and emotional waters. (Even the lower reaches of a river may become unfamiliar and hazardous after a storm, and the world of HDI certainly amounted to a tempest.) He wasn't happy. However, Silversmith hadn't become the managing director of a multinational company for nothing, and had divined what sort of lifebelt to throw him. He resumed in lighter tones, "Nathaniel, I found all your work fascinating. Of course a lot of the scientific details went over my head, but your findings were…ummm…very thought provoking. Could you just clarify for me the impact of poverty? Is it true that all those factors you suspected of accelerating the ageing process were worse for the poor—that you found, for example, that the poor tended to eat less fresh fruit and vegetables, and drink more heavily?"

Nathaniel confirmed this, and Silversmith continued, steepling his thick fingers, "But, even if you took those things into account, they still didn't fully explain their rapid ageing?"

Nathaniel nodded, tight-lipped.

"So, how do you explain it, Nathaniel?" Silversmith had raised his still-steepled fingers to his lips. He leaned forward.

Nathaniel related his ideas about the link between mind and body: when people lived without hope their physical selves disintegrated in sympathy.

Silversmith nodded gently, and was quiet for a few seconds. When he spoke it was in a new voice, altogether quieter, "I think you're right there, Nathaniel. I've always believed that the real heart of the issue, when it comes to health, or anything else for that matter, is what people believe, what people feel….And it applies very much to our business. You know that the word 'image' has…ummm…a pejorative connotation. It's often used against us—you know the sort of argument: 'Beauty is only skin deep so it's immoral for people to spend so much money on something so trivial.' But when people look better they feel better, and the reverse. Now, like other marketers of so-called luxury products, we're in the business of selling dreams. But unlike, say sports car manufacturers, our dreams are affordable. Most women—OK, at least in the western world—can buy at least some of our products, and if they have to save up a little bit for them so much the better…because then our products are valued. They have an aura about them. They become a little piece of magic in a dull life. And part of that magic, part of that dream, is the belief that they will work. And if a woman believes that our products will make her younger, then they probably will! So, if we were to say that scientists had demonstrated that our moisturizers work, that would make it true, and that would improve the miserable lives of thousands of women—a bit of light in their bleak existences….And, lit up, they would radiate…ummm…happiness…to those around them. In the final analysis, our business must be about making the world a better place." Silversmith wondered whether he'd overdone it a bit. He sat back and watched Nathaniel intently.

Nathaniel realised that he was dealing with the sharpest person he'd ever met. Of course he sensed that he was being manipulated, but, at the same time, he could find no obvious flaw in Silversmith's logic. And, after all, he was only being asked to round one figure, and to publish his results in a certain order. The first few words of his reply told Silversmith that he'd won, that he had a lease on Nathaniel's soul: "What's in it for me? If I accept your argument and agree to go along with you, and work on all the projects you have suggested?"

Silversmith tried not to show his delight. "That's a good question. Tell me, Nathaniel, what would you be earning if you stayed in academia? If you did a post-doc, say?"

Nathaniel decided to be optimistic in his response, "Ooh, I should think £18,000 or thereabouts."

Silversmith nearly choked with pleasure, but managed to transmute this into a credibly innocent cough. He was really enjoying this now. "And what would you earn if you were lucky enough to get a lectureship?"

Although Nathaniel knew that he would never be offered one without a substantial number of publications to his credit, and that at his age he would not have commanded more than £20,000, he replied, "Oh, I should think about £25,000."

Silversmith appeared to be weighing up these "facts." He cleared his throat. "What would you say if we started you on £50,000, plus expenses and car, and threw in a 4.5% cut of the profits from your programme and its updates? No, let's make that 5%. Yes, 5%, a nice round figure."

CHAPTER FIFTEEN
Fame

Nathaniel had arrived. It was strange, but even his attitude to his laconic chauffeur was different as she drove him back to Heathrow. Just a few hours had passed, but he was no longer intimidated by her self-contained air, her chic *soignée*-ness. He was now several rungs up the company ladder from her, poor girl. He was downing a celebratory whisky on the flight back to Inverdon, his mind freewheeling, when his intermittent and unfocussed speculations on her taciturnity gelled. Presumably picking up people from Heathrow was all in a day's work for her, and usually these would be important, powerful and wealthy people, mainly men. She had probably been hired as much for her looks, for her "image" as anything else, and one could imagine the crass patronising banter that she'd have to endure, or even have to appear to enjoy, from the bloated chauvinist plutocrats. Now Nathaniel had not been in that category at all, but he couldn't imagine that every interviewee received the red-carpet treatment that he had. Perhaps she had seen him as a rich-bastard-of-the-future, perhaps she had known that his desperate-for-reassurance, bashful-youth demeanour would be transmuted, in the space of a few hours, into the serene condescension of the elite. Imagine how painful witnessing that change would be...if one had extended a branch of amity to an insecure neophyte, only to receive a haughty putdown from the transfigured self-confident version of a few hours later. Nathaniel wasn't sure whether his vague discomfort was guilt. He wondered whether he had been wise to swallow that second malt, or whether, indeed, it would have been better if he had asked for a third.

—

Six months after signing his contract with HDI, Nathaniel's world had changed entirely. He owned a rather nice little cottage in Surrey, and a Porsche. It wasn't entirely new, granted, but it could certainly shift! Not that he had a lot of time to enjoy it—he was working very hard, and was often overseas, visiting HDI's divisions and attending conferences. His face had appeared in a few women's magazines ("Dr. Youth: this man can keep you young!") and he'd appeared on television more than once, even in the USA. His first paper (approved by Silversmith) had just been accepted by *Nature*, and he was hoping that the superb, and horrific, computer images of ageing that he'd sent to illustrate it would adorn the cover.

He frequently visited Saul's, and therefore saw the Tartan Terrors, as he continued to collaborate with Prof. Gnoze on the modification of his famous ageing programme to take account of plastic surgery. He occasionally thought that he felt the beginnings of a resurgence of sexual interest in Melanie, but it was so transient, and she had a boyfriend anyway. He'd not had time to stay in touch with his friends in Inverdon, but he and Mary had managed a celebratory meal at Gerard Paulo-Black's exorbitantly expensive and very much "in" little bistro in Knightsbridge. They'd escaped uninsulted by the notoriously extrovert Paulo-Black, but their assignation had been documented by *Hiya!* magazine. This was the first time that Nathaniel had encountered the words "eligible bachelor" in conjunction with his name. He snorted—little did they know! Unfortunately, or perhaps fortunately, he was still in a state of psychological castration, those rare twinges with respect to Melanie excepted. He could, in an abstract way, appreciate that a woman might be beautiful, but the occasional fleeting awareness of what she would look like on her deathbed (or the fear of such a vision) successfully killed any passion. Besides, he was working so hard, and getting so much fulfilment from his work, that he didn't see how he could fit in anything else.

And so it continued. His paper did make the cover of *Nature*, and it wasn't to be the first time he achieved that. He managed to extract five articles from his thesis, and by the time he was writing the fifth he already had enough data from his new research for several more. His ageing programme had become an international best seller, and a simplified version was due to be distributed for domestic use. By the end of his first year with HDI his 5% share in the software was on the way to making him a millionaire. (He was a bit annoyed, though, that he hadn't insisted on a higher percentage!) The river of Nathaniel Papulous' life was broad and deep and reliable, and seemingly unstoppable. Little did he know that he would soon be tasting saltwater.

One Sunday in April 1993 Nathaniel happened to finish at HDI relatively early (3.12 p.m.). It was a lovely spring day and he wanted to get out and do something exciting. For a long time he'd been conscious that he'd only taken his Porsche to a third of its potential top speed. The birds and the bees, and just about everyone, had a way of enjoying themselves in the springtime that was closed to him, possibly forever. But he had his car, and he knew a quiet and straight stretch of the road. Besides, he had no points on his licence, he was an excellent driver, and he could afford a fine. Nathaniel was ecstatic as he floored the accelerator—this was as near to orgasm as he could get.

CHAPTER SIXTEEN
Crash, and Crisis in the Chrysalis

It was completely dark. Pain. A familiar voice, "Nathaniel?" Nothing. Again. He vaguely remembered encountering this before: pain and darkness. He shifted. Agony! Scream. A warm relief flooding in. Nothing.

Nathaniel drifted in and out of consciousness for five days. A pigeon had hit his windscreen and he'd lost control. An oak tree was the second victim. Nathaniel was lucky, or possibly unlucky to survive. They didn't know how much of him would be left, eventually. At least the morphine could keep the pain at bay. Just.

It was completely dark, but he could see faces. They were spirits...or his imaginings. At least he was sane enough to think he could be insane. Was that Melanie he could see? Old? Young? Then it came to him that he was blind, and it was all in his mind. Even more than before.

The voices might be real. He could converse with them anyway. "Nathaniel, it's Melanie. How are you?"

"What...? Where...?"

"You had an accident...in your Porsche...too fast...."

"Where?"

"...a tree near Frindsham."

"No, where am I?"

"What?"

Nathaniel's face had been shredded, and then burnt in the ensuing conflagration. A full tank of petrol. His lips were hardly there. He was almost unintelligible.

"Nathaniel, the doctors think you'll make it. Ye'll be alright, Nathaniel!"

Then he heard them sing. It was "Auld Lang Syne." Nathaniel felt a strange pain in his face. He wondered if he could still cry.

"Nathaniel. There's something I must tell you. You may never see again." Did this mean that there was some hope? When the bandages came off, he might see again? He didn't, and couldn't ask too many questions. He was so tired.

They gradually reduced the morphine. Nathaniel moved out of intensive care into the burns unit. To minimize scarring they had to apply a new form of dressing—and strip it off. It was agony. And when they moved him Nathaniel didn't know whether he wanted to go on living, if that was what it meant. But as the weeks went by he became aware that there was something else happening. It was almost a miracle, and he tried not to put it to the test, but he couldn't help thinking of it, more and more: he was losing his ability to picture the ravages of age. Was this a compensation for his blindness? When Melanie spoke to him, he saw her, in his mind's eye, as she was, or at least as she had been before his geriatric visions had besmirched her loveliness, and he knew also that another part of his body was working. The picture was steady. Nathaniel wanted to live. Melanie's voice was better than morphine. Her excruciating touch was delicious.

They were able to wheel him into the garden and sunshine now. There were patches of intact skin on his arms and legs, and they uncovered them so that he could feel the elements. There was another "mummy" patient. They wheeled her out too. Lorraine introduced them, rather formally: "Dr. Papulous meet Mrs. Nixon."

It was good to have someone else to talk to. The Tartan Terrors were busy; they had other patients, and, more importantly, Nathaniel was afraid that he would say something to Melanie he'd regret. She had a boyfriend, after all, and, even if she hadn't how could she possibly fancy a complete wreck like himself? Not now, anyway. It was too early. God, would he be thwarted again? Still, at least he had a slight motive there for recovery, and Mrs. Nixon might be a pleasant enough distraction in the meantime—someone in the same boat, so to speak.

Nathaniel was rather pleased with his opener: "So, do you come here often then?"

Mrs. Nixon laughed, to judge by the strange noise escaping from her bandages and penetrating his. "Do you know—that's the first time I've laughed since the accident!" Her voice was pleasant and youngish, and its accent was an unremarkable middle-class home counties one, similar to Nathaniel's. She continued, but the lightness in her voice rapidly drained away, like water leaving an unplugged basin. "God, how could I laugh? They're dead...." Her voice trailed off.

Nathaniel squirmed, and then he remembered from his psychology books of years ago that it was better to talk about these things than bottle them up, so he asked her what had happened.

"My husband and I, and our daughter, Marianne. Oh God, Marianne...." Mrs. Nixon sobbed for some little while, but Nathaniel had all the time in the world. Eventually she recovered sufficiently to continue: "We were driving to Charles' parents for Sunday lunch, and a lorry pulled out in front of us. And that was that. Why did I have to survive, and they have to die? Why?" She cried some more.

That was about the extent of their conversation the first day, and the next day the weather was bad so they were not wheeled into the garden. And then it was the weekend, when the routine was different.

The next time they met, Mrs. Nixon thought she'd better ask Nathaniel something. "So how about you? How did you get here?"

Nathaniel felt awkward about putting his accident on the same metaphorical table as poor Mrs. Nixon's. "Oh, it was stupid. Entirely my fault. I was driving too fast, and they tell me I hit a tree."

"Oh."

That was their second conversation.

The next day Nathaniel was trying to identify the birds he could hear chirping at the bird table not far from his wheelchair, when he heard the squeak of Mrs. Nixon's matching vehicle, and Melanie's voice, "There ye go then, Mrs. Nixon. Oops, deary me, we've scared the birds! Never

149

mind, Dr. Papulous is right there beside you, to keep you company. I'm awa'."

"Lovely voice she has," said Mrs. Nixon.

"Melanie? Yes, she's Glaswegian. She's a lovely person in every respect. Beautiful."

"You can see then?"

"No, no. I'm all bandaged, but I knew her before…before the accident. I used to work here."

"Oh, you're a doctor?"

"Yes. I mean no, not that sort of doctor. It doesn't matter.…I assume you…ummm…you're blind also?"

"Yes. They think there's a small chance for my left eye. To be honest, I don't care anymore. I've nothing to live for. My child is dead, and I'll never be able to have another. Does it matter if it's dark or light out there, when it's always dark in here?"

By the dull thump, Nathaniel guessed she was hitting her bandaged self. He tried, feebly, to cheer her. "There's always something, I think. Listen, the birds are back.…"

It got to the point where Nathaniel was intensely disappointed if the weather were bad, or if Mrs. Nixon had visitors. He really looked forward to their chats. He had listened to Mary's get-well present (her latest compilation of ghastly emasculated music) so often that he could run through the whole thing in his head, every saccharine semibreve. He was still battling not to fantasize too much about Melanie. He couldn't bring himself to ask her about her boyfriend, though this might have been good therapy for his seemingly hopeless ardour. Mrs. Nixon had indeed turned out to be a nice uncomplicated distraction from all this, his relationship with her free of tangled emotional associations. It was strange that they had retained that formality of address: Mrs. Nixon and Dr. Papulous, or, more accurately, Mrs. Nixon and "Dr. Patchulous." Nathaniel wasn't greatly bothered by her malapropism, and as the days went by it became more and more difficult for him to correct it, but the retention of the titles did something for the relationship. It was as if the formality added breathing space, as if it were only a step away from anonymity, and therefore oddly easier to be open about things than if they'd been confined within the narrow amity of Christian names. They approached each other with respect, but candour. Under such conditions was it any wonder that a gentle mutual affection developed? Mainly Mrs. Nixon talked about her husband and daughter, and as the weeks went by her voice lost its rawness. It was as if she were placing delicate paintings of her lost loved ones into frames, and then hanging them on her emotional wall, where they remained part of her but no longer dominated the foreground. As her voice lightened, its youth shone through, and Nathaniel caught himself wondering what Mrs. Nixon looked like, but then realised that this was a doubly ridiculous question—her face had been smashed up like his, and he was, for all he knew, permanently blind. Appearances should not mean anything anymore, but it was nice to know that Melanie would still be beautiful, and, secretly, in his mind's eye, to be able to feast on this beauty, free of his visions of senile decay at last.

One day Nathaniel and Mrs. Nixon were sitting together, discussing their fears and hopes with respect to the forthcoming and possibly ultimate removal of their eye dressings, when Kirsty informed them that Mrs. Nixon's parents had arrived a bit earlier than usual. As Mrs. Nixon was being wheeled away to the lounge, her parents came some of the way out towards their swaddled progeny, and Nathaniel heard them call out to her: "Rosemary…." Rosemary! The voice! Mrs. Nixon was Rosemary Nixon, née Taylor!

Nathaniel's mind was incoherent for minutes. Slowly, his heart rate dropped towards normal. The seething thoughts and emotions were as tangled as Ms. Scraddler's favourite cat's hairs had been. Rosemary!? He needed time. The first thing, then, was to buy some time. He didn't want to have to talk to Mrs. Nixon/Rosemary until he had tamed the chaotic psychological wilderness. How could he arrange not to see her for the next week or so, and yet not offend her? Should he tell the Tartan Terrors? Not if he wanted to keep his options open with respect to Melanie. Did he? And even if he did, why not? It might actually help his chances with her—to let her know that he had been interested in someone else. But what did he feel for Rosemary?

"Melanie?" Nathaniel said, when he had a brief pain-free interlude between dressing removals. "I need to ask you a favour."

"Aye?" said Melanie. "Another to come off…."

"Aaaaargh! Melanie, something rather bizarre has happened. I've just realised that I used to know Mrs. Nixon."

"Oh, aye?"

"Yup. We were at school together for a short while. But, the thing is, she doesn't know who I am yet. And…it's a bit embarrassing, really, but we had a bit of a thing, you know, and I'm trying to sort it out in my head, so I don't want to see her for the next week while I have a think, but I don't want her to be offended. Is there any way you can interrupt our garden sessions without her being suspicious?"

"Oh-ho, that sounds a wee bit juicy! Aye, I'm sure I'll think of something. Leave it to me!"

It was simple, really. When the time came for Nathaniel's eyes to be uncovered it was discovered that his left eye was not nearly as badly damaged as had been feared, although his right eye was beyond salvage. Rosemary had limited vision in both her eyes. Melanie suggested that they tell Rosemary that he was coming to terms with his appearance, and that he felt desperately self-conscious and was indisposed to talk to anyone for the time being. Rosemary understood only too well, although her own gargoyle-shaming frontage meant little to her, next to the loss of her family.

In the depths of his fresh turmoil, Nathaniel had to laugh at himself. No sooner had he started to recover from a major accident, and get over his ageing hallucinations, than he was plunged once again into nightmarish psychotic labyrinths—would he ever be "normal" and "balanced"?

At the time of the crash, and ignoring his sexual hang-ups, the metaphorical river of Nathaniel's life had seemed to be in the mature phase: a mighty, broad, self-confident and unstoppable Old Man River. His career was secure. He was well on the way to fame and fortune. The timid and precarious rills of youth seemed an age away. He could not have imagined that anything would stop him. He could not have conceived of a sea.

There is nothing simple about rivers entering seas. The mixing process is complex and slow, and depends on the temperatures of the two waterbodies, the specific geography of the river mouth, the speed and size of the river, the presence of ocean currents, the silt load of the river, and, not least, the extent of the tides. The fauna and flora of estuarine zones take nothing for granted. Some will migrate to wherever water of the right salinity is to be found, which translates into perpetual nomadism: up and down the river mouth. Some, more sessile, will close themselves off when the mixture of waters ceases to be beneficent (or, indeed, when the water disappears altogether), and wait for better times. A few species are at home in salt and fresh water, some at different stages of their life cycles, like salmon, and others at all times, such as otters and seagulls.

What would Old Man River feel? The first sensation would be that of impedance, of check, of braking. Imagine his surprise on being stalled just when his power seems unassailable! As if that isn't enough, he has the sensation of being infiltrated by something foreign, alien, novel—a new flavour. When all seemed immutable he tastes himself changing, leading to self-doubt and reflection. If an incoming tide is strong, the waters of a river may even find themselves travelling backwards. In a world then, where all the assumed rules are suddenly revealed to have been illusions, and the habitual course is reversed, might not the geriatric waterway dream again of the headstrong self-assured upland becks of youth, and wonder whether they might again be visited?

And then high tide is reached, and when the waters ebb he finds himself once more in customary orientation, only larger than ever, and he may hope at first, and then suspect, that his old ways have won over the new part of him, that they have convinced the strange-tasting infiltrate that there really is only one way to go. On the strength of his first ebb tide then, he may come to believe again that he is the invincible master of all he surveys, that he can overcome whatever has the temerity to attempt to check him. But, lying low, all he can see are his own banks, and the patient and inevitable ocean remains unthought, waiting.

—

Nathaniel had almost died. He was bound to ask himself about the meaning of life, where he had been coming from and where he was going. While, in one sense, lying there swathed in bandages, he had imagined he had found a reason for living, in his re-awakening though confused sexual desires, he also knew that in broader terms, even if he made a reasonable recovery, he would have to slow down a bit. He had been working around the clock, and the very thing that had sat him in the cockpit of his turbo-charged vehicle, that had caused him to push the little pedal to the floor, had been the realisation—subconscious though it had been then—that he would have to change his *modus vivendi*, to take things a bit easier, to find pleasures other than intellectual ones.

Nathaniel's confusion was such that he failed to extricate himself. The currents and counter-currents were beyond his powers of description, analysis and resolution. A week of introspection failed to tell him more than this, and therefore, paradoxically dictated his course by default: he would see how things went. He would tell Rosemary who he was (she was bound to find out sooner or later anyway). If their nascent friendship developed, it could be interesting. If it didn't, Melanie remained a possibility, but then his feelings for Rosemary at their peak had exceeded what he felt for Melanie. As far as his work went it was too early to say whether he'd be fit enough to resume it, but, even if he did, his convalescent health would surely not permit resumption at the same intensity for a while, so there was little point speculating.

On top of all these concerns there was yet another. Melanie's excuse for Nathaniel's temporary withdrawal from hospital society had some truth to it. Nathaniel's "face" was worse than grotesque. He remembered the days when he had been concerned by his weak chin and premature balding; now he had no nose or lips and he had lost an eye! Yes, he was worried about people's reactions, but his intellect was also diverted by the reconstructional possibilities. No one was better placed than himself to direct a salvage plan—his contacts in the field of plastic surgery and the biology and mechanics of skin could not be bettered. If anyone could assemble, and then coordinate the activities of the ultimate face-building team, it was N.E. Papulous, Ph.D., B.Sc. (Hons), B.Comp.Sci.! His supervisors would make a good start: Iolanthe, whatever her faults, was one of the best plastic surgeons in the world, and Prof. Hall-Crumble (or, in truth, Annabelle!) had pioneered the growth of new skin in culture. He could grow a square metre or more from a pinhead in a matter of weeks, and in any shape required! Nathaniel was already imagining how things might fit together.

But before it came to that, he'd need his fractures properly fixed. He'd been too ill to enable more than a couple of the more straightforward breaks to be set, but now he was fit enough for the metalwork to begin in earnest: pins and plates and external fixators and screws and wires.

Nathaniel was jittery as he was wheeled into the garden. It was smaller and more ordinary than he'd imagined it, and most of the birds were sparrows. (This was in the era when sparrows were common.) Where was Rosemary? Was he so anxious because of what she would think of his face, what he would think of hers, or because he was fearful that their new friendship would not survive her memory of what a creep he had been? He tried to tell himself that it was only the latter. And then she was there next to him. They looked at each other. They were not instantly revolted because they had grown used to their own faces now, and the face opposite was no worse.

"Hi!" said Rosemary.

"Lo!" Nathaniel's attempt at wit was probably not understood.

"Nathaniel. I know it's you. My mother always brings me the latest *Cosmo*. She read this article about this brilliant young 'doctor of youth,' who'd had a terrible accident. His name was Nathaniel Papulous. I told the nurses that I'd known you. One of them—I think it was Melanie—said that you'd just realised who I was too, and that the real reason you didn't want to see me was because you wanted time to think. It's alright, Nathaniel, a lot of water has passed under the bridge. You've grown up, and done great things, and I don't care about our childhoods now. It's nothing, is it, compared to what we've been through since? Anyway, looking back, it was quite exciting to be the focus of someone's obsession, to be the reason for someone changing school, leaving the area."

"Do you remember the first time we listened to Gary Glitter together?"

It was OK. They were going to stay friends.

CHAPTER SEVENTEEN
Several Operations and a Wedding

For the second time in his life Nathaniel found himself planning a major project and presenting it to Iolanthe and Hall-Crumble for approval, only this time the project concerned his own face. They were enthusiastic as this would be pioneering work which, if successful, would ensure their places in medical history. They might have waited a very long time to find another fully informed volunteer with that degree of facial damage. What ethics committee could reject a proposal largely drafted by the highly qualified patient himself? But first the broken bones.

Over the next six months Nathaniel became familiar with the orthopaedics team. Characteristically, he studied orthopaedic surgery himself, reading orthopaedics journals to the extent that the team became nervous. For his last two operations they sought his opinion in an almost theatrically solicitous fashion before they dared proceed. The truth of the matter was that although Nathaniel was aware of how things might be done differently, he had no intention of unnecessarily arousing ire. As long as he could walk, use a keyboard, and write again, he didn't care how he arrived at that point, and the team's reputation was such that he was confident of arrival.

Nathaniel and Rosemary continued to see a lot of each other as Rosemary also underwent orthopaedic surgery, although not as extensive as Nathaniel's. She was discharged, wearing a prosthetic mask and a thick layer of cosmetics on those areas not covered by it, two months before Nathaniel's limb surgery had been completed. She

157

continued to visit him at least weekly, often bringing a taped compilation of her seventies singles for Nathaniel's cruelly named "Walkman." This was preferable to Mary's anodyne airs, although Marie Osmond had somehow infiltrated both collections: "Paper roses, paper roses…!" Nathaniel found himself holding Rosemary's hand, listening to her music, and imagining the face of her youth.

At last the day arrived when the metalwork permitted reasonable mobility, and, short of operations to remove the implanted scaffolding once the bones had set, the surgeons could do no more. Nathaniel decided to take a month's rest before returning to hospital for his makeover. Besides, it was Christmas. In this period he agreed to interviews with *The Sin*, *Cosmopolitan*, *Vague* and *The Notional Ink-wirer*, and even allowed some photographs of his face to be taken, on the condition that they would not be printed until after the plastic surgery had been completed. Nathaniel was also able to visit HDI headquarters where he gave his opinion on the ongoing research. Silversmith was delighted to see that Nathaniel would ultimately be able to return to full-time work. Nathaniel was still uncertain about his long-term future, but did not disabuse Silversmith.

The next few months were painful. Unfortunately a vascular supply for the first replacement nose failed to develop, and Iolanthe had to remove the grotesque blackened husk. Hall-Crumble impregnated the next one with a more concentrated solution of vasculogenic factor, and then continued to administer it after surgery, using a chemical called DMSO to aid its absorption. Nathaniel's lips were repaired using a combination of new-grown skin and silicon implants. Facial scarring was considerably ameliorated with new skin, grown both *in vitro* and on Nathaniel himself, by means of slowly inflated subcutaneous cushions which stretched the meagre portions of remaining intact skin. Leeches aided the establishment of the more ambitious grafts, by drawing off stagnant blood until such time as venous drainage developed. Nathaniel couldn't resist having his chin enhanced at the same time.

Ultimately, the surgery was a considerable success. For the first time in his life Nathaniel E. Papulous could be described as handsome, from the cleft of his Kirk Douglas chin, along the classic proportions of his Robert Redford nose, to the Clint Eastwood brow. There were only two slight problems: his entire face was as inexpressive as those of the last-named actors, and a large part of it was entirely insensitive. Nathaniel had to be particularly careful in cold weather, or when sitting near intense sources of heat, as his face could freeze or burn without his knowledge. He decided to have some heat sensors implanted, such that he would experience a buzzing sensation at the base of his neck when his new facial tissues were at risk. (After all, he had gone so far it would be silly not to take that final little step.)

Nathaniel walked from the hospital even more famous than when he'd entered it. His face (before and after) was the first in history to appear on the covers of both *Nature* and *The Sin*. Iolanthe and Hall-Crumble found themselves drowning in new research grants. HDI, as manifested by Silversmith, was ecstatic. Now Nathaniel would fit in with their "young and beautiful" imagery—what an asset for the company to have one of the most famous and gifted scientists in the world transformed into the most handsome as well! Nathaniel was encouraged to baste his new face in the latest HDI cosmetics. That way, his transfiguration might partly be attributed to their supposed alchemical magic.

Seeing the success of Nathaniel's surgery, Rosemary thought she had nothing to lose by opting for similar reconstruction. She wasn't, however, looking for a new face, merely an approximation of her old one. Nathaniel was very enthusiastic. A rebuilt face would be better than her actual old one, because the scale of the work was such that there was no way that Nathaniel could begin to imagine what would happen to it with time. The stretchings, the sub-surface scarring and the implants introduced so many unknown elements to his ageing equations that the new face would, in effect, be guaranteed against his horrible visions of senescence! Beautiful as Melanie was, if she and he had "got things together," Nathaniel would always have lived in fear of the recurrence of those portents of decay distorting her loveliness. Thus the Rosemary-Melanie question was resolved at last. Now all Nathaniel had to do was court Rosemary. This time he would get it right!

—

The buds on the pollarded trees of the boulevards had unfurled to become the pristine leaves of early summer. It was mid-afternoon and the limpid Parisian air wafted through the branches, teasing the young foliage. The shadows danced as the sunlight projected the breeze's antics on the pavements. A pigeon pecked at a crust in the gutter, disregarding the cars, lorries, buses, scooters, motorbikes and cycles on the one side, and the pedestrians on the other: men with jackets slung over their arms; tourists in shorts, carrying cameras; girls in their summer dresses; students lugging books....A tall elegant woman in a tailored black silk trouser suit strode into the Café Faune. She was carrying three large bags bearing the logos of fashion boutiques. Once through the door she looked around, removing her large sunglasses. She shrugged and sat at a table near the window, such that her face was out of the direct sunlight. She ran a hand over her short strawberry-blonde hair, and surveyed the customers on the *terrasse*. Her beautiful face was impassive. She looked about thirty.

"Vous désirez, madame?"

She turned to see a waiter in a black waistcoat half bowing, white towel over his arm.

"Euh...je voudrais un café express, s'il vous plaît." Rosemary was rather proud of her resuscitated school French. Especially the hesitations. A teacher had once made her whole class make the "Euh" sound for twenty minutes, non-stop. It's the little things that count, thought Rosemary. Like being on time! Where *was* Trish? Her coffee arrived, accompanied by a tall glass of iced water. She lifted the espresso to her lips and sipped the fragrant liquid. Oh, never mind about Trish. She would turn up, and she wasn't in a hurry.

It was nice to have a few minutes to oneself and watch the world go by. She should try to keep her mind on the present and the future. In a way that was why she was here. She turned the little packet of sugar cubes in her fingers, noticing that the contents were described in four languages. Sugar—yes, the sweet things of life were what she should concentrate on. She should put out of her mind everything that had preceded the hospital. She could allow herself to think as far back as that moment when she and Nathaniel had discovered their identities. What a surprise that had been! It was funny how she knew intellectually that he was the same person as the gormless infatuated little boy, but she didn't really feel it! He was magnetic now. He knew where he was going, a successful determined man, and yet he also seemed to understand her. She was so lucky that he, too, had had an accident, otherwise she would have been so alone! Should she feel guilty about being glad of his accident? No! That was silly thinking. And he was rather handsome now.

She twisted the new engagement ring on her finger: simple amber set in silver Celtic knotwork. It had been delivered to her by a helicopter timed to land in Nathaniel's extensive back garden at the precise moment of his proposal. (And she had thought she was just invited round for tea!) He could have afforded diamonds, emeralds, anything…but Nathaniel had said that he liked the thought that amber had once been living tree sap, sweet and sticky, and Rosemary did too. Yes, the sweet things of life—like shopping and clothes. Until the accident she'd have felt guilty spending so much on these things: first-class flights to New York, Paris and Milan to shop and party in the company of her new friends. Now she knew that life was unpredictable. She might be dead tomorrow, and she had already lost everything once, so why not enjoy oneself? Mind you, it had taken some persuading at first. When the facial surgery had been completed and they'd had their new images splashed all over the tabloids, they'd been sucked into the celebrity circuit. She'd been sent an invitation to Zander McKing's spring collection show. She hadn't wanted to go, but Nathaniel had thought it would do her good. Then she'd bumped into Trish in Herod's. She hadn't even realised who she was, but Trish had known her and before she knew it they were having a coffee together in the tea shop, and Trish was talking parties and pop stars and clothes and fashion shows, and now here they were, several such events later, ostensibly shopping together for Rosemary's trousseau.

Or at least here she was, waiting for Trish. Rosemary looked at her watch: 3.26. Trish ought to have arrived by three….And then she saw her, waving from across the street, and dropping one of her apparently numerous shopping bags in the process. Rosemary smiled. Good old bubbly bumbling Trish!

"Hi, Rose! Sorry I'm late! My plane got in a bit early, and I'd heard of this darling little shop just off the avenue Kléber, you know, not from the Arc de Triomphe? So I thought I would just go and have a peek, and, well, one thing led to another, and I couldn't stop myself! I am so-o-o sorry, love, honestly! But wait until you see what I got!" Trish giggled and sat down. She was reaching into one of her bags when the waiter arrived. She looked up, "Oh, I'll just have a decaf cappuccino—you do those don't you?"

Rosemary winced at Trish's unembarrassed use of English, but if the waiter resented it he didn't show it, and Rosemary's attempt at eye contact with the man—to show her solidarity—failed.

"It is not a problem, mademoiselle. Would mademoiselle like anything else?"

"Oooh, ah….No, ummm, that'll be fine for now, thank you."

Rosemary winced again—why was Trish "mademoiselle" while she was "madame"? She reasoned with herself: Trish was a few years younger and she exuded an enthusiastic girlishness, something that she herself would not recapture—Trish could certainly not be a "madame"! But that only explained why Trish was a "mademoiselle." Why was she herself a "madame"? She didn't think she looked "old" as such—the surgery had been miraculous. Then of course there was the engagement ring—was that it perhaps? Never mind. She brought her attention back to the present, and the flimsy gladrags that Trish was extracting from her bags.

"And this is what I plan to wear at your reception, Rose. What do you think? Is it too daring?" She held a little piece of shiny material to her breasts. It was clear that not much would be covered.

Rosemary thought of the scars still present on her own body (only her face had been fixed so far) but managed a smile. "It's lovely, Trish." How she loved this glorious superficiality—such good medicine! Even Trish's insensitivity was a tonic—there was no calculation as to what response would be appropriate to Rosemary's history and situation, and this meant that Rosemary too could completely relax in her company. Doubly so, as Trish's boyfriend had become a friend of Nathaniel's.

Devil Halfshed was what the media called a "cerebral" pop star. He worked very hard at his music, not least his lyrics. While many of his songs dealt with the conventional boy-girl scenario, at least some mentioned such issues as unemployment and the corruption of politicians. His *Life in an Outdoor Recreation Area* CD had received good reviews even in the broadsheets. This serious side did not mean, however, that he didn't like a good time or didn't have a mischievous streak. Far from it, in fact. While Rosemary and Trish were enjoying their weekend trip to Paris, he had popped round to Nathaniel's place for a drink.

"Beer?"

"Ta, Nat."

Nathaniel poured the bottle for him, standing behind the bar that was a feature of the "boys' den," as Rosemary called the second lounge in Nathaniel's large and comfortable bungalow into which she had now moved.

"Cheers, Dev. Good to see you!"

"You too, Nathaniel. What's new? How're the wedding preparations?" Dev was sliding open the patio door. He lowered himself onto a lounger. Nathaniel did likewise.

"Well, actually, that's what I wanted to talk you about...."

In Paris they were still in the café. "So, Rosemary, have you planned the honeymoon yet?"

"Yup. We're going to Hysterique!"

"Fab! That's a great place! Catherine was telling me about it. Devil and I were planning to go their next year. Apparently the hotel is just the best in the world—it's got everything, and there's a great beach too!"

"Yes, it'll be nice to take things easy after the wedding, although I'm quite looking forward to it, of course…if Nathaniel doesn't get up to any tricks!"

"What do you mean? Why should he?"

"Well he's being awfully coy about the reception. I think he's got something up his sleeve."

"Oh, I wouldn't worry about it. It's probably some wonderful surprise for you!"

"Mmmn. We'll see."

"I'm sure it'll be fine! Anyway, Rosemary, let's get down to business. There was me talking about what I've bought, but you're the one we should be thinking about this weekend. Let's be methodical about this, shall we? What have you got so far, and what do we still need?"

"This is going to be great! I can't wait to see his face!"

"Well, you won't 'cos he'll be...." Nathaniel was leaning forward he was laughing so much. He was holding the door for Devil, whose taxi had arrived. With some effort he straightened up. "OK, OK. You'd better go. Bye for now!"

Nathaniel closed the door, and stood for a moment chuckling at the thought of what he and Devil had concocted. "I think you could do with another drink, my good man!" he said to himself as he walked to the fridge and extracted a can of draught Guinness. How had he got himself involved in this weird world of pop stars? He sprawled on a lounger and reached across for some peanuts on the side table. He chewed and stared at the mysteriously whirling bubbles of his settling Guinness. Ah yes, it was Rosemary who had met Trish, and then Devil had introduced him to Rob, Rob to Mike and Steve....Ha! He remembered the first time he had met Mike. The wizened front man of The Strolling Bones had approached him in the kitchen at a party at Rob's. Nathaniel re-ran it in his mind:

"So, uh. You're the guy who's the news at the moment?" Mike had sniffed and dabbed his nose. Nathaniel had noticed the creases running down his face from the anxious eyes.

"Well, it seems that way."

"Your face was really smashed, wasn't it?"

"Yep." Nathaniel remembered how irritated he had been feeling with Mike's questions. So many people had asked him about improving their looks. He was sick of it.

"Well, uh, listen...you probably think I want to look younger or something, but it isn't that." He had sniffed again and dabbed at his nose with a monogrammed handkerchief. "Listen, you know, in the biz, sometimes you need something to keep you going, like. You know what I mean, man?"

Nathaniel had just looked at him blankly.

"Snow, man! Cocaine!"

"Ye-es…?"

"Well, it isn't exactly good for the old hooter, man, is it?" Mike had tapped the side of his nose.

Ah ha! Nathaniel had got it.

"So like, do you think you could recommend someone to fix it, discreet-like, you know?"

"Sure!" Even though Nathaniel's range of expressions was limited, he had a hard job keeping his face straight.

From that point a chain of celebrity referrals had gone Iolanthe's way, and Nathaniel's social circle and popularity had increased still further. (Fortunately, the tabloids never did quite divine the reason for it!) The gall of some of these new acquaintances was breathtaking. One of them (Rob Pigwarden, famous for his oft-replaced blondes) had even asked him whether he thought a divorce settlement and a new wife would be cheaper than having his old one surgically overhauled! A consequence of the "cocaine chain," as Nathaniel came to think of his source of new acquaintances, was that there was going to be rather a large guest list for the wedding. Of course this new circle wasn't all sweetness and light. Celebrities are no more likely to get on with each other than are politicians, and one was particularly prickly.

A boxer-shorted Pat Galloper (the lead singer of Some Palm Trees and Camels Around A Waterhole) stormed into the master bedroom of his mansion and hurled the latest issue of *Hiya!* onto the emperor-sized bed. "Fookin' hell! Look at that! Those fookin' swine—that Nose and Rat….They've gone and got the fookin' cover story, haven't they? And our wedding isn't even mentioned in the whole fookin' thing!"

Leanne, in a white satin kimono-like dressing gown, was sitting in the middle of the leopard print bedspread applying nail polish to her toenails. She looked up. "You did remember to slip the reporter the money and made sure he understood what was required?"

"Yes, the treacherous little…."

"Don't worry, Pat! Perhaps we'll be in the next one." Living with a pop star was never dull, but this one's fire and drive certainly outshone the last three. Perhaps it had something to do with his famous "deprived" childhood on a lower-middle-class Manchester council estate? In the year they'd been going out, though, he'd only seemed to get worse. And Devil Halfshed's increasing popularity hadn't helped—maybe that was the main reason? Even though Halfshed's band Obfuscate didn't quite pull in the same crowds, and their album sales weren't (yet?) in the same league, Galloper's resentment of the praise Halfshed's lyrics had received knew no bounds—especially since Galloper's last attempt to venture on to Halfshed's territory (the album *See Hear Now*) had been mocked by all and sundry. Galloper now spat at every mention of his rival's name. To make matters worse he had just discovered (when he had heard about the possibility of having his nasal septum repaired) that Halfshed and that Trish girl of his were mates of Nathaniel and Rosemary's! Now he was keeping score of media mentions of them all— himself and Some Palm Trees and Camels Around A Waterhole versus Devil Halfshed and his band versus Rose and Nat—and his temper was getting shorter and shorter as every day went by. At least, thought Leanne, she and Galloper had received an invitation to the Rose-Nat wedding, and he had been pleased about that. Rose and Nat obviously didn't realise what Pat felt. Leanne hoped it wouldn't be too difficult to keep the warring parties apart—especially her boyfriend and Halfshed.

As far as Nathaniel was concerned, he had arrived. He was fabulously rich, Silversmith was happy for him to cut back on his work when his extra-curricular activities served to raise the profile of HDI, and on his arm was the beautiful and hallucination-proofed Rosemary. The only recent problem had been how to arrange their wedding to coincide with Galloper and Sentup's, as Trish and Dev had requested, thus depriving G and S's ceremony of publicity. And then Rosemary had suggested that perhaps they ought to inhume the halberd of their mutual disaffection, and invite Pat and Leanne to their wedding, but they'd have to be careful about Galloper meeting Halfshed....Life was tough at the top.

The solution to the Halfshed-Galloper problem came to Nathaniel at

4.32 one morning when he found himself unable to sleep. He had kept it from Rosemary, wanting to surprise her, but as his friendship with Halfshed had deepened, he had felt he could relate the gist of it to him. As Rosemary and Trish were away shopping in Paris he had invited him over for a drink—it was an ideal opportunity.

The wedding ceremony itself was a simple small affair in a country chapel near Dawley Crown, a little town not far from HDI headquarters. There were no celebrity guests and no media representatives. Nathaniel and Rosemary joined their parents afterwards for lunch in a private dining room in a local hotel, as the Taylors and the older Papulouses had no desire to attend the huge media fest that was planned for the evening, and they were due some attention. Nathaniel's parents were stiff but did make an effort; Rosemary's parents had the grace and skill to keep the conversation flowing.

"Well your son won her in the end!"

"Yes. He was always keen on Rosemary."

"We took him to see a psychologist once!"

"Nathaniel, remember the tree?"

Nathaniel blushed at Neil's question, but took secret comfort in his brother-in-law's pot belly. How he had gone to seed! "Yes, how could I forget!" Was he going to become a "bother"-in-law?

Mrs. Taylor broke in. "And I wonder what poor old Zebedee would have thought? Never mind. If only Lisa could have come, but Australia is so far...."

Nathaniel exhaled in relief when he and Rosemary were finally away in their chauffeur-driven limousine. They had taken a suite at the Zitz to prepare for (and later recover from) the big night. But before the preparations started they flung themselves on the enormous bed, giggling like adolescents.

"I can't believe it! You're sure it's them? But they've just come in!"

"I'm sure John. 100%."

"F***, f***, f***! It bloody well can't be! They came in four minutes ago and I can see them now: Pratt Bid and Angela Geniston! Clear as

167

daylight! Definitely! Are you having me on? Do you need your eyes checked, woman?"

"How dare you! It's you that's getting things wrong! How much sleep did you get last night? Were you on the razz again?"

John Paulson switched off his mobile phone, swallowed, sighed and rubbed his eyes. He breathed deeply. It was true that he hadn't slept last night, but that had been because he was so excited. In fact, he'd even gone to bed early, fat lot of good….At last he was getting there, he'd told himself. His father would have been proud of him: one of *The Sin*'s chosen few to cover the Papulous wedding. Ever since he'd been a little boy he'd wanted to go into the media.

Paulson Senior had been the brains behind UKBC's coverage of the miners' strikes in the seventies—it had been his idea to switch around the footage of the police charging and the miners responding so that it looked as if the miners were the provocateurs. Very clever. His father had become a hero amongst the media elite, and Paul himself had worshipped him, sitting up for hours as his dad explained how he had doctored the footage. Looking back now, he realised that the subconscious reason for him not going into film reportage was that he felt he never could have competed. But the medium of print had been a field he had known he would conquer, and so at last prove himself to his father. At least the old man had lived to see him distort the anti-capitalist riots in Settee City— the way he had interviewed hundreds of protestors to find the few mindless thugs to profile as "typical agitators: immoral wasters, scum of the earth…." And now it was all going wrong. He was losing it. He'd been so happy to be chosen to work alongside Ruth Lesse on something this major, but the people she saw entering the building were not those he saw coming into it from the foyer….Was it her or him? *Shit!*

Oh no! Here came Nathaniel Papulous himself! Just when he was feeling sick with disorientation—the chance for a scoop of a lifetime and he wouldn't be up to it.

The reporters and photographers had been allowed to attend the reception in the magnificent Macarena Hall attached to the Victor Ear and Herb Alpert Museum, on condition that they stayed outside or up in the gallery and waited for any guests who wanted to be interviewed to approach them. Condenser, parabolic and boom microphones were banned. *The Daily Wail* had commissioned a skilled lip reader, but Liz Birse was looking distraught: "There's something wrong with their lips! There's something wrong!"

And here was Nathaniel. "So, Mr. Paulson," he said, reading the name tag, "have you worked it out yet? Have a press release."

John realised that he hadn't been going mad. There was some explanation!

Nathaniel had had the idea of showing off the skills of Prof. Gnoze's unit, his computer expertise, and the cosmetics of HDI all at the same time. Every guest would have to submit a few recent photographs of themselves, at least those few whose photographs were not already on HDI files. From these his computer programme would build a three-dimensional image of their faces. Iolanthe's team could then rapidly construct silicone models of these faces (in effect, masks), which would be touched up, should this be necessary, using the cosmetics of HDI and the skill of their saleswomen. Each guest would then be issued, on entry to the reception, with someone else's mask, and in this way guests could be reasonably sure of staying anonymous. Not only would people have the thrill of seeing life from someone else's point of view, but they would also see themselves (on other people's heads) as they might look to best advantage, made up with "that magic HDI touch"! What's more, Rosemary and Nathaniel would not then be the only people rigid of visage, and Halfshed and Galloper would certainly have their work cut out to identify each other! Nathaniel was in such a frenzy of self-congratulatory excitement (*No wonder I'm so rich and famous—it's because I'm a bloody genius!*) that he didn't sleep at all on the night of his brainwave. And in the warm light of the spring day, his idea seemed better still. The nuptials of Nat and Rose would be the wedding and publicity coup of the century! Perhaps Mary would let them use the Victor Ear and Herb Alpert Museum for the reception?

When he'd been told of Nathaniel's idea, Halfshed had been delighted. He had immediately conceived a plan to wind up the hated

Galloper. He'd gone directly to Iolanthe and convinced her of his idea for
"…some harmless fun. No need to tell Nathaniel."

"Shit!" Galloper was furious. At least eight of the hundreds of guests
were in Halfshed masks, and mimicking his rival's smug middle-class
Essex-boy tones as they recited Obfuscate lyrics whenever Galloper was
in earshot. Galloper had at first been flattered to be given his hero Wall
Pellow's face but he was the only one with such a likeness and he was
beginning to suspect that all the Halfsheds were in the know—the
bastards had an unfair advantage! The only thing of which Galloper
could be reasonably sure was that anyone who looked like Halfshed
couldn't be Halfshed, but he still couldn't help his visceral reaction
whenever any of the pseudo-Halfsheds hove into view. If only he could
work out who and where Halfshed was!

"Calm down, Pat. It's only a joke!" Leanne was frazzled just trying to
stop him assaulting Halfshed's apparent accomplices. Internally, she was
seething at Halfshed's cunning—the little runt had gone too far now!—
and she would happily murder him herself with her bare hands if she
could identify him. Where the hell was he?

"That you? Pat, Leanne?" It was the familiar voice of Galloper's
drummer, Numbskull. He lifted his Rob Pigwarden mask to confirm his
identity. "Listen, you'll never guess—I thought I saw you at the other
side of the room, but it's a guy wearing your face and doing your accent,
Pat. He really threw me, I tell you, until I heard what he was saying. He
was going on in your voice about how he—meaning you—had the
musical ear of a mature Beethoven, the graceful walk of a Byron, the
literary ability of a McGonagall, the elegance and toilette of Karl Marx,
the culture and sensitivity of Maggie Thatcher….Look I couldn't make
out what he was saying exactly, so he wrote it all down for me. Here."
Numbskull handed over the crumpled piece of paper from which he'd
been reading. "I told him who I was, and he said I should show it to you—
said you wouldn't understand it anyway!"

Galloper understood enough to know that this was an insult. "The
runt! I'll get him, I'll get him!" Galloper was lost in the crowd before
Leanne and Numbskull could move. Numbskull set off in pursuit.

Five minutes later, Pat's familiar face appeared. "Right, luv. Ah've looked fookin' everywhere, the fookin' bastard's fookin' done a bunk. Let's go."

Leanne sighed with relief. No blood had been shed (or even "half shed"!), thank goodness. They would get out of this alive. She would calm him down and they would make love and this whole episode would fade away, and later they might laugh at it and plan some appropriate revenge. She took his hand—and screamed—if it was Galloper's face it couldn't be Galloper!

John Paulson got his scoop that evening. His father would have been proud. Devil Halfshed couldn't resist relating his *coup de théâtre*. When he had identified Leanne sporting the non-features of Catherine Marsh (the vanilla-flavoured urchin-model-of-the-moment), Galloper being nowhere in sight, he had swung into action. His weeks of practice had paid off, and Galloper's slovenly Mancunian drawl had been perfect. Leanne had shrieked and dropped his hand. For a worrying moment he had been incapacitated with mirth, but the fear of Galloper's return had enabled him to regain control. Halfshed's chauffeur was waiting outside the building, the Rolls' engine nicely chauffed. In moments he and Trish were whisked away, cuddling and laughing on the squeaky red leather of the back seat.

One could say that the wedding marked the peak flow of Nathaniel's river. His waters had been augmented and temporarily checked by an incoming tide from the waiting ocean, but now, on an ebb flow, they seemed unstoppable. Virtually every fashion magazine and tabloid featured "The Wedding" as their lead stories, and all the broadsheets consecrated at least two pages. The more serious papers perorated on the evils of "this age of image obsession," and two even referred to the second commandment. The tabloids and pop magazines detailed the determined efforts of Galloper to identify Halfshed, and *The Sin* led with an exclusive on Halfshed's stunt.

Silversmith was in raptures when New York *Vague* displayed paired photographs of wedding guests and their lookalike masks (the former naturally taken on other occasions), with the comment that the masks were more beautiful than the real thing. Shares in HDI were shooting skywards, and he was on his way to becoming a billionaire, and Nathaniel a multi-millionaire. Silversmith would be able to negotiate a merger with Zen-Buddhica on very favourable terms, and then the entire cosmetics and pharmaceuticals world would be at his feet!

CHAPTER EIGHTEEN
Honeymoon Hijacking

Sipping their champagne in the spacious first-class section of the West Indies-bound aircraft, Nathaniel and Rosemary reviewed the connubial festivities. Nathaniel owned up to his Galloper-baiting arrangement with Halfshed, and after his assurance that he hadn't quite known to what extent Halfshed would take it, and an unconvincing show of annoyance from Rosemary, she had relented and giggled—the thought of Leanne almost departing on Halfshed's arm was too precious! Her new husband had such a deliciously inventive sense of humour! She kissed him, almost managing to forget what it had been like to kiss her last man with fully sensitive lips. She and Nathaniel had learnt to juxtapose their remaining areas of sensitive labial muco-cutaneous junction so as to maximise mutual osculatory satisfaction, and now the positioning was almost automatic.

But it wasn't just a case of making the best of diminished selves. Their accidents had afforded them the odd compensatory delight. For example, Nathaniel found it a huge turn-on when Rosemary kissed the eyelid of his damaged eye. He read it as her way of telling him that she loved him completely, scars and all. The more full-blooded erotic pleasures would have to wait until they were in the privacy of their ultra-luxury hotel bedroom on the millionaires' holiday island of Hysterique. It would be so wonderful to be away from cameras.

Naturally the paparazzi were waiting for them at Queensville airport. They had expected this, and they smiled as well as the stiffness of their faces allowed as they ducked into the waiting red and gold stretch limo. Then it was a short and bumpy journey to a little yachting harbour, where a powerful red and gold launch was docked. A high-speed two-hour skim to a purpose-built mooring on Hysterique tested the tenacity of their wigs. Once landed, two armed, red- and gold-uniformed guards ushered them into an air-conditioned four-wheel drive Hiwatashi also resplendent in The Hotel's by now familiar red and gold insignia. (The Hotel was above more elaborate cognomens—all the "in people" knew what "The Hotel" signified.) The armoured gates of the little launch's (dis)embarkment compound swung open under remote control, and they were off. Now they could relax, away from the media circus at last.

Nathaniel asked about the security (which reminded him of HDI) and was told that The Hotel owned half the island, which was entirely fenced off and patrolled by border guards. The other half supported a poor peasant population. Unfortunately the safest harbour on the rugged coastline happened to be in the peasants' territory, and they were "very poor, very hungry." Since a wealthy industrialist had been kidnapped and shot three years ago, the armed escort had been deemed essential. The Hiwatashi was bullet and mine-proof. Nothing could go wrong. The guard smiled as he said this. His colleague smiled back at him, and turned the vehicle off the main track, onto an even narrower and more potholed trail. A gun appeared over the back of the passenger seat. Nothing could go wrong for the kidnappers! Nathaniel and Rosemary clutched each other mutely. Was this a nightmare?

It was a harrowing four-hour journey. Naked pot-bellied kids gawked at the vehicle as it bumped past little shanty villages. Dogs, chickens and pigs scattered in front of the increasingly dusty Hiwatashi. The agricultural clearings trailed off after a while, and the jungle closed in on all sides. Eventually the vehicle could not force its way through the vegetation. Nathaniel and Rosemary, in their smart BCBG clothes, were goaded at gunpoint along a tiny path. Rosemary had to remove her high heels, perfect for the boulevard St. Germain. The kidnappers let her rifle in her suitcase for some gym shoes. When he came to pick up the cases again, Nathaniel found that he no longer had the strength to carry both in his sweaty hands. The gentleman in him compelled him to put his down by the side of the trail and continue with Rosemary's. The shorter of the two kidnappers, who had driven the vehicle and seemed to be the leader, picked it up, grinning. Nathaniel realised how absurd it was to worry about their belongings. Everything they had was, in effect, owned by their kidnappers anyway. What was the point? Nonetheless he continued to lug Rosemary's ridiculously incongruous Vuitton valise. On second thoughts, it wasn't so incongruous—it was snakeskin, after all: coming home!

The kidnappers conversed in what Nathaniel imagined must be some sort of creole. He occasionally caught words that sounded English or French. The squat one gestured at their feet. The tall one nodded. "Now take off shoes!"

Nathaniel remonstrated but a gun barrel in his side ensured compliance. Rosemary's delicate cream feet were revealed again. The erstwhile bodyguards grinned. Two hundred yards of agony later, their torn and bleeding soles felt the welcome relief of a sisal mat.

They were in a two-room corrugated iron shack, some distance up a hill. To one side was what had probably been a field, now heavy with impenetrable secondary regrowth, to the other was a steep and densely forested valley, at the bottom of which one could hear the rush of water. The tall kidnapper had Nathaniel open both their suitcases. The men were delighted by their new treasure trove, and were almost helpless with laughter when they discovered Rosemary's honeymoon lingerie, purchased with Trish on that light-hearted Saturday an aeon ago. The tall one collected all their footwear and took it out in a sack. Nathaniel realised that the confiscation of the shoes and the barefoot march were to make it clear to them that escape was impossible. It was ironic that leeches, which had featured so prominently in the restitution of their looks, and which therefore had made it possible for them to show themselves to the world, were now very much part of the physical and mental barrier between them and the outside world.

Many books have been written about the psychology of captivity, the prisoner-jailer relationship and the paths the mind wanders when deprived of external stimuli. In the last decades of the 20th century a number of high-profile personalities documented the horrors of their incarceration, including Nelson Mandela, John McCarthy, Bryan Keenan and Terry Waite. Patty Hearst's conversion to the cause of her abductors (the Symbionese Liberation Army), and her subsequent re-capture and re-conversion to "normality," dramatically illustrated elements of the peculiar love-hate power game that often develops between captive and captor. Laurens van der Post's spell as a prisoner of the Japanese during the Second World War spawned a book and a film, these touching on philosophical and psychological territory in some ways similar to that of the Hearst case. A hundred years earlier, Victor Hugo had imagined the last day of a man condemned to die under the guillotine, and in the early 17th century Cervantes described the fictional Don Quixote's several episodes of internment, one of which he tolerated thanks to his near-hallucinatory madness rather than in spite of it. Earlier, a man named Daniel reportedly emerged unscathed from a lion's den. Anti-Nasty International's archives on assorted prisoners, incarcerates, hostages and abductees would provide enough material for many doctoral theses.

It is the nature of all these writings, factual, theoretical, and fictional, to attempt to extract general truths from the painful trivia of individual sufferings. It is also inevitable that they highlight the very individuality of suffering, and the individual heroism of the victims. It would be difficult to find two more eccentric hostages than Nathaniel and Rosemary, nor two more divergent outcomes to their captivity, though their cases are easily understood in terms of their biographically shaped psychologies, and, indeed, physiognomies.

The numbness of disbelief was the first sensation. This persisted until they were left on their own in the muggy mouldy atmosphere of one half of the windowless shack, the dividing door having been clanged shut. They could hear their captors' voices, low and urgent, through the zinc-coated metal. A trickle of light and unsatisfactory jungle air seeped in through a cobwebbed gap between the roof and the walls. A fly jigged helplessly in the beginnings of its silken death shroud. Birds and happier insects called and buzzed outside. The sisal mat rotted beneath their feet.

As their non-prosthetic eyes adjusted they could see that the floor was alive with creepy crawlies, chiefly woodlice. A couple of dozen spiders skulked on the walls, and a millipede patiently traversed the damp flooring, waves of movement sweeping forwards along its undulating legs, as mysterious and beautiful as the counter-intuitive swirling of the tiny bubbles in settling Guinness. Rosemary, however, did not appreciate the wonder of that elegantly coordinated locomotion.

Then came the fear. Were they going to be killed/raped/tortured? Nathaniel didn't think so, and tried to convince Rosemary. They were so well known they had surely been kidnapped for a substantial ransom. Their captors would not risk hurting them, or not at first anyway.

Nathaniel strained to make out what was happening in the adjoining room but heard nothing decipherable. It started raining. The noise acted like an imperfect fireblanket, damping down their thoughts but not their smouldering anxiety. Water dripped in from several holes in the roof and soaked into the mat, also leaking in from somewhere at the base of the end wall. Rosemary shivered and started crying, shifting her bloody and muddy feet. Seeing the cheerfully painted toenails, and the tears running down her pathetically inexpressive beautiful face, Nathaniel felt he would burst if he were to love her more. He hugged her. For the time being, that was all he could do—hug her and wait. He would find some purchase, some chink in the armour of misfortune, some means of doing something….

The rain only lasted ten minutes. There was a stirring in the other half of the shack, and the door creaked open to reveal both captors. The smart bright livery of The Hotel mocked them. The squat guard spoke, "Now you take your clothes off. All of them." He grinned, and gestured with his gun.

Rosemary felt a cold terror worse than previous horror—could this be true, was her real life nothing but suffering, and those brief periods of respite merely dreams? She was hardly aware of her actions but watched her arms undressing herself. Nathaniel wondered whether he should rush them, but discretion outweighed temerity. Soon they were both naked. They stood there trembling. Their bodies were a mass of scars. They had intended getting Iolanthe to sort that out eventually, but having undergone so much surgery already they had felt that beautiful faces and functional limbs would suffice for the time being.

The guards were clearly taken aback. They talked in their unintelligible patois, and then the squat one shrugged and pointed at their clothes: "Clean yourselves! Use them!" Nathaniel and Rosemary looked at each other blankly and did nothing. The guard was irritated. He stooped to pick up Rosemary's blouse, and proceeded to wipe her feet, signalling for her to continue. Nathaniel did likewise.

"Good!" said the burly foot-washer, gathering their now blood-stained garments.

Rosemary found herself saying, in old Mrs. Taylor's voice, "Don't forget to soak them in cold water first!" She started giggling. It was not a healthy sound. Nathaniel shook her and then hugged her. Her giggling dissolved into sobbing and then faded.

The tall guard disappeared from the doorway and then reappeared with their suitcases. He brought them in. "Now dress!"

Once more they were left on their own in their little cell. They could hear one of the guards walking away. A few creaks and coughs told them the other had stayed behind. They heard some matches strike, and then smelt marijuana smoke. At least there would be no immediate violence, oh blessed pacific weed! They would have some time to think. Think, think.

Nathaniel was put in mind of those initiative tests, the sort that the more creative teachers sometimes give their pupils: you are locked in an iron shack in the middle of a rugged jungle-covered tropical island; there is an armed guard on the other side of the door; you have the clothes you are wearing and a rotten sisal mat; what do you do? Nathaniel juggled these items in his mind. Could they make shoes out of their clothes and/ or the mat. Could they overpower the guard and use his shoes…or find theirs? And then where would they go? The northeast of the island belonged to The Hotel, so they must be somewhere in the southwest. They were in the tropics, so before noon the sun would be more or less due east, and after noon in the west. How large was the island? Perhaps fifty by twenty kilometres, to judge by the brochure, so they might be twenty kilometres or more from help. They'd be caught quickly if they tried to use the path, and trying to penetrate the jungle was a non-starter.

Would the vehicle still be at hand? Probably the departed guard had taken it. Would the locals help them? It was doubtful. What if they used the river? No, it sounded far too lively—probably nothing but rapids and waterfalls. What then? It came back to waiting, making the best of it. They would be held to ransom. Their ransom would be paid, and they'd be free again. But maybe not!

What if they took their guard hostage and got him to take them back at gun point? It was very risky. If they didn't get the gun off him quickly he could shoot them. Mind you, his reflexes would be dulled by the joint....The joint....How about casing the joint first, so to speak—taking a look around. He'd surely let them out for a call of nature?

Nathaniel called out, "Excuse me! I need to relieve myself, I need a pee! Will you let me out for a moment?" The guard grunted and stirred. He opened the door and signalled with his gun barrel that Nathaniel might exit.

Rosemary was on the edge of hysteria again. "Why have you taken us? What's this for? What are you going to do with us? Please tell us!"

The guard stared at Rosemary, a red-eyed leer, as Nathaniel brushed passed him. His face withdrew, the door banged closed and Rosemary was left on her own, with the spiders and woodlice.

She heard Nathaniel's voice and the low rumble of the guard's. They were talking anyway. Nathaniel came back, smiling. "His name's James!"

"So bloody what!"

"Don't you see? I told him that our names were Nat and Rose. I don't think he knows exactly who we are."

"What!?"

"Look. I've been thinking. If they don't know who we are, and then suddenly discover, it might panic them more than anything. They might shoot us, dump our bodies in the ravine and disappear. There are bound to be people searching for us, after all. If we can just keep them calm, and wait, I reckon things will sort themselves out. That doesn't mean we can't examine all the options, but in the meantime we have to make them see us as people and not as objects. We have to be nice to them, so that they can't bring themselves to do anything too drastic. If we know their names and they know ours that's a start."

Rosemary sighed. "Nice to them!? I suppose so."

"Anyway I had a good look around. I imagine we're pretty isolated here. There is only the track we came on, and that looked as if it hadn't been used for a while. I reckon that this might be an abandoned hemp plantation—perhaps sprayed with weedkiller by the Americans—and it's just gone wild. We might be twenty kilometres from any help. I don't think we'd make it unless we took James or his mate hostage...."

The door burst open and James appeared. "What you talkin' 'bout, hey?"

Nathaniel had been careful to keep his voice low so he was sure that James had not been able to eavesdrop. He turned to James, his voice placid. "I'm just telling Rose that we cannot escape, that we must do what you say."

"Good!" said James. "Now quiet!" He disappeared again.

Presently they heard the tinny sound of a little radio. Nathaniel was electrified. On the one hand he was desperate to hear the news—whether there was any mention of their disappearance—on the other hand he didn't want James & Co. to find out who they were. But of course it was inevitable that they would find out! James' colleague could well be back in civilization somewhere now. It would be best if he told them first. "James!" he called out.

"Yeah? What you wan'?"

"James, I must tell you who we are...." Nathaniel related the essentials: that they were very well known, that they had very rich friends who would pay a lot to have them back safe and sound, but who would exact terrible vengeance if they were harmed. He would personally guarantee them a million dollars if they just let them go.

James just smiled. "You wait for da boss!"

He hadn't seemed at all interested! Did he already know who they were, or was he without any decision-making power himself? Was his absent friend "da boss," or was there someone else? That would put a different light on things! A more organised kidnapping, and therefore in some ways probably less likely to be nastily bungled....What was going on? Nathaniel failed to get any more information from James.

An hour of miserable speculation passed in the horrible confines of the shack. At least it was getting cooler. Were they going to be given something to drink and eat? It was rapidly getting dark now, and the jungle noises were changing. Nathaniel supposed that this would be the time when diurnal birds would make their last territorial announcements. And then they heard a putt-putt noise, and a backfire. It was a motorbike. It stopped outside and they heard the familiar voices of the two guards. Presently the door opened and the burly guard's face appeared in the gloom. "Good evening, Dr. and Mrs. Papulous. Of course we know who you are. My name is Castro. We do not want to hurt you. You will understand tomorrow, or maybe the day after, when the boss comes. Now take this. You are free to walk around now. Here are your shoes." He handed them a toilet roll and a plastic bag containing their footwear, and held the door open for them. His name suited him. He looked like a cross between Che Guevara and Fidel Castro, just shorter, darker and broader, and without Castro's beard.

As they made their way hesitantly to the sheltering shrubs of the forest margin Nathaniel saw that they were not being watched…but then where could they go in the jungle night? A hurricane lamp burned on the camp table, under the projecting roof of the hut. Already a swarm of insects was courting death, and from time to time a little column of smoke or an agonal fluttering on the table marked the end of a short life. Next to this arthropod beacon and nemesis was a battered little motorbike, with bulging pannier bags and what looked like rolls of bedding roped on at the back. Could they steal the bike? No. It was only a couple of yards from where the men now sat on deck chairs next to a little fire, out of the peak insect concentration. The Hotel logo was visible on the back of one of the chairs, although the distinctive colours were not apparent in the gloom.

Seeing that Nathaniel and Rosemary had finished their ablutions, Castro rose and came towards them. He handed a torch and a plastic mug to Rosemary. "Here. If you want to drink you follow that path to the river. If you are not back in ten minutes we will come after you, and we will use our guns." He pointed to a scarcely visible track.

Nathaniel and Rosemary were delighted with this new liberty. It was such a relief to be out! The river was about fifty yards down a very narrow and steep "path," detectable only as a slight reduction in vegetation density. Clearly escape was impossible although temporary evasion would have been easy. The river revealed itself as a small though vigorous stream. The path debouched onto a flat rock, about a yard across, which flanked a little pool at the base of a waterfall.

It was so pleasant to be on their own, and to be able to talk without fear of being overheard. Held in the mug, the water appeared perfectly clear, and being from such a small and lively watercourse it was probably safe. Rosemary and Nathaniel washed their hands and faces and drank deeply. If nothing else it appeared that they would have a little bit of freedom in the evenings.

Nathaniel tried to cheer Rosemary. "Look, this is obviously very well planned. There's someone else giving them orders so they're not likely to kill us at a moment's notice. I reckon the more organised this is, the safer we are. The best thing is just not to give them any excuse to harm us...." They made their way back to the hut.

Castro called to them as soon as they were visible. "Welcome back, my friends! You can take some blankets from the bike. Then I have a special surprise for you." Seeing Rosemary's alarm he added, "Don't worry. It's a nice surprise!" He smiled. Rosemary untied a roll of bedding from the bike and was starting to unfasten the second when Castro called out, "No! That one is for us!" A bit shaken, Rosemary took the bedding into what was the *de facto* honeymoon suite. A plastic groundsheet was included in the roll. The rest was a couple of blankets and cotton sheets, with a freshly laundered smell, and all with that familiar and now hated hotel logo.

Castro appeared at their door, grinning. He was holding something behind his back. "Now what would the lady like as a present?"

Rosemary was aghast, and said nothing.

Castro theatrically produced an aerosol can. "Bang! Bye-bye insect! You see, I know what you want!"

Rosemary had to admit that the present was very welcome. She forced herself to make a little smile of thanks, which was no easy thing given the history of her face.

"Later we eat!" said Castro, still grinning.

—

Rosemary was a bit too enthusiastic with her new toy, and she and Nathaniel emerged coughing into the jungle night. Castro laughed, and James managed a smile. When the worst of his spluttering had subsided, Nathaniel took advantage of the apparent good mood to ask again about the purpose of their kidnapping, and received the same answer: "Wait until da boss comes."

Rosemary and Nathaniel stood awkwardly, not knowing what to do with themselves. Rosemary slapped herself and a red smear appeared on her arm—they were being consumed by mosquitoes! This triggered further hilarity from Castro, who nodded to James. The latter, looking a bit sour, threw them a little stick of insect repellent. It was then that Rosemary conceived the idea that Castro was deliberately withholding succour of various sorts until he had seen them suffer. Nathaniel was thinking how considerate he was, and thanked him.

The meal was served from a pot warmed on some embers. It was a stew which Nathaniel guessed might be based on mango, plantain, okra and chicken, seasoned with garlic, chilli and coconut. It was delicious. Naturally the porcelain bowls in which it was served bore the hateful hotel crest, as did the heavy and ornate Sheffield EPNS forks.

There were only two chairs and Castro had offered his to Rosemary. She had refused, to his inevitable amusement, and she and Nathaniel squatted for a moment until Nathaniel had the idea of retrieving the now redundant mat from their room. He gave it a good shake then folded it double, putting it on the ground such that the least repulsive surface was uppermost. They sat on the mat. There is no cat, thought Nathaniel irrelevantly. His fleeting grin unsettled Rosemary.

After the meal the plates were stacked and left on the table. Within a minute they were seething with insects. Castro said, "We wash them tomorrow. You want a drink, yes? It's good for sleep." He was walking to the bike. He opened a pannier and pulled out a bottle and a couple of mugs, similar to the one he'd given them (and reclaimed) earlier. He splashed a generous measure into a mug and handed it to Nathaniel saying, "For both of you. Drink, my friends. It's good for you!"

Nathaniel thought he was probably right, and took a stout swig. It was rum, but superb, rich, complex rum. Again it must be from The Hotel, thought Nathaniel. Rosemary refused to drink. Nathaniel saw the dispensation of an intoxicant as a good opportunity to improve rapport, and commented on the quality of the spirit. Castro laughed again. "Only the best for you, my friend! This is Mount Gay, very expensive, very good, very strong!"

Nathaniel found that there was little he could say to follow this up, thinking that if he started talking about whisky it might come across as ingratitude, or even one-upmanship. James, looking a bit tense, was leaning forward cupping his mug in both his hands. Suddenly he placed the mug beneath his chair and stood up, walking towards the table, where he picked up the little transistor radio. Blowing and brushing off the insects, he switched it on, tuning from static-obscured station to static-obscured station until he found a strong signal. It was music, rap of some sort, and completely unintelligible to Nathaniel and Rosemary. Leaving it on, James put the radio back on the table and resumed his seat, this time leaning back with his hands behind his head and yawning at the stars, a foot oscillating in time to the beat. The music faded and the immense swell of the nocturnal jungle sounds swam back into aural focus, a mocking background to the puny treble voice of an announcer, and then the word "Beatles" knocked the jungle once more into oblivion. "Hey Jude" at that time and place was the most thrilling and disturbing sound that Nathaniel had ever heard.

As so often in this narrative, the constraints of language demand that what were tangled and transient thoughts, emotions and deeds be related in a reasonably linear and coherent fashion, and therefore necessarily approximated. The fundamental note of Nathaniel's emotional "state" (flux?) at that time is rendered crudely by the English word "nostalgia," more exactly by the Portuguese "saudade." Although Nathaniel and Rosemary had only been away from their native land for a day, the events and the physical distance that separated them from Great Britain seemed an immense gulf indeed. To have a reminder of home unexpectedly thrown to them in the form of "Hey Jude" was the equivalent of a short-term survivor of the *Titanic* floating to within an arm's length of a lifebelt but not having the strength to grasp it. It might also be likened to a distillate of what Nathaniel had felt when chancing on the ceilidh music in London, only soured as if he had been barred from entry to the Burns Supper, i.e. the conjuring of pleasant memories coupled with the knowledge of the impossibility of their re-creation. More than that though, there was a feeling of guilt.

Guilt that Nathaniel had lost contact with—nay, neglected—old friends, and particularly the Barkers. Mr. Barker had introduced Nathaniel to the Beatles after all, and their music had often been the furniture of his emotions. And then Shelagh, Shelagh with whom Nathaniel had cried when John Lennon had been murdered. Shelagh hadn't been able to come to the wedding, and Nathaniel had guessed that she didn't have the money. Although he earned more in a day that she earned in a year, he had not offered to buy her a ticket to London, a "ticket to ride," as the song had it. Shelagh had sent them a lovely watercolour of the beach at Inverdon, beautifully framed too. How many hours of work had she put into it, and what proportion of her barely existent income had the frame cost? Poor poor Shelagh. And, on her behalf, what had Nathaniel done to highlight his discovery of the link between poverty and ageing? Nothing!

And the words of the song….They were Paul McCartney's advice to the young Julian Lennon when his parents' marriage was dissolving, and they were optimistic: they were about starting with an unhappy situation and improving it. Nathaniel was an atheist but he found himself bargaining with God: if you get me out of this one, Lord, I will try and make things better…in every way.

Superficially Nathaniel must have appeared to have been enjoying the music, because James cut through his miasma. "You like the Beatles?"

"Yes" to such a question at such a time seems derisory, but it was all the jolted-back-to-reality Nathaniel found on his numb lips.

Seemingly fully alive for the first time that evening, James switched off the radio (which had abandoned the Beatles for Bob Marley) and continued: "I like Beatles very much! John Lennon, he my favourite." He launched into a creditable version of "Revolution," and when he paused for a moment Nathaniel found himself grasping the lyrical baton and singing on.

The multiple ironies of this anti-revolutionary song, written by the man who had been the most revolutionary Beatle and who had been shot, being sung by a man terrified of being shot and on the verge of committing himself to revolution (as will emerge presently) and by a man who was, in fact, a revolutionary (ditto), was lost on both singers.

For Nathaniel it was, consciously, an opportunity to de-objectify himself—to establish his identity as a sympathetic human being—and therefore, he hoped, to make it less likely that he and Rosemary would suffer early and violent termination. Subconsciously, it was to some extent cathartic, certainly therapeutic by some mechanism. He would not, at the time, have admitted to being happy, but, in fact, the act of singing immersed him in the absolute present, and as long as he was navigating amongst the familiar panoramic scenery of a Beatles' creation, he was blissfully sequestered from his woes. *Saudade* to seraphism in two songs. What he didn't realise at the time was that this superficial bonding with James—to a large extent attributable to the dead Lennon—was a foretaste of Nathaniel's much deeper identification with the poor and oppressed of the world, and that this would ultimately lead to the global Hope-ist revolution, the results of which we take so much for granted in the mid-21st century.

Consciously, Rosemary was aware that Nathaniel was trying to save them. Subconsciously, however, she was reading his body language. She could see him forgetting her and the horrors of their situation, and bonding with a kidnapper! Thus she was unhappy at the cantatory turn of events, and guilty at feeling unhappy. Guilt may be a force for the good, but when its origins are obscure to the intellect it becomes an anti-alchemical poison which strives to eliminate itself by searching for reasons to justify those negative actions or feelings which produced it. Good feelings are driven out by bad, gold is changed into base metal. Put differently, the seed of hatred for Nathaniel was sown in Rosemary that evening. Would she cultivate it, or would it perish?

Castro was not smiling anymore. James and Nathaniel's enthusiastic conversation was interrupted when he stood up abruptly. "Time for sleep, now! Back to your room." James' expression was inscrutable.

The night was a torment. Locked once more in their windowless cell, the humidity was suffocating. Despite the liberal use of the throat-scalding and eye-stinging insecticide, and the repeated application of the repellent, the constant whine of mosquitoes was as disquieting as a quintet of dentistry drills playing an unsuccessful joint composition of Bartok, Glass, Reich and Stockhausen. Rosemary sobbed, burying her head in a blanket which still retained the odours of a more hospitable world. Eventually she dozed off. In the small hours Nathaniel was wet with sweat and slipping in and out of the nightmares of shallow sleep. In the moments when he was awake he wished he were asleep again, but once asleep it wasn't long before a fresh horror woke him.

He saw himself in a classroom. Rosemary was sitting at the farthest desk from his. The teacher was saying: "Now, people, it's the last day of term. We've covered the syllabus already and I don't think any of us feels like starting next term's work, so we're going to do something different. You're going to work in teams to solve a little problem."

Nathaniel found himself teamed with Rosemary, but it was obvious that she didn't want to be with him, and she kept making eyes at Jason.

The teacher explained: "You have been taken prisoner and locked in a little room, full of insects. All you have are some blankets, and your clothes. Except, of course Nathaniel who has a wig and a glass eye, and Rosemary who also has a wig."

The whole class laughed, then they all rose. The intensity of the laughter increased, there were hundreds of jeering evil fingers pointed at them, coming closer and closer. The evil shrillness of it, the malign intensity, forced Nathaniel and Rosemary to flee. They found themselves barricaded in the stockroom, books piled against the door, but it was so stuffy, and they could hear jeering outside, a banshee-bloodhound baying, and there were insects everywhere.

How could they escape? They took books from the shelves and made two stacks and topped each with a wig. Nathaniel removed his glass eye and added this to one of the would-be scarecrows. An insect crawled into his now empty eye socket. He pulled it out. Then he and Rosemary removed the barricading books and knocked on the door, squeezing themselves flat against the wall where they would be hidden when the door opened.

The door creaked and the persecutory keening changed into a panicked howl when the scarecrows were spotted…and then it disappeared, and they were free, and they emerged into the empty classroom and looked at each other, and they were both hideous: faceless, eyeless, hairless, with insects crawling out of obscene and gory sockets, and then they were on fire, and they both screamed.

Nathaniel woke to find Rosemary screaming. She was looking at him in the faint light of morning, horror all over her blood-streaked face. It took them a few minutes to work out what had happened in the night.

The mosquitoes had not been greatly discouraged by the repellent or the spray and had set about filling themselves with exotic English blood ("Fee, fie, fo, fum…"). While mosquito saliva is efficient at preventing blood from clotting, it does not contain an anaesthetic, so a feeding mosquito always runs the risk of being detected and crushed by its involuntary host. During the night many unlucky anophelines had had their repasts prematurely terminated by itch-responsive hands, and the meagre contents of their barely distended abdomens smeared over the skins of their semi-victims. The small amount of saliva injected during these short snacks was not sufficient to cause much of a skin reaction, so their legacy was largely a superficial blood streak.

Unfortunately for Rosemary and Nathaniel, and fortunately for the questing sanguivores, large portions of their faces were bereft of sensation and the meals in these fine restaurants were consequently uninterrupted and edacious. Generous volumes of digestive and anticoagulant spittle had facilitated these feasts, and had caused severe inflammation. The sensory innervation of the Papulouses' faces was thus illustrated by a coloured relief map: a plateau of confluent pink weals where there was no sensation, and a pale lowland area blotched with the dark red of dried blood where the nerve supply was intact. In short, Nathaniel and Rosemary looked horrific for the second time in their lives.

CHAPTER NINETEEN
Another High Tide

James and Castro heard the screaming, and a sleepy-eyed James opened the door. He did not, of course, understand why Nathaniel and Rosemary's faces were quite as they were, but realised that they had suffered badly from mosquitoes. He let them out to wash in the stream. If there was anything good about the situation it was that the worst-looking areas were largely pain-free, and so there was little temptation to scratch. Scratching an itch is not a trivial thing in the tropics, as any wound is a potential access point for infection; traumatising a sore is asking for trouble. When they got back to the shack, Castro was fossicking through a little canvas bag. He pulled out a crumpled tube of ointment and handed it to Rosemary. It was a combination antihistamine-antiseptic and she gratefully slathered it on—her face as well as her feet which were covered with cuts, ulcers and pustules following their barefoot march. Perhaps Castro wasn't so bad after all, she thought.

Any residue of bonhomie from the night before had gone from Nathaniel. He felt headachey, dehydrated and exhausted. He hoped it was just a combination of a hangover and sleeplessness, and not the start of something more serious, a mosquito-borne infection. He tried to cheer himself with the thought that, with any luck, they would meet "da boss" soon and learn why they had been kidnapped.

Breakfast was a mango apiece, organically grown to judge by the insect damage. After another wash in the stream, Nathaniel and

Rosemary found themselves being herded back into the shack, but not before they saw James astride the motorbike. With nothing to lose, Nathaniel called out, "See if you can get us something to read!"

James looked up blankly and Nathaniel wasn't sure if he had heard. James kicked the motorbike into life and was away even before Castro had banged the prison door closed.

"I'm not bloody going through a night like that again!" said Rosemary to Nathaniel, and then raised her voice. "I'd rather they shot us! You hear that, Castro?! If you can't keep the mosquitoes off us then f***ing shoot us now!"

There was no response from outside. Nathaniel was shocked, both by the feral nature of her scream and by her language. If their faces had been capable of complex expressions she would have returned Nathaniel's look of surprise with one of defiance verging on hatred. Nathaniel considered the immediate problem of the mosquitoes: there was only a narrow gap between the roof and the walls. If the worst came to the worst they could stuff a blanket in the gap—admittedly the atmosphere would be even more stultifying. Ideally they needed some mosquito netting….Of course! Rosemary was bound to have some stockings in her suitcase! If they could persuade Castro to let them have them, and if they could find some way of stretching them over the gap. Nathaniel called to him, "Castro! Please! We need some help!"

A suspicious gum-chewing Castro, accompanied by his AK, appeared in the crack of the opening door. "So?" Nathaniel explained his idea to him, and Castro seemed relieved at this apparently sensible request. He closed the door and returned a minute later with some sticking plasters from his first-aid bag and a pair of Rosemary's tights.

Nathaniel set about work but it became apparent that the tension on the plasters was too great—it didn't work—they weren't adhesive enough. Rosemary was crying, and Nathaniel was almost ready to join her when he had another idea. Again he called to Castro, who took the tights from him and returned a moment later. He'd cut the stockings lengthwise, and he also handed Nathaniel a packet of chewing gum. Nathaniel popped a stick into Rosemary's surprised mouth, and she masticated miserably between sobs. Nathaniel took some well-chewed gum from his mouth, wiped the hut metal clean and stuck a piece of stocking in place—it worked!

It took them two hours of patient work, and several readjustments but eventually all possible mosquito access points had been covered, and their handiwork appeared reasonably secure. The task seemed to be therapeutic for Rosemary. Once its likely successful outcome had become clear she had set about chewing and sticking with efficiency and near-enthusiasm.

Castro's curiosity got the better of him and he came in to have a look. He was clearly impressed, and asked that they do such a thing for his side of the hut as well. For Rosemary his polite request was strangely touching. After all, he could easily shoot them (or do whatever to them!) if they refused his least wish, but here he was requesting.

She found herself agreeing, and forcing herself to smile. While they were busy working, this time with the outer door open and Castro sitting outside watching them, the ludicrousness of finding herself willingly destroying her tights in order to give her kidnappers a pleasant night's sleep—*for heaven's sake!*—started Rosemary giggling. Possibly she was also aware of her cud-chewing appearance—a placid cow complacently doing her master's bidding? And would she be slaughtered when the service had been rendered?

Nathaniel was not sure this time whether she was healthily amused or hysterical. He stopped work and looked at her. Was she going mad? He squeezed her arm and asked her whether she was alright. She stopped laughing, jerked free and, by the tension of her jaw muscles and the fixity of her gaze, Nathaniel assumed that she was angry with him. He resumed work, and so did she, but at the other end of the room.

Presumably feeling well-disposed to them after their sterling mosquito-proofing work, Castro let them stay outside the sweltering shack the rest of the day, keeping his gun at hand and his eye on them at all times. Their listless slumping in the shade was broken by the return of James towards the evening.

Castro approached him as he dismounted, and the two men exchanged a few words. Castro shook his head as if disappointed by something. He returned to his seat in the shade of the hut. James reached into a pannier and winked at Nathaniel. He coquettishly hid behind his back whatever it was he had extracted, and, looking immensely pleased with himself, swaggered over to the drained-looking Papulous couple. He stopped in front of them, winked again, and then presented them with a tattered little booklet, bowing theatrically as he did so. It was Machiavelli's *The Prince*, which for Nathaniel vaguely rang a bell. It had possibly cropped up in a conversation with Shelagh or Mary....Well, it was something to read. It was "suggested" that they might like to retire for a while, and from their dark prison Nathaniel and Rosemary could hear their captors walking into the distance. An hour later, when it was almost completely dark, they could hear the men returning. An exhausted-looking Castro let them out of the shack again.

That evening was much as the previous had been, although there was no more Beatles music. It appeared that "da boss" was not to arrive that day. Again James seemed restless, but was unable to find anything on the radio that appealed. He sighed and dumped the little transistor beneath his seat. Stretching himself, he picked his nose and then, with an irritated edge to his voice, asked Nathaniel, "So, you like da book?"

Nathaniel tried to summon some enthusiasm, but on cursory examination it had seemed pretty dull. This lack of rapture might have had something to do with the combination of the tension between himself and Rosemary, and the circumstances of their captivity, which were obviously unconducive to the contemplation of a cerebral though mildewed masterpiece. "The book's fine, James, but I'm saving it for a rainy day." Nathaniel was rather pleased with his repartee. Had his facial musculature been intact, this reply would have been accompanied by a wry grin.

James was unable to fathom these words. He snorted and had another shot of rum, then clenched his eyes closed, pinching the bridge of his nose between thumb and forefinger. Possibly he was suffering from a headache.

The night was mosquito-less but horribly close, and sleep came late. The next day was sticky and slow. Nathaniel found that not only had he nothing to say to Rosemary, but neither did he wish that he had anything to say. Rosemary was no longer hysterical, but limp and passive, as if she had fallen into herself. Nathaniel tried to feel something for her, or for anything or anyone, but felt only dead and empty. He tried to read, but found that he had re-read the first page umpteen times without taking it in. When would this bloody "boss"-guy arrive? Did he—"da boss"—even exist? Did he—Nathaniel—exist? Did John Lennon exist? What about Bright Eyes? Why were they drifting into his apathetic and hazed mind?

Neither of the guards left the camp that day. In the late afternoon Nathaniel and Rosemary found themselves penned again. As evening was falling, and the bird calls were intensifying, a new note entered the soundscape. It rapidly revealed itself to be a helicopter. It came very close, to judge both by the volume and by the movement of the mosquito-excluding tights.

A flushed Castro appeared at their suddenly opened doorway, holding their most sensible shoes. They shod themselves without delay and found they were being chivvied into the overgrown plantation. A few yards of thicket gave way to a circular open area, twenty-five yards across and freshly cleared, to judge by the wilted but still green vegetation carpeting it. Scattered glowing embers at the circumference were all that remained of what must have been beacon fires. A massive helicopter was sitting in the middle. It was blue and white, not red and gold. The ferocious noise and the leaf- and twig-laden maelstrom resulting from the blades were such a contrast to the soft jungle evening that it was almost exhilarating.

Bent double, Castro manhandled them towards the heart of the tempest, and they found themselves sitting in comfortable bucket seats in the middle of a six-seater cabin. James was sitting in the back row with their suitcases, and Castro clambered aboard next to the pilot. The latter was equipped with a headset. A little microphone stood out in front of his moustache like a carrot before a hairy donkey. The helicopter lurched upwards and forwards, and within seconds the feeble glow of the dying fires had been swallowed by the opaque green jungle. This was no two-bit-ha'penny bunch of crooks.

"I have always wanted to say, 'Ah so, Meester Bond, ve meet at last. I haff been expecting you!' but I guess I'll have to content myself with

'Welcome, Dr. and Mrs. Papulous!'" The short and jovial man was sitting in a simply furnished little office, a bare bulb dangling from the ceiling and a rusty angle-poise lamp on his warped desk. He stood and shook the Papulouses' hands.

"I guess I owe you an explanation for all this. Would you like some coffee, or something alcoholic? I think we have some Coca-cola and some rum—you know what a 'Cuba libre' is of course?"

They asked for straight Coke. It arrived in tall glasses, packed with ice and garnished with slices of lime. The waitress was a stoutish middle-aged woman wearing what looked like old-style British National Health heavy-rimmed glasses. Her dark hair was in a bun. The jolly one introduced her as his wife, Gloria, and himself as Alberto.

Rosemary wasn't really following the conversation. The Coke was delicious. Under other circumstances she would have loved that sunset flight, skimming low over a light-sprinkled Caribbean archipelago, particularly if she hadn't been blindfolded for most of it. Nothing was real anymore, except the Coke.

"You know I've been rehearsing this speech for some time, but I don't really know where to start....First of all, let me say that we have no intention of harming you. We have nothing against you people personally, although we resent your...your connections....I say 'we,' and that needs an explanation. We are what you would call 'a terrorist organisation,' the Hysterique Anti-Imperialist Liberation Front. I doubt you have ever heard of us, because we are very small, and very careful, and this is our first major action. Our goals are simple. Do you know anything about Hysterique?"

Nathaniel replied that he knew it was divided in two, one half belonging to the hotel.

"Yes. That's a good starting point. Hysterique is indeed divided in two, by a security fence, into the haves and the have-nots. Almost all the haves are foreigners. Fifty years ago we, the Hystericans, were what was called a backward peasant community. Our ancestors were mainly liberated slaves, just dumped there. Anyway, we grew enough food to support ourselves, we fished and we exported bananas and some coffee. Our lives were not idyllic—there was malaria and other health problems—but things were not so bad either. You would have thought that there'd be nothing particularly of interest here for the outside world, but one day this guy arrived in my home village.

"He was laden with presents: cigarettes, clothes and radios. He said that if we would help him there'd be a lot more to come. He wanted us to grow something for him. He would build us a new school and a hospital. He wanted us to grow coca and marijuana. We'd always grown a bit of marijuana anyway, so it didn't seem such a bad thing, just to expand the area we put under it…and we desperately wanted the school and the hospital. Of course once we'd grown his drugs he didn't pay as much as he'd promised, but we didn't have any choice. We had to sell it to him: we'd neglected our food crops so much that year, and we needed to buy food.

"A young guy, my oldest brother, refused to give away his crop so cheaply, and he destroyed it all in protest. We found him nailed to a tree, barely alive. He had been castrated and his eyes and tongue cut out. He died before we could get him off the tree. We lied to my mother about what had happened to him. I was sixteen and stupid. I went to the police. I was lucky to survive."

Here Alberto paused, looking coolly at Nathaniel and Rosemary, and then continued in the same flat and matter-of-fact way. "Yes, they kept me in detention for three months. They beat me every day, accusing me of murdering my brother and urging me to confess. Of course, they were the ones who had killed him. They were being paid well. So there was nothing we could do. In effect we were all slaves again, and we didn't get our hospital or our school. Of course not!

"Again I was lucky—I had a relative in Jamaica and I managed to get on a boat there. This man, my uncle, was wealthy and I received a good education. I went on to Harvard and then to Oxford. But that is another story. To return to Hysterique—the situation went on like that for fifteen years. The peasants, my people, produced tonnes of marijuana and coca leaf very very cheaply for Papa Ricard. The guy was the president's cousin, and he could do what he wanted. Then one day the narcotic squad arrived—do you know who they are?"

Rosemary and Nathaniel looked blank, and Alberto continued,

"They're the US so-called 'security' force charged with controlling drugs. Anyhow one day they just arrived on Hysterique in their helicopters and sprayed all the crops with weedkiller. That year there were quite a few deaths amongst our people—we had not grown enough food crops and we had no drugs to sell. If you didn't know how these things worked you might expect the guys at the top to be targeted but it never works like that.

"In fact the Yanks made a deal with the government: if they'd sell half the island to them for a luxury hotel development not only would they give them a decent price but they'd give them a cut of the profits. They told the peasants—my people—that they'd build a school and a hospital—that same old story. Of course the money was siphoned off by Ricard & Co. The only provision the hotel builders made was that the government and its lackeys had to guarantee the security of the hotel, and provide cheap labour. So our land was taken away from us. Not only could we no longer grow drugs, but we didn't have enough land to grow even the basic staples. We had no choice but to work for the hotel, and take their near-starvation wages—slaves again.

"Of course there was trouble—you don't take something like that lying down! Some tried sabotage, some tried to continue cultivating hemp in small patches in the most rugged areas, and some tried striking. Papa Ricard's private army, with the training, logistic support and weaponry of the Americans, put down all opposition in the harshest manner: they would raze an entire hamlet if one of its members was suspected of causing problems, rape all the women in front of the men and then kill everyone, babies included. And 'causing problems' could be asking for a decent wage, never mind organising a trade union. No way!

"So things just got worse. Infant mortality is fifty percent, and life expectancy—for those surviving the first year, mind you—is probably about fifty. And, with HIV here now, it's going to get a lot worse. Anyway, eventually, because of the lack of education and the poor physical condition of the local people, not to mention the fears about security, the regime decided to recruit their slaves from elsewhere. So in the end, the local people received nothing—less than nothing—while the Americans and the government got rich.

"To the outside world the picture looks great: international cooperation to control the drugs problem and investment in the local economy, but the only people who benefit are the so-called investors and their crooked local stooges. And let me tell you that the situation on Hysterique is repeated all over the Caribbean and Latin America, and probably the world: southeast Asia, Africa, Bangladesh…you name it. It may not be tourist developments—sometimes it's oil, sometimes it's minerals—but the story is the same: the rich get richer and the poor get poorer."

"So what the hell does this have to do with us?"

"There are many ways I could answer your question, madam, because we are all partly responsible for the state of things, but I think you want me to explain why you have been kidnapped. Very well, I shall tell you. I followed what was happening in Hysterique. I wrote to the president of the USA, I wrote letters to newspapers, I campaigned in every way I could think of but I got nowhere—bland brush-offs or vague promises to investigate. Mostly the media ignored me. The whole island was so sewn-up and terrified that no one dared confirm what I knew. I thought about the problem, and I decided that against a powerful and corrupt enemy one sometimes had to stoop to underhand methods. I needed to do something a bit more extreme.

"I knew of a couple of Hystericans who'd come to Jamaica like me, though more recently: James and Castro. I contacted them and we got talking. The Hotel recruited on Jamaica and they usually didn't bother checking stories too much. They were unlikely to discover that they were originally Hysterican; the fact that they had been trained as security guards—funded, of course, by myself—was sufficient to get them employed.

"For three years James and Castro have served The Hotel faithfully. They are bright chaps and their knowledge and responsibilities grew. The day arrived when they knew enough to pull off the perfect kidnapping. But we needed the ideal victims: very famous people. And then I heard that you were coming, and you know most of the rest!"

"Surely there must have been hundreds of people searching for us, all over the island? How were we not found?"

"Simple. We laid a false trail. The vehicle was driven to a point very distant from where you were detained, and it was burnt. Your blood-stained clothes—which you were kind enough to wipe your feet on for us—were left nearby. We timed your helicopter departure so that the investigation would have time to find the vehicle and concentrate all their forces in that area. In that way we could fly you from the other side of the island with minimal risk. The islanders won't talk. They've already suffered so much, they don't give a damn about rich tourists...and keeping quiet is the safest policy if you don't trust anyone. Now we can announce to the world that you've been kidnapped, and make our demands."

"Which are?" It was Nathaniel who put the question. Rosemary was sinking away again into cold introversion.

"Very few and very moderate: to distribute the money from the sale of the island and the profits from The Hotel more evenly. Pay a decent minimum wage and employ locals, for a start. Let them have a trade union. Build us our school and our hospital. Organise free and fair elections supervised by the UN. Give us a reasonable price for bananas. There's nothing unreasonable in those demands. Once the world knows what's been going on they'll have no choice but to cooperate! I don't think it'll be long at all before we can let you go. But first you'll need to star in a little video...."

Nathaniel was on the verge of conversion. Numerous bells were ready to ring and pennies to drop. The supersaturated solution of his mind lacked only a seed to trigger rapid crystallization: the solute was his by now significant experience of the way men and businesses operated, and Alberto was providing the seed. To use the river metaphor, Nathaniel's river was experiencing its last high tide before it merged with the sea of global consciousness. But it was yet identifiable as a river, and the tide would retreat once more before it merged irreversibly with the ocean, letting it enjoy its last delusion as a separate entity. Or, reverting to the solvent-solute metaphor, the crystallization would be briefly postponed.

What happened next has been described by numerous people—participants and journalists—and no two versions of the event agree. We shall content ourselves with Nathaniel's version, and that of *The Sin.*

The door burst open. Three armed men entered, including Castro. They screamed to Rosemary and Nathaniel to get down. The unarmed Alberto was shot, probably by at least two of the men. Outside more gunfire could be heard. There was blood everywhere, and several bodies, possibly including those of James and Gloria. Rosemary and Nathaniel were rushed outside by Carlos and again found themselves in a helicopter. This time they were not blindfolded. The man next to the pilot turned around and smiled. It was Silversmith! "Relax, we've rescued you! Are you alright?"

Rosemary was sobbing. Nathaniel was numb, as if he'd had too much to drink on a hot day, and had then stood up suddenly. Then nausea overcame him. He threw up into a bag hurriedly grabbed by the still grinning Silversmith.

Two hours later, after a check-up in a state-of-the-art medical clinic, they were in the plush air-conditioned honeymoon suite at The Hotel, alone. The cupboards were full of lovely clothes in their sizes. A waiter had brought them a bottle of excellent champagne. The place was a forest of flowers, and a big bowl of perfect, unblemished tropical and temperate fruit added further colour. They had a bubble-bath jacuzzi together. Rosemary seemed back to normal. Nathaniel was still dazed. Silversmith had said that he would explain everything the next day. HDI was to pick up the bill for the rest of their honeymoon.

"So. How're you both feeling now?" Silversmith had joined them on the patio for lunch. A beautiful and manicured garden rich in bougainvillea and hibiscus lay below them. Little jewelled birds darted hither and thither. A stream had been dammed to create a waterlily pond, with the largest waterlily pads Nathaniel had ever seen: move over Monet! Red- and gold-liveried waiters with dead eyes, oozing subservience, discreetly plied them with superfluous gustatory delights flown from all over the world.

Rosemary replied, "Wonderful!"

Nathaniel was less enthusiastic. "OK, considering. Tell me, how did you know what had happened to us and where we were?"

"Castro has been ours, ummm…working undercover for the

Hysterican government for years. They've been keeping tabs on HAILF for a while now...."

"If you knew what was going to happen, why didn't you stop us being kidnapped?"

"We didn't know what was going to happen! Castro had to be very careful how and how often he communicated, you know. But he was able to let us know where you were. Anyhow it's all over now, and things have turned out very well. There's one less terrorist organisation in the world, and you two are unscathed! The publicity won't do us any harm either...."

The Sin described the events thus:

Dr. Youth's Kidnappers Kaput!

Yesterday, famous boffin, Dr. Youth (Nathaniel Papulous) and his wife, formerly Mrs. Rosemary Nixon, kidnapped three days ago while on honeymoon by the terrorist movement, the Hysterican Anti-Imperialist Liberation Front (HAILF), were rescued. A spokesman for the rescuers, a US-trained hit squad of the Hysterican Army, said that Dr. and Mrs. Papulous were unharmed, but all the kidnappers, who had been heavily armed, had been killed. HAILF was responsible for a number of brutal killings in Hysterique, and the authorities are hopeful that this latest defeat will have destroyed the organisation. The Papulous couple, whose wedding was attended by the rival pop singers Pat Galloper of Some Palm Trees and Camels Around A Waterhole and Devil Halfshed of Obfuscate, are said to be resuming their honeymoon on Hysterique, paid for by Hardley-Dreamlon International, Dr. Papulous' employer....

The article was accompanied by a huge photograph of Nathaniel and Rosemary in wedding garb. How neat. How sweet.

CHAPTER TWENTY
The River Mouth

Of course Nathaniel was suspicious of Silversmith's story. In order for Silversmith to have been in the Caribbean at the time of the rescue, he must have known earlier what was afoot. He could even see him setting the whole thing up for the publicity. Or was that going a bit far? Would he ever know the whole truth? In the meantime he was expected just to pick up the old life where he had left it. In some ways this was to follow the path of least resistance. He didn't have to think much this way, anyway, just try to ignore something nagging there—was it his conscience? Just roll along....He told himself that he ought to be happy. After all, he had Rosemary, the possibly permanently beautiful girl of his dreams, and he was stupendously rich. His life was arranged for him by HDI: the interviews, a ghost-written biography (*Changing Faces*), more interviews to publicize this, some work on further enhancement of the ageing programme, scientific conferences....Why, then, did he dream of Rosemary choking to death on his glass eye? Why did Bright Eyes/The Convalescent come to visit her still form, the red cape of this unlikely angel of death so cheering? Having dreamed this, why did he wake in a warm glow, unbathed in that near-proverbial cold sweat, the faithful standby of thriller writers? And once awake why was everything so grey? Why was John Lennon on his mind, and why had he been unable either to read or to throw away James' present, that tattered little book? It was now more than a year that it had been there on his shelf. Even the development of his paintings-and-grandfather clock story was a meagre joy. Tomorrow he was to hit the road—or rather the rails—again: a trip to Followby to discuss a joint project with Prof. Podd. Then yet another conference, this time in Paris....

Nathaniel found himself walking around the Château de Vincennes on the eastern edge of the great city. He had given his talk, which as usual had been rapturously received. At the subsequent tea break he had been besieged by colleagues with questions, students wanting advice or to work with him, and journalists, always the journalists....He had replied as politely and patiently as ever, and then walked out of the building as the next session started. He had had enough. Amongst the voluminous conference literature was a list of tourist attractions. Nathaniel had stabbed a pen at the list, blindly, wanting to escape the straitjacket of his ordered life. Chance had commanded him to travel all the way across Paris, from the conference centre at La Défense in the west, to the Château in the east. Nathaniel had endured the long Métro journey with equanimity—in fact he had deliberately chosen this rather than the much quicker RER—trying to think of the stations as a string of soothing worry beads, each one carrying him farther from his ill-defined woes: Pont de Neuilly, Les Sablons, Porte Maillot, Argentine, Charles de Gaulle Étoile....

Tiring of this, he had focussed on the people: all the individuals scurrying in and out, under and through this beautiful city, weaving it together with their movements and interactions. How many of them were thinking about the greater organism of which they were part: Paris, France, the world? How many were concerned solely with the minutiae of their petty existences? How many thought only of the next bite to eat, the next can of beer, the next fag, or the next merger?

The Château was right next to the Métro station, most of it clean and bright in the midday sunshine: proud and ancient sandstone, crumbling a bit perhaps but more or less as it must have appeared hundreds of years ago. And then there were the archaeological diggings, going back even further, revealing old foundations in their expected states of senescence and decay. The keep—*le donjon*—was the only building whose appearance would have shocked its creators. It was girt with scaffolding, and this clad with plastic. The interior was being reinforced, the central pillar apparently yielding under centuries of strain, no longer at ease in the old dispensation. Underneath the hideous sheath it was being reborn. Given his history, Nathaniel could not help but identify with the inanimate building. He was far more moved by the ghastly modern chrysalis than by the adjacent elegant cathedral with its headed and time-beheaded gargoyles, or the twinned but resolutely opposite residences of the king and queen: yin and yang? The keep had confirmed the random choice of his pen. He had come to the right place. Vincennes would be the place of revelation. He needed to relax, follow his intuition, and let events take their course. Changes were occurring.

Nathaniel's feet carried him into the bourgeois little burgh of Vincennes itself, full of chic little boutiques and specialist food shops: regional cuisines, patisseries, charcuteries and the like. Amazing how the French turned offal into such attractive delicacies, while all the Scots could come up with was black pudding and haggis! Haggis—*hachis*—mincemeat in French. Of course, that was where the word came from! Elated by this discovery, and further convinced that something very important was going to come out of this trip, Nathaniel transferred his attention from the shops to the people. There were lilac sellers (gypsies?) on the street corners, and a ragged-jacketed beggar sat outside the post office, his left arm trembling, his right pathetically extended, a dirty palm crossed with a few coins. His eyes were on the pavement. Nathaniel gave him ten francs. The multiple mumbled *merci*s told him that such generosity was rare indeed. Wealth and poverty….

Then Nathaniel came to a bookshop. He stopped at the window. Memories of Frillons blurred his view. When he pulled himself back to the present the first book he was aware of was entitled *L'horreur économique*. The author was a Viviane Forrester. It had a simple cover, large blue letters on a white background. Across the lower half was a strip of red paper. Written on this was "Prix de Médicis." This was obviously a good book. Nathaniel knew he had to buy it, and also, somehow, that this was why he had come here. He bought a French-English dictionary as well, and caught the Métro back to his hotel. He was excited as he had never been in his life. Not even when Rosemary kissed his eyelids had he felt this alive.

—

In the next two days Nathaniel did not leave the hotel. Fortunately the embers of his schoolboy French were still glowing, and the enthusiasm of his reading blew them into a passable fire. His river entered the sea. The hyper-saturated solution crystallised. Everything became clear.

PART TWO
The Ocean

CHAPTER TWENTY-ONE
The Ocean at Last

Were rivers animate, one might imagine their entries into the oceans to be shocking, but for any pain to fade as individual riverine consciousnesses became subsumed in the vast saltwater super-being. Nourished by numerous rivers, and by rainfall, and in some aeons by melting icebergs, the oceans are (or were) fabulously rich and productive. Their most fertile areas often adjoin barren western shores, where cold currents sweep nutrients to the surface. Bathed in sunlight, phytoplankton multiply prodigiously, and the rest of ocean life follows. There are great pan-oceanic circulations of life-rich water. Fauna and flora may be carried, passive, thousands of miles around the world, only to end up in the same place, but with vastly greater experience. Theoretically therefore, a little bit of ocean water contains information about many places and phenomena, a rich assortment of vital forces. A conscious ocean would know a lot about the state of the planet. It would constitute a formidable entity.

Nathaniel's reading of Viviane Forrester's *L'horreur économique* marked the entry of his river into the ocean of super-awareness, as the accumulated and formerly seemingly largely trivial, random, and unconnected experiences of his life crossed a quantitative and qualitative threshold and an underlying order became obvious to him, like a revelation to a prophet. His ocean recognised that the experiences of all rivers are similar, that a pattern exists.

In the post-Papulous era it is difficult to credit the widespread ignorance of the late 20th and early 21st centuries. With the exception of a couple of so-called "loony left" political extremists and terrorist movements (for example the Zapatista National Liberation Army of Mexico), the odd maverick journalist (working for low-circulation papers like *The Protector* and *Le Monde Frénétique*) and deservedly acclaimed but not world-changing writers (such as Viviane Forrester and Naomi Klein), the planet was under the sway of multinationals and unaware of its deepening servitude. Protestors against globalisation were effective in gaining media attention, but they were very much in the minority, and the violence attributed to them resulted in most people in the more developed countries viewing them as misguided nutters. Readers in today's enlightened age will have gleaned from the tale thus far some idea of the prevalent near-cataleptic state. However, to appreciate fully the strength of the multinationals' grip on the minds of the public, it is instructive to review Nathaniel's first attempt to discuss his revelation with someone.

Nathaniel was desperate to rouse people, to pass on his new understanding: so little time remained before Big Brother Capital would black-hole all the world's wealth! Already, in the last years of the 20th century, the fortunes of the 358 richest people in the world were calculated to exceed the total annual income of the poorest half of the world's population. He needed to act both quickly and sure-footedly. Any mistake and he would be destroyed, and perhaps with him the last chance for the poor of the planet, for most of humanity in fact. How to start on such a vast task? It would help to talk things through with someone he could trust, someone whose intelligence he respected.

"So, is that what you brought me here for? To tell me you've discovered Marxism? Well bully for you, Nathaniel, most of us went through that phase years ago! I gave it up when I gave up smoking, and I've been a lot healthier in mind and body since! Don't you remember our walks on the beach?" Mary snapped her swizzle stick.

This was not what Nathaniel had expected, but then if he'd thought about it he should have known that she'd changed. "Look, Mary, you don't understand...."

"No, you look, Nathaniel! I've read Marx and Engels. Yes, OK, they had a point or two, but a lot of their so-called research was at the very best distorted, and at the worst entirely fabricated. Now I'm all for having a social conscience and that kind of thing, but anyone who has any sense can see that communism has failed miserably—and that's putting it charitably if you look at the legacies of Stalin and Mao! At least capitalism, while it may be a long way from ideal, actually works. Things are made and crops are grown! Just what are you proposing as an alternative? Have you read *Wild Swans*?"

Nathaniel felt he was drowning.

Mary continued. "I thought you of all people would have been able to see through that left-wing bullshit! Now I'm sorry, Nathaniel, I've really got to go. The director of the Getty is arriving soon."

Nathaniel swallowed. "I tell you what, Mary, if I put together a few hard facts on paper will you check them out?"

Mary sighed. "Huh, 'hard' facts as opposed to 'soft' ones? Tch...yes, I suppose."

The task Nathaniel had set himself was not going to be easy if even someone as intelligent as Mary would barely hear him out!

CHAPTER TWENTY-TWO
Cider with Rosemary

Seemingly helpless with respect to his emotional turbulence, but with a mind—or rather an imagination—still active, it was at this point, sitting there alone in the cafeteria of the Victor Ear and Herb Alpert Museum and watching a drop of condensation trickle down Mary's abandoned glass of Perrier water, that Nathaniel had a vision of his entire life as has been described: as a river entering an ocean. Having a geographical perspective on things made it easier not only to comprehend the exterior world as felt by the waters of his life, but also to appreciate himself, to recognise the patterns in his behaviour. It was obvious from this vantage point that his most creative periods had been born in pain and confusion. Thus far he had succeeded in attaining every self-imposed goal, even in marrying Rosemary. Why should this not continue, even though this time he was facing the biggest challenge of his life? His mission was to break the death-grip on the planet of the oligarchy of multinationals, to counteract their concentration of resources and power. So he had an end in sight, and he could plan for it, ridiculously ambitious as it seemed. Elation and hope defeated frustration and despair.

He took stock. In a way, he was ideally situated to plot the humbling of the mega-corporations. Increasingly trusted and important to Silversmith and HDI, he was already near the core of international business. Just as Castro of HAILF had been a double agent, ultimately bought and controlled by international capitalism, Nathaniel would be a double agent at the service of the world's poor and dispossessed. But, as a double agent, he needed to appear to be faithful to Mammon. He needed to crawl as close as possible to the rotten heart of power as manifested by Silversmith. He knew he had been lacklustre in his performance of late, ever since the kidnapping. Fortunately that had been seen as the inevitable aftermath of such a trauma, and would not count against him should he show himself once more to be an enthusiastic acolyte of avarice. So the old show had to go on, while a new one was secretly being rehearsed backstage.

Part of the old show had been the loving and glamorous Papulous couple. Shared adversity is supposed to bring people closer, but Nathaniel and Rosemary had been strangers since their captivity. One may never understand all the psychology that was at work here, but it is possible that Rosemary had found herself attracted to the enigmatic Castro, and, at the same time, irrationally jealous of Nathaniel's apparent bond with James. Nathaniel, on the other hand, had been preoccupied with the broader moral issues, and consequently unhappy, introverted and far from the model loving husband.

Now Nathaniel's path was clear, or at least its rough direction, and his conscience at ease. It was true that he would therefore be happier, and so automatically more appealing to Rosemary, but he ought to make a conscious effort also to resuscitate the old show. He needed to woo Rosemary, his innocent, beautiful and long-suffering Bright Eyes, once more.

Innocent, yes….It would be better to keep her naïve. That would be safer for both of them. Besides, she had already been through so much anguish it would be unfair to put her through more. Thinking about her in this way, Nathaniel realised that he really did love her.

As he had done years ago, Nathaniel wrote down his goals on a beermat:

> INTERIM PLAN:
> 1. WOO ROSEMARY AGAIN
> 2. GET CLOSER TO SILVERSMITH
> 3. DEVELOP STRATEGY—FIRST GET MARY ON BOARD—IF CAN'T CONVINCE HER THEN WHO CAN BE CONVINCED!?

—

Nathaniel paid the bill, and pocketed the mat. As he was rising from his seat something made him pick up the broken swizzle stick: it was a symbol of…something. He drove back to HDI headquarters, mulling over his multiple challenge. Rosemary was his wife. He saw her every day. He must tackle her first. How to re-seduce her, then? He needed to do something dramatic, romantic, and therefore necessarily out of the ordinary. For a long time, apart from their brief abduction, their lives had been nothing but champagne and caviar, glamour and glitz, so it was no good attempting to buy her with expensive luxuries. It needed humour and ingenuity.

Rosemary was idly leafing through fashion catalogues and wondering whether she could be bothered going to the spring collections, when she heard Nathaniel's car roll up. It was not like him to come home early, especially not lately. Had he forgotten something? Nathaniel opened the door more briskly than usual, and his footsteps were more urgent, and there he was!

Nathaniel heaved the coffee table away from the astounded Rosemary, her glossy catalogues flying. He fell to his knees on the plush child-laboured carpet, grasping her silk skirt. "Rosemary, O Love of My Life, how can you forgive me for my neglect of your lovely person? I have been a poor husband indeed, but I beg your pardon, and resolve henceforth to love you as you deserve!"

Rosemary was predictably astounded, and only managed to gape, a sort of half smile.

Nathaniel continued, "As a symbol of our return to the simple truths, the simple pleasures, I invite you to picnic with me!"

Rosemary found herself seated on a tartan non-child-laboured rug in the back garden, drinking cheap cider direct from a bottle, munching marmite and peanut butter sandwiches, and listening to "Passion Proliferates Where My Rosemary Perambulates" played on a tinny little portable record player. More importantly, she found herself giggling as she hadn't done since her adolescence. Presently they were rolling in a happy tangle. They were in love once more, and it was wonderful.

The next day Nathaniel brought Rosemary breakfast in bed before kissing her goodbye and heading back to HDI, exhilarated and looking forward to his day as he hadn't for a long time.

At the office his new energy and brightness were noticed, and returned smiles snowballed his good humour. A flirtatious exchange with Silversmith's secretary bore the fruit of an appointment with the great man, and, for once, Nathaniel's impetus was such as to assure him of the upper hand in the interview that followed.

"Tyrone," he began, "I'm going to come clean with you. I'm bored. I'm tired of interviews and travelling. I no longer find the science side of things fulfilling either. Now, I know that this might seem like temerity to you, but my mind has been straying to the bigger picture. As I understand it, if we pull off the merger with Zen-Buddhica we become the largest cosmetics and pharmaceuticals company in the world, and I cannot help but think what that will mean…."

Just as Nathaniel had thought, Tyrone, very anxious to keep one of the company's most important assets on board, was only too happy to introduce him to the darker side.

Now he had to devise a means of winning Mary over.

CHAPTER TWENTY-THREE
Making Mary an Insider

It is not easy to describe a comprehensive world view in a few pages, yet Nathaniel understood that this was more or less what he had to do for Mary. He had already annoyed her, and she was a busy woman with a lot on her mind, so what he wrote for her had to be gripping, succinct and accurate. At all costs not insulting or condescending. But how, without offending, could you tell someone that what she had been thinking of as self-evident truths were nothing but lies fed to her by a sophisticated propaganda machine? The phrasing would have to be very diplomatic, unless....Yes, that was a possibility: he could talk about his unease, and what had happened to him emotionally. In that way Mary would perceive no attack. As an old friend, the least she could do would be to show that she cared about his well-being. In fact, he could even phrase it as a request for support, for help. Another idea, perhaps complementary, came to him. What if he asked her to answer a few questions "that he had been asking himself," in order "to put his mind at rest," to "confirm that his fears were simply that, unjustified and irrational fears"? And the best part of it was that this would also be the truth!

Over the next few weeks Nathaniel drafted and re-drafted the letter that was later to be recognised as the first concrete step in the formation of the Hope-ist Movement. Most readers will be familiar with at least some of the text (which gave us the mid-21st century phrase "a Dear Mary letter," meaning a cleverly worded letter with a hidden agenda), but it is included here for completeness:

HDI, Surrey

9 January 199-

Dear Mary

First of all, let me apologise for troubling you the other day. I do appreciate the time you took out of your busy schedule to see me. You were right to be impatient with me—I was not as coherent as I might have been. I hope that this letter will go some way towards explaining my strange behaviour.

I have always admired your ability to see below the surface of things, to see to the heart of the matter in question. I need to call on this perspicacity to help me out of the hole of depression into which I appear to have fallen. Perhaps "fallen" is the wrong word, because, looking back, I have probably been sinking for a long time. Now I have the sensation of waking to find myself in *reality* trapped in a black pit. I am hoping that you, the far-seeing and wise Mary of Inverdon beach, will be able to pinch me, and that I shall wake again, properly, to discover that it was all a nightmare.

"Nightmare" is apt, because you could say that my depression started with images. I'm not sure whether you are aware of my interest in Pre-Raphaelite art? Whenever I felt a bit stressed in Inverdon, and the POW was closed and you or Shelagh were not available, I would go to the art gallery, and lose myself in the paintings. Amongst the collection there are two by John Everett Millais (a founder of the Pre-Raphaelite brotherhood). They appear to be of the same sitter, a young girl. She is possibly nine or ten years old in the *The Convalescent* and two years older in *Bright Eyes*. She is beautiful, with long chestnut hair and big brown eyes looking calmly and appraisingly at the viewer. Her face has haunted me ever since I saw these pictures. As you know I am an atheist, but for years I could not escape the feeling that something or someone was trying to communicate with me through her.

I was only able to understand the "message" (for want of a better word) after I had stumbled across other works from the

Pre-Raphaelite era. You remember that I went to Paris recently for a conference? I'd just visited Prof. Podd in Followby to discuss our latest project, so I was flying from Manchester. I had a few hours to kill before catching the flight and I did what I normally do under such circumstances: I visited the art gallery. As in Inverdon, there were two paintings that particularly struck me.

One of the paintings was again by Millais. I saw that it pre-dated the Inverdon ones by some twenty years. *Autumn Leaves* (painted in 1856) shows four young girls (between the ages of eight and twelve?) standing around a pile of leaves which are about to be burnt. The two girls to the left could well be sisters, and are similar in appearance to Bright Eyes (her mother and aunt?), with long chestnut-brown hair and dark eyes. They are wearing full-skirted dark green striped dresses, obviously of some quality fabric, and are looking out of the canvas with the same serene gravity as Bright Eyes. The leftmost is holding a basket from which her slightly older sister has lifted a bundle of leaves which she is about to add to the already smouldering pile. The two girls to the right are less directly involved. They are shorter and younger and are not looking out of the canvas, but rather downwards, wistfully perhaps. The rearmost has short red hair, is wearing a dull red dress (faded?) and is clutching a broom. The little girl to the right is cradling an apple. Her wide-sleeved purple dress sets off a bright red neckerchief. There is something about the pose of these two on the right that suggests that it is not their place to participate directly in the bonfire.

The other painting that caught my eye is simply entitled *Work*. It was painted by Ford Madox Brown around the same time that Millais painted *Autumn Leaves*. It shows a cross-section of British society centred on a group of workmen digging a ditch. All the social strata are there—from the wealthy aristocrats on their horses to ragged orphans and a barefoot flower-seller—including Thomas Carlyle and F.D. Maurice, who are portrayed as well-to-do men leaning against a fence while presumably discussing the honest labour in front of them. The social significance of the painting is spelled out by the accompanying notice, but, to get some idea of its motivation, it suffices to know that Maurice founded a working men's college, and Brown, the artist, ran a soup kitchen.

You must be wondering what all this is leading to? Don't worry, all will be made clear! I need to add one further element to this story. As the world knows, I am an expert on the ageing process. What most people don't know is that some of my findings have been, at best, "under-publicized," and, at worst, "hushed up." I, myself, have been complicit in this. What no one except myself has known (up to now) is that my research has come very close to costing me my sanity. For a long time I suffered hallucinations, in which I saw people not as they were, but as they would be when they were older, but I'm not going to go into the ins and outs of this long story now. I want to confine my letter to the relationship between my under-publicized findings, my hallucinations and the paintings I have described.

The most striking finding to emerge from my Ph.D. was that the rate of ageing correlates better with socio-economic status than with anything else. A poor diet, bad hygiene, unhealthy housing, smoking and excessive drinking all accelerate the ageing process, certainly, and all these tend to be worse amongst the poor. However, even if these factors are taken into account they are insufficient to explain the rapid ageing and early death of the unemployed, the homeless and those who eke out an existence on slave wages. Poverty itself kills, beyond any of the things that go with it.

During my Ph.D. the beautiful Bright Eyes, whom I visited from time to time, withered in front of my eyes. I was nauseated by the hallucination. Recently, when I saw the Manchester paintings, the effect was similar, but because of the number of portraits on each canvas their differential ageing was clear. In *Work*, the ragged urchins in the foreground and the flower-seller were the first to crumple, Carlyle and Maurice the last, their youth marginally outlasting that of the wealthy riders. *Autumn Leaves* presented the spectacle of the tall and elegant dark-haired girls on the left maintaining their youthful posture and looks well beyond the ugly senility of the apple- and broom-holding ones. Their haughty regard suggested that they were barely aware of the existence of the two other girls/old women. Eventually they wrinkled and crumpled too. I couldn't stop myself from crying (embarrassing in a gallery, so I pretended I was suffering from some allergy). Now this may just be the product of a fevered and overworked brain, but you will at least understand the depth of my feeling and my motivation for taking things further.

It was a few days later, in Paris, that I chanced upon a book which had recently won an essay prize, entitled *L'horreur économique*. I started to read it, and suddenly everything fell into place: the message of Bright Eyes and Co. (of which I have related only the gist in this letter), the kidnapping (I do not want to put anything about this in writing), and even John Lennon's death. It was at this point then, that I experienced the feeling of waking to find myself in the bottom of the pit. What was worse, it seemed as if most of the world was in there with me, but unaware of their plight. The nightmare is summarized by the answers I have found to the questions that follow. I'd be very grateful if you could find the time to do a little bit of research, and independently try to answer them. I hope so much that you will be able to show me that I'm wrong, Mary, but, as far as I can tell, the pieces of the jigsaw fit to make a horrific whole.

1. What has happened to the income/wealth of the rich and the poor in the UK and in the world as a whole, over the last twenty or so years? (Define rich and poor as you will.)
2. What has happened to trade barriers and the taxes businesses pay in this period?
3. Is there a relationship between the number of jobs a

company loses or "outsources" and its performance in the stock market? How does the level of pay affect this?

4. What evidence is there that mergers and privatization benefit the public as a whole?

5. Who is the most powerful media baron in the UK? Of what country is he a citizen? How much tax does he pay and why? Is there any evidence of links between himself and politicians and "their" policies? And the second-most powerful?

6. Look at a range of British newspapers and follow them over several days. Categorize the leading articles and editorials according to their themes:

a) Blaming the rich and powerful for society's problems/ blaming the poor and weak

b) Talking about society's responsibility for correcting problems/talking about individual responsibility

c) Success stories of individuals

d) Other

See if you can find any link between who owns these papers and what they have to say.

7. What is happening to International Labour Organisation Conventions? For example, what is happening in the area of child labour?

8. What is happening to the independence of trade unions? For example, what is the significance of the European Confederation of Trade Unions?

9. What do the letters MAI stand for, and what are the implications of this secretly negotiated agreement?

10. Lastly, is there any pattern to all this? If so, who stands to gain from it and how?

If I am right, the really horrifying and amazing thing about all this is that all the information is theoretically accessible (that is, in the public domain) but that very few people appear to see the whole picture, and very few people want to. Why? There is a lot more I could tell you in person, but I don't want to commit too much to paper. If you want another suggestion, try dipping an investigative toe in the murky waters of multinationals. (Try oil companies and their dealings in the developing world—Colombia or Bangladesh for example!) I suggest we meet once you have had time to make some enquiries. I'll leave you to contact me. Let's hope that I'm wrong!

Love,
Nathaniel
xxx

P.S. You probably won't have time to answer all of these questions—even a couple will do!

On Saturday evening, nine days after posting the letter, Nathaniel received a phone call at home from Mary. Her voice was strangely tense. "Nathaniel. You may have a point. I think it'd be a good idea if we met. How about tomorrow?"

"I'd really prefer for it not to be tomorrow…." Nathaniel was exhilarated by this response, but managed to keep triumph out of his voice. Besides, he was not about to jeopardize his new-found domestic bliss by cancelling a picnic expedition with Rosemary.

"Well, there's a chance I could re-schedule a meeting on Tuesday afternoon. Would that suit?"

"Fine."

"I'll get back to you then."

They met for lunch in a country pub not far from HDI. Mary was almost unrecognisable from the condescending and irritable businesswoman of their previous encounter. She really seemed to need her gin and tonic. "Nathaniel, I owe you an apology. I've done a lot of learning and thinking since I received your letter. There's so much I want to say I hardly know where to begin…."

Nathaniel found it difficult to contain his relief and pleasure at Mary's change of demeanour. He was on the verge of tears. The old friend was back.

"How could I have been so stupid? I feel so guilty for so many things. Poor Shelagh, for one. I was so engrossed in the challenges of my work I didn't see what I was doing. Two hundred multinationals control everything, everything. Bear Mudrock controls our media—41% of the press by circulation for a start—and he's all but got a stranglehold on football. Tory Klaxon only got his massive majority because of his deal with Mudrock: no laws against media monopolies. Mudrock's papers rant on about the undeserving poor while he avoids paying tax because of his subsidiaries in island tax havens…'transfer pricing' and all that….Governments cut company tax because businesses can go anywhere, can pick and choose where they go, bribe their policies into implementation….The Multilateral Agreement on Investment amounts to stripping governments of any rights at all in their dealings with multinationals. The European Union's policies fall right into line via the Treaties of Amsterdam and Maastricht, pillaging—'privatising'—public assets and 'deregulating' basic rights out of existence to remove all obstacles to free trade and frenzied speculation. Even the International Labour Organisation is emasculating its stance against child labour, replacing Convention 138 with a much weaker one outlawing only the worst forms, again bowing to the multinationals….The concentration of wealth, linked to the worsening of poverty, is terrifying. And the whole thing is so unstable—I wouldn't be surprised if the so-called 'tiger' economies of southeast Asia collapse—they're built on a such a tenuous bubble of speculation—and then if Japan goes, and then the next big domino would be the USA! And, of course, you can completely write off all the poorer nations, and Russia's just a…a mafia-controlled nothing! I have been so blind!"

Nathaniel tried to calm her. He reached across the table and held her hands. "I know, I know. How do you think I felt when I realised what's been going on? Or what I've been part of?" He couldn't resist adding, "Or when you rebuffed me the other day? There's more, so much more, Mary….But we have to do something about it."

CHAPTER TWENTY-FOUR
Task One

Both nervous and exhilarated, she touched up her lipstick using the rearview mirror. She stepped out of the BMW, scarlet stilettos preceding elegant long legs. Turning to close the car door, her leather mini-skirt elicited a wolfwhistle from two passing lads. She stood erect and flicked her glossy hair over her shoulders, long chocolate nails contrasting with its blondness. The front view was at least as arousing: the way her skimpy lace-up top tautly presented her cleavage. She wore a blouson jacket over her shoulders, and held a tiny black clutch bag with gold clasps. A supermodel dressed to kill, and by the way she walked she knew it.

It would be a cliché to say that there was silence when she entered the King James. It would also not be true, for it was a big pub with several snugs and only some of the clientèle could see the door. Nonetheless there was "a kind of hush," as the Carpenters would have sung, and most men within eyeshot took advantage of this potential visual access. She stopped just inside the doorway, obviously looking round for someone, large blue eyes blinking. Apparently not seeing him or her, she made her way to the far side of the bar where she stood looking a bit distrait for a moment, before smiling at the barman and ordering a vodka and tonic. She poked the lemon around a bit with the swizzle stick held in her left hand, her little finger arched delicately. The stick's purpose served, she sucked the tip lingeringly. Her eyes drifted dreamily around the room as she laid it on the counter, her tongue playing on her glossy lips. In her line of sight now was a snug in which sat three men and a woman. She held the gaze of one of the men there.

Andy Richards and his colleagues always came here on Fridays. A few pints and then they might go to a nightclub. Liz wasn't too happy with the way the men were ogling the blonde, but she had chosen to be "one of the lads" (not that there had really been much choice). Consequently her only option now was to tease them a bit. At all costs she must not show herself to be jealous.

Andy stood up. "My round!"

"I wonder why, Andy?! You've never been so quick to claim a round before!" said Liz, to Fred and Alan's amusement.

Where at the bar Andy chose to station himself was no surprise. He turned to the blonde. "Would you like a dr—?"

She had extracted a cigarette from her bag and had turned towards him. "Do you have a l—?"

They laughed at the "coincidence." They were both thinking that they were off to a good start. Andy produced a lighter. She held his right hand steady with hers, looking into his eyes as she inhaled. "Thank you! Were you about to ask if I wanted a drink?"

Andy took some time to attract the attention of the barman. This was not unrelated to the fact that he and Lucille ("That's a pretty name…") were getting on rather well. He was jostled by someone pushing to the bar. It was Fred. "Bloody hell, Andy! A woman's a woman but a drink's a drink, man! Don't you trouble yourself, I'll get them!" Andy put on a stage expression of realised guilt, pulling down the corners of his mouth and raising his hands.

Lucille smiled.

Fred looked grudgingly over his shoulder as he made his way back to the snug, having been served almost immediately. Liz and Alan shook their heads knowingly. They had resigned themselves to not seeing much more of Andy that night.

"It's rather hot in here."

"Yes," said Andy. "Shall we find somewhere a bit cooler?"

"My car's just outside."

Lucille allowed Andy a snog before they embarked…and after. It was understood that they were going to her place. Andy had always been "one for the birds" but he had really hit it lucky this night, he was thinking.

What a babe! Between changing gears she was rubbing his thigh, teasingly reaching his groin. He did not notice the old Golf tailing them. In a dark little alley Lucille pulled her car to the side of the road, blue eyes wide with indecent suggestion: she couldn't even wait to get him back! She leaned towards him, lips parted, a finger stroking his cheek....

She screamed, opened her door and ran off into the night. Seemingly simultaneously Andy's door had been opened and a black-clad arm had encircled his neck. A hard object pressed into his throat. "One move, one squeak...!" Two balaclava'd men had opened the front doors. The one who was virtually strangling Andy spoke again, looking sideways at his companion, "How the f**k did you let her escape?"

"It's too bloody late now! Let's get the hell out of here!" The other one spat as he walked round the front of the car to Andy's door, briefly lifting the bottom of his balaclava to facilitate this expectoration, but his face remained hidden. The two of them pulled Andy from the front. He found himself lying on his side on the back seat, bound, gagged and blindfolded, the ever-present presumed gun indenting his temple. "Don't worry. You won't be hurt as long as you stay still and quiet. Listen to the message." Andy heard a cassette being inserted into the tape deck.

The journey must have taken half a day at least. They changed cars twice *en route*, possibly in a garage the first time, to judge by the echoes, and in a remote rural area the second time. Apart from when they stopped, loud music or "the message" was always blaring from the speakers so it was difficult to hear anything outside the vehicles.

The message, which Andy could recite verbatim for the rest of his life, was the following: "You have been kidnapped by The International Hope-ist Movement, for which we apologise. Provided you cooperate you will come to no harm. Our aim is not to spread terror, but to bring hope. In particular we aim to destroy the death grip of the multinational companies on the planet, and restore power to the man and woman in the street. While we detest the economic system, which some might call capitalist ultra- or neo-liberalism, we have no intention of physically harming anyone, even the richest and most powerful advocates of the system which makes the few rich richer and the many poor poorer. We repeat that it is this system that is our enemy, and your enemy too.

"You have been kidnapped because you work for *The Sin* newspaper, which is owned by Bear Mudrock. Mudrock is one of the principal beneficiaries and exponents of the prevailing economic order. Mudrock avoids paying tax, yet his newspapers lecture about the need for the poor to have their benefits squeezed. His British operations pay only about 2% tax, and his global operations only 7.3%. His annual profits are in the region of two billion US dollars. We will release you as soon as *The Sin* publishes the truth about Mudrock. We repeat that we mean you no harm." The voice was female and possessed of a neutral British accent, but sounded as if it had been distorted.

Andy's blindfold was removed. He was in a little sitting room equipped with a blue settee, two armchairs and a camp bed on which a sleeping bag lay folded. The two balaclava'd men were there, dressed entirely in black: gloves, sweatshirts, jogging pants and shoes. One of them spoke, in a rather stilted fashion: "We are sorry to have to do this to you. We hope you will be comfortable. You may sleep when you want but you will have a double guard around the clock. This building is in a remote rural area and no one will hear you if you shout. We brought you here on a roundabout route and we're sure we weren't followed. All the windows are barred and the exterior doors are triple-locked, there are ten of us here, and you cannot escape. If you want something to read there are some books on the shelf there. We will try to satisfy any reasonable requests you may have regarding food and drink. On your sleeping bag you will find a towel and a toothbrush. You may use the bathroom whenever you want, you have only to ask us, but you will only have five minutes' privacy at a time and you must leave the door slightly ajar. You will not be allowed into any other room. We will be happy to answer any questions you might have about the Hope-ist Movement. We will not discuss anything else."

The first the public heard about it was on the Tuesday following the kidnapping. The media lapped it up. *The Sin* had had no choice but to publish. After all, the story had been given to the left-wing *Protector* as well, which had no compunction about printing the Hope-ists' statement. Indeed, it had itself previously revealed details of Mudrock's operations to its small and unfortunately passive readership. The beauty of the Hope-ists' action was that everything in their statement was factual. Mudrock could not sue or deny anything as he would have been torn to shreds by those media he did not own.

The Sin's front page read:

Sin man kidnapped by "Hope-ists"

On Monday morning *The Sin* received a video tape. On this tape the *Sin* journalist, Mr. Andrew Richards, claims to have been kidnapped. Following advice from the police we print a transcript of the tape, on which Mr. Richards reads a statement:

"This is Andrew Richards. I have been kidnapped by a group calling itself 'The International Hope-ist Movement.' They call themselves this because they aim to spread hope and not terror, particularly hope amongst the poor and the oppressed. I have been told that my life and health are not in danger, but I will not be released until the full contents of this tape have been printed.

"I have been kidnapped to draw *Sin* readers' attention to the hypocrisy of the *Sin*'s owner, Bear Mudrock. Mr. Mudrock, who is not a citizen of the UK, controls 41% of the British press. He is one of the most powerful international media barons. His newspapers are full of stories attacking the poor and weak, and blaming them for society's problems. Amongst other people blamed by Mr. Mudrock are single mothers, immigrants, asylum-seekers, the homeless and so-called 'dole-scroungers.'"

The story continued on the inside pages:

"None of this is justified. Studies have shown that immigrants are positive contributors to the economy, and asylum-seekers would be if they were allowed to work. Indeed, our population will soon be failing to replace itself and the UK is already short of the skilled labour these people could provide.

"Mr. Mudrock's lies divert attention from the real cause of society's problems, which is the excessive greed of the very rich, the multinational organisations which control everything, and the international economic system they have designed and which makes this inevitable. As a result of their actions the last few years have seen a great widening of the gap between the rich few, and the many poor.

"A good example of Mr. Mudrock's wickedness was his recent attack on the *Beggar, Shoo!*, a paper sold by the homeless. His story about a vendor earning thousands of pounds was false. Yet because of it hundreds of innocent vendors were assaulted and thousands lost sales—the money they need to survive.

"The sole aim of Mr. Mudrock is to make the rich (himself) richer and the poor poorer. He wants taxes for the rich to be lowered. The best way to do this, he thinks, is to label as many people as possible as undeserving. He wants them to be excluded from society, so that the rich will not have to pay for them.

"Not only does Mr. Mudrock sponsor political parties which promise low taxes for the rich, but he also avoids paying tax by clever paperwork, and by using his subsidiary companies in the Virgin Islands, the Cayman Islands and the Netherlands Antilles.

"Mr. Mudrock only pays 2% tax on his British profits, and less than 8% on his international profits. His total profits are about one billion pounds a year, that is nearly three million pounds a day, 114 thousand pounds an hour, £1,900 a minute or £32 a second, and yet he avoids paying tax! In whisky terms, that's a litre of top quality single malt a second, or an elephant's weight of it every hour. If you converted the whisky into elephants and stood them in a line, within a year the line of elephants would reach all the way from London to Hull, half the length of England. Think of the traffic jams! Despite this, Mr. Mudrock pays almost no tax.

"Mr. Mudrock 'earns' nearly as much every second of his

existence as people on the dole receive every week, and yet he pays virtually no tax. His total profits would pay 100,000 people an annual salary of 10,000 pounds, and yet he pays hardly any tax. Every year his profits could make 1,000 millionaires, yet he doesn't pay tax.

"People who sew T-shirts for Malt Dizzy Corporation would have to work for 160 hours to earn what Mr. Mudrock earns in a second. Think of it: there are people who would have to work ten sixteen-hour days—and they do—in order to earn what Mr. Mudrock earns in one second.... Yet he avoids paying tax.

"How many lotteries would you have to win to get what Mr. Mudrock makes in a week? What do you earn? How much tax do you pay? It is easy to see that Mr. Mudrock is a crook. How can he possibly want or use all that money for himself? Shameful is too weak a word. Let us hope that he sees the error of his ways and pays the British people, and the people of the world, what he has stolen from them, although he cannot bring back to life those who have died because of his lies of hatred, and the poverty he fosters.

"But let us suppose that none of this impresses you, that your only interest is football. Well then, just look at what Mr. Mudrock is doing there: he is about to take over the biggest and most successful football club in the country and take total control of the television coverage of the sport. What do you think will happen to the cost of viewing football? What will happen to the game you love?

"In summary, whatever your interests you can be sure that Mr. Mudrock is harming them. We believe that after taking all this into account, you will decide to make this the last copy of The Sin that you buy until Mr. Mudrock changes his policies. Also we think that you will decide not to buy other Mudrock papers: The Crimes, The Sunday Crimes, Distort on Sunday....There are other papers available. Try them. Additionally we ask you to contribute to the Ex-Mudrock Employees Support Fund, which we shall soon be setting up, as his papers will fail. We must help his employees find new jobs. They are not to blame for The Sin and the sins of their employer."

Then the subject broadened:

"This kidnapping is only the first of many actions which the Hope-ists will undertake throughout the world. You, the people, are Hope-ists too. We aim to take power away from the very few in charge of multinational companies, and therefore in charge of the planet, and give it back to the many. You should not be doing without social services or paying more tax so that they can get away with paying almost nothing. They should not be controlling you. You should be controlling them. You can and you will!

"Our only weapon is truth, and the refusal to buy what they are trying to sell you, the refusal to believe their lies. We, the Hope-ists, aim never to hurt anyone physically, even the deluded super-rich, who, in their own ways are victims of the economic system. Can men as greedy, as selfish, as Mudrock be happy? What does it mean to be a human being?

"Soon we will reveal our next major international target, and you—all of you—will be able to help us change the world for the better. But you can start now. Remember even if all you do is buy one fewer copy of *The Sin*, you are helping, you are already a Hope-ist, and you have stood up against evil. We thank you. The whole world thanks you.

"Finally, please check everything we say. *The Sin*'s words do not stand up to investigation. Ours do."

"Amazing. We planned everything to the last detail, I know, but somehow I never quite believed we'd pull it off!"

"You know the bit I'm proudest of? The takeaway curry wrappers from Margate in the background! I have to say I think that was a masterstroke!"

"Not just the idea of it, though, but the execution of it: the way Stephen pretended to discover that the packaging had been left in shot after the video had been sent off, and his row with Eddie about it...."

"And the police are now scouring Kent...." Mary's words dissolved into laughter.

The first action of the Hope-ists had succeeded. Nathaniel's first biography, a film released fifteen years later, featured an interview with Nathaniel conducted by none other than Andy the erstwhile kidnap victim:

"...What was to become Task One of the British Section must go down as one of our proudest achievements. It is true that later actions were more dramatic, but you have to remember that this was the first action our embryonic movement had taken anywhere. If it had failed the movement would probably have been aborted, so there was a lot riding on its success. We were certainly very keyed up.

"Our reason for choosing the media as a target was simple. If we had chosen anything else then we would probably have been subjected to an avalanche of negative propaganda, which would have buried us. If we wanted to defeat our enemy then we needed to disable his most effective weapons first. My reading of Machiavelli's *Prince* greatly influenced the strategy. Mudrock was the greatest offender so we had to take him out. We had no real choice.

"Why we chose you specifically, Andrew? Well, it had to be someone who worked for *The Sin*. With its massive circulation and mix of reactionary propaganda and mind-numbing cr*p—not to put too fine a point on it, and I'm sorry if I'm offending you, Andy—it had to be *The Sin*, so we staked out the offices for a while, tailed a few reporters. I hope you don't mind my saying so, but your predictability and, shall we say, 'Don Juan tendencies,' marked you out as an easy target.

"So, anyway, we wanted to put several layers of...um, deception into our kidnapping, to be 100% sure that we couldn't be caught. Mary, with brown eyes and black hair, became, with the help of articles purchased by Hope-ists in Scotland, a blue-eyed blonde. A non-smoker since undergraduate days, in preparation for that evening she took up smoking again. We rehearsed the kidnap event itself until it was second nature, and it certainly worked, because you believed that Mary—sorry 'Lucille'—had only just escaped kidnapping herself!

"Her car was hired in Doncaster by a contact there, its plates were immediately changed and it was driven to London where the plates were changed again. Once you'd been transferred from the car yet again its plates were changed and it was driven back to Doncaster, the milometer was reset so that it appeared that it could not have gone as far as London, and the original plates were replaced. It was returned to the car hire firm within twenty-four hours. The other cars used had similar stories. The police never traced any of them, despite a couple being picked out later on motorway video cameras.

"We held you in a cottage in the Peak District, but we decided to make you think that you had been taken to Kent. I'm sure you remember when Stephen 'accidentally' switched on the 'local radio station' and you heard the Radio Invicta jingle from Kent? That was a tape recording. When we practised that Eddie kept laughing when he was supposed to be scolding Stephen for switching the thing on, but, as you know, he got it right in the end!

"Mary gets the credit for the takeaway idea. We had a contact buy some curries in Margate and send us the packaging. We bought you a curry in Sheffield, but repackaged it, after reheating it, so that you believed you were a stone's throw from a Margate curry house. And we made sure the bags were visible in the video shot. Yes, it was a brilliant idea, and when we released you, you did what we'd expected and confirmed the police's fixation on Kent!

"The most problematic bit was how to let you go once *The Sin* had done what we asked. This was the last thing we planned before we kidnapped you. We thought we'd drive you into the back-of-beyond somewhere, dump you by the side of the road, and then tell you in which direction to walk to find a car. The problem was we wanted an untraceable car, as you'd end up in possession of it. As with all good ideas it seemed ridiculously simple once we'd thought of it. We stole your car, which could not be reported missing by yourself, and would also serve to calm early fears about your disappearance….We knew enough about you to know that your colleagues would simply put two and two together and think that you'd struck it lucky with 'Lucille' and had gone off for a long weekend with her! I'm afraid we made some bad jokes about a 'loose heel' having gone off with Lucille! Of course we were right, that's exactly what they did think! So anyway, when we released you we blindfolded you and bundled you back into your own car and drove you hundreds of miles north into the wilds of Caithness. We removed your blindfold, turfed you out and told you where we'd be leaving the car, a mile down the road. By the time you'd reached it we'd long since transferred to another, and you made your way back to civilisation…."

[Transcript from *Changing Faces, the Papulous Saga*, printed by kind permission of International Conscience Digital Resources Cooperative.]

CHAPTER TWENTY-FIVE
Transport of Daylight Robbery/ Transports of Delight

Once Mary had been convinced of the dire state of the world and its cause, or rather had convinced herself, and Nathaniel could talk to her again on the basis of equality and friendship, it became a matter of organisation:

"If we're going to get people to join us we need a clear plan. If we run with *The Sin* idea, then as a minimum kick-off team we need enough people for that. After that it'll be a lot easier. Our blooded recruits can build their own cells, and more people will want to join us. At a rough estimate we'll need...what, ten people at least? So how do we recruit them?"

"Well, I know someone we could count on right away...."

"Shelagh! Yes, a contact in Scotland. Good."

Shelagh was staring, unseeing, through her window. It was raining. The dead flowers on the sill framed the bottom of her view of the drab grey Tillygrime district of Inverdon. They were a treat she'd allowed herself on dole-payment day. Now their withered remnants mocked her earlier attempt at self-upliftment. She could hear fighting again next door, and the bairn wailing.

Dirty dishes stood in the basin, congealed tomato sauce from a tin of Steptoe Supersavers baked beans putting up a good resistance against the unsoftened water. She had already flushed the bottle of washing-up liquid twice; there was no more lather to be had from it. She couldn't afford a new bottle, not even the weak economy stuff, or "false economy" stuff as her mother had glibly called it in her childhood: "This one may seem more expensive, darling, but it goes so much further." Well, Shelagh didn't have the money to buy the "false economy" version, far less what was cheapest in the long run, and she had too much pride to live off her parents. Just to get by until the mythical job came along…ha!

There was still a little knob of soap left in the bathroom, though. She sighed and went to fetch it, her threadbare slippers flapping on the equally worn carpet. The patch of mould on the bathroom wall seemed to have grown—the outline reminiscent of a head in profile, an old woman with sad lips caved in over toothless gums. Her only friend and her future! The impotence, the meaninglessness of it all.

The soap slipped from her fingers and disappeared behind the pipes below the bathroom sink. She reached down to find it, groping around half-heartedly and shuddering at the filth—where did it come from? A rat shot out. She screamed. It disappeared into the hallway. Shelagh's legs gave way. She sat on the edge of the cracked bath, her eyes clouded with tears, her throat on fire with the misery of her existence. It was a relief to cry.

In half an hour she had pulled herself together sufficiently to think straight. She at least had a ten-pence piece so she descended the litter-strewn stairwell, stinking of uncastrated tomcat piss and the vomit of drunks, and the urine of uncastrated drunks and the vomit of tomcats, and went to the nearest relatively un-vandalised phone box—an eight-minute walk through the rain. She dialled the council. She shivered, pulling her thin raincoat around her and trying to avoid the water dripping from the cracked roof as she waited for them to answer the phone. Was that snot someone had wiped on the mouthpiece? An unsympathetic voice announced that they would send someone round "in the next week." No, they couldn't say exactly when, but if she left a phone number….A phone number!

As she made her way back to her phoneless rathole of a flat, she saw that the postman was entering the building; more bills and rejection letters, she supposed. She wouldn't be receiving many more of the latter at least. She could no longer be bothered applying for jobs she knew she wouldn't get, but even if the effort had not been beyond her she couldn't afford the stamps—all of them emblazoned with the bloody queen so haughty and distant and stinking rich. And her mother was nearly a hundred years old and still in good health! Well, she was damned if she were a "loyal subject" of those parasites!

How quickly one's mood can change. Shelagh had never quite managed to extinguish that rush of hope when the mail arrived, but neither did she ever quite expect good news. Today, amongst the red pay-or-else bills there was a large white envelope from Nathaniel. She took it into her bedroom (which she had searched thoroughly for any evidence of rodents) and sat on the edge of her bed to read it.

The next morning—Saturday—a smartly dressed Shelagh was on the way to London. On opening the envelope she had rushed to deposit the generous "expenses" cheque before going shopping, the rat, the rain and the reigning monarch forgotten. After all, she had said to herself, if she were to be a link in their new Hope-ist Movement she needed to look presentable, and by the time her cheques went through Nathaniel's would have cleared. Totally justified. Now Mary wouldn't be the only one in cashmere and Chanel!

Arriving at Inverdon station by taxi with half an hour to spare, she decided to treat herself to a magazine—it had been years since she'd read a new one; her recent contact with such feminine ephemera had been with rather tatty versions in the launderette. A nice new crisp thick *Cosmo* to settle back with while she munched her piping hot BLT sandwich and sipped her filter coffee, and the world rushed smoothly by...marvellous! (Never mind that these would cost what normally sustained her for three days.) A new glossy, a good meal and old friends who needed her—luxury indeed!

As she was leaving the station shop a crackly announcement over the PA caught her attention—had she heard something about the train to

King's Cross? The notice board confirmed it—the stage from Inverdon to Dundee had been cancelled due to works on the line. There would be buses laid on, the first one would be leaving shortly.

Not especially pleased, Shelagh handed her fortunately light suitcase to the old and frail-looking bus driver to deposit in the luggage bay and found herself a window seat. A rather vacant-looking youth wearing the currently *de rigueur* Yike slave-laboured-but-exorbitantly-priced pseudo sportsgear sat next to her and immediately started beeping away on his pocket computer game, occasionally pausing to sniff, clear his throat and cough obnoxiously. Shelagh reflected that reading in a bus always made her travelsick, so that diversion was out. It was going to be a long journey. At least she would really enjoy her BLT and coffee and *Cosmo* when she eventually got on the train. Hunger was the best sauce, they said. What was that song about going to Dundee? Something like, "If ye'll permit me tae gang a wee bittie, I'll show you the road and the miles tae Dundee…."

A few miles down "the road and the miles to Dundee" the beeping of the computer game was joined by the hishtikka-hishtikka-hishtikka of the slave-labour supporter's Walkman. And someone was talking on a mobile phone. At least the weather was pleasant today, unlike in the song: "Cauld winter was howling o'er muir and o'er mountain…."

Distracting her from her distractions, the bus slowed and then swung alarmingly into a narrow country road. Ah, yes, of course—Shelagh hadn't thought about it, but the bus was going to have to stop at all the intermediate stations on the way to Dundee. Well, this would be of some interest as she wasn't familiar with all the by-ways.

Neither, it turned out, was the bus driver. On the approach to Montrose he pulled over to the side of the road to hail a dog-walker. The poor man jumped at the bus driver's quavery but loud voice. "I'm sorry. Can you tell me the way to the station?" Shelagh exchanged glances with other passengers, with the exception of the slave-labour supporter still lost in hishtikka-beep-beep world. Christ, at this rate they wouldn't be in London before nightfall! Couldn't they find a bus driver who knew the route, or couldn't the newly privatised Greater Railways Eastern Ecosse Division (GREED), part of the Ann Gloat and Brian Zooturd transport cartel (famous amongst grateful shareholders for making a fortune out of destroying Britain's long-distance coach services), find the funds after their donation to the Caledonia Liberation Action Party and Zooturd's championing of anti-homosexual causes? You'd think that with the massive profits they'd made from buying the business at way below market value from the last government, and all the redundancies and cutbacks that had followed, they'd still have had plenty of money left over after the political bribes…and the shareholders had had their slice…and the management share options had been issued….*On second thought, perhaps not.* Shelagh sighed.

What had been seen at the time as a probably isolated and most certainly amusing little event—a bus driver having to stop and ask his way, almost worth experiencing for the pleasure of relating the anecdote later—turned out to be part of a pattern. The bus driver really did not have a clue. Increasingly jittery as he sensed his passengers' disquiet, he had to ask three bemused pedestrians and one car driver before locating Arbroath station. Even then he sailed past the entrance on the wrong side of the dual-lane carriageway. He was going to have to attempt a U-turn….

CRASH! Shelagh saw the whole thing happen as if in slow motion. The length of the bus had obliged the driver to approach the break in the middle of the carriageway from the far lane in order to have enough room for a 180-degree turn. He had been late to signal this unorthodox manoeuvre, and a car had come up fast in the inside lane, the driver intent on passing, not realising the bus was about to cut across its path. Both drivers had braked too late and the car had ploughed into the side of the bus directly below Shelagh's window. Now what?

Fortunately—although the car would have needed surgery of heroic Papulousian extent if restoration rather than scrapping had been required—no one was seriously injured, and the bus was only slightly dented. The police arrived promptly and took a statement from the shrivelled and trembling little bus driver. As he sucked desperately on his much-needed fag and, eyes downcast, suffered the imprecations of the irate and bruised young couple who'd been in the speeding Toyota, it was difficult not to feel sorry for him. He looked seventy, but he was probably just coming up to retirement age. Fancy ending his working life like this, with both a bang and a whimper! Shelagh could imagine him being woken by a crack-of-dawn phone call, having already worked a full week (and having enjoyed a deserved—not to say essential—end-of-week drink with his friends), then being ordered to drive this unfamiliar route. "Flexibility" was the thing, after all—the watchword of Tory Klaxon and Brave New Labour—good for shareholders and good for business contributions to party funds....At least funds raised on the strength of this was what had bankrolled their last election success, but now it looked as if CLAP might win in Scotland, and so it was their turn to be suborned by businessmen with an eye for the main chance. Too bad Brave New Labour!

Then it was Shelagh's turn to make a statement to the police—she had been in a prime position to witness the whole thing. She couldn't but be honest, and explain that she thought there was fault on both sides, but she knew who the real culprits were....God, how important it was that the Hope-ists got their message across! But to do that she had to get to London, and to get to London she had to suffer her dependence on the likes of Gloat and Zooturd!

Statements taken, the car was towed away, and the bus driver allowed to drive on to Dundee. Shelagh didn't know whether to laugh or cry when he had to ask one of the passengers to help him find the station there too. Even she knew where that was.

At least they'd had the decency to hold the train, even if they were urged to hurry, hurry, run, run! Because of this delay, the train was crowded with passengers who'd turned up a bit early for the next one. Nonetheless, Shelagh's reserved seat was there waiting for her— something had gone right! It was only when she caught sight of a face she vaguely knew from Inverdon, a face which hadn't been on her bus and which was now sound asleep, that she realised with some bitterness that if she'd caught one of the later buses she would have arrived much earlier. Not only had these had accident-free journeys, but they had also not made the tour of all the little stations between Inverdon and Dundee! Why hadn't anyone bothered to mention this option at Inverdon!? "You tak the high road and I'll tak the low road..." *and you'll bloody well be in Dundee an hour before me!*

At last she was ensconced in her seat. Her breathing settled. High time for coffee, *Cosmo* and BLT! Back from the buffet car, she cracked open her magazine and gloried in the fresh feel and smell of it. Skeletal models were still "in" apparently—she'd heard it called "heroin chic." *Cosmo*, of course, wouldn't dream of promoting such a thing, and skeletal Catherine Marsh (their cover model this month) apparently pigged out four times a day....Now what did the horoscope have to say about the best day to lose weight and eat chocolate while having multiple orgasms with your best friend's boyfriend without damaging the friendship? Sharing Shelagh's table was a young mother and two squabbling brats, but after the horrors of the bus journey, she and her *Cosmo* could just about cope with the train.

Five hours later she wasn't so sure. A rumoured derailment between Berwick and Newcastle (not her train) had set things back a further two hours. The unseasonal warm weather that day would have been cheering had the train's air-conditioning been functional. An announcement told them that it was "only carriages four and five" which were affected and that passengers could move should they wish. The truth was that the air-conditioning in carriage six was also inoperative, and the train was so overcrowded that no one could move anywhere.

Shelagh looked for a blind to pull down, or a window to open. There were no blinds. All the windows were sealed. "Hot" was an inadequate adjective. In the buffet car, the takings of the sweating attendant were breaking all records as he doled out overpriced soft drinks. Looking at the list, after her marathon struggle through ill-tempered masses to get there, Shelagh was damned if she would further increase the profits of the despicable bastards who ran(sacked) this business! Not only were they apparently saving money by cutting back on maintenance work, but the drink sales from the buffet car further boosted the profit margin...and there went the steward again: "Ladies and gentleman, we apologise for the delay and the breakdown of the air-conditioning. The buffet car, situated towards the rear of the train, offers a wide range of cold drinks as well as a variety of hot and cold snacks and sandwiches."

She would drink some water in the toilet. A twenty-four-minute wait in the queue at last rewarded her with access to this privileged private space. It was, of course, disgusting. There was no toilet paper—it appeared to be fully employed blocking the overflowing WC—and the water tap was labelled "Unfit for drinking." Another notice helpfully requested that any problems should be reported. Fat lot of good that would do!

Dehydrated and defeated, Shelagh returned to the lengthening buffet car queue. She must drink, whatever the price. She bought several bottles of water and a couple of orange juices. Her travelling companion— haggard, straggle-haired and red-faced with the heat and with the strain of pacifying the wretched products of her reproductive instincts— beamed huge gratitude at her when Shelagh donated a couple of the hard-won libations. The parent's pleasure was short-lived as the brats proceeded to dispute their ownership of the precious liquid. Would this journey ever end? Did London—O hallowed city with streets paved in gold—really exist?

It was at Newcastle that things really deteriorated. Barely had her sigh of relief at the departure of the quarrelsome family left her lips than an almighty racket reached her ears: drunken male voices singing…"Eskimo Nel"!? Before she knew what was happening she was trapped by a posse of what turned out to be stag-night attendees, largely Australians and New Zealanders on the way back to their jobs in London after a twenty-four-hour jaunt in Newcastle. "Hiya, babe! You're not bad-looking you know! You could do with bigger tits, though!" They laughed. What could she do? The train was packed, there was nowhere to go.

"Here, doll, have a drink!" One of them had a bottle of tequila, a bottle of Coke and a shot glass. He splashed a generous measure of the former onto the table, managing somehow to retain a sample of it in the shot glass. A similar process saw some Coke join the tequila. He rapped the glass on the table. "There ya go, sport! Knock it back!" Shelagh didn't have much choice. If she didn't appear to be a "sport" things might turn very unpleasant. She knocked it back…and forced herself to smile. What more could happen?

"That's-a-girl! Now give us a smile and have another! Say what's your name?"

Their laughter upon hearing it ("Hey this sheila's called Shelagh!") ceded to another loud drinking song.…

Amazingly the train did eventually pull into King's Cross. Woozy and headachey, and sticky with spilt Coke and tequila, Shelagh waited in the taxi queue, just managing to force a smile in reply to a wave from the antipodean crew piling into a pub across the road. What a relief it was to get out of that train! Thank goodness Mary had booked a hotel.

The *en suite* bathroom with the wonderful hot shower and the crisp white towels, the thick pile carpet, the smug hum of air-conditioning…all these restored her spirits considerably. A couple of aspirins washed down by a fresh orange juice (and it was!) delivered by a prompt and smiling room service almost completed the recovery process. A good night's sleep and she'd be entirely rehabilitated, but first to phone Nathaniel and Mary.

Sunday morning was wet and windy. A Burberry-coated and cashmere-sweatered Shelagh breezed out of the hotel, the girlish etiolated nature of her elfin features strangely emphasized by the smartness of her new clothes and by the way she'd tied her freshly hairdressered hair back. She was intent on keeping her shiny new calf-length boots out of the puddles and divided her attention between this and avoiding other people's umbrellas with her own. So it was that she walked smack into a dark young man clutching a camera. He too had not been keeping a good look out. He'd been tracking a young woman on the pavement on the far side of the road. The collision brought them both up short.

The study of feminine appeal through the ages—fashions, "in" people, "looks," body shapes and weights, lips, hips, eyebrows and their various modifications and modes of presentation—is fascinating. One theory is that the way women are portrayed, or present themselves, reflects the status and needs of contemporary men.

The apparent exception of the flapper phenomenon of the 1920s, in which women bound their breasts (thereby assuming a more masculine conformation) and simultaneously became more assertive and extrovert in their public behaviour, is interesting. The dearth of young men in the wake of the Great War meant a relative abundance of women and femininity. What better way to balance society than to masculinize women?

By the end of the 20th century the glorious domination of "market forces" over compassion, humanity and commonsense had undercut the role of the labouring man. In the UK, coal mining, ship building, heavy manufacturing and the like had virtually disappeared. The few areas of traditionally male and working-class employment remaining had been deregulated to the extent that those working in them had no quality of life, being virtually on twenty-four-hour standby for miserable little sub-contracted and non-union-represented scraps of high-pressure unpleasant work. Women on the other hand—less aggressive and with better communication skills—were ideally suited to the abundant "information age" posts. They were not well paid and the hours were cruel, but at least they could find steady-ish employment, clamped into their telephone headsets or metaphorically chained to their keyboards.

Unsurprisingly, the psychological and physical health of men suffered. By the mid 1990s studies had shown that the blood-testosterone level of football supporters rose and fell in line with their team's success. While some drug companies in the late 20th century (including HDI) were racing to find a male contraceptive (yet another "symbol of female empowerment"), ironically there was also widespread concern about falling sperm counts. Numerous theories did the rounds, most of which related to oestrogen-like pollutants in the environment, some of which related to the wearing of tight undergarments. It was only in the aftermath of the International Hope-ist Revolution that the real and obvious explanation became widely acknowledged: the lack of a decent job, and thus of a perceived valued role in society, was even more devastating to one's reproductive soundness than one's team conceding a home game. The tragedy was that any zoologist familiar with the link between status in the hierarchy, stress and reproductive success in social mammals would have been able to have enlightened and warned the apparently baffled medical community decades earlier. They did not seem to want to listen. Could this have had anything to do with the fact that drug companies and environmental pressure groups could see no way of profiting from such an explanation?

Be that as it may, men in the dying years of the millennium were in desperate need of re-asserting their remaining masculinity, feeble though this was. There were no more river sources to find, and only the craziest artificial and bizarre "firsts" ("the first blind diabetic paraplegic to climb Everest single-handed and without oxygen..."). The media images of women at this time accurately reflected this male need. Healthy, happy, well-built, strong and assertive women (acceptable, with shoulder pads, in overconfident yuppie circles of the 1980s) would have been intolerable to the average male of the 1990s. Images of such women would have screamed: "You're not man enough for a real woman like me, you miserable little failure! Not only do I earn more than you, but I am highly fertile and I have an enormous libido. You can't fulfil my sexual needs!" No, the images required were of frail, gaunt and abject femininity, forever cowed, easily dominated....It so happens that the body-mass index of slim women is highly correlated with their fertility (and also, therefore, with libido). The sexual appetites of seriously undernourished women therefore posed no threat to the egos of broken men.

So what about breast size? Confused and stressed masculinity did often desire large-breasted women, but whether mammarily well-endowed or not, the rest of the body had to be marasmic, and therefore easily dominated, infertile and sexually unthreatening. The problem was that emaciation does not predispose to breast development. QED, then, the appeal of the silicone-breasted stick model. (The lesser known and more drastic alternative was to eat oneself obese, and then have liposuction performed everywhere except on one's bosom.) In many ways the silicone sylph was the ideal woman for turn-of-the-century man: not only was she unthreatening because of her general thinness, but

243

she had demonstrated her willingness to bow to the whims of masculinity to the extent of having her body mutilated. A woman like that was the ultimate trophy, the ultimate masturbatorial fantasy.

Correction. To make a woman like that, in all senses of the word, was the ultimate fantasy.

Ernest J. Clackworthy was wedded to his camera. Introduced to photography by a schoolfriend, he had abandoned other hobbies and interests shortly thereafter. He was one of the relatively less miserable few in that *fin de siècle* world as he knew what he was meant to do in life. Never mind that his chosen profession could be accused of distancing him from it (life, that is). Never mind that he was never able to detach himself from his mobile phone for fear of missing the next contract. He had an eye for it, as they say. He saw the world through a rectangular frame and that suited him. Well, almost.

Whatever else the tribulations of a professional photographer's life, it did offer the not inconsiderable compensation of frequent contact with pulchritudinous specimens of the opposite sex, even if this were, at least initially, with the interposition of a Penon, Nikpus, Olymon or Cantax. (No, don't be ridiculous! Of course there wasn't one called "Penus"!) There was always the hope that things would develop, so to speak.

Sunday morning found EJ, as he was professionally known, in paparazzo mode, long-lensed Nikpus dangling from his neck. Friendly interaction with his subject was not on the cards. There would be none of the sometimes sex-charged banter that went with a *Cosmo* shoot, for example. After the untimely death of the Princess of Dolpins, the gutter press (most of the press, in other words) had yet to decide on a single hot substitute, but the actress Lisa Beverley was as much in the running as Leanne Sentup and the rest of them, and there was usually a lot of running. The strange mutually dependent but seemingly often hostile relationship of "celebs" and journalists/paparazzi was discussed *ad nauseam* in the media following the princess' death. The art, from Lisa's point of view, consisted in always appearing to be trying to escape but never trying quite hard enough.

Sunday morning, therefore, found Lisa secretly/publicly on the way to a brunch liaison with the new "love of her life," the mysterious musician known only as Chemistry Navigator, recently signed to the Roar-Curse label, and much sought after by the media. EJ did not know whom Lisa was on her way to meet, but, having followed her often enough in the past, he could tell from her pseudo-furtiveness that a story was afoot. If he got the shots he'd be a few thousand quid to the good. He was acting today on his own initiative.

The penetration of Cupid's arrow into the juvenile Nathaniel had probably been helped by the backfiring of the Taylors' station wagon through the intercession of the lubricant adrenalin. In the case of Shelagh and EJ, this ardour-enhancing catecholamine was triggered by the shock of impact. In EJ's case, the penetration of the missile was doubtless further aided by certain psychological factors pertaining to late 20th century masculinity.

CHAPTER TWENTY-SIX
Good Hair Days, Dreadlock'n'roll

These little islands in Rosemary's existence were important. Once a month or so, the opportunity to relax away from it all. The soothing touch of professionals, competent and calm. The gentle music. The murmur of their voices, the solid wholesome clunks as they put their instruments down. The order and method. The familiar scents which distilled the muted pleasure, permeated it, transcended it....The knowledge that one was at the centre, one was the focus, and yet not under pressure to do anything, be anything, say anything. Just to relax and keep still and take pleasure in the knowledge that one's beauty was being enhanced. Away from it all.

Away from the nest she was building. Strange. Why was that a relief? Was it because her instincts' heretofore hidden purpose was slowly unmasking itself? Was her body aching for children...again, and did she not want to admit this? It was true that she did not want to make herself vulnerable once more. Yes, it was true that the nest was complete, and she could no longer ignore its painful emptiness now she was without the diversion of acquiring more twigs. All the same, it was less painfully empty than it would be if more chicks were to perish.

What about love? Did she love him, and did he love her? She knew he was working hard, bringing in the money. (Up in Inverdon this week.) She accepted that their time together was limited, and that this was sufficient for him. And she had always known that his existence was a more abstract one than hers. He could lose himself in intellectual games, which is what his work amounted to. Funny, he effected to despise men who were interested in sport, but what was the difference when you came down to it? It was all an avoidance of…intimacy. That being so, could he ever really love her? Certainly he gave the appearance of loving her. Always a kind word, a "loving" touch. But there was something mechanical, planned about it. As if he were acting the role. Or was it her imagination? Did the problem lie within her? Had the loss of her family cauterised her? Were her suspicions merely the mind's way of preventing joy from crystallising, joy which could so quickly turn into pain?

Pain / *du pain*: pain was the bread of her existence. Maybe that was why she liked coming here. When the blood ran she could feel something…reliable. The local anaesthetic was never 100% effective. The physical pain was a distraction, a comfort. Just like the sugar of her clothes shopping and her superficial friendships with the likes of Trish. Rosemary realised with a laugh that she went for plastic surgery the way other women went to the hairdresser. And when she emerged—or rather when the minute stitches came out—her body had fewer scars. Every time, fewer scars. What would she do when the only scars left were the emotional ones?

But what was life, after all? It was a never-ending attempt to distract one's mind, to stop it going too far…from asking what the purpose was, because there was none. Terrible deprivations with no obvious escape pushed one towards suicide, of course, but so did the absence of even the least obstacle or problem: the mind should be employed in solving little problems, or drowned in love. The former was Nathaniel's apparent attempted solution. Rosemary understood that the latter had always been hers. Not exclusively, of course (nothing was ever that clear!) but largely. Now she felt she had nothing tangible. She was suffocating, suffering the *ennui* of Madame Bovary. What did she want?

Of course, there was always another way of looking at things. Forget the heavy analysis. Forget the *angst* and the *ennui*. (Foreign muck, after all!) Plain good old-fashioned Anglo-Saxon boredom had a lot to do with it. What could she expect after years of turmoil and adventure? She was used to it, and now she'd hit a calm patch in her life and its novelty had gone. Of course she was bored. She needed to get out more, a job, sport,

R. Eric Swanepoel

something, somewhere, somehow. A fresh start.

If she could only return to her girlhood and re-run her life, so as to avoid all the heartache, and open new pathways, new possibilities. Maybe she could at least recapture the spirit of those days. The happiest she'd felt for a long time had been when Nathaniel had surprised her with the picnic and the song from her girlhood—perhaps she could go through a sort of rebirth by dosing herself with music from those years. Maybe everything would seem new again. But where was she to get this music? She'd long since given away her record collection. Nathaniel only had "Passion Proliferates Where My Rosemary Perambulates," and there was a limit to how often one could listen to that.

Rosemary switched her computer on. As she waited for it to boot, she hitched up her skirt and distractedly examined the site of the latest scar-removal operation on her right thigh…*mmmn, not bad.* The computer stopped its whirring and the screen settled. She typed "seventies music" into the web search engine she'd chosen: Excite. That was what she needed after all, a bit of excitement. The dozens of responses amazed her—there were obviously many people out there who shared her interest. She would have to limit her search. She added the words "Surrey music shop" and hit the enter key again.

Wearing Sophia Loren sunglasses and a headscarf, Rosemary *incognito* Papulous walked down the basement stairs, pushed through the bead curtain and entered In The Groove Records. The patchouli incense hit her at the same time as the music of Satin Subterranean. This was her place, OK! A dreadlocked and nose-ringed male Caucasian of indeterminate age was sprawled in a fraying cane chair, his feet on the counter, nodding time to the music and puffing on a roll-up. "Hi!" He raised a hand slightly to accompany this minimal and informal salutation. The lighting, from a single bare bulb, was dim. As Rosemary's eyes adjusted she saw the narrow space was packed with trestle tables, each laden with splitting cardboard boxes stuffed with old records in tattered sleeves. Beneath the tables were more such boxes. In the corner a portable record player was Rude Lee-ing away: "…nothing was happening, b***er all, b***er all. Then one shiny dawn she tunes to an

248

NY station. Well, she couldn't credit what she heard—so cool! Commenced humming to that fab, fab music. See, she was redeemed by that pop and soul!"

Amen.

CHAPTER TWENTY-SEVEN
Mary, Mary, Quite Contrary

It wasn't exactly a state of cognitive dissonance—Mary's research had convinced her of the justice and urgency of the Hope-ist cause—it was just that the momentum of her job seemed to be carrying her in the opposite direction. Government funding for the arts (and for everything else) had long since been cut to the bone in the interests of complying with the Maastricht Treaty and meeting the convergence criteria for the single currency (even if the United Kingdom's entry into this was to supposed to be "decided on its merits when the time came"). Museum directors and the higher echelons of their staff were thus primarily occupied with fund-raising, there being a limit to the amount that could be indirectly extracted from the desperate poor by means of the lottery. As in the field of education, in practical terms this meant cosying up to big business and offering it one's premises and public as advertising territory in return for the wherewithal for survival. As there was so much competition for sponsorship from all the formerly public-funded institutions, the terms were not usually particularly favourable. One took what one could get and used every trick in the book to get more.

So it was that at the time Nathaniel was posting his fateful letter to her, Mary was sending invitations to company directors to come to a gala evening. The Victor Ear and Herb Alpert Museum was, under Mary's direction, about to prostitute itself, as if it hadn't done enough of that already.

Mary reasoned with herself: what better cover could there be for a founder of the Hope-ist Movement in the process of planning the first

Hope-ist action than her continued toadying of the business elite? Besides, she was responsible for the livelihoods of her staff, and, come to that, she needed to earn a living herself. And such hobnobbing with the wealthy and powerful would surely offer the opportunity of learning something useful, or possibly even of turning one or two of them? Matahari Mary or not, the show must go on. After all, Nathaniel was still working for HDI.

Most importantly, if what she and her staff had achieved were half as major a breakthrough as they imagined, this would be the last time they'd have to kowtow to anyone, and that might not even be necessary when the bigwigs saw what she had in store. Potentially she and her staff would never have to work again.

So, on the day that Shelagh was conducting an unpremeditated investigation of what privatisation had done to public transport, Mary was putting the final touches to the VE and HA Museum in preparation for that evening's *grande fête*. The staff were to act as guides and personal servants to the illustrious and potentially lucrative guests. Each had been assigned a particular magnate, these assignations signalled by their garb in the appropriate company colours, logos displayed boldly front and back. Roar-Curse Records, a very late addition to the list, had caused a bit of a panic, but Mary had solved the problem by buying some of this label's album covers, scanning them and transferring the images to large pieces of card, which she had then had fashioned into a suitable costume.

Apart from the usual superabundance of vintage champagne, caviar, etc., Mary had decided to give the expropriators of wealth personal demonstrations of what their "sponsorship" might buy them, and she had re-jigged all the displays to this end.

Despite all the artistic and creative frenzy (or right cerebral cortex stuff) that this "re-jigging" had entailed, she had not forgotten the baseline information crucial to advertising investment decisions. On huge display boards in the museum's foyer was a socio-economic and psychological breakdown of the public which the VE and HA could serve up. In this regard she had excelled herself, presenting not only a profile of the visitors in the last few months (such data culled from videotape analysis, interviews and questionnaires) but also the projected visitor profile, according to what steps she might take to advertise the VE and HA and the exhibits she might put on. These potential steps and exhibits were, of course, all costed. Statistical analysis notwithstanding, anyone could see that it was highly speculative, but at the very least it would have been an indication to the targeted plutocrats that they were dealing with a highly intelligent and resourceful woman, someone who would take their money seriously, and someone who could use both halves of her brain.

However, the real meat of the evening was not contained in the *vol-au-vents*, nor the visitor profiles, nor the displays, clever and attractive though they were. No, the real knockout stuff was on the computers, innocently sitting there, apparently normal in every respect.

Jim Mud, the managing director of Roar-Curse Records, was happy indeed to be going to the VE and HA. Two days previously he had being analysing his group's sales and had come to the conclusion that a recent entrant into the music business was making inroads into his market share. What was especially strange and sinister was that his apparent opposition's style could not have been further from that of Roar-Curse. What on earth was turning a significant proportion of his customer base—lovers of your basic raunchy, rough-and-ready, gut-wrenching, heavily blues-influenced garage rock'n'roll—into admirers of insipid spiritless drivel!? The Internet informed him that the Bland Band label had its origin in the VE and HA, and its CEO was none other than the director of that museum: Mary Mackenzie. Jim had not lost much time in phoning this mysterious competitor and arranging a meeting. He trusted his instincts to be able to derive some benefit from such an encounter.

As it happened, Mary had just been phoned by Grope Four, the big nightclub security group, and been told that their CEO would not be able to attend the party, as they were heavily involved in a legal case involving assaults committed by one of their subcontracted bouncers. (*Subcontracted or subhuman?* thought Mary.) On the spur of the moment, then, she had invited Jim Mud to come in Grope Four's stead. Given the shortage of time, she had not been able to do her usual extensive background research on Roar-Curse's corporate structure and history. All she'd had time to gloss before the party was the immediate story of Roar-Curse itself. She trusted her instincts to benefit from the encounter. And at least she would have some good news to give Mr. Mud.

Tyrone Silversmith was also pleased with his invitation. He knew Mary from Nathaniel and Rosemary's wedding, and had rather taken a shine to her at the time. Mary had not given him the impression of being wholly impervious to his charms either, but one could never really tell with these businesswoman types—if they weren't after your personal resources, they might be after your company's. Still, the wife wouldn't be going. Not least, he was looking forward to putting the enigmatic Ms. Mackenzie on the line a bit about the apparent correlation between the declining sales of HDI tranquillizers and the increasing popularity of— what did they call it?—"blandified" music. Not that a few thousand pounds lost here and there meant much to a company the size of HDI, but it would at least give him a teasing edge, that essential ingredient of seduction. And in any case, there would be other good points to the *soirée*: wine, cigars, good company of the old school tie sort, and possibly other totty. After all, it was his firm (a good word!) that had developed Priaptra, the new wonder drug for male impotence. If anyone had a right to benefit from it, it was himself!

Tactfully, Mary had chosen not to play any of her music that evening. She had decided to concentrate on the aural aspects of the Internet, or more specifically on how the skills of the museum staff in this rapidly developing area could be used to push a company's products. Once the guests had been provisioned with the first of many beverages, and the *canapés* had made a round, Mary commenced her introductory speech:

"Most of you will know of our founder's sad story and his interest in the human ear. All of you will be aware of the growing potential of the Internet as a tax-free haven for reaching markets, for conducting business. With ever-increasing bandwidths and baud rates, improved system architecture, and the international agreement to keep cyberspace tax-free for at least another year, the information superhighway connecting you with your clients has never been more accessible; it has never been cheaper.

"This potential is, however, a long way from being fully realised. As of yet, only 20% of the British public enjoys access to the Net. As of yet, the transmission of sounds via the Net is in its infancy: most Internet imagery has no aural accompaniment. Those sites that do, require that a specific request be made by the Internet user for the sound files to be downloaded and played. The software for doing this has, until now, failed to keep pace with the hardware, and the process is often slow and painful.

"Chat sites, however, are very popular, and the Internet is increasingly replacing the telephone. Yet with the longstanding acceptance of expert systems and with the voice analysis software available, we at the VE and HA had the feeling that there was a lot more that could be done. This evening we would like to show you what that is. Your guides will take you to your terminals.

"Before you disperse I would ask you to look at the more conventional displays as well. These are, of course, real possibilities in terms of pushing your companies' products and services using our more conventional resources, but we think that after you have seen our computer demonstrations they will seem of rather secondary importance. They are not. Their purpose is to give you something to talk about to those who will expect you to report on this evening. What you see on the computers is of such import that we think you will want to keep it to yourselves. I wish neither to appear hubristic nor condescending but I believe it will take a while for the magnitude of it to sink in. You will probably not want to trust anyone with what you have seen until you've had time to think carefully. Thank you, and enjoy the evening."

Silversmith found himself guided to a private booth. He had been disappointed to discover that the HDI logo was displayed on the torso of a male staff member, and not on the bosom of one of the nubile cybernettes that most of the other captains of industry seemed to have landed. Still, his intellectual curiosity had been whetted by Mary's portentous speech, hype though it almost certainly was, and one must take the rough with the smooth, after all: his guide seemed personable enough, and there would be an opportunity to meet the women later.

The wrong-gendered one requested him to sit. In front of him was a computer. A Cyberbabble Web Browser Icon was the sole occupant of the screen. Familiar with Will Doors' InterWeb Voyager and its rival, NetScrape, he did not recognise the Cyberbabble symbol. So, they'd developed a new browser had they? Already this was interesting....*Come to think of it, they must have dispensed with Doors' eponymous operating systems as well! My, o my, o my!*

Mary's first instinct had been to approach Jim Mud immediately upon finishing her speech. He was the only one of her guests whom she had never met, and also the only one without a customised display awaiting him.

He had an engaging lopsided smile and a strange but not unpleasant accent: "Nice place you got here!"

"Yes, we do our best! Forgive my curiosity, but where do you come from?"

"Oh, I was born in Australia, but mainly grew up in the States. Now I live here. You know, to...uh...to get the British wing of my record business off the ground."

"Yes. How's it going?"

"Well, funny you should say that...."

Of course by accusing her of stealing his clients he was also paying her a compliment, and Mary's blush was not entirely one of shame. Mary explained the thinking behind blandification. As she was talking she was aware that the soma-like pacification of the masses by the means of blandified music hardly sat well with her developing Hope-ist outlook. Although highly self-aware and a gifted controller of body language, she could not quite dissimulate her unease, and Jim was fast on the uptake: "If you ask me, there's something not quite right about doing that to people...." It was not so much what he said, it was the way that he said it. It was obvious to Mary that he really didn't like the idea, and what's more, that he had divined that neither did she.

There was a lull in the conversation, a mutual appraisal. Mary was tempted to tell him more. She decided to take it slowly. "Yes, I'm not that…ahh…sure about it either. I have some good news to tell you in that line anyway…but, you know, it could be argued that to make people happier with their lot in life can't be entirely bad…."

Jim decided to be frank. "Sometimes, Miss—I assume it is Miss, or do you prefer Ms?—Mackenzie….Mary then, thank you! I think this whole business of making money stinks. And yet ostensibly that's why we're all here tonight. Philanthropic sponsorship of the arts, of public education, doesn't come into it."

Mary wasn't sure what to say—this guy didn't mince his words! Fortunately Jim continued. "You know, I was brought up in a family where money-making was everything. My father….Oh, I must stop myself, he's the last person I want to talk about….No. Let me just say that my father and I haven't always seen eye to eye. I disapprove of his politics and his…ah, shall we say, relative deficiency of scruples when it comes to business tactics. I often wonder about the consequences for society….Anyway, I dropped out of business school, and started mah own 'thang,' in James Brown-speak! It's done well—my business—and it kinda gave me some satisfaction when my father saw that and wanted me to come into his fold. He almost begged me, and I knew it was only because I was so profitable—nothing to do with paternal affection. The terms were OK. I get total freedom. I'm still in charge."

Mary thought there was something a bit pathetic, not to say desperate, about the way he had ended his little speech. Did he want her to acknowledge what a success Roar-Curse Records was…thanks to his genius? (It was true that it had been a clever and original idea to bring back vinyl and sell discounted Roar-Curse brand phonograms to the disenchanted ex-hippy market, but this was obviously an idea with an expiry date on it. That generation wouldn't live forever. And the other arm of the business, focussed on the younger market's taste for the rough stuff, no longer seemed to be a growth area either.) She was itching to ask who his powerful father was—"Mud" rang no bell—but she didn't want to offend him by bringing up this obviously touchy subject again.

Whatever else, it was clear that Jim wasn't "one of them," in the

Thatcherite sense. Dare she tell him about what she, Nathaniel and—
soon—Shelagh, were hatching? At the same time as this question was
taking shape in her mind she heard herself saying, "I have to say, I tend
to share your scruples about the way a lot of business is conducted, and
its consequences…and things seem to be getting worse. Do you know
about the Multilateral Agreement on Investments, for example? There
are some of us who—"

Mary stopped short. She'd better wait until she'd discussed it with the
other Hope-ists, and in any case it was time to do the rounds. "Sorry I'd
better stop myself there. I really could talk all evening but I'll have to
go….Lots of flesh to press, as they say. Listen, Jim, it's been great
meeting you! I'm glad you came, and I can give the good news that the
Bland Band label is winding up—we'll sell it to you cheap if you want the
assets. I think you'll understand why we're no longer interested in it when
you've seen what we've been working on. Felicity here will give you a
rundown. You may be interested…."

A fetching young lady swathed in Roar-Curse record sleeves put her
arm through his. Jim raised no objections to being swept away. In one
swallow he downed the champagne that had been gently tickling the
atmosphere with its bubbles over the last ten minutes. Without releasing
Felicity, he deftly swapped the emptied vessel for another glass on a
passing tray. *Interesting, interesting….What had Miss Mackenzie—Mary—
been about to say? That woman knew so much about so many things.*

"So, Mr. Silversmith, how are you?"

His calculations as to the obviously astronomical value of a fast and
effective browser which bypassed the Doors operating system were
interrupted. "Ah, Miss Mackenzie! I'm fine, thank you. Very well indeed.
And how are you? It's always a pleasure to see you. Nathaniel keeps me
informed about your doings to some extent of course, but he never
mentioned that you were heavily into computing and the Internet!"

"No. Well, no one outside of the museum knew about it until now. We
couldn't take any risks until the project was well advanced." Mary
noticed that the browser icon was still on the screen. "But you haven't
seen anything yet. Believe me, you'll understand why we kept it secret

until this point. Put the headset on, adjust the microphone and hit enter."

Silversmith reluctantly tore his eyes off the slender straps of her scarlet evening dress on the fine skin, the delicate collarbones, the elegant curve of her lips as they gave birth to soft Scottish phonemes....

The icon disappeared. Otherwise there was no change. A blank screen.

Mary spoke, "Demonstration mode. General familiarisation." Lines divided the screen into three columns. A voice came from the computer, "Good evening." In the leftmost column the same salutation appeared.

Silversmith raised his eyebrows and looked at Mary. He loved her authoritarian manner. Mary indicated that he should reply. His "Good evening!" appeared in the right column. For a few seconds, nothing else happened, and then more text appeared in the middle column: "Male, 56 +/- 4 years." Mary explained that these were the ninety-five percent confidence intervals for his estimated age, and that the computer would modify and improve on this the more he spoke. Further text appeared on the screen: "Southern English accent, possibly Oxford, upper middle class. Slight apprehension. Reassurance required."

Mary murmured to Silversmith's guide, "That's the Pygmalion module working there, Glenn...good."

The computer spoke again, its words echoed in the left column: "Yes, it is surprising. Is there anything you would like to talk about?"

Silversmith laughed. "But this is a childish confidence trick—you knew I'd come to this computer so you've just programmed all this in— you could have used a tape recorder for this sort of stuff!" Mary raised her eyebrows slightly but said nothing, keeping her gaze on the screen.

In the central column were the words: "Incredulity. Subject addressing third party." The computer spoke again: "What can I do to convince you?"

Silversmith replied immediately, "You'll have a hard job. For all I know there's someone sitting somewhere listening to me and typing all this right now...."

The central column showed that his age was now estimated to be 56.7 +/- 0.35 years. "Logical scepticism" was appended to the text. It spoke, "Yes, we could play games for hours and you would not be convinced. Try asking for something on the Internet."

"Find me the HDI website." No sooner had Silversmith spoken than the text had disappeared and he was looking at the familiar logo.

Glenn could not resist calling out: "Snap!" He was, after all, HDI'd from head to toe.

Thinking quickly, Silversmith decided to try something crafty. "Summarise the profits over the last ten years. What are the company's strengths and weaknesses?"

Before he'd finished, the computer was speaking, "Your question was ambiguous. Firstly when you say 'the company' are you referring to HDI? If so, are you referring to the entire HDI group, including all its subsidiaries? Would you want to include its clandestine units, and its drug-smuggling links? Secondly, the concept of strengths and weaknesses is a subjective one. This part of your question is too vague. Please re-phrase it."

Silversmith blushed and let out an involuntary laugh. He turned to Mary and smiled. "I can't believe this!" he said, meaning that he was, in fact, starting to believe it.

As before, Mary raised her fine dark eyebrows a fraction. "You still haven't seen anything yet. Computer! Sophistry mode. Psychological counselling. Push HDI products. Subtlety five."

The computer's screen cleared and then turned pale blue. Silversmith could hear gentle (blandified?) music in his earphones. On the top of the screen were the words: "Marital counselling." The computer spoke in an unctuous voice, "So. You have come for marriage guidance. That is already a very good step. Well done. Now, is there anything in particular that you'd like to tell me to start off with, or would you like me to prompt you by suggesting some areas you might like to discuss? Take your time."

Silversmith laughed again. Immediately the computer replied, "I know it can seem a bit strange to be talking about your intimate life with a computer. Please be assured that your communications and my response are fully encrypted and therefore it is unlikely—though admittedly not impossible—that anyone will breach your privacy. Shall I suggest some topics?"

Silversmith spoke, "No. That's alright...." Despite himself he couldn't help slipping in a thank you. With a quick wink at Mary, he continued, "Tell me. I no longer find my wife particularly attractive. What can I do about that?"

Mary struggled to keep her face straight: predictably arrogant and sexist pig this guy was! The computer was silent for twenty seconds. "There are so many ways to approach a big subject like that. You are nearly fifty-seven years old. How old is your wife? Are you both in good physical health? How long have you been married? Do you find other women attractive? What turns you on? When last did you have an erection? Do you think your wife finds you attractive? Are you employed? If so, do you enjoy your job?...I am rattling off all these questions merely to give you an idea of the enormity of this subject. You may answer any questions you want to. I can give you more or you may just want to tell me what is bothering you most...."

Silversmith winked at Mary, and touched the side of his nose, to make it obvious to her that what he was about to say wasn't true. "I haven't been able to have an erection for years. What can you advise me?"

"First, let me congratulate you on having the courage to admit it. Erectile difficulties may have both psychological and physiological causes. You need a full medical examination as the first step. But may I suggest, that if it turns out that you suffer from performance anxiety, you suggest to your doctor that he or she might want to prescribe Relaxedil. If the problem is more physiological—circulatory—but you do not require cardiac medication, you might want to try Priaptra. Do you require more information on these drugs?"

Silversmith was grinning broadly—both drugs were HDI products. He was beginning to understand what Mary and her team had developed. He called out "Subtlety zero." The computer replied, "Sorry I do not understand." Mary explained that if it suspected that the user had divined what it was up to it would stop. The program would only respond to commands of this nature given by herself. She continued: "Computer reset. Sophistry mode. Music discussion. Full web use. Push HDI products. Subtlety zero. Continue."

Now this was fascinating! As far as Silversmith knew, his company had nothing to do with the music business, so how on earth could this work?

The screen was constantly changing now. Various musical instruments from all over the world were drifting over it, together with maps of where they came from. At the same time Silversmith could hear little pieces of music dominated by the instrument closest to the centre of the screen. Now there were clips from music videos, pop, jazz, blues, traditional music of various sorts. Now there were various forms of musical notation. Now there was a lab-coated stern-looking woman twanging away at a string whose tension she was adjusting by adding weights to a dangling little tray. The screen cleared again. The computer spoke: "That was to give you some idea of the topics we can discuss, the subjects covered by websites. What would you like to know or see or hear?"

Silversmith decided to start with something familiar, a site he had visited more than once: "Smylie Minnow."

Instantly the familiar pixie face of the Tasmanian songstress was there...but what was happening to it? The make-up was changing. She was becoming...even more beautiful! Arrows and labels were appearing. "This is how Smylie would look if she had requested an HDI cosmetics expert to make her up for a night on the town. The eyeshadow is HDEye No. 3B, the lipstick...."

Silversmith's delight spilled out in laughter. He was hooked. He appeared to Mary like a little boy surrounded by presents at Christmas time. He clicked on "music tracks" and the familiar download option was there. All her songs were listed, from "I shouldn't be so mucky..." onwards, but in place of all the usual advertisements, such as "Do you want the best in hi-fi equipment? Visit our sponsor Hitakyo. Click here..." there were only HDI ones! The software had somehow superimposed HDI advertisements on all the ads supposedly integral to the site. This was commercial dynamite! Silversmith clicked on a song-download icon. Instantly the familiar chirpy little melody commenced, but what was happening? Smylie was coughing! Now a voice: "This wouldn't have happened if Smylie had been vaccinated against Balinese flu. Ask your doctor for the HDI vaccine against this potentially lethal virus now." Smylie's singing voice returned to normal, and then was overlain by the same voice as before, "But even if Smylie were feeling poorly, Bronchylin cough medicine would have helped...." This was, of course, an HDI product. Now Smylie was wrinkling up. "This is Smylie at fifty, having had average Tasmanian sun exposure and having failed to use SunOut, the revolutionary new HDI sunblock."

Silversmith sat back open-mouthed, shaking his head. He couldn't think of anything to say. This was INCREDIBLE! The commercial clout that this would give HDI was incalculable.

Mary let it sink in for a minute or two before she spoke, exchanging a wry look with Glenn. "Now the beauty of this is that we don't necessarily have to let people know the extent to which the browser is biasing their exposure to the Net. What one might do initially is offer the browser as a free download. It not only doesn't require DOS and Doors to run, it actually runs faster if computers don't have these....we've made sure of that. So what we're talking about is not only edging out Doors, InterWeb Voyager and Netscrape—but also swamping their advertising with whatever you wish to put in its place. Individual users' computers will automatically be assigned Cyberbabble gateway addresses when Cyberbabble is downloaded. What this means is that the advertising—or 'Intelligent Sophistry' content as we call it—of what the individual user experiences can be regulated by us...or by you, centrally. It would be up to you what you did, but my suggestion would be to start with minimal tweaking, and then gradually increase the content of—in your case—HDI-warped content. It might be better even to wait a year or two until Cyberbabble has a sizeable share of the market. To be completely honest with you, our biggest worry is that the opposition will develop a way of detecting whether a user is operating through a Cyberbabble browser, and then block access. At the moment our browsers can be made to appear as if they are NetScrape or InterWeb Voyager...."

If Silversmith had been gob-smacked before, he was pole-axed now.

Mary continued, "As it works at the moment, we can harness all the best resources of the Net. In other words Cyberbabble makes intelligent use of all the online translators, speech synthesisers and expert systems available. We have not wasted our time re-inventing the wheel where the wheel has already been invented, so to speak. If you like, to extend the vehicular metaphor, what Cyberbabble does is to select the best wheels, seats, chassis, engine and transmission system. It then assembles them elegantly, and then puts you, the paying advertiser, in the driving seat, all the time letting the user think that it is him doing the driving!"

Silversmith turned from the screen towards Mary. This would make more than a fortune. This could make or break any number of HDIs. This was probably the most significant advance since the discovery of DNA. This was mega-bonanza time!

And Mary….Mary was the most beautiful woman in the world. Ever.

CHAPTER TWENTY-EIGHT
Hope-ism Shapes Up

It was noon. At least according to Big Ben. Nathaniel and Mary had arrived simultaneously at La Dolce Vita Cafeteria and Brasserie, Mary on foot and Nathaniel by taxi. Mary was tired but elated after the previous evening's *tour de force*. It had been refreshing to walk in the rain. Now she would have to reveal all—or a bit anyway—to Nathaniel...and to Shelagh. She ordered a cappuccino. Nathaniel had a tomato juice with "the works."

"She should be here by now." Mary glanced at her watch. She had done as much toying with the remaining foam in her cup as she decently could. She didn't fancy another coffee. She wanted to eat.

Nathaniel grunted as he licked his cocktail stick. It had been pleasant just making occasional small talk and watching the world go by. Heaven knew it happened seldom enough. "It's difficult to understand what could have gone wrong. She seemed clear about things when she phoned last night, and this place isn't difficult to find. I vote we give her another five minutes and then phone the hotel."

Nathaniel was just searching for the hotel's number in his wallet when Mary stopped him. There Shelagh was, running and waving. She arrived panting. "Hi, you guys. Sorry I'm late."

"Hi, Shelagh! It's been a long time, far too long..." said Mary. She was thinking, horrified, how thin she was looking. Even the glow of exercise couldn't mask the pellucid fragility of her skin.

"I'm really sorry. I sort of had an accident. I bumped into someone, literally...."

Was she blushing now? Nathaniel decided not to pursue the matter. "Never mind, you're here safe and sound. That's all that matters. Something to drink?"

"Would I? Hell!"

Over the course of the meal the story of Shelagh's nightmare journey emerged. A few delicate questions from Mary elicited enough information for her to imagine Shelagh's recent life—or rather existence—in Inverdon. Mary was quiet after this. Guilt? She wasn't exactly sure what she was feeling. The atmosphere was awkward anyway. And as yet no one had broached the real purpose of the meeting. In the broad daylight and in a public place with people going about their ordinary business the whole thing seemed ludicrous. But facts were facts, Mary told herself. It was Nathaniel who suggested they retire to a snug in a pub he knew and get down to the nitty-gritty. He paid the bill, and in silence they rose to leave, Mary and Shelagh each contemplating her own secrets and wondering how much to reveal.

The Galway Bay was a good idea. The Celtic atmosphere recalled jolly times in Inverdon's drinking establishments, and the dark nether regions were conducive to frank interchange. Neither did several excellent pints of "t'black stuff" impede matters.

Nathaniel started by sketching the background to Hope-ism for Shelagh, occasionally glancing at some notes: "According to the latest UN Development Programme report, 13.5% of the UK's population lives below the recognised poverty line, defined as half the median personal disposable income, but if one takes into account life expectancy, knowledge deprivation and social exclusion, 15% of the UK's population can be considered to live in poverty. The United States—the richest country in the world, by the way—is worse. More than a fifth of Britons are functionally illiterate, and one in ten will not live until the age of sixty. The gap between the rich and the poor is growing across the world. More than one billion people lack the means to meet their most basic needs. Twenty percent of the world's population consumes 86% of goods and services, and nearly half of the world's meat and fish. And, far from this situation improving, people in Africa consume 20% less than they did twenty-five years ago...."

Mary and Nathaniel took it in terms to outline the state of the world, occasionally interrupting each other to embellish and support what the other was saying. Shelagh did not seem surprised by anything, occasionally grunting in agreement. "Yes, it just confirms what I've been thinking. I hadn't quite put it all together, but it's really pretty clear, isn't it? So what do we do?"

"Well, to me it's obvious we must nail Mudrock first, and I'm going to tell you a bit of a story about how I came to that conclusion." Nathaniel was enjoying playing them along. Intrigued, they watched as he pulled a plastic bag from the pocket of the jacket lying crumpled on the bench next to him. It was a Frillons bag. He took out four little softbound booklets, three identical and brand new, the other old and tattered and sealed in transparent polythene. He handed a new one each to Shelagh and Mary. It was *The Prince* by Niccolò Machiavelli.

"This little booklet," said Nathaniel, holding up the tattered one, "was given to me by one of my kidnappers on Hysterique. Somehow I could never throw it away. Well, the other day I was sitting in my office wondering just how the hell we could ever hope to save the world, because, let's face it, that's exactly what we're setting out to do. I mean, we're going to need to build a massive power base, recruit many people....It's a huge and complex thing. To give you one idea of the sort of issue we might face: if we're going to win people to us we need to tell them what we're up to, what we're doing. But that immediately exposes us to the risk of betrayal. So how can we contain this risk?

"Another thing: initially, of course, we'll be a small and weak grouping, and yet to make any sort of impact, to attract publicity and therefore to grow, we need to attack something big! How is David to defeat Goliath, and which Goliath should we pick? It's all very well knowing what's wrong with the world, but it's another matter putting it right. Just consider how many hundreds—thousands probably—of organisations are already trying to do that, from Anti-Nasty International to Verdant Pax....They all have a little corner of the truth, but they haven't changed much....So what will make us any different?

"Anyway as I said, I was sitting in my office thinking about all these things, and—to be frank—slipping deeper and deeper into despair, when my eye caught this miserable little booklet here. I'd jammed it between a couple of books on my shelf and forgotten about it. I don't know what made me take it down then. I suppose I was just so fed up and depressed and wanting some sort of distraction.

"It turned out that this little thing held all the answers, or rather it turned out to be the muse I was seeking, a source of inspiration, and a sort of...um...touchstone, against which I—or we—could test potential strategies.

"*The Prince* is a manual of power. Machiavelli believed that fragmented sixteenth century Italy would have been better united under a single strong ruler. His experience of politics led him to devise a treatise spelling out how this could be done. *The Prince* is, in effect, Machiavelli's recipe for uniting Italy.

"Now you may not think that this is very relevant to what we're trying to do, but if you read the book with a bit of imagination you will see that the situation of sixteenth century Italy can be likened to that of the entire world today....Except that the powers struggling to control the world are not rival warlords but multinational companies.

"If you like, you can read it as the means by which one company might rise to domination. But—and this is what is so exciting—you can also read it as the means by which another force might be able to take advantage of the rivalries between the diminishing number of increasingly powerful multinationals to wrest control of the world from them!

"There's a lot of food for thought in here, but if there's a single principle above all others that emerges it is either make potential enemies into friends, or destroy them absolutely: do nothing to antagonize until certain of victory, and then strike immediately with overwhelming force.

"To cut a long story short, this book got my mind working again, and I came to two main conclusions.

"The first conclusion was that there are two reasons why all the 'do-gooder' organisations have failed in their quests to prevent wars and famines, protect the environment, ensure that human rights are protected, and what have you.

"The first reason is that many of them have not sufficiently understood the common root of the world's problems, namely the economic system tied up with the multinationals. In *Prince* terms, if you don't even recognise your various enemies' territories, how can you hope to even begin to hatch a plan to defeat them? Indeed, if the various do-gooders are not tackling the common root of the problems they are trying to solve, then, far from helping they may even be aggravating things in the long run…by uselessly wasting the energy of good people, and thereby promoting disillusion and apathy, for example.

"The second reason these do-gooder groups have failed is that those few who have understood the underlying cause of the world's problems—or in other words the identity of the enemy—have diffused their efforts over such a wide front, even at this deeper level, that their impact has been negligible. In *Prince* terms again, if one little group is besieging Enemy A, another little group is attacking Enemy B, another C and so on, then they are far less likely to succeed than if they were all to select one common enemy and attack him together. And, having vanquished him, move on to the next. This next one, having seen his powerful neighbour defeated, may even wish to avoid bloodshed and surrender on the spot.

"The pathetic fragmented approach, of attacking multiple enemies on multiple fronts, is typified by the various green consumer guides you can buy. Not only are there several of them, but each is chock-full of various goods to be boycotted or supported. Now, who, other than a tiny minority of militants, is prepared to wade through all that information, and weigh up every potential purchase in the light of it? I don't decry the intention or the integrity of those behind these things, but this approach just doesn't, won't and cannot work! It fails to understand human nature, which is fundamentally lazy, and, let's face it, often dispirited and drained by socio-economic conditions, if not deprived of choice altogether. If I were in charge of a multinational, supplying supermarkets or clothes shops say, then I would chuckle to myself every time a new green guide or whatever came on the market: more confusion amongst the poor huddled masses, ha, ha, ha!

"I suppose you could add—if you go in for conspiracy theories—that some of the disunity amongst do-gooder groups will be the consequence of the manoeuvres of the multinationals, or of *their* Machiavellian strategies, if you like, of divide and conquer....But I don't think it's even necessary to evoke this to explain what's happening, tempting though it is, but that's another story...."

Shelagh and Mary were transfixed, occasionally mechanically raising their glasses to their lips. They were no longer conscious of tasting the Guinness, the delicious product of yet another multinational.

"Be that as it may, if all the world's problems stem from the multinationals and the economic system, then it seems to me obvious that we should try to convince all the do-gooder groups of this...to educate them. And then, instead of each of them fighting their own tiny corners, their own little aspects of the behaviour of the ravening swarm of multinationals, we need to get them to work together, and work together systematically.

"In short, we should target the multinationals individually, one at a time, and we need to bring as many of the disparate and sometimes feuding do-gooders as possible into the same struggle. Fortunately, neo-liberal capitalism being what it is, once a company is targeted I think its competitors are unlikely to rush to its rescue. Indeed they are more likely to go into a shark-like feeding frenzy and finish the job for us. Nonetheless we shall probably need to think of ways of ensuring that they do remain divided.

"The second major conclusion I came to was that unless we disable the media at the outset—our enemies' major weapon—we're sunk. Fortunately, as a result of the very processes we are trying to defeat, a significant proportion of the potentially hostile media is controlled by one multinational, and that by a single man: Bear Mudrock. We need to strike him hard, take him out of the game. This first action is the most crucial. If we fall at this hurdle then we'll have lost any hope of gaining credibility and it's all over."

A specific bit now between their teeth, the Shelagh-Mary-Nathaniel magic-circle-of-three found itself instantly re-constituted. Within two hours a few possibilities for the first Hope-ist action had been drafted. Each had a list of investigative tasks.

With all of them happy and excited, the conversation broadened. "You know, we'll probably manage this first action with the help of the few people we've mentioned, but obviously the Hope-ist Movement needs to recruit and expand hugely after that. Remembering what you said, Nathaniel, it's all very well us personally explaining things to the first few recruits, but it won't be long before we're going to need to formalise things...."

Shelagh was right. If the organisation were not to disintegrate into some gigantic pantomime version of Chinese whispers they would need to lay down a framework. They would need formal guidelines, principles....It was decided that together they would draft a general introduction to Hope-ism which would take as its point of departure the effects of the current economic system on health and longevity; Nathaniel would then write a tract about Hope-ism from a biological perspective, using metaphors from the science of evolution to cast light on economic systems, and Mary would look into the Hope-ist approach to potential allies: political groupings, protest groups, and NGOs such as environmental and human rights organisations. With her recent experience fresh in her mind, Shelagh was more than keen to tackle the subject of transport.

Mary judged it a good moment to reveal what she'd been up to. "Nathaniel, do you remember Geoff Winwood?"

"Mmmn, rings a bell. Yes, he was just finishing a Ph.D. at the Three Cs when I was starting mine. A bit of a miserable bastard, I recall."

Mary smiled. "Yes, he does have his moments, but he doesn't seem to remember you as being entirely full of light and joy either, you know! Bloody bright, though. I've only just learned that you two knew each other. I suppose he never thought to mention it as he didn't know that we knew each other! Anyway, he's been working at the VE and HA for the last couple of years."

"I didn't realise that you did anything that required a computing boffin?"

"No. Well, I wanted to keep things hush-hush. The fact is I had a hunch about the Internet and browsers, and I paid Geoff to organise a little team to look into it, and, in a nutshell, it's come up trumps...."

Now it was Nathaniel's turn to be agog, and Shelagh experienced a second dose of agoggedness, as Mary summarised her recent doings. Nathaniel was even quicker on the uptake than Silversmith had been. "Mary, the potential is limitless! You've given us our victory on a plate! The media are where all battles are won or lost; in fact their conquest IS the battle! If we can disable Mudrock we'll effectively have taken out the printed media, television and cable…and if we can use your—what was it?—Cyberbabble browsers once they've become widespread, then the Internet is ours too! Yes! And it's not just a question of disabling it either, if I've understood you properly, but of making it ours in the fullest sense. Oh, the beautiful irony of getting companies like HDI to pay for and push Cyberbabble, only for it to turn around and bite them a year or two down the line!"

Eyes shining, they parted on that note. Shelagh had decided to keep quiet about her rendezvous.

CHAPTER TWENTY-NINE
Funny Business

The telephone purred as she was putting the finishing touches to her make-up. On getting back to the hotel, she had swallowed two ibuprofens, downed a pint-and-a-half of water, and gone to bed for a couple of hours to sleep off the alcohol. She had roused herself at 6.30 and taken a long shower, luxuriating in the foam and aroma of the gel.

The phone would be reception letting her know that EJ had arrived. Ten minutes early. He was keen! Shelagh asked the reception to tell him she'd be down in five minutes, knowing it would be nearer fifteen. *Treat 'em mean and keep 'em keen and all that!* God, it had been a long time!

Downstairs EJ's right eye was twitching. The contact lens had slipped out of position. *Damn!* Why did this sort of thing always happen when he was about to meet someone who got his juices flowing? Scleral congestion, unilateral or not, was not especially a turn-on for the opposite sex. He told reception that he would be in the toilet, in case Shelagh were to appear. Looking at his tear-streaked visage in the mirror, he wondered whether the bottle glasses of his youth would not have been better. He shrugged. Lens adjusted and face sponged, he ventured into the lobby again. If he smoked he'd have lit a cigarette. As it was, his only nervous habit was nail-biting. This he resorted to, although his teeth had difficulty finding purchase on the unseemly stubs. The receptionist, a seasoned people-watcher, had the situation sussed. She allowed herself a little grin. *Poor boy.*

Shelagh had decided to descend the stairs, thereby slowly and regally entering EJ's field of vision, rather than simply popping out of the lift like a puppet in a Punch-and-Judy show.

EJ heard a female throat being softly cleared, and turned to the stairway. A smart little pair of black medium-heel shoes was followed by sheer stockings, a wide knee-length multi-layered creamy chiffon skirt and a neat black bodice. Her hair was up, as when he had last seen her, but this time the childlike delicacy of her features was emphasized by little-girl pink lipstick, subtle blusher on her oh-so-photogenic cheekbones, sky blue eyeshadow, and little pearl earrings and necklace. A trim Chanel jacket completed the picture.

EJ's heart was racing. He affected his pose suavissimo, and, left hand in the pocket of his sports jacket Prince of Dolpins-style, extended the other one, intending to bring her hand to his lips. Shelagh gave it a gentle squeeze and released it before he knew what was happening. He stood there for a second, not sure what to do now that the gallant gesture he had so carefully been rehearsing in his mind had been summarily rendered redundant. A bad start.

Shelagh was sure she was going to enjoy herself with this one.

"Business, business, it's just business…." Mary said to herself as she pulled on her green velvet Guccaci evening dress, the one that went so well with her fair skin and raven hair. She dabbed some extra perfume behind her ears and checked her lipstick again. "Business, business meeting only—he's a married man after all!"

Silversmith's taxi drew up. Silversmith told the driver to wait. He alighted, bunch of flowers in hand, and rang Mary's doorbell. Mary, a bit disconcerted by his gift giving the lie so early to her comforting little story, and simultaneously uncomfortable about how pleased this had made her, took the flowers from him and left him on the doorstep for a minute. She plucked some older blossoms from a vase, throwing them in the bin and stuffing Silversmith's offering into the vacated container. She noted with approval that he'd had the good taste not to go overboard— just a simple and subtle little mixed bouquet, none of your crass, enormous and unambiguous bunches of mutant roses.

Silversmith took her arm in a way there was no gainsaying. It was good to have a man be a man, even if he was a married one, and a sexist bastard into the bargain! Most of them were so pusillanimous these days. Was it she who had become intimidating, or had men just lost their balls? Ah, never mind. Now she was with one who knew what was what. With men like this she knew how to play it too.

The meal was an exercise in sophisticated flirtation, in practised foreplay. Yet a stenographer's transcript of their conversation would have been passed by the most po-faced of mother superiors as fit for her convent's English classes, although admittedly the technological references would have baffled the less computer-literate of these worthy women. No, the frisson was in the pouting of the lips, the raising of the eyebrows, the pauses in the conversation, and the languorous extension of the words: "Well, perha-aps, Mr. Silversmith, sir...we mi-ght just be able...mmmn...to come to some arrange...ment. You re-ally want...you really want Cyberbabble then?" The longest of these pauses coincided with particularly pleasurable sensations arising from the friction of his foot on her leg, or *vice versa*...and, towards the end of the meal, with the mutual tickling of each other's feet, and then the gentle teasing of his groin by her wonderfully prehensile toes.

Yes, Silversmith knew all the best restaurants with private tables and oversize tablecloths.

Over the six months between the posting of Nathaniel's fateful letter to Mary and the first action of the Hope-ists, Rosemary's interest in music developed considerably. Nathaniel's frequent absences bothered her less as her music collection and knowledge expanded. But it was probably not so much these that made the difference, as the people she was meeting.

Even people as apparently taciturn as Spider (for such was the dreadlocked one's cognomen) are inclined to open up when repeatedly exposed to an unthreatening presence clearly sharing an interest and appreciative of a guiding hand. The dim and smoky interior of In the Groove Records was a breath of fresh air to Rosemary. She looked forward to their relaxed chats about Robert Johnson, The Clash, The Floyd, The Doors, Jimi Hendrix, Neil Young, Eric Clapton, Robert Fripp...while sipping instant coffee from a cracked mug, her be-jeaned legs up on the counter next to Spider's. As far as she was aware, Spider had no idea who she was and she was happy to leave it that way. They were friends not because of her fame, her image, but because of who she, an individual human being, was. "A man's a man for a'that," as Nathaniel was fond of saying, and so was a woman.

Nathaniel was aware of and approving of his wife's new interest and the pleasure it seemed to give her, and him too. He began to look forward to coming home and seeing what new aural treasures she had acquired. Barker would have appreciated this, he would say to himself as he put this one or that on the turntable.

Rosemary's weekly visits to "The Groove" (as she learned to call it) became twice-weekly, then sometimes three times. She came to realise that her initial impression of a relaxed atmosphere had been misleading—Spider had a nice little business, thank you very much! Nonetheless, he always found time to discuss music with her. Indeed, unbeknown to her, and perhaps also to himself, he was systematically teaching her everything he knew about blues and rock music. In effect, she became his protégée. She would leave the shop weighed down with a selection of listening homework, her notebook full of subtleties to observe. Sometimes he would have to go out for an hour or so, and he would ask her to stand in for him. Although more than half his stock was old vinyl, Spider had a good selection of recent Indie releases, and many friends and contacts in the industry. An ever-widening circle in fact. The Groove was on its way to becoming an "in" place. NME wanted to do a feature. The day they were due to take the photographs Rosemary took care to be away.

Not long after the NME article it became obvious that they would have to move. The current premises were too cramped for the business they were doing. It also became apparent that Rosemary's assistance with this relocation would be appreciated, if not essential, and Spider was moved to consider formalising their relationship and appointing her his salaried assistant. Rosemary was flattered, but also worried. With the higher profile this would entail, not to mention the necessary paperwork, she would be forced to reveal her identity. That not only incurred the risk of distorting, at the very least, their business relationship-cum-friendship, but also of attracting what would be for her unwelcome media attention. And what would Nathaniel think about his wife working in a music store?

As it turned out, Nathaniel wasn't bothered and congratulated her on Spider's offer. He recommended that she reveal her identity to Spider, because, he reasoned, Spider was bound to discover it sooner or later (if he didn't already know) and a secret of that magnitude between business associates could only prove dangerous. Secondly, he suggested she use her maiden name in all her business dealings, and try to handle more of the background work. If Spider understood her position he might well be willing to deal with all the more up-front stuff. There was, of course, a good chance that the media would "find her out" anyway, but would that be so dreadful? Compared to all the exposure they'd had in the past what did a little bit more really matter? And, after all, it wasn't as if there would be anything scandalous in what she'd be doing! Rosemary kissed Nathaniel. All things considered, she wasn't too badly off with him, even if he were away more often than not!

Nathaniel was indeed very busy. Attending scientific conferences the world over, overseeing further research on ageing in Inverdon and London, and fitting in Hope-ist meetings in preparation for the strike against Mudrock were taxing in themselves. In addition he was trying to learn as much as could about the business side of HDI. It was a delicate game: he had to show enough interest so that Silversmith would let him into the dark realm where the real decisions were made, without probing so deeply and eagerly that he might betray his motives. Industrial espionage—for that was what it amounted to—called for a cool head and a subtlety that was extraordinarily draining, yet knowledge of the strategic thinking of the multinationals was crucial to the success of Hope-ism. As he learned more, Nathaniel began to suspect that there might well be a conspiracy after all. The Multilateral Agreement on Investment, which he occasionally heard Silversmith mention on the phone, might be the topic of those mysterious meetings in Paris and Geneva he claimed to be attending. Nathaniel thought it would be worthwhile checking on the whereabouts of other multinational bosses at these times.

Nathaniel was also working on the formal texts that were to be the basis for the expansion of Hope-ism. It was important that these be accessible to a wide readership. Mary, Shelagh and himself had decided that a variety of tracts ought to be written, dealing with various subjects and written for people of different backgrounds.

All these things took their toll. He had enjoyed the evenings at home listening to music with Rosemary, but now either he was away or she was. The only genuine moments of relaxation, so it seemed, were his chats with Michelle on his journeys to or from Heathrow or Stansted. Michelle was a lovely girl. So easy-going.

EJ had left his car outside the hotel. It was a beat-up old VW Minto— "the car with the hole in it," as the advertisement said, referring to the sunroof. The trouble was there wasn't a great deal of sun in the British isles; there was a lot of rain, and EJ's sunroof didn't close properly. He'd jammed several old plastic bags in the crack, and taped another over on the outside, but the tape had perished and water found its way in in the worst weather (most of the time). The consequence was a healthy fungal population in the upholstery and a horrible musty smell. EJ had only become fully aware of it when he was about to take Shelagh out. Normally he was so intent on some project or other that such trivial issues escaped his attention. Of course he was also so used to the smell that it hardly registered anyway. But that evening, on his way to pick up Shelagh, he had realised that it might be considered off-putting. In a panic he had pulled in at a garage and bought a couple of dangly car deodorants to hang from the rearview mirror, a Snoopy dog one for the dashboard, and a spray as well. All of these fully deployed, he had grunted in satisfaction and driven off from the service station. Thirty seconds into the journey it had dawned on him that there was such a thing as overkill. In fact the atmosphere was marginally less choking than would be found in the aftermath of a peaceful demonstration in East Timor, for example, when the survivors of a massacre perpetrated by British weaponry in the hands of the Indonesian armed forces were being driven off with teargas and smoke grenades. He had opened all the windows and driven on, wet and freezing. *How one suffers for love, or for money!*

Shelagh had noticed that he smelt rather strange, but had put it down to a poor choice of aftershave. The car made things plain, however. Had he spilled some milk in it, that he needed all these deodorants? He apologised for the perfume factory smell and the wet seats. Shelagh responded gracefully. Of course, with the clothes she was wearing he would have no idea of the way she'd been living for the last few years! It did her good to be with someone who obviously had as much of a struggle as she did (or had had), someone with whom she could feel comfortable. When the rain started again, and EJ had to lean out of his window to wipe the windscreen as the wiper on his side of the car was broken, she couldn't suppress a giggle. EJ looked at her, a bit startled, and then laughed too. They hit on a more romantic and drier solution. EJ would lean across Shelagh and look out of her side of the windscreen, her arms propping him. "You really should get the wiper fixed, you know."

Over the meal, in a cheap, friendly and dimly lit little Greek restaurant, dolmades and retsina coming out of their ears (or at least Shelagh's—she noted with approval that EJ was going easy on the wine), EJ talked about his work, and then some. His eagerness was almost infectious, but not quite. Shelagh yawned. EJ sensed it was now or never. "Anyway, what I'm trying to say is that I've worked with any number of models. I know what works, and what doesn't work, what the agencies, the media are looking for these days. And you're it, Shelagh, you're just right…."

Shelagh's guard was up, but she thought she might as well hear him out.

"So what I'm proposing is this, that you let me put together a portfolio for you. I have contacts that would lend you the clothes. I have a friend who's a stylist and she'd lend a hand, and then I'll send the shots around, and believe me, with a face and figure….Well, that's something else…."

What? Did she have to lose weight? The last time her mother had seen her, she had almost fainted!

"The thing is, as you are, we can find you lots of work. But I think you have the potential to go right to the top, the very top! All that would be required is a very simple minor little thing…."

He was taking his time to work up to it, thought Shelagh.

"Well the problem many girls have is their weight. In your case that's not an issue, although it does surprise me that you can eat so much...."

Shelagh grimaced.

"No—no insult intended. Look, let's face it, a girl has to do what's she got to do. I mean I suppose if you take the right pills, or make a trip to the bathroom. And it doesn't have to last forever. You know what you earn in five years can set you up for life."

What was he on about?

"But look, obviously you have your weight sorted and it's not my business how you do it. No, what I would suggest, and this isn't to imply that there's anything wrong with you as you are, it's merely a suggestion as to how you could enter the big money, you understand, and I'm talking about page three *Sin* stuff...."

Shelagh knocked her glass over.

"Look, I know what you're thinking, it may not be what you would call upmarket, an intelligent girl like you, but you get voted *Sin* page three girl of the year—and I'm sure you would be—and we're talking millions. And then sponsorship deals, a move into showbiz when they can no longer be bothered to Photoshop out the wrinkles. Pop stardom, for example, and don't worry if you can't sing, they can fix that....OK, OK, OK, if you want to look at it that way, then yes, they are exploiting you, but you're also using them! It's a two-way street! And you drive away with loads of money!"

"Hey, hold it, EJ. You still haven't told me what it is I have to do!"

"Well, there are lots of scare stories, but really the risks are tiny."

"Look, just calm down. Tell me what it is!"

"Well, it's only a suggestion, and don't take it personally, but I think a boob job would make a huge difference to your prospects. Look, I tell you what we'll do. First we'll put together a portfolio. I'll show it around and we'll see what happens, see what the boys think. I'll certainly do this for nothing. You're special, Shelagh. I may have made some mistakes in my life, but this I know for sure: you can make it big!"

What he meant to say was, "You can make them big!" thought Shelagh. Could she really make millions? No more flushing of economy washing-up liquid bottles then, no more rats in the bathroom....Well, there were two ways to handle what the filthy rich were doing to the world, if you weren't to let them walk over you: you could attempt to destroy the whole system, like this Hope-ist Movement thing, or you could grab the first opportunity that was presented to become one of them. Imagine going back into the dole office, having spent five times what the sour-faced bastard behind the counter made in a month, on breakfast alone, and reminding him of times gone by. *Yes, yes, yes!*

EJ—a curious bird indeed. The strange thing was he'd never once asked her about herself, or even what she thought about anything, other than this modelling thing. She was relieved, in a way, that the subject of her current employment had not come up. What could she have said, after all? What should she do? Anyway, no harm in having some more fun this evening. And no harm in having a few photos taken later, was there? No commitment for the time being.

Mary was returning to the table after powdering her nose when she saw Silversmith take what was probably a tablet from his wallet and pop it into his mouth. He took a slug of coffee and swallowed. Was that a leer on his face? Though startled by her arrival, his expression quickly reverted to benign solicitude. "Well, shall we go then?" he said, patting her hand. The £5 note on the table was clearly the tip—he had paid the bill in her absence then—good man! The taxi was waiting.

This was always the most awkward part of the evening. What now? The old ritual, as if she didn't know: "It's been a lovely evening. Would you like to come in for a coffee?" No matter how many times one had been through it....

Her front door closing behind them, all awkwardness vanished. He was upon her, the strength and enthusiasm of a man half his age, and, promising much—even through the layers of clothes—a delicious pressure.

Definitely the best lover she'd had, thought Mary, lying drowsy-eyed. It was seven in the morning. Silversmith had just left her; she'd woken to the sound of the door closing, and had turned to find a note on her bedside table:

Mary had a little lamb
His name was Tyrone S
And Tyrone thought that Mary was
The sexiest and the best!

See you soon I hope!
TS xxx Baaa....

She smiled. *The endurance of that "little lamb"!*

The new Groove premises were purpose-built. They had decided to retain, as far as possible, the subversive, seedy and other-wordly atmosphere of the basement original. At the same time they had wanted to give the impression of a "forward-looking modern and dynamic young business" (indeed, it was with these buzzwords that they had described themselves in their recently drafted "mission statement"). In the end they had opted for a hub-and-spoke arrangement, a low-ceilinged passage leading from the street to a bright high-ceilinged ultra-modern and glitzy central area, complete with a mini-cybercafé-cum-listening facility on a mezzanine floor. This was equipped with the latest terminals and headsets. Conventional tills and two customer help desks failed to clutter the spacious ground-level central concourse. Leading off this hub were eight wedge-shaped rooms. Six of these were near-replicas of the original shop and dealt with various musical genres. One was divided into offices. The last was an exhibition space and entertainment suite.

Today they were throwing a party in the latter to celebrate the opening. This was an exclusive private do, for invited guests in the music business only. There were to be no reporters or cameras. Rosemary was looking forward to taking a full part in the proceedings, and meeting all the people about whom she had heard so much. She was now Spider's official assistant. As Nathaniel had predicted, he hadn't been bothered about her identity, or about her desire to keep it semi-secret. The public launch party was set for the following Monday, when Rosemary would be safely out of the way in the offices.

Among the guests, Spider was particularly pleased to welcome Jim

Mud of Roar-Curse Records. Not only was this an important new Indie label, but Spider greatly approved of Roar-Curse's commitment to earthy "real" music. He had spoken to Jim Mud on the phone a couple of times, but had never met the man in the flesh. He would have to prise him away from Rosemary.

Rosemary had never "fallen in love" with anyone in the Mills-and-Boon sense, at least not unless one were to count her adolescent crushes on first-team rugby boys back in Thrackston days. Her first husband had just been there, the right man at the right time. She'd wanted children. He was a "solid respectable man" with a good salary. All her friends were getting married. Why not her too? She'd been as happily married as anyone, she imagined, and she'd trained herself not to think about love.

Nathaniel had been slightly different. He, too, had been there when she needed him. He'd come as close to understanding what she'd been through as anyone. At times she had thought she loved him, it was true—that afternoon on the rug, for example—but there had never really been that lightning bolt in her life. Until now.

Jim Mud had everything. An international glamour and sophistication delightfully belied by his little-boy smile. A delicious accent. A sense of humour. He must be a wheeler-dealer, she thought, but he seemed entirely guileless, straightforward. He was so at ease and yet also so touchingly bashful, modest. He was gorgeous, utterly gorgeous! And, what's more, he was so interested in her. She found herself telling him her life story. Of course when he realised who she was, the conversation became slightly stilted. And the way he was looking at her—was he looking for scars? He felt compelled to ask after Nathaniel: "…your husband." She explained that she didn't see much of him "these days…" and let the words linger as she looked into his eyes. He must get the hint, she thought. A rush of red to his face confirmed that her meaning had been registered. Her face incarnadined in sympathy. They haltingly restarted the conversation and got on to music. He asked whether they had any original Robert Johnson pressings, something he would give his "eye teeth to see." She took him to one of the spoke rooms, with its dim and delicious atmosphere.

The United Kingdom may not have had a "special relationship" with the United States of America, but The Groove was certainly set to have one with Roar-Curse Records.

Nathaniel's flight touched down at Stansted. It was noon, a sunny day in June. The first Hope-ist action was still a month in the future. Nathaniel was returning from Inverdon. Officially he'd been there to consult with Hall-Crumble and Annabelle about a sub-contracted HDI project. In reality, Nathaniel had engineered the visit so that he could chase up a few loose ends with Shelagh regarding the kidnapping. And, maybe, subconsciously, there had been another reason....

Michelle was there waiting for him in the arrivals lounge. This was her first day back at work after a holiday in Majorca, Nathaniel seemed to remember. Unusually for recent times, her smile had not accompanied her. What was wrong?

"Not much of a tan then, Michelle? Good to see at least someone takes what I say about UV seriously!" Nathaniel said jokingly. Not even the flicker of a quarter smile. Within a minute Nathaniel realised it was nothing to do with work. Usually she told him about that sort of problem directly and immediately. Something else then. Barely had they exited the airport car park than she started sobbing. Nathaniel insisted she pull over. He hugged her and stroked her hair. What on earth was it? She continued sobbing, "Oh, Nathaniel...."

Nathaniel's mind was working. "Listen, Michelle, I don't know what's bothering you, but I imagine it would do you good to talk about it. Now it so happens that I don't have any deadlines to meet today. Do you have anything urgent this afternoon?"

He could feel her head shaking a negative against his chest. She sniffed.

"Well then, why don't we go to a nice quiet country pub for lunch? I know a good one only twenty minutes away. I'll do the driving of course. You can have a drink when we get there. That'll help you calm down a bit. Doesn't that seem a good idea?"

The muffled "Mmmn" and the positive shake of her head were strangely arousing. God, her hair smelt good!

Fortunately it had stopped raining by the time EJ and Shelagh had finished their meal. EJ could assume the normal DVLA-approved driving position. Where to?

"Tell you what, Shelagh, I happen to have the keys to a studio. You know we could take some shots tonight for the hell of it?"

Why not?

Behind the camera EJ was transformed. Calmness and control, humour and *je ne sais quoi* oozed from him as Shelagh pranced and primped to the strains of M.C. Solaar's "Victime de la Mode." What magic was worked by a Nikpus and tripod such that he became so sensitive? He could yabber on for hours across a dining table, boring you senseless, and yet, give him a camera and stand him a couple of metres away, and it was as if he could read your mind, and he was so interested in everything about you. Had he been saving his questions for this?

"Tell me about your birthday parties when you were a little girl. You know your face has an innocence, a fragility, a goodness that can only come from a good heart, Shelagh. You have suffered, too....Mmmn, I can't imagine how I would have reacted to the rat!" And Shelagh laughed, and her eyes shone, and the flash went off, and she cried and the flash went off, and she pulled herself together and the flash went off, and she talked and talked, and the flash went off...and the atmosphere changed. EJ had stopped taking photographs. He was looking at her coldly....Almost angrily?

"Hey, Shelagh. Look, I don't know how to tell you this but it's a simple fact. I think the best thing is for me to be absolutely straight with you. You're too old."

Shelagh gaped. Did she look it? Heavens, only a year ago she'd been asked to prove her age when entering a pub! Then it hit her that in sketching her life story (omitting Hope-ism, of course) she had indirectly enabled him to calculate her age.

"Look, I'm really sorry, but if they find out that you're in your thirties they'll laugh in your face. It doesn't matter that you look like you're seventeen, because, with the right lighting, you do. They'll find you out, and it'll be obvious enough soon anyway. I'm afraid that's just the way it is. Look, these shots will be great, and you'll easily get catalogue work. I'll pass them round for you if you like. You could at least earn some decent pocket money, but making the big time is out of the question. Besides, if you're thin because of all the hard luck, because of what you've been through, although usually poor people are overweight, and your luck has changed, and you don't have a...a way of keeping things under control, then, to judge by the way you eat—even if age weren't the issue—you'd never make it....Sorry, but that's how it is."

A cold rage swept away her initial impulse to cry. "With the right lighting...the way you eat...!" he had said! *The goddamn cheek of the man*! Shelagh rose from the beanbag on which she had so recently been coquettishly disporting herself for his ogling lens. She stood there a few seconds, malevolent eyes piercing the now silent EJ. He blinked. She took a step towards him, her tight lips writhing in fury and loathing. Another step. EJ's eyes opened wider. He was unable to move. Shelagh's face was looking up into his, a few inches away now. She snorted and shook her head from side to side. "I pity you," she said. "You must be a very unhappy person. I wish you a happy life, all the same." She picked up her jacket and was gone.

EJ stood on the spot a further ten minutes. He could feel his breathing modulated by each beat of his heart. He was definitely, completely, 100%, head-over-heels in love.

Shelagh hailed a taxi, had to be reminded to get out when the taxi stopped at her hotel, abruptly demanded her key from the startled receptionist, marched up the stairs, unlocked her door, threw herself on her bed and cried herself to sleep, unexpected waves of homesickness adding to her confusion. Life had been so simple....Her and her rat.

Mary stretched luxuriously. *Who has had whom?* she asked herself. Was there likely to be a conflict of loyalties? No. She liked Silversmith, at least in bed, but not what he did for a living, and the two things for her were separable. She didn't want him to suffer as such, but if he didn't change....What she ought to do was try to persuade him to change HDI's policies without giving away what the Hope-ists were planning. In any case, he was an intelligent man, and HDI wasn't at the top of the hit list, so he would quickly see which way the wind was blowing. As a matter of interest, what would they expect a company like HDI to do in order to obtain Hope-ist approval? Certainly the usual stuff about decent pay, job contracts, and union representation, but also they ought to be doing more research on malaria, TB, and river blindness—the so-called "Third World" diseases—and the prices of drugs (especially HIV treatments) and vaccines for the poorest nations should be considerably reduced....Ultimately she might be able to turn him.

In the meantime, if she could gain Silversmith's confidence, she might be in a better position than Nathaniel to find out what they were up to, pillow talk and all that....

And wouldn't it be funny if she were able to tell Nathaniel about his boss? Mmmn, she'd keep this affair quiet and shock him with her insider knowledge. That would be a laugh!

And, then, if she took a dislike to her "little lamb" there was always blackmail. Life was great!

The novelty of a new man kissing her, his fresh carnal yearning—mixed with the desire to please her—failing to target his lips and tongue on her few sensitive areas which he struck only occasionally and by chance, was somehow overpoweringly moving and wonderful. Nathaniel's love-making, practised though it was in the realm of her senses—accurate even—was nothing compared to this raw passion. "One Roar-Curse raw kiss for a million expert ones!" Rosemary giggled delightedly to herself. And this was potentially only "The first of a million kisses." "Kisses sweeter than wine...." *Wonderful! Thank you, Robert Johnson and Fairground Attraction and...whoever it was! My old friend, the blues!*

They turned off the single-track country lane on to a gravel driveway. An old sign hanging on rusted chains signalled that they were at The Ploughman's Halt. A friendly looking, ivy-covered redbrick thatched bungalow lay before them, its mullioned windows ajar. Nathaniel parked the car on the grass verge: singingly brilliant verdure in the early afternoon sun, dotted here and there with yellow lotus flowers, white daisies and purplish clover blossoms. Five other cars were similarly parked along the driveway. Trellises and arbours heavy with ivy and honeysuckle broke the garden into separate little enclaves. Nathaniel pointed out the rockery in one, the pond in another, the flower garden in a third. Each was furnished with at least one wooden table, the sort with integral benches. Bees and butterflies busied themselves here and there. Some sparrows were building a nest in the eaves of the old building. Even the distant hum of the motorway added to the impression of seclusion and peace. The murmur of voices, the clink of cutlery and glasses, the smell of roast beef and potatoes spoke temptingly of lunch. Still a bit red-eyed, Michelle smiled at Nathaniel's expression of enquiry—yes, this would do!

They took a table next to the rockery. Here they were fairly private and could watch the lizards. Nathaniel left Michelle in their charge while he went to fetch the drinks and a menu. As Michelle sipped her dry white, and Nathaniel his Aythorpe Best Bitter, Nathaniel mentioned that he'd come here once or twice in his Ph.D. days when he'd been based at Cambridge. They examined the menu. Nathaniel happily observed that his favourites were still there. Michelle chose the traditional farmhouse pâté and Melba toast, to be followed by a baked potato with fresh basil, tomatoes and buffalo mozzarella "drizzled with olive oil." She looked up playfully through her fringe as she announced this, eyebrows lifting, as if she were a naughty little girl chancing it and half expecting to be scolded for being so greedy. Nathaniel managed the required indulgent smile—she was so lovely and so obviously trying to put a brave front on something terrible he almost wanted to cry. He plumped for the ploughman's lunch with Stilton. Perhaps because of the pub's name they made a special effort with the ploughman's, he explained, besides which he always liked to eat something local wherever he went. Stilton was only half an hour up the motorway, just south of Peterborough.

With the gentle warmth of the day, the gentle conversation, the second glass of wine and the good food, Michelle felt the remaining tension drain from her. Nathaniel was a good man, a good friend, even if it was a strange sort of friendship that only existed in cars on the way to and from airports. They'd known each other for years now. It was good to have him opposite her for a change. It was good to look at him. Heavens, the poor man had had his problems too, and there must be so much on his mind, and yet here he was giving of himself for her. She at least owed him an explanation for her tears.

Back in Inverdon it was raining. Shelagh's flat smelt musty, as it always did. She walked into the kitchen. The table was heaped with open baked bean tins, largely empty, leaking tomato sauce. A huge rat sat on the only chair, man-size it was, and rubbing its belly and burping. "Ahh, hallo Shelagh, welcome back! My, I've had a job preventing you putting on weight! You know if you keep on eating the way you do you'll never make it….Never mind. Would you like some chocolate? Ha, ha, ha…!" The voice was EJ's. The rat was knocking the table and laughing.

Shelagh woke, initially surprised and relieved to find herself in a sweet-smelling hotel room. Then memories of EJ flooded back. *What a bastard!* There was someone knocking at the door. "Who is it?"

"Room service, madam. Your morning tea."

Ah, yes. She needed to get started. She had a train to catch. "Come in please!"

A smiling fresh-faced young woman came in. On the tray beside the tea was a huge bunch of red roses and a card. "Looks like you have an admirer, madam. A gentleman was very insistent that you get these this morning."

As soon as she was alone, Shelagh tore open the envelope, hands trembling. There was a greeting card, a horrible soppy one with a big-eyed basset puppy and the words "I'm so sorry!" A message was scrawled inside in ghastly spidery writing:

Dear Sheila [sic]

How can I begin to apologise for my behaviour? I made the terrible mistake of confusing my private life with my work. Something stupid took me over and I spoke to you as I would have spoken to a model asking my advice. How incredibly stupid of me!!! I have not slept all night. I am in agony over my appalling behaviour!

I really think you are wonderful. You are one of the most beautiful people I have ever met. I know I haven't known you very long but I sense you are a very, very special person. Please, please, Sheila, at least—even if you never want to see me again—let me know that I am forgiven. Please!

With extreme contrition and affection
EJ x

He had enclosed a business card with his address and phone number. Shelagh wasn't sure what she was feeling, but she put the greeting card and the business card back in the envelope and popped it into her handbag. During the course of the next three quarters of an hour, between showering and dressing, and then while dressing, she took it out again and re-read it several times. By the time she went down to breakfast there was the hint of a smile on her lips. She ordered a full English breakfast, and then having eaten it and nicely replete, she ordered some extra toast. *Just for EJ. Mmmn—delicious fattening food!*

CHAPTER THIRTY
Michelle: My Hell

"Nathaniel, it's a long, long story. I'm not really sure where to begin, or how much to tell you." Michelle sighed, rubbing her eyes with the heels of her hands. "Well, perhaps I should say that I haven't been on holiday in Majorca, and that's why I don't have a tan. Despite that, you'll be receiving a postcard from there, if you haven't already. All the postcards you and everyone else have received over the years have been lies. I haven't gone overseas for ages. I keep…kept a big stock of cards from all over the world and I had an arrangement with a couple of close friends. I took my holidays at the same time they did and I filled out some cards for them to post.

"So why did I do this, and where did I go? Until recently I had a sister…." Michelle's voice broke. She took a sip of water.

Nathaniel squeezed her shoulder. "It's OK. Take it easy. You don't have to talk about it now if you don't want to."

"No, no, thank you, Nathaniel, I think I probably should. It can't make things worse. So, anyway, whenever people thought I was away on some exotic pleasure trip I was visiting my sister…and my mother." A cloud passed over the sun, a gust of wind rustled the foliage around them, and the lizards were gone. Michelle shivered.

"I think we should go inside, don't you?" said Nathaniel. Michelle assented and they found themselves a settee next to a grand old fireplace, stacked with wood but unlit. "Wait here a moment, Michelle." Nathaniel came back in a few minutes, two glasses in hand, to find that the fire had been kindled, small flames apparently from buried firelighter blocks were starting to gain a purchase on the wood. It crackled and settled a bit. Outside it was starting to rain.

Michelle accepted her cognac gratefully. Clasping it with both hands, and taking the occasional sip, she stared into and beyond the fire and continued her story: "Our parents didn't get on very well. I was too young to remember it clearly but I was able to piece things together later. I imagine there was fault on both sides....

"My father came from a very poor background and a broken home. Fortunately, an aunt who took him under her wing encouraged him. He worked very hard. He won a scholarship to a public school, then went to Oxford and never looked back, in the sense that he was very successful at what he did. But I don't think he was ever able to relax or take anything for granted. He may just be getting to that point now, but that's another story....

"Anyway, although we were very well off financially, we almost never saw him because he was always working. I think we were all in awe of him at least—maybe even scared. It wasn't as if he was violent, but, you know, one look from him could burn you in two. There was kind of...an unspoken expectation that we would do brilliantly at everything. If we did well he would say nothing—things were OK. If we didn't then the shame was....I don't know how he transmitted his scorn to us, because he almost never raised his voice or anything like that, but it was as if he could fill the whole house with it."

Nathaniel was thinking that his parents hadn't been too bad after all.

"My mother wasn't exactly a strong person. She came from a similar background to Dad, but she never 'bettered herself'—what an awful expression that is—and the longer the marriage went on the more my father grew to despise her. By the time I was five and my sister was two he was moving in uh...well, I suppose you could say in fairly high society. I think he must have resented the fact that he felt he couldn't take my mother out in that world, or invite any of his contacts home. He was ashamed of her. A common story, that kind of thing, I believe. My mother took to drink and sleeping pills and she was diagnosed as suffering from severe chronic depression.

"Fortunately—if that's the right word—the electroconvulsive

therapy actually seemed to do her a power of good. It's true that her memory wasn't what it used to be, but the damage was pretty minimal really. And Mum got some good counselling. She emerged a much stronger woman—at least for a while. I think it became clear to her that the root of her problems lay with Dad, at least that's how she saw it. She tried at first to get him to see a counsellor, but he laughed in her face. He could be pretty nasty at times....

"One evening, after he'd said something particularly cutting no doubt, and had gone off for a meeting, my mother appeared at our bedroom door and told us that we were going away. She'd packed two suitcases with her things and ours—my sister's and mine—and she wanted us to leave there and then. My little sister was half asleep and didn't really understand what was happening. I started to cry. I didn't want to go. I think Dad had just started to make an effort with me. He'd given me a teddy only that week, and he read the occasional bedtime story. I was nine then, and Yvonne was nearly six. I suppose I was becoming someone he could have an intelligent conversation with. I made a scene and refused to go. I can remember my mother trying to persuade me, tears running down her face, but I refused, absolutely and utterly, to budge. Then, a sort of...of coldness—a hatred—swept over her, and I can remember to this day what she said next: 'Very well then, Little Miss Daddy's Girl. You stay with your God's gift of a father and we'll see what becomes of you. Just don't make a noise, and go to sleep.'

"I can't really remember what happened in the next few hours—I don't think I went to sleep, I imagine I cried—but they left and Dad came home and went absolutely berserk....There was a letter telling him not to bother looking for them, that they'd gone to stay with relatives of hers that he wouldn't be able to trace, and that he'd never see them again. He calmed down enough to phone the police and anyone he could think of who might be able to help. The police came round and interviewed us, and looked for possible clues I suppose. Nothing."

Nathaniel was thinking how little he had known the seemingly imperturbable Michelle. How many stories there were under the surface of people! The barman came over, put some more logs on the fire and gave it a poke. "Yes, nothing like a good fire," he said.

Nathaniel could see that he expected some kind of acknowledgement so made an effort to pull himself into pleased-customer mode. "Mmmn. It's great. Fancy needing a fire at this time of year, though. That's England I suppose!" The barman seemed satisfied with this, but, picking up the vibration that he had interrupted something, withdrew.

Michelle continued, "So he tried every means he could think of, of contacting them, offering a reward, putting advertisements out, and so on and so forth. Nothing doing. It was a horrible, horrible time. I cried constantly. I did badly at school where my life was hell—I was teased mercilessly about being abandoned by my mother. Can you imagine what that does to a child? Eventually Mum phoned. She was staying with relatives in Sunderland. She wanted a divorce. Dad was so angry with her he not only agreed immediately, but he made her promise never to contact him again.

"The only good thing, if there was a good thing, is that my father really tried to do his best for me. Although I didn't appreciate it at the time, he made considerable sacrifices to be with me more often. He'd never been shown any love by his own parents, and even his aunt had been a strict disciplinarian so I can forgive him for lots.....Anyway, he really made an effort to be warmer towards me. He resigned from one company and moved to another where they were less demanding of his time, but of course he had to take a cut in salary. On top of that he hired a governess to teach me at home, to help me catch up. We moved to a new area. I started in a new school where no one knew me. The story faded from people's memories. My father met someone else. Because of my mother's desertion, he had obtained a divorce without too much difficulty. He re-married.

"My stepmother is a gentle sort of person. She certainly isn't the archetypal wicked witch sort. It must have been difficult for her, because I'm sure I resented her, but things very gradually picked up for us.

"There was never a word from my mother or sister, and I was forbidden to mention them. And then one day, there was a letter for me. I thought at first it might be from a boy I fancied at the time—I was sixteen and my head was full of boys. It wasn't. It was a very strange letter. There was nothing to say who it was from, and no return address.

The postmark suggested it might be from somewhere in Wearside, but it was too blurred to be certain. All the letter said, in bad handwriting, was that I should be in the house at five p.m. and answer the phone, and that I should be on my own and not tell anyone about it. I was quite excited. I cancelled my piano lesson, and sat by the phone. Of course Dad was at work and Sal, my stepmother, was visiting a friend so no elaborate schemes were necessary to have the house to myself.

"The phone rang, exactly on time. There was this strange voice, with a strange accent, almost a Geordie accent. It was a young girl, who claimed to be an 'Yvonne.' It took me a second or two to work it out. Of course it was my sister. She sounded frightened. That was the first time, the first time I'd heard my sister's voice in seven years." Michelle was finding it difficult to continue. She had put down her empty glass and was pinching the bridge of her nose between the thumb and forefinger of her left hand, her eyes closed. Her mouth was working.

Nathaniel placed a gentle hand on her back. "It's alright, Michelle. No hurry."

She swallowed, and started speaking again, "She told me…she told me that she thought about us night and day, but that she could no longer remember what we looked like. That Mum forbade her to talk about us. That life wasn't very easy. Mum's relatives weren't any help, the few that were still in the area. They were all very poor and busy with their own problems. Yvonne had used directory enquiries to find us. She wanted to see me, but didn't want Mum to know about it. She couldn't talk long. They didn't have a phone, but she would wait in the phone booth at the same time every Thursday, seven o'clock. She gave me an address but told me to disguise any letters I sent so that if Mum saw the envelopes she wouldn't suspect who they were from. I could hear some shouting in the background. She said there were some people impatient to use the booth and she'd have to go.

"Can you imagine how upsetting that was? Years of nothing and then a conversation which left me with the feeling that something was wrong. The first thing I wanted to do was to speak to Dad, but then I thought no, better not. After all, he had forbidden me to mention Mum and Yvonne. I had once raised the subject hypothetically, you know, like…if, just by chance Yvonne or Mum happened to get in touch one day....He hit the roof. So Yvonne and I were in the same boat: we had to keep our parents out of it. I thought how dare they forbid sisters to know each other! It wasn't our fault, what had happened. Actually I suppose on a deep level I did blame myself....I think children do. I had done for years. I kept thinking if I'd gone with Mum I could have talked sense into her later. But then I was only nine. Anyway, by the time I was sixteen my guilt was changing into anger, resentment.

"But there was more than upsetting Dad at stake, 'cause I think if it had just been that maybe I would have said 'To hell with you!' I was also worried that if contact with Mum were re-established then it might upset my stepmother Sal, and I didn't want Sal to suffer. She was as innocent as Yvonne and myself. Anyway, I kept the secret, and it kind of ate away inside me.

"I wrote to my sister, putting a false name and address on the back of the envelope. I sent some money also, although I didn't have a great deal; Dad never believed in spoiling me, and I was still at school. Every Thursday I tried to phone, but either there was no reply, or there was some stranger, or it was engaged. I wrote several times and heard nothing. Then, two months later, she phoned again. Dad was home so it was a bit awkward. I think I kept calling her Sandra or something and she got the hint and I gave her a safe time to phone.

"I think it was at that point that I started to suspect that whatever was wrong was seriously wrong. The whole thing wasn't doing me any good either. Everyone was worried about me, but I felt I couldn't tell anyone. It was dreadful. They called in the school shrink, or 'counsellor' I think the title was. Her name was Ms. Wood. In fact I was itching to tell someone, and when Ms. Wood assured me that anything I told her would remain confidential I told her almost everything. It was a massive relief to confide in someone. She was quite a wise woman. I think she knew that as soon as I'd got the money together I was intending to go and see Yvonne, come what may, so she did a very good thing. She told me not to do anything in a hurry but she led me to believe that she would come with me. She said she had an idea and would get back to me in a few days.

"She was as good as her word. Ms. Wood was what you might call a polymath—she had so many interests and activities. One of them was art history, and indeed she'd organised school art trips before. Anyway, she came back to me with a clever idea. She had been speaking to the teacher who ran the history society and thought she could organise a joint trip to the northeast. There were lots of museums and galleries and sites of historical interest and what-not in the Sunderland-Newcastle area, but, more specifically, it so happened that the history people had been looking at the death of traditional industries in Britain and there was a museum in Sunderland that apparently had excellent exhibitions on coal mining, ship building and glass blowing. Ms. Wood saw no reason why the arts society shouldn't study glass blowing and moulding. She suggested I join the society and then I would have a legitimate, uhh…a natural reason to go up to the northeast the next long weekend.

"Having that to look forward to was such a good feeling. And actually I enjoyed the arts thing as well in the meantime!" Michelle laughed. Nathaniel smiled, remembering their conversations on this subject.

"So when my sister eventually phoned again I explained what was happening. She sounded a bit doubtful but she didn't have much choice really. She asked for more money. I sent her what little I'd saved since I'd last raided my savings for her. I thought I might have to borrow some money from Ms. Wood.

"Dad was really pleased with the idea of me going off on an arts and history trip with some school friends. Besides, there were two teachers going with us, the history teacher—Mr. Hardwick, I think his name was—and Ms. Wood of course. Dad was so delighted with my enthusiasm for something—there hadn't been much of it for a while—that he ended up giving me quite a generous sum of money, telling me to really enjoy myself. I think he also saw the trip as a sort of coming-of-age thing….

"Well, it certainly was. To cut a long story short, there were two museum-art galleries in Sunderland. Ms. Wood arranged for me to have half a day off when they were going around the transport museum, which wasn't particularly interesting for us art people anyway. She insisted that I give her an address where I was going, and told me to phone her at her hotel if I wasn't back by five p.m. I promised.

"Well, it was a shock, Sunderland. Particularly the area where my sister and mother lived, a big rundown estate. Very bleak. I won't bore you with the details, I'm sure you can imagine them. Anyway, I eventually found where they lived. It was an old tenement block. The ground floor door was hanging open, the intercom thing didn't work. My sister had told me that Mum would be out and that I could go up and knock on the right door on the first floor. I can't tell you how nervous and excited I was as I walked up those filthy stairs.

"I knocked on the door. This ill-looking creature with dirty brown hair opened the door, keeping the chain on. 'Yeah?' she said. She coughed. I thought I'd come to the wrong place as this looked nothing like my sister as I'd imagined her. She sounded aggressive, and looked distrustful. I apologised and said that I must have come to the wrong place—did she know an Yvonne? The door banged closed and I thought that was that. I'd come all this way for nothing. I was never going to find her.

"But there was a rattling noise and the door opened wide and the odd-looking creature was crying. And she threw her arms around me. It was…it was Yvonne!" Michelle was weeping.

Nathaniel could see the barman eyeing them. This sort of thing wasn't good for business.…Nathaniel, sitting next to Michelle on the settee, leaned across and put an arm around her shoulders. The sobbing subsided. They'd been occupying the settee for some time and the barman was restless. "Michelle, let's go somewhere else. I know a nice place we can park the car." They stood up and left, Michelle with lowered head and biting a thumbnail, guided by Nathaniel's arm around her waist.

Nathaniel swung the car onto the shoulder of the narrow country road and switched off the engine. There were a couple of poplars on the slight rise where they now found themselves. All about them the fens stretched flat and green and dull, quartered by ditches dug long ago by Dutch drainage experts, some of whom had settled in the lands they had reclaimed. It was still raining, a steady dispiriting drizzle. The nearest village was hidden in the murk.

Michelle continued her story, "I went in. There were ashtrays full of cigarette butts. There was a threadbare sofa and an easy chair, and not a great deal else really. The place had a stale smell. The windows were closed. A small black-and-white TV was on the floor in the corner. Yvonne sat on the sofa and indicated that I should sit next to her. She was trembling, terribly thin and small, and wrapped in several baggy jumpers. She was only twelve. She lit a cigarette and offered me one, as if it were the most natural thing in the world. Neither of us knew what to say.

"I started speaking, just blurting things out, stupidly....Things like 'So, how's school then?' The vehemence of her reply shocked me: 'It's f***ing shite!' Slowly I worked things out, put the story together. In fact it was only much later, when she was in hospital, and I started making enquiries and looking for records that all the pieces fell into place.

"Anyhow, it appears that when they first arrived in Sunderland, Mum had not wanted to let the authorities know where she was, because she didn't want Dad to track them down. For a few weeks they'd lived with Mum's sister and her husband but it had been made clear to them that they would have to move out and look after themselves. Of course they couldn't remain hidden if they were to claim dole, etc. Mum had to contact Dad and get an official divorce. She was so proud and angry that she refused to take any money from him. That's how stubborn she was. I think Dad had, in his worst moments in the past, called her a parasite. She was determined to prove herself, to make her own way....The trouble was it wasn't just her; she also had to support Yvonne, and the dole and child allowance were barely enough to live on. The only jobs available amounted to slaving long hours for the same money.

"They got this terrible flat. Fortunately there were some friendly neighbours—Indians who had fled from Uganda. They used to come round with offerings of their food. Yvonne used to play with the kids and Mum would sometimes leave her with them to grab a moment for herself, and a bit later to work. She found a clandestine job in a fish-and-chip shop. It was very badly paid, but even the few pounds cash-in-hand made a big difference....

"Then the kids at Yvonne's school got to hear that they were friendly with 'Pakis.' She was bullied and teased. They would wait for her outside the school gates and they would set about beating up the 'Paki-lover.' They put dog shit through the letter box, and their neighbours', and foul graffiti was daubed everywhere: 'Go home Paki parasites and take your

Paki-loving friends with you!' That sort of thing. And Yvonne had just adopted a little stray kitten. When Yvonne and Mum were out the bastards caught the kitten and cut it open so that its entrails were hanging out. They tied a hate message round its neck and nailed it by its tail to the door. It was still alive when they came back home. It was just about the only thing that Yvonne owned, the only thing…the only thing she loved…." Michelle was struggling to maintain her self-control.

Nathaniel clasped her hands in his. "God…."

"Mum had a nervous breakdown and went into hospital. Yvonne was sent to a children's home. Yvonne never really talked about it, but I gather she, she…." Michelle was battling not to cry. Nathaniel hugged her as best as he could in the confines of the car.

"Oh, Nathaniel….I'm pretty sure she was abused. She was only eight!" It was clear that Michelle would not be able to talk again for some time. Nathaniel kept hugging her and rubbing her back. There was nothing he could think of to say. His mind was numb. This was going to take a long, long time but he had to hear it all out for Michelle's sake.

"When Mum recovered sufficiently to be discharged, Yvonne was allowed to join her again. Unfortunately she had to go back to the same school. They couldn't afford to move. They were still living next to the Indians but they simply could not take the risk of associating with them again. Can you imagine how they all felt? I think Yvonne, for her own survival, was forced to take part in some horrible act against them. I guess this happened….

"Anyway, despite this, school was simply intolerable for Yvonne. She repeatedly played truant. There was nothing Mum could do, she was out working whenever she could. Yvonne started drinking and smoking very young—glue-sniffing, dope, petty crime….It wasn't long before she was in the juvenile court. The judge, I can imagine, made some derogatory remark about single mothers living off the state and not assuming responsibility for their children. Yvonne had a criminal record by the time she was ten.

"Of course she was disruptive whenever she was in school, desperately seeking attention. She was expelled, and was supposed to receive special tutoring or something, but this was only for a couple of hours a week. Nonetheless she got on well with her first tutor. I think she really looked up to her, and she was just about coming out of her shell when the tutor was moved elsewhere. Everything went downhill again. Most of the time Yvonne was left to her own devices—her only friends were kids like herself, illiterate vagabonds. She was in court again. Nothing really changed. Then one of her friends, the only one with a real talent, let her have a go on his beat-up guitar. She absolutely loved it. She was a natural, if there is such a thing. She had virtually no education, and supposedly couldn't concentrate on anything. 'Attention Deficit Disorder' or some nonsense like that—but there she was borrowing this guitar whenever she could, which wasn't often, and practising, practising, writing songs even, although she could barely put a pen to paper. That first time I saw her she had the guitar and played me one. It was really good, as if there was another person inside this frail messed-up little sister of mine that the guitar released. It was…it was really beautiful. You know I heard a Negro spiritual the other day, and it had something of that in it!

"Anyway, that visit was the first time I'd seen her since they'd left. Of course I only gathered a small amount of her past then, but it was enough to really…umm, turn things upside down. You know, all the sorts of comfortable judgmental attitudes to the poor which I had unconsciously been absorbing, they were all destroyed. When I got back to cosy little 'Middle England' I was a different person. My friends seemed alien. It was really difficult. I was determined to do everything I could to help my sister, and my mother, even if she didn't want anything to do with me. I insisted that Dad let me take on an evening and weekend job. Well, of course, my schoolwork started to suffer, and before long he forced me to stop, which I only half resented because I also realised that there was no point destroying my own future also. Dad wanted to know why I seemed to need so much money, because I never had anything to show for it. I couldn't tell him anything. He thought I must be taking drugs. Ironic, really. And the thing was, the more depressed and upset I got about the impossible situation, the more I was tempted! That would have been the two of us down the tubes. But of course I never took anything. Somehow I muddled through, managing to visit Yvonne every few months in one sneaky way or another, and give her what little I had. But I couldn't go often enough or give her enough to make a real difference, and I was just watching things fall apart, really.

"Anyhow, Mum heard my sister playing this old broken guitar in her bedroom one day, and told her how good she was. I can imagine how happy Yvonne must have been, I can imagine her face all…all lit up. I'm sure no one had ever said much complimentary to her. For all Mum's bad points she has—or had—some very good ones, and I'm sure she really loved Yvonne. She decided to buy her a guitar, a really nice one. This would be her salvation, she must have thought. Of course good guitars don't come cheap, and Mum certainly wouldn't have been able to borrow money from the bank, but she saw this advertisement, offering loans to anyone, no credit checks….

"You can guess what happened. It was a loan shark thing, with an interest rate of virtually fifty percent. Mum must have been so happy to be offered the money that she didn't read the small print. I can picture her coming out of the office with the money in her purse, and going into the music shop, and going home with the guitar, all glowing and excited and humming to herself, and then Yvonne's little face when she saw it." Michelle buried her face in her hands, her shoulders shaking.

Nathaniel was moved as deeply as he had ever been in his life. He was not only appalled at the story of Yvonne's life, he was in awe of Michelle. This young lady was the most impressive, truly good human being he had ever met. If he had ever entertained the notion of an "affair" or a "fling" with her, that thought had gone from his mind. *Let nothing cheap or nasty ever sully her.* He realised that he loved her in a transcendent, pure way. He knew, too, that he was in the presence of not just a natural Hope-ist, but someone with the integrity, compassion, intelligence and drive to significantly shape the dawning movement. He too was crying, openly and unashamedly as he hadn't done since he'd been a little boy. It was as if with this woman he had come home. To a home he had never known existed. He kissed her, very gently, on the cheek. She turned towards him, and put her arms around him. They held each other. The tears on their faces echoed the rain on the windows.

CHAPTER THIRTY-ONE
Yvonne Worse, and the Michelle Shock

It was getting late. They had to get back to HDI headquarters. While Nathaniel drove, Michelle continued the story: "So of course Mum couldn't keep up with the repayments. At first she tried to hide it from Yvonne, but Yvonne couldn't avoid noticing that Mum was even more depressed than usual, there was nothing on the table but expiry-dated stuff…and then she came across one of the threatening letters. Yvonne, although she wasn't exactly literate, put two and two together. I think she probably felt guilty.

"She sold her guitar and gave Mum the £50 she'd got for it. Of course the guitar had cost Mum a lot more than that, and the debt was running into hundreds. I think they had a blazing row, and from that point things really went downhill. It was seldom that I managed to contact her after that. The debt collectors came round and took what few possessions they had. Yvonne stayed away from home more and more—sleeping rough, shoplifting to feed herself….She was in the juvenile court more than once. In and out of children's homes, which she would always escape from. Not long after she reached the age of adult responsibility, in the eyes of the law, she was caught stealing food from a supermarket skip. I think they'd dumped a load of cheese that was approaching its sell-by date—presumably they wanted to replace the line with a faster-selling more profitable one. It's actually an offence to take dumped food, if you can believe it! Anyway she was fined. Can you think of anything more stupid than fining someone so poor that she has to steal dumped food out of a skip? Of course she couldn't pay the fine.

"To make matters worse she fell pregnant. I don't really know what was going through her mind at the time, but I imagine she wanted to make a fresh start, well away from everything that had so many unpleasant memories. Maybe she just wanted to evade the fine. Maybe a friend of hers had moved...but she hitch-hiked to Glasgow. She somehow found a squat and moved in with a group of other young homeless people. They would busk and beg for a living. When I spoke to her later about it she gave me the impression that this was one of the happiest times of her life, those few months. She always liked talking about that time, the little community they established for themselves, the parties....That time and the day Mum had given her the guitar. I always tried to change the subject when that came up because I knew where it would lead.

"The time came when she was due to give birth. She didn't want to go to hospital because she was afraid the authorities would identify her, and she'd be in trouble for not paying the fine. I can imagine that her squat-mates weren't too happy about her giving birth amongst them, but she could be very insistent, my little sister. So she started to give birth in the squat. It was a breech presentation and it was obvious that unless she got medical help she would die. She got to the hospital, but it was too late to save the baby. I believe it was badly underweight anyway, and so was Yvonne.

"She was in the hospital for a few weeks. Of course her identity had come out and she had given them my phone number. I went to see her. By this time I was working for HDI and had more money so I stayed up there a week. That was the first time I pretended to be overseas on holiday, by the way.

"Yvonne was horribly depressed, I could see that. The one good thing was that they had decided to quash her fine for stealing from the skip. That was the only time when the law wasn't an ass in her case. Anyhow, it was obvious that she was in no state to look after herself, but for some reason, after a brief stay in a psychiatric ward on antidepressants, they insisted on releasing her. She was supposed to report regularly to an outpatients clinic. No one bothered to tell me any of this, and Yvonne was beyond having the sense to contact me. She went back to the squat. I can imagine her trudging down Sauchiehall Street, in her three worn jumpers, with her ragged little knapsack, containing almost nothing...."

Michelle stopped talking. She was blinking and looking out the window. She cleared her throat.

"Of course her friends had been expelled and the property had been boarded up. She knew no one and there was nowhere for her to go....She was really on the streets now. I don't know how she managed....Well, actually, I can guess.... Months...a year went by and there was no word from her at all. I imagined she might be dead. Then she phoned. She was in hospital once more. Not for the same reason. She'd been knifed and beaten.

"I went to see her immediately, of course. I pretended that a friend was seriously ill...which was near enough the truth anyway. It wasn't just the wounds that were shocking. She was throwing fits as she was coming off heroin.

"For the next few years she was in and out of the hospital. Methadone was never enough. She was injecting and swallowing jellies, of course, but heroin was always the big one. She was certainly on the game by this time, I suspect she had been for a long time....You know, even the bits I witnessed get all confused for me, because there was so much that happened. I know she went on a couple of de-tox courses. The first time she overdosed on heroin not long afterwards....She was in hospital for weeks. She also picked up various STDs along the way....The second time she went on a de-tox course, the same thing happened and she very nearly died. Methadone does more harm than good in my opinion....You know if they gave them a set dose of clean heroin every day they'd be fine, the pushers' and smugglers' market would collapse, and everyone would benefit in the long run...but the politicians are too lazy to explain this....Oh, what's the use? Hell.

"Anyway, there was a sort of semi-independent drug advice centre that seemed to help her for a while. They had a soup kitchen which they tried to make welcoming—you know cheerful pictures of flowers on the walls, that kind of thing....You could go to their little hall any time for a cup of tea and biscuits and some company. There was even a guitar there. I could see her putting on weight and I started to hope that this was the light at the end of the tunnel. And then there was an article in *The Sin* about how impostors were making a fortune selling the *Beggar, Shoo!*'

Nathaniel was so startled to hear Mudrock cropping up in this story that he almost drove into the car in front. He braked sharply and the car behind hooted.

Michelle was so wrapped up in her story that she didn't even seem to notice. "Well, the centre was largely funded by the *Beggar, Shoo!* and because their sales plummeted after the *Sin* article the centre had to close. Once more Yvonne had been let down at the moment she most needed support. She was pregnant again.

"Not long after that she was fined a couple of hundred pounds for stealing a jersey worth twenty-five. She couldn't pay, of course. She was arrested. She was detained at Risleyton Vale. I don't know whether you've heard about it?"

Nathaniel admitted he hadn't.

"Well, it's pretty grim I can tell you. The place is horribly overcrowded and the staff are overworked. There is a shortage of basic clothing. At times Yvonne was shackled, can you believe it? At that point there weren't even any private washing facilities or toilets for the women. The male officers used to watch through the cell doors, and award the women points out of ten."

Michelle broke off again. She was biting her knuckles. The windscreen wipers clacked away. It was a few minutes before she found her voice. "They put Yvonne in with some real hard cases. Yvonne was obviously a hopeless loser through no fault of her own. Her cell mates made her life hell. She was forced to do all the little chores in the cell. She was bullied mercilessly. She virtually stopped eating. As it was, their diet was unhealthy—the men cooked the food and they used to shout that they'd...that they'd put shit and piss and semen in the custard and gravy...any sloppy food they claimed to have contaminated. The women would only eat chips and pies. Yvonne was wasting away, a pregnant woman. And then she attempted suicide. All she had was a knife she'd stolen from the dining room table and sharpened on a wall. Imagine her sawing away...." Michelle broke off and coughed.

"It was messy, lots of blood spread around, but they told me her life had not been in any real danger—huh! When she came out of hospital, a day later, with her arms all bandaged they put her in the strip cell.

There's this procedure, or umm…programme or whatever, called 'SPS,' 'Suicide Prevention Strategy.' They dress you in an uncomfortable loose T-shirt and skirt made from some special blue material you can't tear. The sheets are the same. The bed is just a concrete block. There is nothing else in the cell apart from a cardboard bedpan. You can't kill yourself because there's nothing to do it with. Basically it's cheaper than trying to solve people's problems, much cheaper than counselling or occupational therapy or anything…and while you're in there they don't have to worry about you. So you're shut up in this room with nothing but your problems. Of course if you are really suicidal and determined, you pretend you're not so that they'll let you out…and that room makes you suicidal. It is so…." Michelle was crying again. Her voice was hoarse. Nathaniel decided to pull into a motorway services area so they could have a cup of tea.

Michelle sat herself at a table while Nathaniel went to queue. He added a packet of shortbread to his tray. He paid at the till and turned towards the table. She had gone. In the few seconds before he spotted her a dozen appalling scenarios flashed before his eyes, but there she was on her way back from the toilets, having touched up her make-up. She flashed him a brave little smile, but it only involved her mouth. Her eyes were so sad.

They drank their tea in silence. With all the hurly-burly of the contents of several dozen motorway vehicles eating and talking, and laughing and crying (there was a baby at the next table) it was the wrong place to continue the story, and more trivial conversation was impossible now. They sipped and chewed in silence. The refreshments finished, they sat there for a moment. There was a strange tension. Although they both knew that it was therapeutic for Michelle to tell her story, and Nathaniel wanted to hear it, it was also an ordeal for them both. Sitting in silence in the middle of the indifferent crowd had afforded a little island of relief, but they had to leave it and strike out once more. Nathaniel squeezed Michelle's hands and smiled. "OK, come on, girl, we can't sit around all day!" As they walked out they passed a young man reading *The Sin*. Nathaniel tried to get between Michelle and his table so that she wouldn't see it. But how silly—the wretched *Sin* was everywhere!

—

The car picked up speed and merged with the flow. Michelle started speaking again, "Eventually the trial came up. The judge was merciless this time. He looked at her long record—I was there—and said in view of the 'apparent ineffectiveness of previous punishments' he was going to give her 'a lesson she would not forget.' He sentenced her to two years. The smug fascist bastard. I knew, in my heart of hearts, that he might just as well have sent her to the gas chambers. I knew it would kill her." Now Michelle seemed to have a new energy, there was anger in her voice.

"I tried to hide my horror from Yvonne. I tried to get her enthusiastic about having a baby. I visited her as often as I could, sent her lots of presents. I had an interview with the new governor of the women's wing and pleaded Yvonne's case. She was a really nice friendly, approachable, capable woman. She arranged for Yvonne to have some counselling, tolerable cell mates….And she started a course in basic mothering skills. She turned a lot of things round in that prison. The male mafia that ran the show didn't like it. They trumped up some accusation or other against her and a male governor took her place, but, anyway, Yvonne seemed to benefit from her influence. Of course her educational programme was disrupted due to overcrowding and staff shortages, but Yvonne managed to stay off drugs during the rest of her pregnancy, which can't have been easy, because heroin was widely available. You know I heard it just used to be good old dope in the prisons in the old days but the new urine tests detect it. God, the idiocy…." Michelle sighed.

"So, she had her baby, a healthy lovely little girl she called, she called…Michelle." Michelle buried her face in her hands, breathing deeply.

"Of course they had her in shackles as she went into and came out of the hospital, but, never mind, for the first time in years Yvonne was happy. They let her look after the baby. She had a common interest with the other mothers in the prison. I was amazed, you know. Given Yvonne's history I thought she might go into postnatal depression or something, but no, she was fine.

"It was then that I decided to risk telling Dad. He…he said, very coldly: 'I only have one daughter. As far as I'm concerned Yvonne died a long time ago. I'm really disappointed in you lying to me all these years, Michelle. I don't suppose there is any point telling you to have nothing to do with her, but I never want to hear about her or her baby again, or even know that you are seeing them. For your sake I shall give you some extra money. You can give it to the baby if you want.' That was all he ever said on the subject.

"I never understood how he could be like that—so inhuman, brutal....The next year was relatively good for Yvonne. I saw her four times. The baby was fine, and she was a surprisingly good mother. And then I had a phone call—she'd attempted suicide again, this time she'd tried to hang herself. Apparently mothers can only keep their babies for a year, and then they are taken off them. That pushed Yvonne over the edge again. I was so angry I wanted to kill them all, all those f***ing bastards that had no idea about anything....I went up there and visited Yvonne in hospital—she was delirious on sedatives and raving about how they had disembowelled her kitten—and then I demanded a meeting with the prison governor and kicked up all hell. I suppose that did my case no good. Once I'd calmed down I investigated the possibility of adopting her. No go—they didn't think I was suitable, and they wouldn't even tell me why. I blew my top again, big style....Nothing changed. They wouldn't tell me where little Michelle was even, my own niece! I tried to contact Mum also, thinking that she might rally round under the circumstances and somehow might be able to adopt her, but Mum had disappeared.

"Yvonne came out of hospital and went into the strip cell for two weeks. When she came out she wasn't speaking to anyone, except that if you asked her how she was she would say, 'I'm fine. I'm really fine.' I knew she wasn't, I knew she was going to attempt suicide again.

"Two weeks ago I received a phone call. They said she was very ill in hospital and that I should go and see her. I had been about to go up anyway—-the postcards had all been arranged with my friends. I knew immediately that Yvonne was dying. She had apparently hoarded some paracetamol. It destroyed her liver. By the time they worked out what she'd done it was too late. It was hideous....At the end she was a horrible dirty yellow and vomiting and convulsing....Oh God, I couldn't believe it—paracetamol that you can buy on supermarket shelves! It was….Seeing her like that….

"You know, when she died I was actually relieved, Nathaniel. And, by the way, they told me, in passing, that they wouldn't have considered a transplant, because she was HIV and Hepatitis C positive." Michelle seemed strangely bright-eyed. "As I was standing there, holding her dead hand, all yellow and withered, on the end of her scarred arm, I realised something that I'd never thought of before, but it was obvious: if Dad had given her a teddy bear, and not me, then it might have been me lying there, and her thinking the same thought. Such a small thing….It was so weird to think that a teddy bear was all…." Michelle sighed. She didn't speak for a while.

"I phoned Dad. He looked at me, kind of coolly. Then he said, 'Well, I'm sorry.' That was it. When I got back from Scotland yesterday evening I went straight into HDI, into Dad's pharmacology library…."

Nathaniel turned round in his seat, the car almost crashing into another attempting to pass them. "What! Your dad works at HDI?"

It was Michelle's turn to look surprised. "Of course he does, Nathaniel! He's your boss, after all!"

Nathaniel pulled into the next layby. He sat gaping, still clasping the steering wheel.

Despite the horror of her story, Michelle seemed slightly amused at Nathaniel's ignorance. "Well, we never made a thing of it, you know— accusations of nepotism and all that….It is a relatively cushy job I've got, after all. Oh, come off it, you must have known!"

"No, honestly! I had no idea!"

"Anyway I went into his library and I looked up paracetamol. Do you know what I discovered?"

"That it's lethal, but that it could be made harmless….I did a course in biology you know."

"Exactly. If they mixed a sulphur-containing amino acid in with the paracetamol! It would only increase the cost slightly. I was so angry I did a little bit of research—on the Internet, and by phoning a few people. Apparently it's elementary pharmacology and they've known it for years and years….Every year there are probably thousands of people the world over who die needlessly and painfully from paracetamol, many more than from ecstasy, or anything like that….But they won't make it safe because the improved version would cost slightly more and the publicity surrounding the new combination drug would frighten people off paracetamol altogether and harm their profits! Their f***ing profits, Nathaniel!"

Nathaniel was rapidly overcoming his shock at Michelle's identity. From the way she was speaking he knew that his earlier feelings about her remained valid. She had to join the Hope-ists. She was a Hope-ist! She was pure gold. "Michelle, I can't begin to tell you how moved I am by what you've told me. I…uh, it sounds so lame—but I admire you so much….But, you know, you're not the only one with a secret. Listen, it's…what…it's just gone six. What do you say we take the car back to HDI, and then go for an early meal somewhere? Can you make it tonight? I think Rosemary's got some meeting connected with her music shop, and I really need to tell you something very important. And I think you'll find it a comfort."

So it was that Michelle Silversmith joined the International Hope-ist Movement. It was her voice, distorted a bit, that Andy Richards had listened to on his long car journey to the Peak District. She was the one who dug up most of the information on Mudrock used in Task One.

CHAPTER THIRTY-TWO
Sheep and Satin Slash

Having finished breakfast, Shelagh went up to her room to collect her things. She was about to leave when she remembered the roses. She put down her case and approached the dressing table. She hovered over them for a few seconds, her face working, before pulling one from the bunch, wrapping it in some dampened tissue paper and then a plastic bag, and stuffing it into her handbag, the long stem protruding. She picked up the rest of the bunch. The receptionist might like them.

The journey back to Inverdon was relatively incident free, apart from a forty-minute unscheduled stop south of Edinburgh due to a suicide on the line (a previous train). Shelagh couldn't help thinking that if one thing were certain, it was that the suicide wouldn't be that of a GREED shareholder!

So much had happened in the two days since she'd left Inverdon, especially in emotional terms, it seemed that she'd been away for months. She was coming back with money in her pocket, and a major job to do to justify it. Depression had been replaced by nervousness, apprehension....And she wasn't sure at all what emotion would eventually drop out of her confusion over EJ.

The rose replaced the faded flowers on her kitchen windowsill, and sat there for days, gradually wilting, next to a large bottle of highly concentrated dishwashing liquid. Now that she had money, Shelagh had a telephone connected and chased up the council to do something about the state of her flat. A buildings inspector came round: it was to be fumigated and damp-proofed. She was offered emergency accommodation while this was being done, but decided to stay with her parents. Some impulse made her pop the almost dry rose into her suitcase.

The three days with her parents were all her nerves could stand. They would persist in asking awkward questions! And the phone calls on Hope-ist matters hardly dampened their curiosity. It was good to get back to her own wee place, re-painted and rat-free, even if the neighbours and the stairwell remained the same. Now she could concentrate entirely on the Scottish wing of the Hope-ists.

But she couldn't. The rose was still there, trying to tell her something. EJ had been gauche in the extreme, but his card had a truthful feel to it. And he was so funny in some ways. Should she write to him?

She was sitting at her kitchen table, turning the rose in her hands, when the phone rang. It was Nathaniel. "Hi, Shelagh. Listen, I've just had a package for you forwarded by the hotel. I suppose my address was easy to trace as I paid for the room. Anyhow it's fairly bulky. The strange thing is the name on the back of it is the same as that of someone I knew when I was a kid. This E.J. Clackworthy, it wouldn't by any chance be Ernest Jason Clackworthy, would it?"

Shelagh laughed. "Yes! He's a photographer I met when I was in London. A strange guy...."

"A photographer! I don't believe it! With curly black hair and glasses?"

"He might have contact lenses, but yes!"

"God! It was a long long time ago, but there's a really funny story attached to him...and to photography. Well, it involves me and Rosemary—wait till I tell her! We'll all have to meet next time you come to London. You'll kill yourself laughing when you hear it, it's best to wait until we're all together. I'll drop the guy a line right away!"

Shelagh was astonished at how happy she was.

The package arrived two days later. It was a set of the most exquisite photographs of herself she had ever seen. She really did look beautiful. The best one was framed. The card was simply inscribed: "Please forgive me, gorgeous! I hope you're eating well! Get in touch, plee-ee-ease! EJ x"

Shelagh wrote to him immediately, a postcard showing the four seasons in Scotland: a sheep in near-horizontal rain (spring), a sheep in near-horizontal rain (summer), a sheep in near-horizontal rain (autumn), a sheep in near-horizontal snow (winter). Shelagh annotated the front: "NOT the place for photographers' cars!" On the back she wrote: "OK, forgiven, but watch it next time! I'll look you up when I'm in London."

As it turned out, Rosemary had no great desire to meet Jason/EJ again—at least she never appeared to be available on the evenings that suited Shelagh, EJ and Nathaniel. Nathaniel went for a meal with him and Shelagh, and talked of old times, but two hours was enough. In EJ's company Nathaniel and Shelagh could not talk about Hope-ist matters, the largest part of their overlapping pre-occupations, and Nathaniel suspected that she and EJ wanted to be on their own. But it was more than that—there were only so many paparazzi anecdotes he could listen to. It was exhausting pretending to be impressed by how much *The Sin* had paid him for the latest Lisa Beverley-Chemistry Navigator scoop etc., etc., when one was on the point of blowing that whole rotten ship out of the water, but how could one decently break away when EJ never stopped speaking?

"So, after I bumped into you that day, Shelagh, I was kind of dazed for minutes afterwards, and it wasn't just the physical impact you know. But I was standing there like a zombie when I remembered what I'd been doing. And I really panicked that I'd lost Lisa, but she was looking into a shop window. She didn't want to lose me! When she saw that I was free she started off again. So she arrived at this café, and went up to this guy sitting at a table just inside the window and they kissed each other, and that was my first shot—I got a grand from *Screws of the World* for that....Now there were two tables just inside the window, and the one where he was sitting was half in shadow, but the other one was brightly lit. She seemed to be gesturing and they moved to the brightly lit table. 'Good girl, Lisa!' I said to myself. And it was a perfect situation for me. I sat at the place opposite: I could have a coffee and rest my camera on the back of a chair so I could get great shots with my longest lens, and I was even a bit higher than them. *F***ing ace!*

"Now I had no idea who the bloke was, but by the way Lisa was acting I could tell it was really important for her to have some shots taken with him, which probably meant he was big news—which was great for me too—so I just kept shooting away. You know there was a shot when they were looking into each other's eyes, all adoringly, and I got five grand from *The Sin* for that one? And you'll never guess why! Well, of course, it later turned out that the guy was the Chemistry Navigator geezer who's made such a big splash and hardly anyone has any shots of, but it wasn't just because of that. In that picture Lisa was holding a cigarette and you could identify the packet on the table: Satin Slash. The guy who bought the photo from me explained—and I'm not sure he should have—I think he got carried away a bit he was so enthusiastic. Anyway, because there are so many restrictions on fag advertising—and it's looking as if even bribing the government by laundering money through sponsored companies can't last much longer after that Formula One thing—the tobacco companies only have one option left, what they call 'product placement.' The way it works is if *The Sin* publishes a picture showing a young person's role model-type smoking identifiable fags then they get a back-hander—all very under-the-counter stuff, of course, but this shot had everything—really first-rate glamour product placement, personal interest, and it was perfect technically. Hell, I was chuffed! So this meal's on me! And I've got a new car, Shelagh, with a roof that doesn't leak!"

Maybe, it hadn't been such a waste of time after all, thought Nathaniel. Shelagh was looking a bit uncomfortable. She liked this bloke, and yet she didn't. Well, sometimes he was a laugh.

When Nathaniel had excused himself, EJ took up the story again. "And another thing, Shelagh. Lisa was so pleased with the whole thing—I think Chemistry Navigator wanted some publicity for his new album, she wanted to keep her profile up so that HDI would renew its 'Face of HDI' contract with her, and I wouldn't be surprised if Empire Tobacco slipped her some dosh as well—but she was so pleased she's posted me—it must have been her—a photographer's pass to the launch party for Chemistry Navigator's new album, and there's a guest invitation as well—so would you like to go?"

CHAPTER THIRTY-THREE
Reflections

Rosemary

It amazes me how it came together. Looking back, it appears as if every meeting, liaison and apparently chance event had a purpose. Yet if we had all known what everyone else was doing at the time who knows where the world would be now? It's likely that the shock would have destroyed the Hope-ists: animal jealousy could have prevented the world from being saved! If I had known what Nathaniel felt for Michelle I would have....Yes, even though I was being unfaithful to him in more than thought!

As it was, until that famous first Hope-ist action (the kidnap of Andy James) I was unaware that the Hope-ist Movement even existed, let alone that Nathaniel had anything to do with it. I avoided anything to do with politics. I think part of it was that I was trying to screen out what had happened in Hysterique. Before that, even, I had needed to go almost as far as I could into the world of materialism and "the beautiful people" in order to give myself an emotional break from the loss my husband and child in the crash, but, inevitably, this set the pendulum swinging in the opposite direction. There was a natural reaction against the spiritual junk food, and it started with my growing interest in music.

I was immersed in the world of rock music—literally if you consider my involvement with Jim Mud! Since the picnic on the lawn Nathaniel and I had drifted apart again. One's emotions are sometimes too complicated to describe, but something had gone wrong between us on

Hysterique, and the bond we'd re-established on that tartan rug seemed to fray as Nathaniel disappeared into his work and I was beginning to get some fulfilment, some direction, from The Groove.

When I met Jim Mud I experienced something I hadn't felt since girlhood. To be honest, I hadn't thought I would ever be able to feel that stomach-churning face-flushed thing again, but when I met Jim I felt alive as I hadn't since the accident in which my child died. My horizons were wide, and life was new once more. I didn't give Nathaniel or our marriage a thought. And Jim was a hell of a nice guy. Still is, not that we see him so often these days.

Anyway, at the time of the kidnapping, Nathaniel was supposedly away attending to one of his projects in Inverdon. I invited Jim round to our place. We were between the sheets when his mobile phone went off. The ring tone was "I can't get no satisfaction." I didn't know whether to curse or giggle at the time—things were just getting interesting in bed and the irony wasn't lost on me. We could hardly carry on making passionate love with that thing chirping ridiculously in the background! So Jim got out of bed, trying to hide you-know-what. (Which I thought was rather silly of him! Endearing too….) And he went through his jacket pockets, muttering oaths all the while. He found his phone at last and put it to his ear, looking at me apologetically and raising his eyebrows the way he does.

And then his face changed.

Shelagh

EJ was such a strange guy! At times he came across as incredibly shallow, materialistic and self-seeking, but there was a sort of unguarded charming enthusiasm with it. At other times he seemed so perceptive and intelligent. You had the feeling that he understood you completely. In the days before the kidnapping I veered between a sort of girlish delight at his attentions, repulsion at his apparent manipulativeness, a feeling of superiority at the superficiality of his motivation, a motherly feeling towards him when he seemed so hopeless with things like his car, and a more distanced, analytical attitude: that he was a worthwhile human being who could be brought into the Hope-ist fold. He just needed to be made aware of the bigger picture into which his small ones fitted, so to speak. Yes, I was fascinated by him. He was a challenge.

I decided to keep him in the dark about my involvement in the Hope-ists, but to gently introduce related topics into the conversation, both to get a feel for where his sympathies might lie, and to steer him further in the direction of a Hope-ist view of the world. I didn't do this too often. I have to admit in some ways it was quite nice to have a boyfriend uninvolved with Hope-ism—sometimes I needed to escape from the intensity of it. It was, of course, very intense a lot of the time, and in more ways than one.

I suppose if you admire someone, and spend a lot of time with them, then sexual attraction can spark up. I know that Nathaniel felt something along those lines for me, and I did at times for him. I think we both decided to let ourselves enjoy a bit of flirtation and to leave it at that. If anything, it enhanced our working relationship. Perhaps part of it was that we were both trying to do our best to impress each other. As if saving the world wasn't enough motivation in itself!

During the kidnap all that teasing and flirtation stuff fell away. We were so wired—high on adrenalin—that our focus was total. I was responsible for organising the Scottish Hope-ists. I took some time off work, pretending to be ill....God, how my life had changed in just a few months: from only being responsible for myself—basically collecting a dole cheque and working out whether to eat, wash or heat my water—to being a lecturer at Robert Gilbey's and an active Hope-ist!

When *The Sin* printed the story and we knew we'd succeeded we were so elated! We all kissed each other.

I knew at that point that I loved EJ, because I was so desperate to tell him about it. I took a risk—I wish I could say it was calculated, but in truth it wasn't, it was driven—and I arranged to meet him as soon as possible afterwards. I suppose he might have sold the story and wrecked the Hope-ists, but I knew I had to tell him.

I told him everything. He sat there—in that same Greek restaurant where he'd told me to have my boobs enhanced—he sat there like a proverbial goldfish, gaping and gasping, bless him. I knew when I saw his face that it would be alright. I knew he was one of us. I think he must have sat there for a good five or ten minutes, paralytically gormless. I was giggling into my Retsina and the other diners and the waiting staff were beginning to stare. Eventually he closed his mouth, picked up his drink and clinked my glass. There was so much admiration beaming from him. I think he was crying in a kind of controlled, manly way—ha, ha! He didn't need to say anything. Then I started crying too. Quite a scene really. We were so happy.

I had found my life partner, and the Hope-ists had acquired a genius of a photographer, with a great knowledge of the advertising world.

Sometimes you have to follow your heart, you know.

No. You should always follow your heart. It sometimes just takes its time to give you a clear message, that's all.

Nathaniel

When we knew the first action had succeeded we were thrown, amazed, rudderless....We had rehearsed what we would do at that point, in a very business-like manner, but when the time came we felt as if we were drugged. I felt both as if I were living only in the moment, and as if I were living in all time—past and future. All the events that had led there—my whole life in fact—were simultaneously in my consciousness. So was the future, which I saw as golden and nostalgic! It was all upside-down.

It was as if I had crossed some threshold, beyond which everything would take place automatically, and the rest of my life were as good as acted out already. I felt tremendously powerful, but also very distanced. I felt as if I were an eternal being, put on earth for a purpose which I had sensed before, but only on a certain level. Now I beheld this purpose from a vastly elevated perspective. I belonged to another realm.

This feeling didn't last. The details fled my mind immediately. Mundane exigencies brought me back to earth: we needed to cover our tracks and lie low for a time. In practice, this meant that we had to resume our "normal" routines as quickly as possible and act as surprised as everyone else about the Hope-ists' actions.

It was some comfort that Michelle was a Hope-ist—I wasn't totally isolated at HDI. We were both intrigued—to say the least—about how her father would react to the kidnapping. Michelle was so lovely in that state of confusion of apprehension and triumph. I was hovering on the very edge of taking my feelings for her further, but I held back. I just didn't feel it was right. It would be easy for me to say that I didn't make a move because a scandal and the wrong sort of media attention might have wrecked everything (infidelity with Silversmith's daughter!), or because I felt it was morally wrong to commit adultery, but it wasn't really that, I don't think. Perhaps I was just in awe of the purity and goodness of her. Perhaps I knew that she was destined for someone else. Maybe I knew deep down that Rosemary was my ideal, and that we would connect again. Maybe I was terrified of rejection.

Mary

It was the best of times, it was the worst of times, as they say. So much was happening on so many levels that part of me was watching from a distance. Almost as Nathaniel describes himself feeling at the time we knew the first action had succeeded, I felt that way most of the time. I suppose I always have to some extent, but it was never more essential to me than then, helping to maintain my equilibrium. Heavens, I was sleeping with the enemy, I was developing the most sophisticated software in the world while hiding its real (Hope-ist) purpose from the developers themselves, I had been an actress in a real drama (which might have gone horribly wrong), I was involved in the strategic planning of the Hope-ist Movement, I was running a museum, and I was a saleswoman—selling the museum's services, and especially the Cyberbabble software. Looking back, I did a damn good job!

Silversmith was old-fashioned, like Old Spice aftershave—a relic from a chauvinist era when men made all the money and were the bosses, both at work and also (or so they thought!) at home. He was, I felt, really rather a simple man. Not simple in the sense of stupid, of course. I mean he was simple to understand in terms of his desires and motivations.

Business was a game to him. Money and power were only the tokens he used to measure success. Before the first Hope-ist action I doubt he ever seriously thought about the consequences of all his machinations for the world at large—for him the world was just a gaming board. And up to the time of the second Hope-ist action he probably only thought about the consequences of his actions in terms of how the Hope-ists might perceive them, and so target him. It wasn't that he was positively evil—I wouldn't have found him attractive had that been the case—no, he was just locked into a view of the world that happened to be inseparable from evil, that sustained and promoted it. He was blind to this fact.

Did I want to reform him? On one level, yes of course—I think most women want to remake and "save" the men they find attractive—but I didn't believe it was possible. I just enjoyed his predictable masculinity, and I used the relationship to obtain information for the Hope-ists, of course.

Now Jim Mud was different. I really fancied him in a multi-dimensional way. If I had known about Rosemary's relationship with him I might have done something stupid. Maybe I would have told Nathaniel. I don't know. I'm so glad that I only found out about it later, when so much had happened that it ceased to matter. Jim was a good guy. He had a great sense of humour. He could keep you entertained, and his conversation was so unpredictable, but you sensed he was genuine. I wonder what would have happened if he hadn't been so taken with Rosemary?

Michelle

It was as if I had lanced a boil. Telling Nathaniel about Yvonne was cathartic—not only did I need to talk about it, but I also needed to regain trust in humanity. Nathaniel's openness and impeccable behaviour released me from the prison of fear and negativity that would probably have seen me becoming a druggie or an alcoholic like my sister. Then, when he showed me a way of fighting the system, of putting the world right, I was truly happy for the first time in my life. I was part of a group of people who cared both about me and the world…and about people like my sister.

Yes, I fancied Nathaniel like anything. I suppose I had cut myself off from this sort of feeling throughout the hellish school years and my early adulthood. When my prince came along (as I saw him) I was desperate to have him. Yet I knew he was married, and I respected him too much. Besides, I was terrified of losing him as a friend. So I was happy and frustrated and sad. At least we both had Hope-ism to distract us, and within this framework we had a degree of intimacy. Now I'm so glad that nothing ever happened between us. It's all worked out so well.

CHAPTER THIRTY-FOUR
Whisky in Mud, and Clarity in Gin

"Dad!?" Mud's face went pale. "Christ! Shit! Jesus! Yeah. I see. OK." He chucked his phone onto a chair and pulled on his trousers. "Rosemary, we're watching TV." Rosemary knew whatever it was, it was serious.

As Nathaniel had insisted that the bedroom was a TV-free zone, his adulterous wife and her lover learned of the Hope-ists' first action from the settee. Rosemary had never seen Mud so fraught, all poise and humour gone. When they had watched enough of the story—playing on all the channels—to have the gist of it, he muted the sound, punching the remote control. He turned towards Rosemary, his mouth working. She had been transfixed by the story, but just why Mud was so disturbed was even more intriguing—frightening even.

At last he managed to find his tongue. "Rosemary, Bear Mudrock's my father."

They sat a long time in silence, looking at each other. Rosemary felt she should speak. "So, uh….How do you feel?"

"I don't know. We…we weren't that close. I mean I knew some of those things about him, and I didn't approve. But he's my father, and I thought we'd made up some of the distance. He was starting to believe in me, you know? Now the bastard's been shafted. I just don't know what I feel. I just don't know. Christ." He sat there breathing deeply through his nose, lips compressed. "I need a f***ing drink, Rosemary."

Rosemary poured two whiskies. No ice, no water.

They needed time apart. To think. To digest the news. Rosemary had butterflies in her stomach, as what she learned of Mudrock and his doings resonated with and re-awakened some information she'd gleaned at the time of Hysterique and stashed in her subconscious. Perhaps it was more a feeling than information, a feeling that there was a big black iceberg beneath the surface of her world, and that sooner or later she would have to deal with it. She had lost her kids and her former husband, but a time for facing horrors had come again. First she needed to purge herself.

After two days of pacing and drinking and hand-wringing, and just before Nathaniel was due back from Inverdon, she phoned Mud: "Jim, listen—I think we should stop seeing each other. No. It's not that I don't love you, or that I blame you for your father. It's just that….Yes. Friends. And, Jim—I'm thinking of joining them."

Mud whistled, lowering himself into his swivel chair, phone clamped to his ear. He spun this way and that, staring unseeingly out his office window. "You know what, Rosemary? I think I will too. They're goddamned right, after all."

When Nathaniel arrived, Rosemary didn't even notice the change in him, so wrapped up in her own turmoil was she. It wasn't her short-lived affair with Jim Mud that bothered her. That seemed trivial now. No—how to tell him that she wanted to become a Hope-ist? Working in a record store was one thing, but would he be happy with her throwing in her lot with a radical campaigning organisation? Especially one that would not be overly enchanted with HDI and the apparently standard multinational tricks of which it undoubtedly would be guilty?

For his part, Nathaniel was elated but frustrated. He could not tell Rosemary what a major coup he had just pulled off, no matter how much he itched to share his excitement. He had to protect her—and himself—for the time being. God, if she suspected his involvement and leaked it!

"It's good to see you, stranger!" Rosemary had opened the door to him as soon as she had heard his key in the lock. She kissed him, her long hair enveloping his face in the wonderful scent that always hung about her. Nathaniel was suddenly weak with compassion for his wee Rosemary. He couldn't talk to her about his state of mind, but he could press her close and sigh. How much this woman had gone through—his own sweet

Rosemary, her body still firm, despite the child it had fruitlessly borne and the mangling it had undergone. She was gorgeous and he loved her.

Rosemary was surprised at the passion of his greeting. Initially desperate to talk about the Hope-ists, to probe into his attitude to them before possibly revealing her decision, she pulled his arms from about her and held them by the wrists at waist level, but he was looking into her eyes, and his lips pursed, and he planted another quick kiss on her lips. She giggled, and led him to the bedroom.

Jim, Nathaniel. Nathaniel, Jim. Life was strange, thought Rosemary. *Dare I tell him about the Hope-ists?*

Michelle, Rosemary. Rosemary, Michelle. Life was strange, thought Nathaniel. *Dare I tell her about the Hope-ists?*

Lying on their backs afterwards, looking at their perfect faces side-by-side in the ceiling mirror, Rosemary murmured, "So what do you think of the Hope-ist thing, Nat?"

"Mmmn. Well, I don't really know...." His pulse was racing again. This time it wasn't sexual arousal.

"Oh come on, an intelligent man like you—you must have an opinion!" Rosemary turned and looked at him directly, his face in profile.

Nathaniel swallowed. This was rather aggressive—had she suspected? Christ! He fished for a convincing reply. "I can see their point, but, but, uhhh...they're running a tremendous risk." He looked at her, happy with the way he'd put it. He hadn't lied, as such. Now would she reveal that she knew of his involvement?

"Mmmn." Rosemary was disheartened. How could she tell him she wanted to join them? He would object on the grounds of safety. She turned away from him and closed her eyes.

Nathaniel breathed deeply. No, she didn't know, but how could they be close with this secret between them?

In the wake of Andy James' kidnapping, Rosemary and Mud weren't the only ones keen to join the Hope-ists. But how did one join them? The problem for the founding Hope-ists had been to build a large and coherent international organisation without exposing the leadership—

they were only too aware that they risked assassination. The Internet, in the state it existed before Cyberbabble had become widespread, provided a partial and interim solution. Mary had enough expertise to set up a few untraceable websites on which the tenets of Hope-ism were posted in the world's major languages. Emphasis was placed on the fact that Hope-ism was incompatible with violence and the destruction of property, and that such acts were disowned by the movement. Suspecting that enormous efforts would be made to identify and neutralise the core of the organisation, Mary, Nathaniel, Shelagh, Michelle, EJ and the thirty or so others involved at the time had reluctantly decided that initially there would, in fact, be no coherent, continuous organisation. Until Hope-ism became so popular that membership was the norm, they advocated (through their websites) the establishment of no more than local discussion groups, or cells. The next action would be planned and executed with the help of a select few international contacts, whom they knew personally, and with whom they communicated covertly using encryption technology. Their websites simply stated: "Be ready to act when the next Hope-ist action—Task Two—takes place. It will be obvious what you need to do."

"They came just after midnight. There were four of them, she said. Big, ugly, no more than twenty-five. Dark clothes. And guns. Her husband—Ricardo we shall call him—tried to resist and was rewarded with a Colombian kiss: a shotgun smashed into his face.

"They dragged him out of the house and beat him senseless. He was found the next morning, battered and bruised, his face barely recognisable through the coagulated blood. But at least he was alive.

"His crime? His wife, between sobs, can think only of this: Ricardo had been on strike at the ___ plant in Casanare, a poor, lowland area in the shadow of the Andes, in eastern Colombia.

"She and local community leaders suspect he was attacked after ___ passed details of strikers to the Colombian army's 16th Brigade—which ___ pays to protect its personnel, installations and pipelines. The army then used paramilitaries to encourage Ricardo not to strike again."

[© OBSERVER, Extract used with permission from an article by David Harrison which appeared in *The Observer*, 3 November 1996]

There had never been any serious argument about which multinational would be the major focus of Task Two. DAP was a natural. As a target it fulfilled all the criteria: guilty as sin of acts which could only be described as supremely evil, super-rich and powerful (and therefore sufficiently Goliath-like for its demise to *encourage les autres*), but not in possession (yet) of such a stranglehold on the market that consumers would find it too inconvenient to boycott. Perfect.

The only contentious point had been whether it was sufficiently represented throughout the world to kick off the international phase of Hope-ist action. It was important to give as many people as possible an early taste of success. Once they had participated in a successful action, they would be committed: a blooding of the spears. If relatively few people or countries took part then a chink of opportunity for the Big 200—the covert strategy-developing organisation of the largest companies in the world—might open. There was no telling how they might exploit any perceived lack of universality. Would they, for example, consider in some way "rewarding" countries in which no anti-multinational actions occurred?

Eventually the committee (steered by Nathaniel, admittedly), had opted for a dual action against DAP and Axon. Both were hypocritical if one considered the faces they presented in the developed countries and their actions in the developing world. The bosses of both were buddies of the directors of the IMF and the World Bank. Both operated a violent anti-union policy. Both paid their workers derisory wages, and sponsored political systems which ensured that Third World populations would remain abject and subservient scrabblers after the subsistence crumbs the multinationals deigned to throw them.

One was as guilty as the other when it came to wrecking the

environment. They had made a fine art of portraying environmental activists as anti-progress Luddites who would rather see people starve than see a tree cut down. DAP and Axon were happy to see both, of course, as long as their major western consumers didn't find out, and there was little chance of this, considering who controlled the media. In fact, a Hope-ist researcher had unearthed evidence that they had been amongst the major sponsors of a recent television series which had used twisted arguments, out-of-context quotations, and slick innuendo to blacken the green movement. In this way they were enjoying considerable success in setting the political left (what remained of it) against the greens. Divide and conquer. Goebbels would have learnt a thing or two.

What was important, however, was that one or other of these noxious mega-corporations (if not both) was present in all the countries in which the Hope-ists had established a foothold. No Hope-ists need be frustrated onlookers.

That the CEO of Axon had been particularly rude to Mudrock at a Big 200 meeting was not entirely irrelevant either.

"We need to get as much information on DAP and Axon as we can."

"State the obvious, Nathaniel!"

Mary's acerbic edge sometimes irritated him, but Nathaniel decided to ignore it. "I once had a god-awful job with DAP. I had no idea at the time how useful it might turn out to be. They wanted me to develop a sort of database which would enable them to find the most profitable countries in which to operate, and it dealt with such things as how exploitable the labour force was…."

"Hmmn. I vaguely remember—just after you got your first degree? Did anything come of it?"

"I couldn't stick it, but I think a guy called Fred East took over. That's all I know. These things are not advertised."

"To be honest, Nathaniel, I don't think the fact that they were toying with this idea umpteen years ago is of much use to us—I mean we already have concrete evidence of some pretty rotten stuff they've done more recently—but if we can get hold of this East guy…."

"You mean prove that they're using it now?"

"Well no, actually. I have another idea, and I think it could be a big one. I just might do a wee bittie head-hunting in Inverdon. With the Cyberbabble sales taking off, the VE and HA could afford to hire another boffin. Let me run with this a bit, will you?"

"Okey dokey. 'Nuff said, and all that. So anyway, Cyberbabble's selling? That's great! When can we use it?"

"Well," Mary exhaled in irritation, "you know full well it would be self-defeating to activate the Hope-ist part before it's the standard web browser. I would think that'll take another few months...."

"After the next action?"

"Yes. After Task Two." Mary delicately swallowed the last mouthful of gin and tonic and set her glass down, the ice clinking. The condensation sparkled in the sunlight.

"Another one?" Michelle smiled. They were sitting on the patio of her small apartment in Chelsea. Below them the London traffic struggled past a stricture in the route. This was due to a deep hole in which two men were doing something with cables and pipes. Nathaniel thought of Ford Madox Brown's painting of workmen, and had a rush of excitement as he identified himself and the other two Hope-ists looking down on this scene with Carlyle and Maurice considering how to better the lot of the poor. One could even see a beggar further along the pavement....

They were not on the balcony solely for the view, however, or on account of the weather. They were more comfortable sitting outside with the rush of traffic drowning their speech, just in case the flat was bugged. If they had noticed the slight movement of the curtains across the road, they wouldn't have been quite so relaxed.

Michelle set the bottle of tonic down. "You sure you won't change your mind and have a little splash of gin in there, Mary? No?" She handed the glass over. "Excuse me if this sounds a stupid question, but this Cyberbabble thing—surely anyone with the least knowledge of computing would be able to download the programme and know immediately what you were up to?"

Mary and Nathaniel looked at each other to decide who would answer. Nathaniel spoke, "The beauty of it is that what people download onto their computers is minimal. All the intelligent software is web-based."

"Well then, can't people just contact the controlling sites and use ftp or whatever, and work out what's happening?"

"Good question. No, they can't. The secret is a method of rapid switching between host computers. Not only can we pull in computing power from mainframes throughout the world, and use them for things like speech analysis and synthesis for example, but we can also hide the controlling software by dispersing it between machines. It's quite complex, but essentially each terminal is sent a coded list of addresses and switches between them. The coded list itself is constantly modified, at our discretion. When we want to change what Cyberbabble is doing we can direct terminals anywhere to go to certain host computers and access certain software. At the moment we're just letting the purchasers receive minimal advertising material of their own choosing. When the market penetration is sufficient, however…."

"Market penetration! You've certainly picked up the biz-speak, Nathaniel!" Mary laughed. "Do you know, I think I shall have a splash of gin, Michelle."

Michelle's smile faded as she poured. She froze as she was about to put the bottle down, her brow furrowed, and then she sat upright. Her eyes moved between Mary and Nathaniel. "I've just had an idea. As I understand it, there's nothing anyone can learn of any importance from the browser programme that sits on people's PCs. Is that right?"

"Yes," they chorused.

"And am I right in thinking that Doors is the main opposition to Cyberbabble?"

"Correct."

"And that Doors is a ruthless operator and is probably scheming like mad to thwart you?"

"Yes."

"And am I also right in thinking that your profits on Cyberbabble are likely to be vast?"

"Yes."

"And that if and when we do have adequate 'market penetration'"—

at these words she smiled and looked at Nathaniel—"then the sky's the limit and we can do anything?"

"Just about—yeah."

"Well, how would it be if you offered Doors a slice of the action? Sell some of the marketing rights to Cyberbabble to him—give him a big cut seeing as your profits will be huge anyway—and let him do half your work for you! You know, like *The Prince* says, we can turn the enemy's strengths against him."

Nathaniel and Mary looked at each other: "Brilliant!"

Michelle tried to hide her delight and pride. "I wonder what EJ's up to. He said he had an important mission this weekend, but he was very coy…."

CHAPTER THIRTY-FIVE
Share Hell, and Security

"...and shares in Mudrock companies continue to plummet. In the City, News Irrational shares have lost 230 pence in the last twenty-four hours and there is no sign that the bottom has been reached. Wall Street reports similar losses, and a spokesman for News Corruption, the US wing of Mudrock's media empire...."

[Radio X, 3 July 199-]

"The leverage this gives us, Shelagh! It's incredible!"

"It's also incredible that none of us thought what would happen to the stock market. Supposedly intelligent and well-educated...!"

"Yes, but do you realise how we can use it?"

"No, but after your Doors idea, Michelle, I'd be surprised if you didn't!" Shelagh laughed, her nose crinkling.

The International Hope-ist Movement had rapidly evolved methods of evolving rapidly. That is, they had realised that there were two sorts of meetings that were particularly productive. The one was unsurprising: people who knew each other, and had worked together successfully, met to brainstorm an issue. What they had also discovered was that when two people who barely knew each other (and it had to be limited to two, or shyness inhibited the process) came together to "blue sky," as they put it, creativity was boosted. Strangely, it happened even if one party was non-contributory—there was a magical chemistry between committed Hope-ists that could be tapped. The "random information input"

331

method was a refinement: they would take a newspaper, or watch a television channel (any channel, but they had to stick with it), or go to an art gallery, or for a walk in the park, and just let the ideas come. Relaxed creative space was vital in an organisation that planned to tackle more than a handful of short-term tasks. Space for synchronicity and serendipity, some would say.

Michelle and Shelagh, who knew each other largely by reputation, had met for such a session. They were sprawled on Michelle's thick living room carpet, propped on oversize cushions. The curtains were closed against the wet grey day and the mock coal fire glowed. It was early Sunday afternoon and Shelagh had a few hours before the flight to Inverdon. They had elected to listen to Radio X. (In any case, it was useful for someone to monitor news bulletins.) Shelagh had rolled a joint, and they passed this between them. Their conversation was murmured and the radio was turned up to thwart bugging devices.

Michelle took a drag and exhaled in the direction of an incense vaporiser. She tapped the ash into the shell ashtray. Another draw. "Look at it this way, with people buying and selling shares it means that a company can be successful or fail, not on the basis of anything concrete, but on the basis of rumour. You know, they don't have to actually produce more goods more cheaply or whatever, they only have to make people think that they will, and then the value of their stocks shoots up...."

Shelagh took the joint, nearly down to the roach. She took a final pull and stubbed it out. "So what you're saying is that we won't even necessarily have to take action against a company....If we can make people think that we're going to, then the market, the shareholders, will take the action for us and they won't have much choice but to do what we say!"

"Exactly!"

"We'll have to be careful, though...."

"What do you mean?"

"We wouldn't want to be caught crying wolf."

"But if we told people why a company was going to be targeted, then the action would actually become what the shareholders did!"

"If enough people were on our side, Michelle."

"Don't you think they will be?"

"Fingers crossed. Fingers crossed….Shit!" Shelagh had started as the doorbell rang.

Michelle sprang to her feet, gesturing to Shelagh to hide the ashtray and her dope under the sofa. She sprayed air freshener around the room before running to the intercom. "Yes?"

"Check your post."

"Hallo?" Whoever he was had gone. Michelle called to Shelagh to run to the balcony and see if she could see anyone below.

Shelagh went out and looked up and down the street. "No one there. No one I recognise. No one suspicious." She came back into the room, dripping. The front door was open and Michelle had gone. "Michelle?"

A voice answered from the bottom of the stairs. "It's OK. I'm here." Michelle came into the room clutching something. It was a video cassette. Just a video cassette—no box. "Michelle" was written in clumsy marker pen lettering on the label. "Well, only one thing for it." She put it in her video recorder and pressed play.

"Well then, can't people just contact the controlling sites and use ftp or whatever, and work out what's happening?"

"Good question. No, they can't. The secret is…."

"Oh my God, Shelagh! It's a film of the meeting we had yesterday. You can hear every word. Someone's been spying on us—shit! Taken from across the r—." With that, Michelle dashed onto the balcony. There, waving and smiling from the window of the B&B opposite, was EJ! "The little bastard!"

At the exact moment that Michelle spotted EJ, Shelagh called from the living room, "Michelle, Michelle, it's EJ!" And there he was on the screen too, a big smirk on his face, "This tape will self-destruct in five seconds. Five, four, three…." With that, the screen EJ broke into laughter, and continued speaking, "Seriously, if you don't already know it, I have appointed myself security officer. Listen, we're going to have to be a lot more careful about how we conduct ourselves. With the right microphone, or even with a bit of lip-reading skill, it's easy to tell what people on the balcony are saying. Another thing, for all you know this tape might have been booby-trapped. Look, I know there's a danger of becoming too paranoid, but the stakes are pretty high here and we're dealing with some desperate people. I think we're OK so far, but you never know. I don't think your flat is bugged, Michelle, because I broke in and scanned it when you were out one day. All part of the journalist's trade. Oh and by the way, watch the dope, too—any excuse....Wipe this tape when you've seen it. Don't burn it—that's what the amateurs do— any remains will arouse suspicion."

Mudrock sat at his big desk with his head in his hands. "Jesus wept!" he hissed. Just a few weeks ago he had been on the brink of owning half the world's media. Now his empire was crumbling away to nothing. Ninety-five percent of him was in despair, but he hadn't come this far by giving up when things got tough. A small corner of his soul relished the thought of battling against nigh insurmountable odds, or even of starting afresh...a blank sheet. But the nightmare wasn't over yet. It had never been this bad. He couldn't go anywhere without a posse of bodyguards. Demonstrators and journalists hounded him—including those who were ostensibly his employees! Even his new trophy wifelet seemed to treat him with disdain. Where had all the love gone? *Jesus wept!*

A knock at the door, and a secretary entered—these days even they didn't bother waiting for permission to enter. She dumped a looseleaf file on his desk with the words, "The latest developments as requested, Mr. Mudrock. There's an analysis appended." She didn't wait for an acknowledgement, but did close the door gently as she left. Leaving him to stew in the juice of his own making, he imagined her thinking. *Cheeky bitch!*—why had she accepted a job with him if that's how she felt? All his employees were bastards and idiots—everything the Hope-ists had announced had already been in the public domain. If they had f***ing bothered to do any research, the cretins! How dare they act all high and mighty and surprised all of a sudden! God, people were insufferable. *Thick as pigshit.*

Sighing at the rage he realised was futile, Mudrock shrugged and, without much interest, opened the file and glanced at the sheets of paper it contained: shares in freefall, shareholders up in arms, most subsidiaries threatened with takeovers….Ho, hum.

So what were these Hope-ists demanding then? Mmmn, Melanie had included that too: sixty percent tax to be paid on profits, guarantee employees' union rights, minimum wage £5 an hour worldwide, permanent employment as far as possible rather than temporary contracts, change of editorial policy….In return? They'd urge their followers to support his companies, rather than the opposition.

Well, on the surface of it he didn't have much choice, but there had to be some way….Just maybe the Big 200 could come up with something, but most of them wouldn't give a damn about him, that's for sure. He sighed again. Much as he hated what was happening, and despised most of mankind, there were some people he did admire: his enemies, the Hope-ists. If only his own employees had such courage, integrity and initiative, the pathetic unprincipled opportunists….

Fred East was looking east, standing at his window and surveying the North Sea as he had so many times before. His tenth-floor office gave him a marvellous view of that ever-changing vista: sky and water, water and sky, ships and oil rigs so puny against them, but, alas, not insignificant…pollution, the exhaustion of natural resources and global warming, and DAP had a major responsibility. If only it were just these. Just! He laughed at the word. They were important enough, but his guilt was more directly to do with people. He had confronted his boss about the newspaper story on Colombia, and by the evasiveness of the answer he knew it was true. How had he been so stupid as to take on this job without considering its implications? His joy in the intellectual challenge of the statistics had long evaporated. Still, one could be too hard on oneself. He had children and an ex wife to support and he would never subject them or himself to the degradation of living on the dole if he could do anything about it. But what about the worse degradation to which he was subjecting other families? F***, life was a matter of filthy compromise. Fred West was a convicted murderer, and was he, Fred East, any better?

At least when he got home he could forget such questions while he kicked a ball around with his son, or showed him how to fly a kite, or lost himself in watching his daughter at play with the dolls' house he had built. Thank goodness for the kids. But Colombian kids?

In the last few months, hours had been swallowed by such circular and depressing thoughts, but no solution presented itself. Sighing, Fred tore himself from the window and plumped down at his computer. Then the phone rang.

CHAPTER THIRTY-SIX
Mudrock-ing the Boat

Nathaniel was feeling good. No barriers existed between himself and Michelle now, and the frequent journeys between HDI, Heathrow and Stansted were both relaxing and exciting, as they exchanged Hope-ist ideas as easily as anecdotes about their pasts. Having decided not to have an affair with her, he was free to reveal everything and anything about himself—no need for any particular presentation, no need for a front, no worry over seduction tactics. So airport journeys were fun, and how many people could say that? Not only that, but in those heady first few days after Task One it seemed that their plans were unfolding well, even though every day, every step, was make-or-break. Perhaps that was why he felt so alive.

At least this was how Nathaniel explained his mood to himself as he boarded the plane at Stansted. It had been a year since his last visit to Inverdon. So much had happened since. It'd be good to see Shelagh on her home turf…a relaxed drink or two in the POW. Groups were all very well, but no matter how democratic or fair one tried to be, there was always that lingering feeling that not everyone had voiced all his or her thoughts. As the tacit head of the Hope-ists, Nathaniel felt it his duty to try to speak to at least the main actors on an individual basis (and "actors" they sometimes were!), to nip any disenchantment in the bud and glean any fresh ideas which people were too timid to voice more publicly. (Was "real" democracy attainable, and what was it anyway?) But with Shelagh it was also the opportunity to renew an old friendship. This would be the first time for years he and she would meet without at least one of them being a bit down.

But, if he were honest, he wasn't completely happy. Beneath the glow of the moment, there was an unease. Rosemary was drifting away from him again, he could feel it. He wanted to talk to Shelagh about that. The relief of unburdening himself was already almost tangible. He might have been mistaken not to have told Rosemary about the Hope-ists. Rosemary was sensitive to his lack of complete candour, he thought. Was this eroding their relationship? Besides, one day she was bound to discover that he wasn't at work when he said he was.

Putting Rosemary aside, there were important and genuinely exciting Hope-ist developments to discuss with Shelagh. Inverdon was to be the site of the second major action, or at least the focal point of the British part of it. Shelagh would be coordinating it. It was asking a lot of her— all this on top of her job. Funny how she'd been unemployed for years and then a few weeks after the foundation of the Hope-ists she'd been successful at an interview and was now a junior lecturer at Robert Gilbey's. Or maybe it wasn't so funny. Of all the people in the world, after the research he'd done, he ought to have some insight into the negative effects of unemployment on morale and ability to cope, and therefore, conversely how positive Shelagh's key role in the Hope-ist Movement had been for her psyche. Her whole attitude to life had changed. Happy, not feeling she had to prove anything to herself or anyone else, she would have shone at her interview. The old Shelagh again, only *sans* "desperate edge," or whatever it was that Mary had accused her of!

Then there was the "official" HDI reason for his visit: to see Prof. Hall-Crumble about the tissue culture experiments. These days it gave him a smug pleasure to see the old man. Hall-Crumble was no longer offhand, now that not just some, but most of his research funds were dependent on Nathaniel and HDI.

Of course there was Annabelle too—always a pleasure to see Annabelle, who didn't treat him with that deference or awe that some of the others oozed, and which Nathaniel found uncomfortable. He felt good when he was with her, rather as he did when he was with Michelle. No embarrassment either about his changed appearance. In fact, he'd be lucky not to be teased anew! *Good old Annabelle, and good young Michelle!*

—

Throwing its weight in on the cheerful side, Inverdon was doing its best to welcome him. It was clear and sunny, and not especially cold. Partly for old times' sake he decided to wait for the airport bus rather than catch a taxi. In any case, he had a few hours before the first of his meetings was due, and it was always a good thing to support public transport, even if it had all been privatised. He'd drop his stuff at Shelagh's place (she'd be at work but she'd sent him a set of keys) and then he'd stretch his legs in the Granite City.

Had he known where they would take him? East along Junction Street, past Steptoe's (a quick look in—no one recognised him and he didn't bother identifying himself—just a smirk in the direction of old Mr. Tough, chiding some poor assistant at the end of an aisle, *plus ça change…*) and then to the art gallery. He wasn't sure if he really wanted to go there or not, but his legs didn't seem to give him a choice.

Good. Bright Eyes was still there, her young and confident self. Nathaniel sat down opposite her and gave himself over to daydreaming. More than anything, he supposed, she was a symbol of human potential. She was what the Hope-ists were about—letting people live out their potential. It was good to come back here and touch base, to clear one's mind of its quotidian pre-occupations and focus on what had become the purpose of his life: enabling others to live out theirs with some dignity, or even just to live.

Bright Eyes was beautifully posed, poised between a happy but disciplined childhood and an adulthood of which she had certain expectations. Given her background (well, her class) and the times in which she lived, she would have been well versed in the arts and music, but probably not the sciences. For the likes of her a career—or employment of any sort—would not have been an option. A good marriage would have been the thing, whereas many of her countrywomen would have been working from dawn to dusk, or even dusk to dawn, in the mills, or gutting fish, or as maids. Strange—it would have been socially difficult for Bright Eyes to have worked, but it was impossible for her poorer contemporaries not to! But for all of them, constrained as they had been in their own ways in the Britain of the mid-19th century, things were better then than they were in the late 20th century for much of the world's population. Already Bright Eyes was older than many children, born say in the 1980s, ever got to be. And she'd never had to walk miles carrying a heavy bucket full of dirty water on her head.

Nathaniel wondered what she would have said if she had known that 150 years after her picture was painted, sitting pretty (or rather standing pretty) at the heart of the great British Empire, four-fifths of the world's population would have been living in poverty, and at least a quarter of humanity would not have access to clean drinking water? That eighty percent of disease in the developing world would be caused by dirty water, and that ten million people would die every year as a result, many of them children? And that the situation would be deteriorating, and even in Britain the cost of all the basic services would not only be absolutely more expensive for the poor than for the well-to-do, but also increasing disproportionately?

And, speaking of children, that some of the richest men in the world would be working to weaken the international convention against child labour, despite the frighteningly high levels of adult unemployment (once one saw through governments' massaging of the figures) in order for the wealthy to become wealthier still? They wanted to re-institute the child labour of Bright Eyes' time! Well, not if Nathaniel could help it: for the sake of all the potential Bright Eyes, he would succeed!

Positive feelings continued: Professor Hall-Crumble was positively tepid in his welcome. What had come over the old boy to humanise him so? What was more, Hall-Crumble had kept himself up-to-date with Annabelle's progress in the laboratory, to judge by the congruence of their reports. Wonders would never cease.

Annabelle was enthused. "Aye. I wouldn't be surprised if we've got something this time, Nathaniel. We've a whiley to go yet, and then we need the image-processing results and the electron microscopy to be certain, but as far as I can tell, simply by eyeballing it and by the rate of passaging, there's something going on. It's all randomised, right enough, but I've never seen a clone produce such apparently varied strains. Some of them are forty generations down the line and still dividing like embryonic tissues. We're having to come in at night to re-bottle them. And yet they differentiate as soon as we try the maturation medium! I've never seen anything like it—those chemicals must be working! You know when I was a lassie I used to dream about the elixir of eternal youth, and now I might be about to find it."

Nathaniel tried to contain her zest but as he too realised how massively significant this was, he had a hard job keeping calm himself. It had largely been his idea after all. Big money could be made from this telomere modification experiment—Mudrockian-Silversmithian amounts in fact, even dwarfing the income from Priaptra, HDI's best-selling treatment for erectile dysfunction—and the security of Hall-Crumble's laboratories had been stepped up. It wasn't quite at HDI levels of fortification, but nonetheless one had the feeling of having traversed an obstacle course by the time one reached the inner sanctum of the laboratory, Queen Annabelle's domain. Add to that the fact that the key information was known only to himself, to Annabelle and to Hall-Crumble.

He was waiting for Shelagh in her flat when she arrived. She was glowing with vitality, and dying for a drink! She showered and changed into fetching non-lecturer garb, and they were off to the POW.

Once again rumours about its imminent closure were circulating, as were the petitions to stop the mysterious and malign developers from knocking it down. If it had not all happened before, Nathaniel would have been upset. As it was he found it funny, but dutifully signed his name. Some wag had selected the old Terence Trent-D'Arby number most appropriate for the occasion: "Sign Your Name." Shelagh and Nathaniel laughed simultaneously as the penny dropped (or rather, just after the 20p dropped into the juke box). "…Sign your name across my heart, I want you to be my baby!" Their eyes met. It was as if no time had passed since their undergraduate years, and was there an additional buzz?

There was a lot to discuss. Where to start? Nathaniel asked how Shelagh's lectureship was going—and soon regretted it as she ranted on: "Oh, very well—I'm enjoying it, but it's certainly not all roses. There's a maddening amount of bureaucratic junk. If only I had more time for preparing my lectures, instead of all the 'auto-assessment' crap! There's not enough money for building repairs, and we—the lecturers I mean—are paid badly, atrociously compared to our equivalents in industry, and we're expected to pull in research grants right, left and centre, on top of everything! But they can bloody afford to employ all these admin. people, efficiency assessors, etc., etc.,—f***ing parasites if you ask me—although I don't suppose it's their fault as individuals, they're just earning their living.

"But I tell you something, Nathaniel, the thing that upsets me the most—and don't get me wrong, on the whole I'm enjoying it!—but the thing that upsets me the most is the students. They've changed so much since our day, and it wasn't that long ago. Do you remember we used to complain about how passive our classmates were, how uninterested they were in politics and so on? Well, if you can believe it, if we were passive then, they're moribund now—basically, they're dead to anything outside of exactly what is required to pass the exams. They've zero interest in debating things, zero tolerance even for anything that isn't strictly required by the syllabus. They want everything dictated, or, better still, printed and handed out to them. They seem to be totally lacking in spirit. Defeatist, broken….And when you hear what they talk about amongst themselves—apart from relationships and exams of course—it's just mental junk food: soap operas and the latest constructed-by-numbers insipid pop drivel for heaven's sake! The 'cream of the nation's youth'!"

Nathaniel knew all this only too well, being in frequent contact with academia and students, and was bored, but it was clear that she needed to get it out of her system. He rubbed his eyes and sighed.

Unfazed, Shelagh continued: "At times I despair of changing people's views, of reaching people. You know I once set them a little general knowledge quiz, just for interest. None of them knew where Algeria was, far less what was going on there. Less than a quarter could name and spell the three main political parties in Britain. And half of them read the damn *Sin*. Let's face it, whether its politics have improved or not, it's still all tits and star signs, and these are supposedly educated people reading it! We have such a long way to go.

"I don't suppose you can blame them, mind you. They don't know whether they'll ever have jobs, far less be able to make any sort of impact on the world, so what can they do but spot for exam questions and divert themselves from the horror of it all? But, boy, have we got a long way to go! There's so much riding on our next action, Nathaniel. If we fail, then the world's down the tubes!"

Christ, thought Nathaniel, as if he needed reminding!

"In fairness, I suppose there are some good developments. I've been able to…umm, gently introduce our view of things to a couple of the lecturers. Basically, when they're blowing off steam about how much time they're wasting on useless administration I gradually steer the conversation on to why all these changes are happening. There's one who's well along the road to Hope-ist thinking. I plan to tell her about us in the next few days…."

Nathaniel shifted in his seat, toying with an empty peanut packet. On such a person-to-person level the process was insufferably slow, but he didn't want to stem Shelagh's enthusiasm. "The more the merrier, but I agree this next action is make-or-break, and the sooner we get it off the ground the better, and I'll tell you why. I have some pretty interesting news, in fact. You remember I was going to cosy up to Silversmith? Well, it's come up trumps, he sees me as his little golden boy! The other day we went for a little walk together—the guy's paranoid about being bugged—anyhow we went for this little stroll round the gardens at HDI, and he told me some things that confirm our fears. There is an alliance being constructed, one we're going to have to break pretty damn soon. Apparently the Big 200 met recently…."

"You mean there really is such a grouping?"

"Well if there wasn't before, there certainly is now. Yes, the 200 CEOs of the biggest multinationals got together to talk about how to carve up the world, according to Silversmith, who was positively gloating that he'd been invited, by the way, the odious little….Anyway, they were worried about us, which is good, but they were moderately confident that soon everything would be sewn up. They just had to step up the pace a little bit."

"EMU, NAFTA…?"

"Yes, that's part of it. They reckon that once they get rid of the last residues of social services, statutory workers' rights, etc., and they've forced the trade unions into the corporatist straitjacket, and brought in the private sector to all but take over public services, then it'll be a piece of piss to play the citizens of various countries off against each other, and even within countries it'll be easy to set the worst paid workers against the unemployed, the unemployed against the workers, and all racial, national and religious groupings at each other's throats. In fact, from what I can make out it was more or less admitted that behind the scenes they were manipulating—sponsoring even—the fascist groups to divert attention from what they, the multinationals, were up to! Then they'll be able to continue de-regulating to their hearts' content in the name of the glorious 'market forces' without a significant word being raised against them. They even plan to launch a campaign of 'solidarity against fascism' just to show what good blokes they all are, and to divert the energies of the multinationals' natural opponents into anti-fascist protests! Very clever, but the hypocrisy, the stench of it all! They're even worse than we suspected!"

"But what do they say about us specifically?"

"They've more or less made a pact not to cave in to any demands we might make. They've already guessed roughly what we're going to do, and they're talking about setting aside money to compensate any of their number affected by a boycott, a 'capitalist solidarity fund' if you can believe it—what an oxymoron for those who praise competition! They're determined, under no circumstances will any of them fail to toe the 'market forces' line—you know the stuff: 'Market forces must be obeyed. The only way to create jobs, and improve living standards is to dismantle all barriers to free and fair trade, blah, blah…free and fair competition…' they say, when what they're working towards is cartels, oligarchies and monopolies! A 'solidarity fund' indeed!

"The incredible thing is that people still believe them, despite their day-to-day experience. Absolute bloody victims of consumerism! Oh, God, Shelagh, I know you've heard me go on like this before, but it never fails to astound me that people can be so…stupid!

"To get back to what I was saying, they have sworn not to raise wages, not to allow their employees representation by non-corporatist unions and all that kind of stuff. They reckon that if they all collectively withdraw advertising from non-supportive press, the press will be forced to print their propaganda, and as we know they already have all the mainstream politicians in their pockets.

"Anyway, sorry, to come back to your question, more specifically they're going to cast doubt on our motives, accuse us of speculating on the stock exchange, of using our insider knowledge to benefit from the ructions we're causing. In short they are going to make us appear to be acting like capitalists and exploiting others' misery, while they continue to do precisely that, entirely unhindered and unquestioned!"

Shelagh's fingers were drumming on her almost empty pint glass. "But surely we can simply get the news of this meeting out now, before it's too late?"

"Well, they'd probably work out where the leak came from, and at the best we'd no longer be able to spy on them....At the worst I would have an 'unfortunate accident.' But who would publish it anyway? And if we published it, would people believe us? You know their propaganda's already starting to bite. I think we just have to go ahead with our planned campaign right away, and hope that they're not yet organised enough, or united enough, to withstand us. I still think we're in with a better than even chance."

"Would they believe us? Mmmn. That's a point, Nathaniel. You know I find it a bit difficult to believe that 200 men can be so, uh...of one mind. Especially not the egotistical and driven types that make it to the top of multinationals. There must be some divisions that we could work on."

Nathaniel snorted. "Yes. Apparently Mudrock is the dissident. Silversmith thinks his nose is still out of joint at having been seen to give in to our demands, that his ego is bruised and therefore he's making a lone stand against the other multinationals to show he's a real man! I'm sure it's ego alright, but I think there's a bit more to it. You know he was always against the European Union and EMU?"

"Who could forget?"

"...At a time when all the major multinationals were wholeheartedly in favour, he was playing the xenophobia card, in his so-called 'news'papers....But for once, whether you agree with his reasons, his policy was actually right. Never mind the fact that he was mainly against the EU because they were then marginally more socialist in their policies than ultra-liberal capitalist Britain, and because his own particular media empire would suffer...and that he'd failed to understand that the whole idea—the whole direction of it—was towards more extreme deregulation than he'd ever had wet dreams about...."

"Yes, yes, Nathaniel! I'm not thick you know! Tell me what happened! Or better still, while you think of the words I'm off for another drink! Same again?" She smiled as she rose, pinched his cheek, and then sashayed over to the bar, smiling again *en route* as she stood aside a moment to let a bearer of multiple drinks pass.

Yes, "sashayed" was the word for it, thought Nathaniel. God, she looked sexy in that slinky silk outfit—what was it, a cheong-sam?

Nathaniel could never resist drawing a face on the creamy Guinness froth. A half-smile this time, a wink. He could rarely resist at least one pint of Guinness upon which to draw it either, however politically incorrect the Guinness dynasty might be, although one of them was an expert on red deer, he had heard. Interesting how the imbibitory history of each glass could be read in the frothy relics left clinging to the side. You could look at your emptied glass, and think back on the big gulp that had started the whole delicious experience, and then lower down, where the hemi-rings were closely bunched, was when you'd been eking it out, consciously metering your pleasure to keep pace with your slower drinking partner. It was a relief to dwell on such simple joys from time to time, even if only for a few seconds of diversion.

"So Mudrock is still opposed to the EU, and to the single currency in particular. According to Silversmith he was unable to justify his opposition in terms that made any sense, but part of it must just be that he doesn't want to have to make another climb-down. They apparently savaged him. You know, in his own perverted way the guy has a bit of pride, and doesn't want to be seen to contradict himself. Funny, considering his newspapers are happy to change their tune if it'll make more money...."

Shelagh was smiling again, but this time it was a corner-of-the-mouth, glint-in-the-eye affair. She had an idea. "Well, Nathaniel, I think we should help him. Don't you?"

"What do you mean?"

"He was opposed to the EU, and to EMU. He wants to stay opposed to it. We are opposed to it also, though for different reasons. But if I know anything about human nature, if Mudrock was humiliated at the meeting he'll want his own back, and he won't worry too much about reasons."

"I think you might be on to something! What would you say to a trip to London this weekend, more specifically to the Budgie Docks Building?"

"Mmmn....Which just happens to house the offices of a certain newspaper, which just happens to be receiving a visit from the big boss at the moment, a certain Antipodean by birth and American by citizenship, and whose name rhymes with Woodstock and also has something to do with mud, but who couldn't be further from the spirit of said event?"

"Ye're nae sae glaikit are ye, quine?"

"Ye ken fine ah'm nae sae green as ah'm cabbage-looking!" They laughed at their attempts at the local dialect.

"Did you know that the French word for 'cabbage' is a term of endearment, Shelagh, *mon petit chou?*"

"If you don't watch it, Dr. Papulous, I'll give you shoe!" Shelagh mimed kicking him with her ankle boots. She was pouting with pretend fury, underneath which a smile made its presence known. There was no way of hiding the blush.

Nathaniel decided not to bring up the subject of Rosemary.

CHAPTER THIRTY-SEVEN
Crises

HOPE-ISTS ACCUSED OF INSIDER DEALING
Adrian Blacklink, chairman of the US Federal Bank, has voiced suspicions that the recent stock market chaos initiated by the so-called International Hope-ist Movement may have been motivated by insider dealing....
[The NY Gazette, 24 July 199-]

HOPE-IST SITES ADVOCATE VIOLENCE—PM RESPONDS
The proliferation of self-proclaimed Hope-ist websites advocating civil unrest and violence is alarming in the extreme," the Prime Minister, Mr. Tory Klaxon announced at an emergency meeting of international leaders....
[The Daily Wail, 29 July 199-]

INTERPOL GEARS UP
In the wake of widespread rioting and a spate of assaults and letter bombs targeting multinational bosses, international police co-operation is to be extended....
[The Daily Torygraph, 30 July 199-]

COMMENT: ENOUGH IS ENOUGH!
While we support the aims and methods declared by the so-called Hope-ists at the time of the Andy James kidnap, we deplore subsequent developments. We suspect that the movement may have been sabotaged by right-wing forces, and that many of the statements attributed to the movement

**are in fact the work of provocateurs. However, until the
founders identify themselves, they must take responsibility....**
[The Sentinel, 31 July 199-]

Mary had set up an encrypted Hope-ist Internet chat room. It was
inaugurated at the end of July. Disconsolate, the founding Hope-ists
logged on at the arranged time. None of them had anticipated the
ruthlessness and speed of the enemy's response. Nathaniel started by
expressing what they were all thinking.

Nathaniel: "So, do we throw in the towel?"

Nathaniel: "Come on, people. Any ideas?"

Mary: "No, but news: Cyberbabble almost there—within a week we
can launch."

Nathaniel: "Good. Something they won't be able to corrupt. We'll
have a clear communication channel."

Everyone breathed in relief. Nathaniel's reply had implied that they
would fight on.

EJ: "For what it's worth, there's a good side to this. With so many
pseudo-Hope-ists, the chances of us being identified are not great. As
long as we continue to take the precautions I've suggested, I don't think
we need worry about security."

Michelle: "So we're not identifying ourselves!?"

EJ: "If we do, we'll be behind bars immediately...and it's goodbye to
everything."

Michelle: "But if we don't then people will continue TO BE KILLED
in our name!!!"

Nathaniel: "We must deliver knock-out ASAP. If we can perform
Task Two this weekend and get Cyberbabble synchronised...."

Michelle: "There must be some other way we can make our message
clear—that we have nothing to do with any of the violence. Is there some
branch of the media that we could trust? I mean if we could convince the
owner of a broadcasting company or something of our bona fides, and get
him—or her—to pass on our message: 'The Real Hope-ists Speak'-type

of thing. That way we might avoid public identification."

Nathaniel: "Bingo! I came to the same conclusion! I know this chat room is encrypted, but all I'll say for now is that Shelagh's working on this. So watch this space, fingers crossed and all systems go for Task Two!"

Shelagh: "Wish me luck, guys!"

Nathaniel logged off, sat back in his chair, and ran his hands through his hair. He was in his study. Rosemary was out at The Groove and for the next couple of hours there was nothing he had to do. For once. He breathed deeply—in through the nose, out through the mouth—trying to relax. Annabelle had just phoned him—Hall-Crumble had died—a massive stroke. Nathaniel reflected that for all his professorial status and his interest in "saucy" literature, his life had been relatively uncomplicated and low-stress. What would it be like to have an ordinary life with no major pressures? Say he had become a low-ranking employee of Doors, for example, or had stayed in the bookshop, or had become the manager of Steptoe's? A nine-to-five job, coming home from work and switching on the telly for an hour or two, a beer in hand. Watching the news half awake, awaiting the soaps, and the football matches, and the weekends, and his pension, and relaxed overseas holidays. (Short ones that he could afford, of course, once a year.) And then death—slipping away in his sleep. A little announcement in the paper. A few families and friends lamenting his passing at a quiet funeral. No. Such a life would be empty, meaningless. He'd be bored stiff.

How about cutting and running now? Abandoning the Hope-ists, who might well be defeated at any moment? He was already wealthy, and if the elixir of youth project turned out to be as successful as it was promising to be, a third share—no a half share!—in the patent would in all probability make him one of the richest people on the planet! With that kind of money he could set up his own paradise anywhere. He could buy Hysterique, for example, and convert the whole island into a real heaven on earth....He could take Rosemary away and protect her from all the horrors and tawdriness of the world—to hell with everything and everyone! After all, had it not been said by someone—Maupassant?—

that life was neither as good as one thought it was, nor as bad? Did this not mean that most people, no matter what their external circumstances, hovered around the same emotional mean? The wealthiest people in the world complained and were miserable when their cars were stuck in traffic jams, or when their relationships went wrong, and the poorest were happy when it rained, or when it didn't, or when they got a handful of grain in a refugee camp. In that case why burn himself up over the state of the world and other people? Had generations of sages (and bookshelves of self-help books) not advised that the only thing one could be reasonably certain of changing was oneself, one's own attitude? He and Rosemary could run away and stay young and beautiful, possibly for centuries, and live even longer than that! He would at last have the time and the opportunity to close that gap between them, the gap that was still there and still hurt whenever he stopped and listened to his heart. Gorgeous Rosemary in his arms forever! So why on earth was he wasting his time with this ridiculous Hope-ist thing? Why?

But there was some other yearning within him, as yet inchoate. What had happened to the clarity and sense of purpose that had come upon him in Paris not that long ago? Why this feeling of immanence and imminence? He knew that some revelation was near, but this knowledge was not enough to give him peace. "God," he said, for once not blaspheming, "help!"

Nathaniel wept.

Shelagh had decided on the frank approach. In the worst case scenario at least their actions would be well advanced by the time the papers came out. Also, there was no need to reveal logistic details, so even if Mudrock got on the phone immediately to DAP and Axon....

Mudrock was the model gentleman as he ushered Shelagh into his office, on the surface unruffled in his impeccable suit and dull tie. Shelagh knew this was an act. He asked if she would like a cup of tea, coffee, a cigar? He smiled slightly and shrugged when she declined all three, as if to say, "Well, you never know....I'm not a chauvinist and don't make such assumptions."

Shelagh didn't waste time. "Mr. Mudrock, I have come to offer you the biggest opportunity you will ever have in your life. What I'm about to say must remain between you and I for the time being. I'm afraid I cannot take any chances with regard to us being overheard, or bugged. Would you mind removing your jacket and accompanying me to the roof?"

Not used to taking orders, Mudrock's self-control frayed slightly, as evidenced by a slight twitch at the corner of his mouth and a moment of hesitation. This gave way to a "Sure, I'm-just-a-regular-bloke-happy-to-go-along-for-a-lark-to-please-a-lady" smile. "It is the middle of winter, you realise?" he said.

Shelagh debated whether to come on tough at this point, and say something like: "You won't feel nearly as cold as you'll become if you don't do what we say!"…Or even something cryptic along the lines of: "Hell, they say, is the coldest place, Mr. Mudrock." In the end she settled for the factual: "If you are really concerned about the cold, Mr. Mudrock, then you might be interested in doing something to help those who are forced to sleep rough, instead of sending your fascist thug readers to beat them up." She was thrilled to hear the power and confidence of her voice. Lecturing had helped.

Mudrock could not maintain his air of *sang froid* now that he was genuinely cold. Ironic, thought Shelagh. He grasped the railings, shivering, looking out over a grey miserable London. Now he was doing a good job of appearing to be a frail and tired old man. "Great view!" he said, as if he were showing it to her, trying to regain some command. Pathetic. "Now what have you got to say? You people have caused me enough trouble already—what more can you possibly want?"

"Mr. Mudrock, we know all about the meeting of the 200. We could expose the lot of you tomorrow.…Only we agree with some of your views, which we heard didn't go down too well. We too are opposed to the EU, to the EMU, though our reasons are different."

Mudrock straightened. "What are you offering me, and what do I have to do for it?"

"Mmmn…interesting, the order in which you asked that. It says a lot about you.…Anyway, to answer: if we succeed in our plans, and if you cooperate, then the media you control are guaranteed the lion's share of the market. This is not something that we would give you, as such, but it would happen as a matter of course. You would emerge as the moral leader and popular hero of the age. You would go down in history alongside Saint Paul, Gandhi, Martin Luther King and Che Guevara. There's no doubt about it."

"I'm not sure I'd choose to 'go down in history,' as you put it, alongside those particular gentleman. And if I don't agree to whatever it is you want me to do?"

Shelagh snorted. "It's likely that you won't be able to make any more business decisions in your life, Mr. Mudrock. You have no idea of the scale of our movement, and the advanced stage of our plans for our next action."

"I think you'd better tell me more, Ms. McPherson...."

CHAPTER THIRTY-EIGHT
Suspense

Hanging. Forty yards to the ground and thirty to the top of the building, like a lifeboat on the side of the Titanic. Only it was him and the entire Hope-ist cause that risked sinking. Stuck, well and truly. There was no escape, no possibility of denial or credible explanation. When the sun rose, or perhaps sooner, they would spot him there, train cameras on him....And this time there were more than Rosemary's affections at stake. What madness had brought him here? *Zebedee!*—what bizarre twist of his psyche had made him take that damn cat's moniker as his codename?

CHAPTER THIRTY-NINE
Red-faced

Shelagh emerged from the Budgie Docks building. Her demeanour, her briefcase and her smart suit would have signalled "businesswoman" to the casual observer. The air of calm belied the stakes at hand. She had played all her cards. She could do no more. Mudrock had not given her the smallest clue as to what he would do. He had simply told her that he would give her "offer" due consideration, and that his answer would be evident in the morning papers. The self-control he had ultimately managed had been impressive, and the meeting had ended in an atmosphere of mutual respect—two powerful people recognising each other, an electric feel to the moment. The addictive properties of such power games! Mudrock could blow their cover completely if he chose. He could hand them over to the police. She wouldn't put it past him to have them assassinated.

These might be the last moments of her life. The air was good to breathe. The noise of the traffic was intoxicating. The iridescent sheen on that pigeon was beautiful. Why had she never really noticed these things?

Que sera sera. The die was cast.

She phoned Nathaniel in Inverdon. He sounded resigned. Well, that was all one could be. He told her he was sure that she had done her best. He informed her that everything was running according to plan, that the service station demo teams had all presented acceptable plans for the morning, and that he was confident that the operative codenamed

"Zebedee" would manage the DAP building, and that she wasn't to worry. She could stay in London with Mary if she wanted, to catch the first edition of *The Sin*. And not to worry, he said—what a daft piece of advice!

"And, Shelagh...."

"Yes?"

"I should perhaps tell you...."

"Mm hmmn?"

"No. Sorry. Forget it."

And so on the eve of Task Two, sleep impossible, Mary and Shelagh sat up together, drinking coffee at first, and then gin.

"We've come a long way...."

"Do you remember the first time we met Nathaniel?"

"Yes. The ceilidh...."

"Strange to think that that funny-looking guy, as he was then, has had such an impact on our lives...."

"Mmmph. Do you remember....?"

Calum Mackay was pissed off. Thoroughly. Life had not been good to him. Ever since he had been sacked for drinking a lager in Steptoe's supermarket. It had been dented anyway—at least as far as they knew—and it was only one can! Then he'd been on the dole for a couple of years, got a girl pregnant—her fault. Days at the slot machines. Can or two of superstrength in the evenings. Street corners. Fights. Then his uncle had got him a job with the electricity people. Sweeping the floors at first, but he liked his boss—they both supported the Dees and went to matches together—and he suggested an HND. Well, he'd never passed anything before and didn't think he could do it, but this guy was insistent and said he'd give him a crate for every exam....Helped him with his studies too. Third time round he got it. Maybe they were sick of his face, but he got it. So then a job pressing a few switches, and basic maintenance. First time ever he'd enjoyed his work. Got to see "the ween" a bit too—at school now—nice wee boy. Then the company had been bought up and he'd had to work longer hours, and now his job was gone. Just like that.

This would be the last switch he would flick. Off. What was the f***ing point of anything? Och well—at least there'd be no more night shift.

What Calum didn't know was that the loss of his job was the least of it. Scot-El-Gas was a massive private company, linked to an American utilities corporation which had vacuumed up, at rock-bottom prices, many of the small gas and electricity companies resulting from the privatisation of the state-owned power monopoly. Scot-El-Gas had then "rationalised" their operations (sacked thousands of employees) and consequently been spectacularly successful upon their entry into the stock market. Scot-El-Gas had not stopped there.

Their dealings (as members of a covert utilities cartel) with the impoverished health service had been particularly shrewd, forcing hospital authorities to sign contracts allowing them to interrupt gas supplies for up to ninety days. Hospitals not prepared to sign such "interruptible" contracts had had to pay sixty-six percent more for their gas. This had effectively enabled Scot-El-Gas to supply gas at a moment's notice to the highest bidder, dumping the poorer clients.

The consequences for the hospitals had been disastrous; for Scot-El-Gas, sublime. Its managing director, Sir Dreadmond Filcher (knighted for donations to a political party), had, of course, awarded himself a few million pounds in bonuses, and raised his salary by a similar amount. To add to the sordid tale, the company paid tax at a rate of only 6.7% (the salaries of its tax lawyers alone would have settled the foreign debts of more than one African country).

Then, one day, Sir Dreadmond, addressing a small gathering of shareholders, made his fatal mistake, adding that last straw to the camel's back of public tolerance. In response to a question about the morality of the hospital issue, he had replied, "Well, let's face, we're in it for the money. If we cared about the poor we wouldn't be in business. F*** them, and sign up with BUPA, that's what I say!" This, and the chuckle that accompanied it, were captured for posterity by a dictation machine nestling in the pocket of a would-be Hope-ist who had infiltrated the meeting.

Clever and successful men are often let down by their hubris. The recording was not of high quality, but the words were distinct, and the entire Scot-El-Gas story thereby rendered clear and digestible: screw the poor, avoid paying tax, slip a few bob to the politicians, and you'll end up a knight. The Hope-ist wannabe in the audience was Internet literate and posted the story, complete with transcript and streamed audio file. The stock market consequences scuppered Scot-El-Gas. Sir Dreadmond was at first "unavailable for comment" and then "could not be reached."

Sir Dreadmond and Scot-El-Gas employees and shareholders were not the only people to be unhappy at the effects of that tape-recording. Dr. Nathaniel Papulous was considerably dismayed in the early hours of a chilly morning in Inverdon when a green button failed to make his window-cleaning cradle descend from its position forty yards up on the DAP building.

What could he do? If he called the security guard he would notice the windows. *Calm down!* Presumably it was just a temporary powercut. Judging by the extinction of all lights in the district it was a central fault which they would fix pretty much immediately. All he had to do was wait a little.

But what if it took a few hours? Was there any way of climbing down? *No, forget it!* Red paint dripped from the paintbrush he still clasped. He put it down—it was perishingly cold and his hands were painful. He thrust them into the pockets of his overall, pacing up and down the two yards available to him, trying to stay warm and to make sense of things and come up with a plan. The temperature-monitoring sensors he'd had implanted in his face at the time of his surgery so many years ago triggered the warning vibrator at the base of his neck—his insensitive face was in danger of freezing. He pulled his slightly warmed and paint-tacky hands from his pockets and buried his face in them. There was nothing for it— if he were going to be caught red-handed he might as well be caught red-faced too. A seagull squawked near his ear, making him jump. *Shit!* What was that on the top of his head? *Shit.*

So if he was still there come the dawn what would happen? His cover would be blown. The Hope-ists would be dealt a severe blow. If Shelagh hadn't succeeded in rallying Mudrock to the cause, he sure as hell wasn't likely to support them after such a fiasco....

CHAPTER FORTY
Forever Dirtying Windows?

While Shelagh was in London, meeting Mudrock and consulting with Mary, who had become the *de facto* international coordinator of the Hope-ists, Nathaniel had continued with his dual existences in Inverdon as scientist and activist. It was amazing, he thought, how volatile emotions were. Suddenly the tension, caused both independently by his two roles and which existed between them, had never been so difficult to handle. The elixir of eternal youth and the salvation of humanity were potentially in his grasp—they had flowed from his imagination. Were they compatible? Did this even matter? He could have sold what he knew about either of them for virtually any figure. He could have disappeared off into the sunset with Rosemary (or virtually any woman, or women, of his choosing!), bought a whole archipelago of paradise islands, and founded a dynasty, and yet he knew that this was impossible. His conscience, his damn conscience, would have destroyed any pleasure. That, perhaps, was the real secret of life: how to kill one's conscience.

As he didn't have this option he had to follow the dictates of the wretched burdensome thing. This was all very well when simple decisions had to be made, but in the "real world" few decisions were simple. Every potential action had innumerable consequences, and these had consequences in turn, most of which one could not hope to predict, so one's mind was exhausted. It was a gigantic game of chess where the edges of the board ran off into infinity and there was nothing so definite to aim for as a checkmate, nothing so definite as a time limit for each move, merely an awareness that one had to act quickly, a nauseating pressure.

He couldn't help but think of his more youthful dilemmas—in the bookshop, for example: which books to read? How had he coped with that? How had he coped with Rosemary's girlhood rejection of him?

He had done…something. That was it! One simply had to act, take some physical action. In the bookshop, instead of forever agonising about optimising his choice of reading material, he had just started reading the ten bestsellers of every month and those books of which the author's biography/photograph had appealed. Instead of pining away over Rosemary, he had programmed her image into the computer. As soon as he had been physically doing something he had felt better. Automatically then, it had seemed, he had stopped trying to analyse things beyond reasonable limits. And, come to think of it, when physical situations had become trying he had performed the reverse trick— thinking in an abstract way about height when he'd been stuck in the tree, for example. So, unpleasant physical circumstances demanded mental diversion, and mental strife demanded physical action. Balance and harmony. *Mens sana in corpore sano.*

So how did this help him now? It was obvious that instead of taking a back seat and worrying about the outcome of the actions to be undertaken by others, for the sake of his psychological well-being he ought to take part himself. But he had to maintain his cover. If he were exposed, then he would no longer be able to spy on the multinationals from the inside. That would harm the movement considerably. And besides, would many of the Hope-ists, unaware of the identity of their mysterious founder, consider him a hypocrite once they knew for which organisation he was working? He had to be careful.

At 11.15 p.m. according to the video's clock, Dr. Nathaniel E. Papulous Ph.D., B.Sc. (Hons), B.Comp.Sci. entered the University of Inverdon Medical Faculty Cytology Laboratory. His non-vitreous eye had been recognised by the retinal scanner, and he had correctly punched in two codes at the inner security barriers. Then, while she worked, he talked to a Mrs. Annabelle Jane Stewart about the progress of a "telomere modification experiment." Eleven minutes after he had entered, Dr. Papulous left the laboratory. Mrs. Stewart left a few minutes later. At

2.35 a.m. flames from the burning laboratory could be seen eight miles away. By the time the fire brigade arrived nothing salvageable remained. The cause of the fire was suspected to be a malfunction in the central heating unit, but it was never proved.

Nathaniel walked to his vehicle. He felt alive, alert and vigorous, much as he had done many years ago in the same city after walking out of the office of a certain Morgan. This time he was heading towards that same office.

A Ford Transit van sporting "IHM Window Cleaners" in huge black letters, pulled up outside the DAP building. A good-looking man of average height and early middle age—or late youth—with a receding hairline and dressed in a blue overall, reported to the security guard. The guard would later be able to give the exact time....

"Evening. Identification?"

"F**k! Do you mean to tell me that not only do I have to work at...f**k knows what time of the night it is...."

"It's just gone eleven-thirty."

"Not only do I have to work in the bloody middle of the night, but I need to prove who I am for the pleasure of it! Can't you read what's on the van, mate? I'll give you three guesses why I'm here...."

"The windows have never been cleaned at this time before...."

"No. I'm f**king sure they haven't. But we—or should I say the f**king c***s in charge of this crappy business have just won the contract, and how do you think they did that? They charge less, that's how. And how can they charge less? Because the government is forcing me to take this job, or I lose my dole anyway, right? So they can pay me almost nothing and I have to work whenever....What do you think the wife thinks of that? I work all night, every night, and sleep all day, when I'm not working then too. And they couldn't even be arsed to tell me that I needed ID...."

"Alright, alright, keep your hair on. Ah, sorry....You know how the cradle works?"

"Show me." Nathaniel hadn't even noticed the reference to his baldness. A piece of piss—it was all going swimmingly! He should have been an actor. And the worst was already over—the next bit wouldn't be a problem at all. If he tried hard enough, he could just about empathize with his juvenile self feeling a touch of vertigo up a rotten old poplar, but here he was on a solid platform, with a security rope around his waist to boot, and if he wanted to go down he had only to press the green button, and for up, the red. All he had to worry about now was the artistic, literary, and political challenge of filling the huge canvas of the building in the most effective way.

Dawn came. Earlier than usual owing to the absence of clouds. The sun would soon take the edge off the cold. The seagulls had long since breakfasted on their usual pavement pizzas (the spilt and regurgitated kebabs of late-night over-indulgers, of which there were many in this northern town) and even their morning snacks of fish heads and guts were a distant gustatory memory. The sun's rays and the first of the human tide of morning office immigration arrived almost simultaneously at the DAP building.

Nathaniel had had time to review his life. Ironically, his desire for action to release him from the tyranny of thought had resulted in a period of forced inactivity and isolation, such that—if one ignored the seagulls—all he had for company was his own mind and his thoughts. There was nothing he could do but think.

A truth had struck him as had looked back on earlier predicaments: lessons recur until one has learned from them. This episode was too like the abortive cat rescue of his youth for it not to be significant. Mulling on this, he had concluded that his self-image had been the real reason for his earlier failure. If he had cheerfully and confidently explained to the Taylors what had happened when they had found him stuck in the tree, they might well have believed him. If he had laughed at his foolhardiness he would have won them over. He re-played that scene in his mind, and saw Mr. Taylor affectionately ruffling his hair rather than chiding him: "You're a right little tearaway, Nathaniel, and no mistake!" Instead of widening the rift with the Taylors, it might have brought him closer to them, and to Rosemary in particular. But then the course of his life would have been altered, and Hope-ism might not have existed.

Now, like then, he had no control over the externals, but he might be able to change his own attitude to them. What if being up in the cradle, forty yards from the ground, had been his plan all along? Well, he was bound to get wide publicity, stuck there on the platform...the very public platform.

Rosemary, tucking into her breakfast grapefruit, had been watching her husband for several seconds with the sound turned down, before it registered: Nathaniel! Dressed as a workman and covered with paint! In a cradle, halfway up a building festooned with huge painted messages—and the Hope-ist symbol! He was talking, shouting! A man was abseiling down to him from the top of the building, but Nathaniel was oblivious. He was apparently addressing thousands of people standing in front of the building. They were cheering and clapping! Tens of microphones and cameras were trained on him. Rosemary had leapt to her feet (although she was holding the remote control) and was feverishly trying to turn the volume up—then she remembered that she'd pushed the mute button: "...have never advocated violence and never shall. All we believe in is in providing useful information to you, the people of the world, so that you may make informed decisions and democracy may flourish, because without information—and for that matter education, understanding and analysis—democracy does not exist.

"They tell you that this is the information age. They say that there is as much information out there as you could possibly want or need. They tell you that you already have freedom and choice. In a sense they are right. But which of us has the time and the energy to sift through it all, to know what is relevant and important? So we, the Hope-ists, and our friends, such as Allies of the Planet, Verdant Pax, and Anti-Nasty International, have made a start at sorting through the information about companies and their products, and condensing and summarising it."

Mary turned towards Shelagh and smiled—Nathaniel was getting on to what she had been working on! Fred East had been only too happy to resign from DAP and accept a job with—as he thought at the time—the VE and HA. Mary had subtly assessed his attitude to Hope-ist issues

363

before taking the plunge and telling him what she was planning. Fred had revelled in the opportunity to use the software he had developed for DAP to enable the Hope-ists to determine how DAP—and other companies—operated. He had also provided valuable information regarding access to the DAP building.

The environmental and human rights groups had been another story. At first they had been intensely suspicious of her, and of the notion of cooperating with each other. Indeed, more than once Mary had feared that they would shop her to the authorities. Throughout, she had striven to maintain a serene and self-assured air, and the strength of her arguments had won through: by most objective criteria the world was getting worse and the organisations' impact as fragmented and disparate entities was, at best, limited. Why not cooperate?

Mary had been at pains to let them think that the "Boycott Index" was their idea: all the information regarding a company's employment and environmental policies, tax affairs, charitable donations, attitude to bribes, donations to political parties, etc., had been reduced to numerical values. Ultimately these had been condensed to a single figure. This amounted to a summary of a company's net contribution to human happiness (or misery). Low values indicated that a company was performing poorly, and therefore worthy of boycott.

The wrangling over this essentially subjective formula had been intense, verging on acrimonious. Verdant Pax had wanted more weight to be given to environmental factors, Anti-Nasty International to human rights ones. Mary had tactfully pointed out that oppressed, poor and abused people were not known for their concern about the environment (or about the welfare of animals, for that matter), and so the compromise arrangement had marginally prioritised human rights.

"All those using Cyberbabble will find that every time they click on an advertisement or a company's name, a figure appears—this is the Boycott Index. You may find the formula on our official website, which is the only one...."

Rosemary had phoned Jim Mud, and, that task done, was sitting entranced, her knuckles to her lips. Nathaniel had been a Hope-ist all along! God, he looked handsome—despite the red on his face, the silly boy!

"Of course you are free to do what you want with this information, but we suggest that any boycotts or protests, which must be peaceful, are restricted to the two companies with the lowest BI scores. These are named on our website and their scores appear in red...."

Shelagh was restless—*The Sin* had not appeared yet! What was happening?

"Click again and you will see that a map of the company structure appears. You may then investigate any subsidiary...." At this point Nathaniel became aware of the abseiler. The latter let himself down on to the platform. It was EJ! They talked to each other, smiling and patting each other on the back. Nathaniel shook his hand. EJ appeared to nod, then hand something to Nathaniel, before standing to the side of the cradle and pressing one of the switches. The cradle moved slowly down—power had been restored. Nathaniel tapped EJ on the shoulder and made an admonitory gesture. The cradle stopped. Nathaniel resumed speaking, but this time his voice was crystal clear, and he was no longer shouting. EJ had handed him a radio-microphone, and the forest of parabolic and telescopic microphones in front of the DAP building was now redundant and disappearing, like Birnam Wood preparing for Dunsinane. Someone was relaying the signal to a portable public address system. The electronic assistance was immediately exploited by Nathaniel. No longer having to shout, his address took on a more intimate tone.

Rosemary was transfixed. Having rushed to her sitting room, she was sitting forward on the sofa, elbows on knees, chewing her knuckles now. She had never really known Nathaniel! The telephone burbled. It was a friend telling her to watch television. Rosemary hurriedly thanked her, trying to keep the irritation out of her voice, put the phone down, and then, after a moment's reflection, took the handset off the hook.

—

"What if a company wishes to improve its BI rating? Is there a quick way it can redeem itself and avoid being targeted?"

Frantic with apprehension, for the umpteenth time, Shelagh got up and ran out of Mary's flat to the corner shop to check if any of Mudrock's papers had come out. The delivery van was just pulling away as she arrived. The turbanned shopkeeper knew what she wanted by this time, and smilingly handed over the thick bundle he'd assembled—she'd paid in advance. Shelagh was too desperate to get back to Mary's to notice the lack of traffic and pedestrians. She stopped herself peeking—she had to share the moment with Mary, good or bad.

"So we have set up a fund distribution network, and money donated by companies wishing to improve their ratings will be channelled to local co-ordinating groups in developing countries. These will not only pay for the schooling of girls, but will even pay their families to allow them to attend. You may think that focussing on women is sexist, but we know that educating girls is by far the most effective way to improve quality of life, to say nothing of eliminating the widespread practices of female infanticide and selective abortion...."

Television forgotten, Mary and Shelagh competed to read headlines and editorials to each other.

If they had been watching the box they would have seen someone, bag in hand, running through the crowd to the DAP building, shouting and gesticulating. The cradle was lowered. The bag was handed over. The cradle ascended. Nathaniel started speaking again; he had taken what looked like a newspaper from the bag. "I am happy to announce that today's issue of *The Sin* spells out Hope-ist philosophy in more detail...."

CHAPTER FORTY-ONE
"We are living in a non-materialistic world."
(Lyrics from song by Mud Honor, © Roar-Curse Records 2004)

As early as two months after Task Two, the Hope-ists knew beyond all doubt that they had won. Faced with an international boycott and thousands of protestors blocking the forecourts of their petrol stations, DAP and Axon capitulated in days. Their lower-ranking employees received pay rises. Union membership was encouraged. Victims of harassment and their families were compensated. Environmental and educational funds took the place of bribes to government officials.

Other companies saw the light and followed suit, at first in dribs and drabs, and later in their thousands. Even the hundreds of thousands of Hope-ist volunteers who came forward in those early days to help with Hope-ist administration could not keep pace with the rapidity of change in the Boycott Index ratings. With companies falling over each other to improve their Hope-ist credentials, the Boycott Index had to be temporarily suspended. Voluntary tax donations flooded government coffers. Third World debt was cancelled and expenditure on health, education and welfare rocketed.

Mudrock's contribution was invaluable. His famous words, which appeared in all his newspapers and on all his television channels on the fateful day, are recited by schoolchildren to this day: "I have come to understand that the concentration of money and power is not compatible with the greatest happiness for the greatest number of people, an ideal for which we should all strive. I beg forgiveness for much that I have said and done, and I hope that my actions from this moment will lead to a more just and compassionate world...." His media became the *de facto* voice of the Hope-ists. The circulation of his papers doubled and the letters sections became the forum for the liveliest debates.

Michelle was not idle. Her sister's legacy was a massive restructuring ("The Yvonne Reforms") of the educational and criminal justice systems of the UK, and thence, by example, of the rest of the world.

Cannabis was legalised and taxed. The possession of small quantities of hard drugs was decriminalised. Addicts, after a week's hospitalisation and full medical and psychological examination, became eligible for free prescriptions. Heroin addicts, receiving regular and consistent doses of heroin, backed by counselling, were able to lead functional lives. (Methadone was discontinued.) Drug-related crime disappeared and the consequent benefit to the economy more than paid for any care that addicts received. With no incentive for anyone to push drugs, rates of addiction declined dramatically. The illegal drugs trade, and all the economic distortions that went with it, vanished virtually overnight.

Penal institutions rapidly became unrecognisable. The emphasis was placed on the diagnosis of behavioural and learning problems and their treatment. Education was prioritised, as was re-integration into society. It seemed that no matter how much money was thrown at this, the return, in terms of the money saved by the prevention of future offences, always exceeded the expenditure. Not only this, but as prison populations fell substantially (due both to a drop in re-offending and to lower rates of first offences secondary to enhanced levels of welfare and lower unemployment) the total cost decreased.

Teachers' salaries were increased to the level of company directors' (whose pay was now effectively capped by Hope-ist criteria applied to their companies). Class sizes were reduced to a maximum of eighteen. The number of exams and assessments was reduced, and teachers found themselves with much more respect and latitude to exercise their professional judgement in the classroom.

Emphasis was placed on drama, art, music and language skills, as research had shown that concentrating on these had remarkable spin-off effects on self-confidence, social skills, achievement in other subjects, and general happiness. With more outlets for self-expression, creativity, and high-level social interaction, materialism declined remarkably: kids discovered that there was more pleasure to be had from playing an instrument than from possessing the latest designer goodies. A saying from that time still with us today is: "If you want a scientist tomorrow, make an artist today."

Bilingualism, as a minimum, became the norm, and parents, should they require nursery care for their offspring, were encouraged to place them in a non-mother tongue environment. As soon as they were old enough to write, children were encouraged to maintain correspondence with a pen pal in another country and of another culture, and to provide a monthly report on their pal's life. Exchange visits were routine.

Racism declined substantially. In debates on the subject the word "tolerance" (which carried the dangerous implication that people were not liked or valued, but stoically endured) came to be replaced by the word "acceptance." Even Tory Klaxon, in his last speech as prime minister, was recorded as saying: "From this day we shall no longer 'tolerate foreigners,' we shall embrace our fellow and equal human beings." (A showman to his dying breath, he milked the pause in the middle to the nth degree.) He was as good as his word. Immigration policies were relaxed, immigrants and asylum seekers were welcomed and given full citizenship. As the standard of living in developing countries rapidly improved, immigration proved not to be as great as had earlier been anticipated. New citizens (as, in fact, had long been known but had been hushed up) were found invariably to work hard, pay tax, and on balance make a positive contribution to the economies of developed countries. "Strength in diversity" was a popular slogan at the time.

Shelagh initiated a transport thinktank. With companies obliged to operate under Hope-ist criteria, the solely financial incentive for the best brains to work exclusively for the private sector diminished at the same time as those same Hope-ist criteria effectively brought the private companies under a form of democratic control. Countrywide monopolies for the various forms of transport were felt to be more effective than a system based on competition, as the subsidy of less-profitable (often rural) services within a single organisation was easier than establishing inter-organisational compensation funds. In the end, companies competed on the basis of Hope-ist criteria to run the transport system for twenty-five-year periods—enough time for them to benefit from long-term strategies and investment, but not so long that there was no opportunity for creative shake-ups to have an influence.

Greater public awareness of companies and how they operated soon exposed the military-industrial complexes of the developed nations for what they were. Hypocritical and counterproductive sanctions against such countries as North Korea and Cuba fell away and were replaced by aid programmes. With no Uncle Sam-type bogeymen to whip up their cowed populations, dictatorial regimes quickly collapsed as their corruption and inefficiency became apparent. On the other side, with no Saddam Hussein-like bogeymen remaining for the developed nations, massive "defence" expenditure could not be justified and the vast sums of money released were ploughed into international education and health care. As arms production and exports dwindled, and the levels of education and welfare increased in the developing nations, regional conflicts dried up.

Silversmith, a wary and defensive man, strongly argued that drug companies must be allowed to patent and make large profits from their successful products or there would be no incentive for further research and development, the costs of this being substantial. A compromise was arrived at. A team of medical representatives drawn from both developed and developing nations divided drugs into three categories: those of primary interest to developed countries (cosmetics, treatments for obesity and heart disease, drugs for the diseases of old age…), those of primary interest for developing nations (parasiticides, anti-malarials, TB and AIDS remedies…) and those equally important in both spheres (many vaccines, antibiotics, analgesics and anaesthetics). Drugs in the second and third categories could then be paired with those in the first category. A company which had developed a good malaria remedy, for example, had to provide this at cost price and allow other companies to produce the generic equivalent, but would then be allowed an extended patent and a substantial profit margin on one of its drugs in the first category—no other company anywhere would be allowed to produce it. In this way there would be an equal incentive to research and develop drugs in all categories.

In the pre-Hope-ist era a major problem had been the way natural disasters had been tackled. Well-paid foreign aid workers often did not have any awareness of local culture and traditions. These, vital to a people's self-esteem and viability, were often considerably damaged, and local expertise was wastefully neglected. Well-meaning donations of food and emergency aid often put local farmers out of business, and increased the long-term dependency of the population. Hope-ist reforms emphasised that aid should mainly take the form of buying up food and materials from as near the disaster area as practical, under the guidance of informed locals, who would also be employed to distribute it. Every country would be required to draw up lists of local experts and resources. Disasters were viewed as opportunities to improve the infrastructures of affected countries: often the legacy would be better roads, water supplies and education programmes. As with penal reform, higher expenditure in the short term reaped dividends in the long term, and developing countries became better trading partners.

The most significant effect of Hope-ism was that on values. It is difficult for us to comprehend now, but in pre-Hope-ist days many thought of life primarily as an exercise in the competitive accumulation of money and material goods. The possession of these was assumed synonymous with happiness. Indeed, those who owned less by choice were considered "poor" in every sense of the word, regardless of the cultural richness and fulfilment of their lives. Their occasionally self-evident happiness did not prevent them being considered "weird"—perhaps it even increased the likelihood of this opinion.

In the mid 21st century we take much of the above for granted—Hope-ism is so much part of us. Let us never forget the courage and wisdom of those first few brave souls, struggling against great odds in what to them must have seemed a benighted world.

CHAPTER FORTY-TWO
A Cliffhanger Ending

In the days after Task Two, euphoria gave way to exhaustion. Demands on the time of the founding Hope-ists and their partners were cruel: committee meetings, press conferences, "exclusive interviews," and numerous national and international events and deadlines drained their energies. For weeks they did not even manage to meet for a decent private discussion.

Nonetheless, Rosemary and Nathaniel were inseparable, and felt themselves bathed in a blessed light. They had found each other properly and finally, and relished the uninhibited sharing of their deepest thoughts and feelings. Their love for each other was truly radiant and struck all who saw them. It left one with a feeling of awe, humility and inspiration. The drop in the rates of divorce seen in the aftermath of the International Hope-ist Revolution almost certainly had more to do with rising standards of welfare, the global alleviation of the pressures of materialism, and improved levels of education, but Rosemary and Nathaniel's example did permeate the literature of the time in various guises.

Despite the pleasure that their healed relationship gave them, the longing for a relaxed social gathering with all the early Hope-ists intensified—a proper celebration away from the public eye to chew over the past and congratulate themselves on the present, but, most of all, just to be friends and human beings, rather than media sages, economists, politicians, computer boffins and social scientists.

"This must be it!" Rosemary pointed to a cluster of balloons dangling from a post next to the carriageway. Nathaniel swung the car onto the narrow track. Fifty yards along, a boom across the road brought them to a halt. Two overcoated men emerged from an adjacent kiosk. Nathaniel wound down the window.

"Evening, Dr. Papulous, Mrs. Papulous." Calum had been glad to find employment with a security company, even if it meant a lot of standing around in the cold. This job was quite a coup—he'd be able to tell his friends he'd met them all! Already he'd more than once dined out on his doctored recollections of his one-time fellow Steptoe's employee, and now they met again. He chose not to remind Nathaniel of their acquaintance.

The boom was raised and they drove on. Nathaniel had thought there was something familiar about the face, but couldn't place it and dismissed the idea.

It had been Shelagh's doing. Friends of her parents owned what had been a small farm just south of Inverdon, and the large stone outbuilding on the property was a great venue for a ceilidh. Apart from anything else, the sea cliff reduced security requirements.

Among the cluster of cars, Nathaniel recognised Jim Mud's convertible (he must have driven all the way from London!) and Shelagh's little hatchback. It would be so good to see them! Opening the doors, they could hear the band tuning up. As that familiar sound hit him, Nathaniel almost collapsed with nostalgia—how he had missed this! His anticipation was all the greater as he knew what an impact his first ceilidh had made on him, and now Rosemary was about to experience it. He smiled at her. She raised her perfect eyebrows (yes, the latest medical developments had made this possible, although other women were then starting to inject "botox" to paralyse their faces!) and stepped from the vehicle. Clad in a simple and chic knitted black dress she had never looked lovelier. Despite the chill of the evening there was a vital glow about her. He helped her into her coat and kissed her on the cheek. How he loved that woman!

Lined with gas heaters, the high-ceilinged granite hall was cosy and welcoming. Trestle tables laden with food and drink stood at one side.

Across the way there were bare tables and chairs where the early arrivals were sitting supping the first beverages of the evening. There was ample room for dancing in the middle. At the far end a platform had been erected for the band. Tune-up and sound check completed, they were coming down from this stage and making their way directly to the drinks table. *Musicians never change!* thought Nathaniel with a smile. A burst of giggles from the entrance distracted him—the Tartan Terrors had arrived—and hot on their heels were Trish and Devil Halfshed!

Friends old and new were pouring through the doors, the band had struck up a blistering set of reels, and Nathaniel and Rosemary found themselves high on a cocktail of banter and music—contributed to in Nathaniel's case, no doubt, by the first Guinness of the evening. The atmosphere-setting music came to an end and his laughter-punctuated conversation with Jim Mud and EJ was disrupted by Mary, who spirited the two of them away to join her in the first dance of the evening, the Dashing White Sergeant. Nathaniel took Rosemary's hand and walked over to the Tartan Terrors, asking Melanie if she would join them.

"Sets of three, facing each other. Anyone short of a partner raise your hands! They're looking for a lady over there...." The second fiddler, an amiable-looking fellow with glasses and a crewcut, was calling the dances for the benefit of the novices. Nathaniel, imagining how the instructions so familiar to him must sound to Rosemary's ears, was enjoying it as much as he ever had.

Rosemary looked at Nathaniel, mock apprehension on her face. He squeezed her hand. "Don't worry. It's easy—Melanie and I will show you how it's done." Melanie, in a green bodice and short tartan skirt, smiled acknowledgement.

"Hold hands in a circle, round for eight and back for eight...."

Dutifully they shuffled and skipped round and back. Nathaniel couldn't wait for the dry run to be over and the dance proper to start. After what seemed an age, the time came.

"Got that? Great—you're on your own now. Shona will give you a couple of bars of introduction and you're away...." Everyone looked beautiful that night, and the lead fiddler was no exception. In her early twenties, her easy confidence as she took her fiddle under her chin and swung her shoulder-length fair hair out the way in the one relaxed movement suggested a lifelong familiarity with her instrument. Nathaniel nearly missed the start of the dance, so rapt was he at the elegant tremor of her left hand as she added vibrato to a sustained note.

And they were away. A progressive dance, the successive trios of faces that met them during the course of it were a delight indeed. Here was Mary, sandwiched between EJ and Jim, and having a struggle with both of them by the look of it! Now it was Mudrock—had he come!?—grinning impishly and looking years younger, next to Michelle and Fred. Then Shelagh, Geoff and another of the Tartan terrors—Kirsty....

Rosemary seemed born to ceilidh dancing. By their third dance (the Boston Two-Step) Nathaniel had given up instructing her. Her lightness of foot thrilled him—he had never enjoyed the Schottische so much.

Whew! It was time to sit down and have a drink: orange and soda to rehydrate. Just as Nathaniel was about to deposit the drinks on the table, he saw an old couple entering the room: his parents!

They looked small and frail and bewildered. In an instant Nathaniel was with them. Rosemary turned around at his sudden disappearance. Soon all four of them were seated together. Nathaniel was astonished at their acceptance of his invitation to this event in what was to them the wilds of Caledonia, and not less surprised by their acceptance of the whisky he offered, but the world they had known had changed so much that old rules no longer applied it seemed. They clasped their glasses as if their lives depended on it, mute and lost, sipping tentatively and stealing glances at the strange new sights. Nathaniel enquired about their journey, and they seemed relieved at the easy topic and told him almost eagerly about their drive to the airport, the flight and their taxi ride. Nathaniel was touched by the way the one would stop and look at the other for confirmation, and by how the narrative baton passed so naturally between them. How they had altered! Setting down his glass, his father spoke directly to Nathaniel, "Son, we just want to say that we're terribly proud of you and of what you've done."

His mother's turn: "We couldn't have wished for a better son...."

"Or daughter-in-law," added his father, looking with obvious affection at Rosemary.

It was time for another dance. This time it was a waltz, and all four Papulouses took to the floor. Mrs. Papulous Senior was seen to smile.

The next one was a Strip-the-Willow. Shelagh's parents came over and chatted easily with Nathaniel's, while the younger people whirled and "hooched."

Returning to the table, Nathaniel felt a tap on his shoulder. He turned round: the Barkers! Greetings over, Nathaniel beckoned Rosemary to meet his former teachers. "And this, Janet," he still thought of her as Mrs Barker and felt a bit uncomfortable with this name, "this is what your good advice finally won me. Meet the famous Rosemary!"

A couple more dances, and then it was time for the band to take a break. Silversmith had put in an appearance, and was laughing and joking with the best of them. Since Task Two, Nathaniel had been a bit uneasy in his company, as Silversmith must have realised that the information he had given him and Mary in confidence had been used against him. Still, he hadn't shown any obvious signs of bearing a grudge. As if he could read Nathaniel's mind, he approached, hand extended. "Listen, Nathaniel, I know you hated what I seemed to stand for. I just want to say that I was wrong, and I think you did the right thing. Well done, lad!"

Feeling giddy at the welter of reconciliations, Nathaniel sat down next to Rosemary. In the far corner by the food, Jim Mud and Michelle seemed to be getting on famously, the former gesticulating with a paper plate, the latter laughing uninhibitedly. Mary was deep in discussion with Spider, which surprised Nathaniel—what could they possibly have in common? EJ and Shelagh were nowhere to be seen. Rosemary broke into his thoughts, "Nathaniel, what happened to that colleague of yours in Inverdon—Annabelle I think you called her?"

"Mmmn….She came into some money I believe. Retired to the south of Spain." Nathaniel wasn't looking her in the eyes. His mouth twitched after he had spoken.

"It wouldn't be 200 thousand pounds that she inherited, would it?"

Nathaniel turned quickly, mouth open.

"I think you forget that we have a joint account." Rosemary smiled and tapped his nose with a forefinger. "Pity the secret of the elixir of youth was lost in that fire, wasn't it?"

Beautiful, and exceedingly clever too! Nathaniel's grin was huge. He squeezed her hand.

Nathaniel's parents returned from the drinks table, whiskies recharged and the pallor gone from their faces. They looked at home now, and smiled as they approached. Rosemary shifted to the right on her chair and Nathaniel moved to share it, freeing a chair for his mother.

Shona had returned to the stage alone. She placed her bottle of beer at her feet and picked up her fiddle. Staring into the distance she began to play a slow and lovely melody. Both her serene and pensive face and her music spoke of long-ago deeds and faraway places, of hopes, dreams, memories and fears. One by one the gathering fell silent. All eyes were on her, but she was clearly oblivious. She had gone to that place where all great musicians go, and was incidentally taking her audience with her.

For Nathaniel and Rosemary only three things existed: the two of them and the music. Rosemary was leaning against Nathaniel's right side, her left arm around his waist, her right hand holding his left one in her lap. Nathaniel nuzzled her hair, breathing the wonderful scent of it deeply into his being. His right hand massaged her waist. Niel Gow's "Farewell to Whisky" had never before been this exquisite, this…spiritual. It was as if all of mankind's longings had been lent wings by those deft young fingers, so assured and leisurely. Rosemary was sobbing quietly. Nathaniel felt the little shakes of her body against his. A tear ran from his good eye. If they had been able to look around they would have found that they were not the only ones so affected. For a full ten seconds after the last note had faded, rich in compassion and understanding, there was not a sound to be heard. No one moved.

Her eyes still focussed on the infinite, Shona raised her bow again. Another soul-nourishing melody oozed from her magic instrument, a music of the spheres: "Pachelbel's Canon." The second fiddler had joined her. But what were they doing with it? It was speeding up, they were teasing it, injecting it with humour and vivacity…"Pachelbel's Frolics." Transcendent joy and universal love. Most were openly weeping now. Nathaniel experienced the same state of yearning, immanence and imminence he had felt in his study what seemed an age ago. He knew that some profound revelation was about to strike him.

When they finished, the silence was holy. What could possibly follow? Again Shona raised her bow, wand of the gods. This time the tune was both moving and rousing, and rhythmical and Scottish. Full of the love of wild places and of passion for life: "Hamnataing," a tune from Shetland. This time, after a long living silence, Shona received a standing ovation. Nathaniel thought that he had witnessed the Martin Luther King of the fiddle, Hope-ism in music. Cheers, smiles and laughter swept away the tears. Shona, smiling too, was joined by the rest of the band. The next dance was about to start.

Nathaniel and Rosemary turned to each other. "Let's go for a walk." If they had looked, they would have seen three couples embracing just outside the door: Shelagh and EJ, Michelle and Jim, and Mary and Spider. A limousine with the numberplate DEV-1L was rocking mysteriously. They didn't look, and found themselves drawn to the sea, walking along a rough path towards the edge of the cliff. Hand in hand, occasionally releasing each other to negotiate a tricky bit, they made their way by the light of the half moon, which was clearly visible through the thin cloud. Unusually for northeast Scotland, it was a still night, and the sound of the gentle surf tickling the foot of the cliffs reached them as they neared the edge. The turf sounded hollow under their feet. They carefully lowered themselves into a sitting position. Arms round each other's waists, their feet dangled in space. An anchored ship's lights could be seen on the horizon. To the left the glow of Inverdon was visible in the sky. A coconut smell, from the little yellow flowers of the clifftop gorse, sweetened the chill air.

"Rosemary, I've something to tell you."

"Mmmn. And I've something to tell you."

"You first!"

"No, you."

"I'm going to learn the fiddle. Hope-ism can manage without me. And I never want to be away from you again."

"That's nice."

Nathaniel was taken aback by the apparent indifference of her response, and looked at her in alarm. Rosemary laughed, squeezed him and kissed him on the nose. "Wait until you hear what I have to say!"

"Go on then. I'm all ears."

"Can't you guess?"

Nathaniel struggled to make himself think. He hated the games women played. "No."

"Did you notice I haven't had any alcohol tonight?"

"I thought that you were going to drive back!"

"Mmmn."

"Well what is it then? Go on, tell me!"

"Nathaniel, do you remember when we were in hospital together?"

"You mean the clinic at The Hotel after we were kidnapped?"

"No, after our accidents."

"What about it?"

"Do you remember what they told me about my injuries?"

Something was clicking into place. "Rosemary! Don't tell me they were wrong! You're not...!?"

"Yes, Nathaniel. All going well, you're about to become a father!"

Suddenly Nathaniel knew what it was that had been bothering him all those years, or rather what he had not allowed to bother him. He knew why he had been so enthusiastic about the elixir of youth, and why, subconsciously, he had gambled on destroying it. He knew why he had been attracted to other women, but had resisted. He was now a full participant in creation. He was in the stream of it. He was alive but would die, and yet live forever, and it didn't matter. He and Rosemary would grow old and wrinkled, but it didn't matter. Young Bright Eyes flashed into his mind, smiling a benediction. He was kissing Rosemary. His cheek was wet.

It had been a night for crying. It would be a life for loving.

The ocean hissed its approbation from the void below. A lone seagull cried, "Kittiwek, kittiwek, kittiwek...." The wind picked up and the moon disappeared behind thickening clouds.

Printed in the United Kingdom
by Lightning Source UK Ltd.
101673UKS00002B/130-228

9 781413 717563